D0407953

Mrs Einstein

Also by Anna McGrail
BLOOD SISTERS

MRS EINSTEIN

Anna McGrail

W.W. NORTON & COMPANY, INC.
New York . London

Copyright © 1998 by Anna McGrail

First American edition 1998

For information about permission to reproduce selections from this book, write to
Permissions, W. W. Norton & Company, Inc.,
500 Fifth Avenue, New York, NY 10110.

The text of this book is composed in Ehrhardt
Composition and manufacturing by Quebecor Printing Group

Library of Congress Cataloging-in-Publication Data
McGrail, Anna.
    Mrs. Einstein / Anna McGrail.
        p. cm.
    ISBN 0-393-04611-7
    1. Einstein, Lieserl, b. 1902—Fiction. I. Title.
PR6063.C478M7 1998
823'.914—dc21   98-14264
                                                  CIP

W. W. Norton & Company, Inc., 500 Fifth Avenue, New York, NY 10110
http://www.wwnorton.com

W. W. Norton & Company Ltd., 10 Coptic Street, London WC1A 1PU

1 2 3 4 5 6 7 8 9 0

For my own mother and father

Acknowledgements

This book was completed with the generous help of a grant from the Kathleen Blundell Trust, administered through the Society of Authors, London, for which I give my grateful thanks.

My first intimation of the existence of Lieserl came from *The Private Lives of Albert Einstein* by Roger Highfield and Paul Carter, Faber & Faber, 1993. The letters which contain the clues to her existence are quoted extensively in that book, and also in the catalogue which accompanied the Christie's sale of the letters, as part of the estate of Mileva Einstein-Marić, in November 1996.

A very useful book, when considering what was known about light, gravity and the universe prior to the twentieth century, is *Schrödinger's Kittens and the Search for Reality* by John Gribbin, Weidenfeld and Nicolson, 1995.

The information about the safes used in the Manhattan Project was gleaned from an essay entitled 'Los Alamos From Below' in *Surely You're Joking, Mr Feynman* by Richard Feynman, published by Norton, New York, 1985.

The German phrases were given to me by Peter Fox.

Thanks to Caroline Dawnay and Jo Goldsworthy for their support and encouragement.

Contents

The Beginning

The laws of science do not distinguish between the past and the future. What has happened, what might happen and what might have happened are indistinguishable. In time, anything is possible.

But all stories have a beginning. So here is a beginning.

In a dark, dark wood, there was a dark, dark house, and in that dark, dark house, there was a dark, dark room, and in that dark, dark room, there was a dark, dark daughter.

Lieserl.

Mrs Einstein

CHAPTER ONE

The Farm

4 June 1910

EVERY MORNING, THE LONG LOW LULL OF OXEN, THE STORKS crying on the river. Outside, in the yard, the clatter of iron milk pails. Every morning when I woke, Desanka was bringing in the milk, warm from the cow, before the first mists of the day had cleared. I opened my eyes.

Today was different. It was still dark, the farm quiet. What had woken me was cooking. Desanka was frying potatoes with sliced onion and ham, in a heavy iron pan, on the stove.

'Is this breakfast?'

I slept in a corner of the kitchen, in a nook between the outside wall and fireplace, so that I might be warmed by the damped-down coals in the winter nights when the snow was waist-deep, and cooled by the hint of outside in summer evenings, so I didn't have to move to ask this question, merely shout from the shelter of my blankets. I shouted not only because Desanka was a bit deaf, but also because I thought I might still be dreaming and that shouting would wake me up.

I thought I might still be dreaming because I had often dreamed of breakfasts that needed cooking. If I was telling the stories that Desanka sometimes told me, of Ruritanian princesses in their high castles, I would have allotted those spoiled princesses breakfasts of ham, eggs, onions and warm potatoes daily. A paradise.

On the farm, I had cornbread and sometimes butter before the day began, butter only if I had been good.

Desanka, busy over the stove, made no reply. I wiped the white crusts of sleep from the corners of my eyes and shouted again. Not too loudly, though, because I knew that princesses didn't shout and today, I thought, on the evidence of all this cooking, I might be on my way to being noble, if not a princess at last. After all, in the stories, it was always the most unlikely changeling child who was revealed to be a true princess before the end.

Desanka chose not to answer. I knew she had heard me because with a jerk of her head she indicated that I would have to leave my snug nest of blankets in the cosy corner of the kitchen and get on with my usual morning round. By now she was clanking and banging the ironware about with gusto and there were other smells, other pans that needed tending beyond the onion and potatoes, other tasks to be seen to besides me; today Desanka had other fish to fry.

I got up, shook out my skirts and went into the farmyard for the water and the eggs.

When I got back, shivering, for the mist still lay white in the yard and there was no warmth to the place in this darkness before the sun, Desanka was broaching the topic of onion soup. She slid a slow knob of butter into a pan and watched it whiten and bubble. In the tin washing dish on the table there was a trout, brought yesterday from the river by Milos. I knew what Desanka liked to do with trout: dill sauce and cucumber salad. I put the pail of water down on the floor with a heavy clang.

'Desanka . . .' There was something not right going on here. It wasn't the Emperor's birthday.

'Get me three onions.'

'Desanka . . .'

'Now.'

Dismissed, I put the basket of eggs on the table and went outside again. Desanka had placed long strings of onions and garlic to dry outside the window and they were covered in red dust. There were two sisters at the next farm, Helena older and Silvja younger than me, girls who took up the clapping as our rope turned in the patch of flat ground in their yard, over and over, kicking up red dust: Apple, peaches, lemon pie, who's the one you'll love till you die?

I blew the red particles off the onions. There had been no rain for weeks. I could see how it would all end in a storm. The clouds would bank from the west, the way they always did, the chickens would huddle and peck at one another and the storks on the river would grow quiet.

I pulled three onions from the rope and stared across the field. The plain went on and on. I had sat on the back of the wagon with Desanka from time to time, and knew that the fields, green in the summer, white in the winter, just kept on going past. An occasional farmhouse. A church. That was it. There was no reason to suppose that anywhere in the world was any different.

It was different somewhere, though. I knew that from Desanka's stories. In amongst what I took to be factual accounts of princesses who danced all night, kings' sons in disguise, witches and goblins and children who got lost in the woods, there were tales of fine houses, grand dinner parties and a farm transferred against all legal precedent into Desanka's name, so that it could not be sold by her brother Ferdi to pay his gambling debts. Sometimes there were darker stories of how such precautions had been a waste of time anyway as Ferdi had drunk himself to death and squandered the family fortune – Desanka's dowry against the day she might become a bride. They were stories that made me believe, as Desanka obviously believed, that one day a rightful inheritance would be ours again.

The sun was coming up. I imagined Ferdi stumbling to his death in the bright morning, scattering gold coins.

* * *

'Morning.' Helena had been foraging for wild strawberries. She must have been up early to get down to the lake and the river where the willows trailed long branches in the only cool water for miles, even in the summer so dark and cold it took your breath away when you jumped in, down where the earliest berries grew. The basket with its red prizes was heavy under Helena's arm and she put it down with a sigh.

'What are you doing here?' I said, surprised to see her.

'Desanka asked my mother. Paying, too. For your visitor.'

I went back into the kitchen and brandished the onions at Desanka. 'Who's coming?'

Desanka hurried away my bedding from the side of the chimney breast and scattered damp tea leaves over the tiles of the floor.

Desanka would have liked radio, if it had been available. She would have liked swinging the rhythm of her mornings along to a dance tune. Big band music. Lots of trombones. Romance novels, too, in the evenings, if she had the time to read them. If there wasn't too much mending to do. But in those days, she had to hum along as best she could to a tune that existed only in her own head.

'Brush,' she said to me, taking the onions and gesturing at the tea leaves. 'Helena . . .' Helena was dragging her basket in over the floor. 'Helena, hull the berries.'

'Mother says I'm to be back by noon.'

'Plenty of time yet, then.'

Helena fetched a bowl from a high shelf, sat on the floor and began.

Desanka never allowed me to call her mother, so I was the only person I knew who did not have one. Millie Lanic, who was once at the school with me, had had a mother and did not have one now only because hers was buried in the churchyard. This was a source of much sympathy for Millie at first, and I envied her. Mind you, she had the worst of it later when the younger children, two sisters and a sickly brother who had been the cause of his mother's childbed death, needed so much looking after that Millie did not come to school again.

I missed her. She had been able to read almost as well as I could and took a good hand in turning the rope at break times. It had surprised me, and Desanka, too, that I had learned to read, for not many people expected, then, to learn how. Once I had accomplished this task, Desanka had wanted to withdraw me from the Mehanovics' school, claiming that there was more useful work I could be doing, even if I was only seven years old, in Ferdi's rescued inheritance. I had dug my heels in, mainly because I would miss the mathematics too much. I was nearly top of the class in mathematics and it was the only time in my life I ever felt like I had done anything remotely right. Although I didn't enjoy the rest of school very much, even I could see that sitting in a room and reciting the names of the emperors of Austria was a better option than cooking and cleaning all day like poor Millie Lanic.

Unlike poor Millie Lanic, however, I knew I had a mother somewhere in the world, and a father, too, as Desanka had made that clear to me right from the start, though she was remarkably close-lipped about both. Knowing this, I had worked out that it was only a matter of time before they came to claim me. Desanka hadn't exactly said as much, but it seemed only logical. Why else would she have mentioned them? If they weren't going to come back one day, why wouldn't she just have let me call her Mama like everyone else?

I sometimes wondered what cataclysm could have occurred to separate me from my parents. Earthquakes, fire and flood were all possibilities. Although I had often mentioned these and other disasters, in an enquiring tone, Desanka wouldn't say.

I had badgered her, once, for news about them, gossip, information, any fact which would fill in the picture, and Desanka, in the middle of harvesting, the busiest time of year, had stopped long enough to say, 'Your father is a Technical Officer in the Berne Patent Office.'

'Oh.'
She knew that would shut me up.

By noon we had egg dumplings and stuffed peppers, smoked
sausages and spice cake, trout with dill and cucumber, and strawberry pancakes arrayed under a muslin cover on the wooden kitchen
table. Desanka, Helena and I had stopped for about ten minutes to
eat the potatoes and ham that Desanka had cooked for our breakfast, but apart from that break to keep our strength up, we had
worked all morning. Over the fire the onion soup simmered, the
savoury white broth already delicious just from the smell, ready to
be ladled into the freshly wiped earthenware bowls as the grand start
to Desanka's banquet, and I felt that we had finally earned the right
to know in exactly whose honour Helena and I had been working all
morning.

'A friend.' Desanka sniffed then said, 'A friend of a friend. Wash
your hands, Helena, before you go home.'

Helena put on her bonnet to walk home in the midday heat and
pocketed the coin Desanka handed over. She made an extravagant
smile at me, an invitation to come and tell her all the details of the
mysterious visitation the instant it was over and I grimaced back at
her in assent.

When Helena had gone, I was taken to the pump in the yard and
washed, scrubbed and combed. I then sat in the kitchen wrapped in
a towel while a heated iron seared into cotton.

'What's that?' I said to Desanka. Even I could see that the
garment in her hands was serviceable rather than decorative, not
the sort of dress a princess would wear, though the cotton was
considerably finer than any I possessed.

'Millie Lanic's old Sunday dress.'

Everything I wore that day was white and starched and stiff
beyond recognition. There was a tiny brown scorch mark on the
pleat at the back where Desanka had overheated the iron and she
cursed.

'Make sure you don't turn your back,' she said, draping the dress over my head, 'and no-one will notice.'

I let her tie the sash at the back in a rounded bow.

'Sit there,' said Desanka, placing me on the wooden bench by the table, 'and don't move. I'm going to get washed myself.'

The door banged.

Of course, as soon as she was out of sight, my body began to manifest mysterious itches at all its extremities and in its secret places: nostrils, the back of my neck, in the recesses of my armpits. But I sat there on my wooden seat and did not move an inch. I forbore to scratch even the largest, most scabrous itch. I bore my suffering like a badge, for what, I did not know . . . beyond Desanka's temper if instructions were left unobeyed and a vague sense that something so important was about to happen that I dare not risk disaster. The spice cake was already lavish in its dish and, although I was hungry, I did not dare disturb Desanka's finely displayed slices. So I sat, and I watched as Desanka came in and made herself ready in a clean apron and put the last sprinkles of dill on the trout and the last pinch of salt in the soup and then she sat on the bench beside me, too, her headscarf square on her head, to wait.

I imagined that the Berne Patent Office had turrets. Battlements. Crenellated towers. A drawbridge, possibly, and a moat. My father, one of the Patent Officers, was in charge of a brigade of cavalry. Admirals. Patents, perhaps, and he lined all the patents up every morning to inspect their medals and spurs. My mother . . . Desanka had been a little more vague on this point, so all I could do was imagine her in a white floaty dress sighing into a handkerchief and bewailing the fire, flood or earthquake that had wrenched their true daughter, the princess, from them. I looked forward to the day I lived in the Berne Patent Office, didn't have to go to school any more, wore white dresses and had ham for breakfast every morning.

*   *   *

In the early afternoon, when every square inch of my body had itched into submission, the wooden seat was at its hardest and the peppery scent of the white oleander was at its strongest, we heard the unmistakable sounds of a pony and trap at the furthest reaches of the farm. 'Come on,' said Desanka, hearing the clatter of wheels against the hardened ruts. She gave the soup a final stir and, lifting me down off the bench, took me by the hand. We went outside, into the hot sun, into the red dust.

A carriage drew up at our doorway. It contained one lady dressed in black, a parasol against the light, and a mountain of boxes. Desanka and I waited like good peasants for this lady to greet us, to notice us, for so far she had not even looked in our direction. She held her head high. A regal bearing. The carriage stopped and finally she turned to us and smiled.

'Shall I curtsy?' I whispered to Desanka.

'Serbs don't curtsy,' said Desanka, so I didn't.

As the woman descended from the carriage, however, Desanka relented somewhat.

'Reckon they could kiss, though.'

I was turning to interrogate her when the stranger from the carriage bent down and put her arms around me, all dark hair and fine embroidery and lawn.

'Lieserl . . .' I had never been clasped to a bosom before but there was no doubt that this was what was happening. I spluttered a bit and didn't kiss anything except a shred of embroidery, though I felt a cool cheek against mine. I was so filled with excitement I thought my feet must leave the ground and I would float up in the air. How could I not have realized what was going on? This wasn't the Queen herself, she wasn't wearing a crown. This must be a royal messenger, returning from the Technical Department of the Berne Patent Office with news of the rightful inheritance. The changeling was going home. Why else would Desanka have gone to so much trouble? Scorched dress or not, I was finally on the way to being a princess at last.

'Lieserl...' There came a spate of strange sounds. I stepped back and looked at the dark stranger blankly. Without hostility, to be sure, for she had done nothing yet that would make me actively hostile, but suspicious, nevertheless. For a start, apart from not making sense, she wasn't bearing a royal proclamation.

'Lieserl...'

I shook my head at her and backed away further. This wasn't right. Was the Queen on her way? Where was the Patent Officer?

'She does not know you, Mileva,' said Desanka, putting a steadying hand on her arm. 'Why should she? Give her time.'

The stranger nodded her head and bestowed her full attention on Desanka. 'You are right.'

Now I could understand her. She was speaking a language I knew. She took Desanka by the hand and the two women embraced, as if they were old friends, Desanka completely unawed by the regal bearing and the parasol.

'Come here, I have things for you.' And without a further look at me, she drew Desanka closer into the magic circle created by her magic carriage from which she began unloading gifts. I watched, unsure whether I would ever be noticed again, taking in all the details.

Now that I could see her properly, our visitor was tall and strong. She had wide-boned cheeks and wide-boned hands, dark eyes in a set face with a flat forehead and a mass of black hair held only insecurely by a galaxy of pins at the nape of her neck. She wasn't what you would immediately call pretty but she was striking. Dark eyebrows and a definite nose. She also had what I at first assumed to be a hard look about her. It wasn't. It was a hard-done-by look. More, it was a look that, now I watched her, was a hard-done-by-and-I-want-you-to-know-it look. Not everyone who was hard done by wanted you to know it, after all. However, I was distracted from weighing in the balance the full implications of that stranger's particular look because my eyes, like Desanka's, were drawn to the stranger's stomach, which became obvious as she took off her cloak

and bent to retrieve a small silver-wrapped box from the mountain
of parcels.

'Seven months gone,' whispered Desanka to me as we smiled for
the anticipated gift, 'if she's a day.'

I knew what she meant. I grew up with cows.

'Chocolate,' said the stranger and handed the box to me. I bobbed
my head. Forbidden to curtsy, I did not know what else to do. It
never occurred to me to smile.

'Little girls like chocolate, don't they?'

She looked encouraging. I shrugged. I had no idea. I had never
tasted chocolate.

'We kept it in the shade and ice to keep it from melting . . .' The
woman waved her hand, as if the chocolate wasn't important. I held
the silver box tightly in my hand, half hidden behind my skirts,
guessing at the treasures it might contain, hoping Desanka would
forget about it and I could open it secretly, all to myself, later, in the
night, this gift from the palace, the crenellated towers of the Berne
Patent Office.

Desanka did forget. She was bowled over by treasures of her own.
As well as the chocolate, our visitor brought with her Swiss cheeses
and fruit, produced from beneath the carriage seat, German
sausages, Italian cornmeal and a side of ham. There was bread, and
a basket of hothouse plums, and several books with coloured
pictures over incomprehensible writing – I recognized all the letters
but none of the words. And she also brought with her a small fair
boy, about five or six years old, only visible once the last of the boxes
had been safely handed over, sitting as good as a statue on the far
edge of the seat.

Although I hadn't seen the chocolate in the silver box yet, and
so was reserving my judgement until then, I thought the boy was
the strangest thing I had beheld so far in my life. Everyone
Desanka and I knew had hair that was almost black; this boy's was
a colour I could only think of as white, though later Desanka told
me that the correct term was blond. I thought he was simply ill. I

watched in concern as he stood and negotiated the step.

'This is', the woman stole a glance at me to see how I was reacting, 'Hans Albert. My son.'

'*Guten Tag*,' said the boy formally, and held out his hand. Both women's eyes shone with approval. Here was a boy who knew his manners. A little prince.

'*Szervusz*, Hans Albert.' Desanka took the proffered hand gravely. I declined, despite a glare from Desanka.

'We cannot stand here in this sun,' said Desanka. 'What am I thinking of? Come in, please, Mileva. Hans Albert.' Desanka bustled, picking up parcels. 'Come in, come in, please.' She ushered us all, people, the cheeses, the ham, the plums and the cornmeal, out of the heat and into the low kitchen. My eyes widened; 'please' was a word I did not think Desanka knew.

In the kitchen it was cooler, despite the cooking. 'Sit down, sit down.' Desanka waved her hands. She was all hospitality. Our visitor, I noticed, watching her walk across the swept floor, had a slight limp. She was not well then, either. What was this band of invalids doing in our kitchen?

The visitor sat on the wooden chair Desanka held out for her. The small boy sat on the visitor's lap, which confirmed his illness as far as I was concerned. In the commotion, I hid the box containing the chocolate behind a box of cherrywood for the fire, in the nook that would later that day become my bed. Then I sat, too, in my accustomed place on the bench, even though Desanka hadn't included me in the invitation.

'Wine,' said Desanka.

It was not a question. Both the small boy and I looked expectantly towards the stranger to anticipate her answer with our heads already beginning an eager nod.

'I don't think . . .' The stranger waved her strong embroidered arm but Desanka was stronger. Desanka's hospitality was not going to be thwarted by polite niceties. Earlier that morning I had buffed to a shine on a muslin cloth the crystal from Budapest, the

few glasses Desanka had taken down from above the dark rafters
where they usually hid, safely out of harm's reach. Whether wine
was a proper offering or not, Desanka was going to offer it because
then she could show the shine of the crystal.

Desanka poured the cold red wine and lifted her glass. It glinted
in the sunlight from the window. 'Mileva,' she said. 'We are glad to
have you here.'

The woman took a sip, reluctantly, dismissing any notion of a
celebration, and thereafter her wine remained scarcely touched. She
wanted tea, instead, which Desanka heated the kettle to provide.
Throughout the rest of the meal, through the egg dumplings and
stuffed peppers, the smoked sausages and the spice cake, the trout
and the strawberry pancakes, that Budapest glass of wine shone red
on the table. The woman had the tea, and some of the onion soup
and a little of the trout and then declared it enough. In her delicate
condition, she said, she had to be careful not to strain the abdomen.

Prince Hans Albert and I had some of everything. Mainly the
pancakes, and a sort of lemon squash that had come from the
carriage. He had a stronger constitution than I had given him credit
for.

We ate for the most part to a conversation between the two
women of harvests and haymaking and whether there would be
fighting, though I could not tell where and I could not tell why.
There was talk of cold mountains and faraway places and then
suddenly . . . 'All this food . . .' said the stranger, gesturing at the
table. 'It reminds me of home.' And for a moment I thought she was
going to burst into tears.

'Mileva . . .' said Desanka, but the woman ignored her, pushed
aside her plate and said something to me in the same language she
had used before, the language Hans Albert had used, and I stared at
her.

Desanka said, 'Why go on at her like that, Mileva? You must
know she can only speak Hungarian.'

'Hungarian,' said the woman. She rolled the vowels round on her tongue as if they were turnips and she was coughing them out. 'The girl must have German, Desanka.'

Desanka sliced a piece off an apple more violently than I had ever thought possible. 'German.' She spat back her disgust. 'What is wrong with good Hungarian?'

The visitor was undaunted. 'German lessons. The mother tongue. The language of the Empire. We don't want her growing up *stupid*, now, do we?'

Desanka shifted uncomfortably in her seat. I wondered whether the visitor was going to ask about the Mehanovics' school and was opening my mouth to tell her about the mathematics when she said, 'We shall pay for the lessons, of course.'

Desanka put the apple down again, sparing it more violence. 'Pay for them? Yes?'

'Once a week. Twice a week. The girl must know how to talk to her mother. Is that not so, Lieserl?'

'She can talk well enough already . . .' Desanka turned her face away and did not finish.

The fact of a mother, my mother somewhere, hung shimmering in the air. A mother in a white dress speaking a language I could not understand.

'In our family now', said the woman, 'we speak German.'

The thought of my mother would not go away. How could I speak to her if she didn't speak Hungarian?

'And later piano lessons. Yes.' Mileva was brightening. She turned to me. 'I played the piano. I still play. Your father plays the violin. He went at five to the Volksschule and started music at six. There must be music in your blood. Now you must be . . .' She hesitated.

'She's eight,' said Desanka.

'Eight,' she said. 'You could play the violin.'

I was entranced. Not only did I have a mother who spoke foreign languages, but I had a father, too, who played the violin. A violin that I might play, one day.

But first I wanted to establish the facts.

'I really have a papa?'

'Yes.' Mileva nodded. 'Of course.'

'Is he still a Technical Officer in the Berne Patent Office?'

The woman laughed and turned to Desanka. 'You haven't been keeping her up to date.' Desanka shrugged. 'But perhaps I didn't write . . . Your father', she said, turning to me, 'is a professor in Zurich.' She must have noticed my bewilderment. 'A professor is like a teacher.' I was severely disappointed by this. The only teacher I knew was Frau Mehanovic and she wasn't very exciting.

'Does he teach sums?'

'In a way. Physics. His work is physics. He has had papers published, in the *Annalen der Physik*. One on the nature of light.' The nature of light? Light was light, surely, and there was very little more that could be said about it. 'And now he is working on gravity.' She could see that she had lost me. Physics. Gravity. The nature of light. All these things I didn't know that she simply took for granted. No wonder she was worried about me growing up stupid.

'Gravity,' I said, repeating the word back to her, fishing for further information.

'Gravity,' she said. 'It is the key to everything. In theory. Very complicated theories. That's what your father does. He writes down all his ideas on pieces of paper.'

I paused for a moment to dispose of the image of the Patent Officer inspecting his massed brigades of patents and tried to replace it with a picture of my father spending his days writing very long and complicated sums on pieces of paper. As an image, it might have been accurate, but it lacked the glamour I had always associated with him. However, all was not yet lost. My mother's role in this was still not clear. 'My mother,' I said. 'My mother, too? Does she write down ideas?'

'No, sweetheart. Your mother just does your father's mathematics. He thinks she has too little learning to do more.'

'I'm good at mathematics,' I said. I thought of those mornings spent with the Mehanovics, while the other children scratched columns on their slates, adding rows and carrying little numbers across, operations that I never needed to bother with. I only had to look at the numbers and I knew the right answer. Just look. Frau Mehanovic called it good, but it was strange to be called good at something that required no effort at all, no effort, and I whiled away the minutes it took the others to catch up by watching the motes of dust floating in the shafts of sunlight that came in through the high window at the end of the room. 'I do my sums in no time at all,' I said.

'So does your mother,' said Mileva.

'When will she come for me?'

Mileva looked at me and looked away.

'Will she come when I speak German?'

Desanka scowled.

'When I play the violin?'

Desanka stood up and began clearing dishes. 'Why don't you go outside, you two?'

'What about if I come top of the class in mathematics?' I tried as a parting shot.

Hans Albert struggled off his mother's lap.

We went. I sidled out so no-one would see the scorch mark in the pleat at the back of my dress. We went because we were children. We knew when we weren't wanted and we left them to it.

The sun was at its hottest and the only shade was behind the barn. The little boy seemed very lost and very bored. He had the air of someone who knew he'd been brought on a long journey only to prove a point. He had a blue suit as starched as my dress and a shirt that was preternaturally white. His hair reflected back the sun.

'What's wrong with you?' I said, hoping to get to the bottom of the mystery about his hair. Had it been an accident? Had he been born that way? But he looked blank. It was the first time I realized not everyone in the world was going to understand everything I said.

I decided to be patient. I decided also that he might be sensitive on the subject, given his illness, and so changed tack.

'There's a rabbit in a hutch back here,' I said. 'Come on.' I jerked my head and my thumb and he followed like a lamb.

'*Hast du Hunger?*'

'No,' I said. 'We're keeping it for Christmas dinner.'

'*Nein*,' he said, rummaging in his pristine shirt. '*Choko.*'

And in his hands he held out towards me the silver-wrapped box, stolen from behind the cherrywood in the nook in Desanka's kitchen in a sleight of hand that I would not have dreamed possible if I did not have the evidence of it right before my own eyes. I was impressed, but I was not going to hand over my treasure without a fight.

'That's mine,' I said, and took a step towards him. I was a good head taller than him, and my arms, strong from fetching water every morning, could knock him to the ground in less than half a minute, I reckoned.

Hans Albert held up his hand, put the silver box down on the floor and reached into his pocket. Out of it came the usual mess of objects small boys collect. A piece of string, a snail shell, a knife. I admired his ingenuity in smuggling it all past his mother and into the pocket of the best suit. He held out the collection to me, inviting me to choose. I shook my head. There was nothing there I wanted. I wanted the chocolate.

He held up his hand again and rummaged further. This time, even before he brought it out, I could tell he had come upon something that was a particularly fine treasure. He hesitated a moment, but I took a step nearer. He shrugged, gave up, and opened his hand to show me.

A stone. A black stone. I looked at him with withering contempt.

'*Nein, nein*,' he said. '*Du wirst sehen.*'

He looked wildly about, then, picking up the box, walked back across the yard looking at the ground. Suddenly he bent down, looking at a rusty nail fallen on one of the cobbles.

'*Schau mal.*'

He put his array of objects down, beckoned me closer, and waved the black stone towards the nail.

When it was still a distance away, the nail left the ground, leaped towards the stone and stuck there.

I was transfixed. I gazed at him and the stone alternately. This boy had had a magic stone in his pocket all through lunch.

Hans Albert looked at my wide eyes with glee. '*Ich gebe ihn dir.*' He held out the stone in his palm, with the nail stuck to it.

'I still want half,' I said, gesturing with my hands before I took it, and he nodded in assent.

I showed Hans Albert the loose brick in the lee of the wall, where I had always thought I would put my own treasures, if I ever had any, and he watched as I pushed the stone and the nail to the back of the dark hollow.

Then we opened the silver box together and divided the chocolate, half each, out of sight in the safety of the lee of the wall, behind the barn and the rabbit hutch. I was not quite sure what the substance was, but it had an undeniable allure, a scent of sugar, and I could tell that whatever we did with it, we would have to do it quickly, for the block was already turning molten in the heat, losing its appealing shine. We ate it without stopping, until it was all gone, and our hands and mouths and hair were sticky, and our ironed white clothes were streaked and hand-printed brown.

I stood up. I felt slightly queasy. I was not sure that this new experience entirely agreed with my digestion, especially on top of the dumplings, puddings, sausages, spice cake, trout, strawberry pancakes and onion soup. Hans Albert, I surmised, was thinking the same. His white hair seemed tinged with green. Suddenly he was violently and dramatically sick, over any remaining whiteness of his shirt, over the polish of his shoes, the neatness of his stockings and the stones of the yard. In solidarity, and dismayed by the smell of the oleaginous vomit, I was immediately sick, too. Hans sat down against the wall and groaned.

From the barn I fetched a broom, and Hans watched as I swept the dust of the yard over the still recognizable dumplings and cherries in a glazed pool of liquid chocolate. And then I was away, across the back field, and he was with me. In the field we could have soldiers, forts, we could have our own towns and countries, adventures, alarms.

We were children. Whether we spoke the same language or not, we knew how to play.

Hans Albert and I built a farm. We constructed, out of water from the ditch and dust, a place where we all could live: Desanka and I in the north-east corner, the animals in the south, a big house in the west for Hans Albert and his father and mother and the child that was soon to be coming and which Hans Albert made faces about. We scored a channel through the mud, shored its banks and poured in water to make a river for the oxen to drink at, and Hans was just about to construct a major crossing of this river using planks and bits of old wood when the day, in a cry from the house, was suddenly declared over.

I looked up. We had been out there a couple of hours, I reckoned. Hans Albert had a sunburned pink tinge to his skin and his nose was red. The sun had begun to move down in the sky and the two cows we kept were lowing, already past their milking time.

Hans seemed to be used to these arbitrary curtailments and wiped the mud from his hands along his short trousers without protest. There wasn't much clean space to be found on the trousers but he did his best.

'Hang on a minute,' I told him, pushing him down again. 'We haven't finished yet.'

'Hans!' The voice was distant but insistent. 'Hans Albert!'

The hand-wiping on Hans' part became more agitated.

'Let me have a look.' I put my head above the parapet of the world we had created – the bank of the ditch before the field of corn – and saw Desanka striding and Mileva limping towards us. I said to Hans, 'They're coming to get us.'

'*Wir sollen gehen*,' he said.
'If you say so.'
'*Sie sagt so.*'
And then, before I could make a move, he took the plank of wood that was going to be his bridge and smashed it into the houses and the fields and the cattle pens that we had made, and used the heel of his vomit-stained shoe to grind out of existence the last of the houses where we would all live.
'*Alles fertig*,' he said. He seemed satisfied.
'Why did you do that?'
He shrugged and waved his hands. From this I understood that next time we would build the world better and bigger.
We walked towards the angry shouts that greeted the appearance of our once-white apparel.

We stood for a moment awkwardly before the carriage. The woman had held Hans Albert under the pump and scrubbed at his face and neck with a rag from Desanka and he was now moderately clean again.
'Say goodbye, Lieserl,' said Desanka in her warning voice. Her warning voice meant that I had to remember all the manners she had taught me, all the formalities she had drummed into me, all the niceties by which she, ultimately, and not I, should be judged. 'Say goodbye nicely.'
I remembered my manners and held out my hand, though I was at a loss for suitable words. Desanka stepped into the breach. 'Thank you, Hans, for a lovely play,' she whispered in my ear.
'Thank you, Hans, for a lovely play,' I said, copying the heightened vowels which had crept into her speech.
Hans, similarly prodded, managed a, '*Danke*, Lieserl.' He shook my outstretched hand formally and gave a small bow. '*Auf Wiedersehen*.'
'*Auf Wiedersehen*, Hans Albert,' I repeated, twisting my tongue to get round the unfamiliar sounds.
He climbed into the trap and sat on the seat, silent, knowing there

would be further words about the shoes and the state of the suit.

Mileva lingered a moment longer in the yard. I watched her trying to think of something to say to me, something that would explain everything, this visit, my family's absence, the day when my mother and father would come and take me back with them.

'Lieserl . . .' After my name, there was nothing.

I had thought of something, though. 'Can I read them?' I said.

'What?'

'My father's papers.'

She looked at me strangely. 'One day,' she said. 'Maybe.'

'Are they in German?'

'Yes.'

'About gravity?' I didn't have the slightest idea what gravity was. It was just the word she had said.

'If you want to know anything about gravity', she said, 'start with Newton.'

'I will.'

She stood a moment and looked down at me. I could tell she believed me. Good. I meant her to.

'Do you know, Lieserl?' she said, bending down and taking one of my hands in hers over that softly swelling mound of baby. 'If you had been a boy . . . I sometimes think . . .'

Her voice trailed away. She could think of nothing more to say, just moved her fingers over mine.

'Shall I see my father one day?'

'One day.'

'My mother?'

'Yes.'

'Promise?'

The woman squeezed my hand in hers. 'I promise.' And then she let my hand drop and turned away.

'Be a good girl, Lieserl. Be a good girl for Desanka.'

She climbed awkwardly onto the seat next to the pale boy and the driver took the reins. Hans Albert waved solemnly at me. Mileva resumed her regal bearing, one arm round Hans Albert, the other folded carefully over her stomach, head held high under the parasol, and steadfastly refused to look any further in my direction. I looked carefully to see if she might be crying, as this was what Desanka did when, overwhelmed with sorrow about Ferdi and the gold coins, she sometimes turned away from me, and Mileva was, just a little. The tear sparkled in the low sun.

I watched as long as I could the stranger and the little boy swaying from side to side as the wagon bounced over the sun-hardened ruts of the farm track. Then she had gone.

'Who was that, Desanka?'

'Don't you know?'

'You didn't tell me. She didn't tell me.'

Desanka shrugged. 'I thought it would have been clear. That was your mother.'

I felt a wave of terror wash over me. I looked down at my grubby hands, the stained dress, turned again to look at the track where the carriage had driven, wanting to run after her, knowing it would be useless. I had already watched her go.

Desanka said, 'I'm going to milk the cows.' And she went.

I couldn't speak, I couldn't move. I just stood there in the late afternoon sun with the red dust on my shoes and watched the track for a long time, hoping against hope that my mother would change her mind and come back for me.

I waited and waited but there was no clatter of carriage wheels, no delighted cry of voices returning. Just the oxen lowing, the storks on the river. I shivered, though the warmth of the day held, and finally came back to the house, full of things that needed answers, because there was nothing else I could do.

Desanka was nowhere in sight and I had no-one to ask all the questions that teemed through my head. I kicked through the empty kitchen where the plates were uncharacteristically still adrift on the tables, the trout and the cucumber salad melting into oil in the early evening heaviness. I picked at bits of sausage and batter, newly hungry. I had eaten nothing since the disaster with the chocolate. I ate, thinking about everything I had seen and heard and trying to make sense of it. Apart from the fact that I was clearly not going to be a princess before the day was over, it didn't make sense, not any of it. On the table was the glass of wine which Desanka had insisted upon and which the stranger had left untouched after her first mouthful.

Guessing correctly that Desanka would now be too flustered or too angry to notice, I picked up the crystal glass and touched it with my tongue. On the fine rim from Budapest I could taste her skin still, Mileva's, my mother's salt and scent. Salt like the one tear she had shed for me. The one tear I was worth. I breathed in the grape scent of the wine and the salt scent of her skin, then I licked the rim of the glass completely around, taking into my mouth every last scrap of her that I could find. Then I drank.

The wine was like sandpaper and vinegar, and in the pit of my stomach it burned like fire, so much that I thought at first I would be sick again, incurring Desanka's end-of-the-day wrath, but then the stumbling sensation settled down into a warm dizziness, disorientating but not altogether unpleasant. I drank it all.

I left the plates where they were and got out my blankets and tucked myself up in my bed. I watched the ceiling, which was twisting and turning, and waited for sleep, even though it would not be full dark for hours yet and I knew I was supposed to clear the plates and dishes and cover the leftovers with muslin, but I could not face the spurned spice cake, the rejected strawberry pancakes. Besides, the world was spinning and I was watching it.

I stared at the spinning wood of the rafters, the beams where kitchen smoke had blackened the wood, and I curled deep inside myself with my questions. I had drunk the wine that belonged to my mother and made her part of me. She couldn't ever be lost to me again because I had her scent now and the taste of her tear on my tongue and I would carry it with me always.

*   *   *

In the night, when it was dark, Desanka woke me when she leaned over to tuck in my blanket. The fire was damped and red, and in the glow from the oil lamp she carried, she looked like the only mother I would ever want or need.

'Was that my *real* mother?' I asked Desanka.

'Yes, little one. That was your real mother.'

'Am I going to live with her one day?'

'Not soon. Perhaps not ever.'

'Why?'

'Money.' Desanka wiped her hands on her apron. 'There is no money.'

She looked round the kitchen. The table was now cleared, the covered dishes would be lined up neatly in the larder. Wherever she had been, and I did not know and could not guess, Desanka would not go to bed without tidying her house.

I snuggled back on my pillows. I didn't see what money had to do with it. We had no money either. Desanka often told me so. She told everyone so. But there was more. I knew there would be. Adults always had more than one excuse.

'They have much work to do, your parents. Your mother says they have written a paper that will make them famous some day.'

'Do you think it will?'

'Who knows? Your mother is a very clever woman. But Mileva has her hands full, and the new baby will come next month, maybe the one after. She shouldn't be travelling so far in this condition.'

'Then why did she?'

Desanka sighed. 'I don't know.'

'I do, I think,' I said. 'It was to say goodbye.'

Desanka didn't deny it, but she kissed me hard and patted the blankets down around me before she left.

I couldn't sleep now. The fire and vinegar of the wine was in my mouth and even though Desanka had tucked me in tight, I was restless. The heat of the day had lasted enough for me to go outside, so

I took my blanket from my nest and wandered out into the yard. I went to the lee of the wall, took out the loose brick and extracted Hans Albert's magic stone.

I waved it at a dandelion growing up between the cobbles and nothing happened. I waved it at a passing snail and nothing happened. It was as I suspected. All the magic had gone out of it with Hans Albert's departure. All the magic had gone out of everything.

I shook my blanket and placed it on the ground. I lay on it, flat on my back, and looked up at the sky. The distant stars made me feel small.

Was this all there was for me? To be for ever abandoned, shut out? If it was, I wasn't going to be happy with it. But, given the weight of that unremitting sky, I didn't see what I could do about it.

In the dark I finally let the tears spill over and fall on my hair and over the blanket, as if tears could still work magic, as if I still believed Desanka's fairy stories. I knew now that I was never going to be the Princess Lieserl. I would always be the changeling child and I would never be rescued to take my rightful place in the royal palace, the lofty heights of the Berne Patent Office. Never.

As far as my family were concerned, I might as well be dead. As far as the stars were concerned, I might as well not exist. They would shine on and on without end, or at least until the Day of Judgement, anyway. And the planets would move in their stately orbits, with or without me.

I wondered, not for the first time, why the stars didn't fall on me, on all of us, and crush us out of existence. I shut my eyes, overwhelmed by the weight of it all.

So what was I now? Nothing. Nobody's daughter, nobody's joy.

I fell asleep under my blanket and under the weight of that sky and the stars, with the taste of my mother in my mouth and Hans Albert's stone in my hand, crying because I was utterly alone.

CHAPTER TWO

The Athens of the North

12 October 1910

THE MONEY. THE FIRST MONEY HAD ARRIVED FROM BERNE,
along with the news that I had a new brother, Eduard. Mileva had
sent it, as promised, for the lessons – music and German.

'Mother and baby are doing well. All are doing well,' said
Desanka, putting the letter down on the table and returning her
attention to the money.

'Does she ask about me?'

'At the end. She says, "Hope you are all well, too."'

'That's it?'

'That's it.'

Desanka fingered the money over and over in the kitchen, at the
table, counting the notes, the coins. I left her to it and slid out of
the kitchen, putting a knife in the waistband of my skirt for show. I
had promised Desanka I would cut the last of the peppers and
onions for pickling, but Frau Mehanovic – against her better judgement, I think, for fear that I should damage it – had lent me a book
entitled *Practical Mathematics for the Common Man*, and I was
working my way through it in secret in the hay barn. Desanka would
have preferred pickled peppers to percentages any day, and I knew
she would resent me spending time on the latter, so it was prudent

to keep it to myself. Anything beyond addition, subtraction and compound rates of interest was of no practical value when it came to running a farm.

I sat in the hay barn, floating along on square roots, vulgar fractions, and the Italian method of decimal division. When I did mathematics, I was beginning to learn, I could forget myself. Lost in the numbers, I no longer knew who I was. I forgot the time, the hours passing, forgot anything of who I had been – all that was left was the shining thread of numbers, sometimes twisting and turning on itself, sometimes doubling and redoubling, but I could follow it along until I arrived at whatever answer was to be found. When it came to numbers, I could *see*. And with that sight, I was immune to the world. Immune, because I could leave it.

That afternoon I succeeded in losing myself in incommensurable numbers to such an extent that for a short while, at least, I managed to forget that I had a new brother.

But the fact of it kept hammering back in every time I lifted my eyes from the page. I couldn't forget it, and I couldn't forget the fact that the successful arrival of Eduard made it less and less likely that I would be summoned to the family home. For a start, there would be even less room now. I inspected my nails. Quite clean. Since my mother's abrupt departure, I had been keeping myself reasonably presentable on the off chance that she would appear again, just as abruptly, and this time I didn't want her to be put off by my appearance. It was a constant source of regret that her last memory of me was irremediably tinged with the fate of the chocolate.

After an hour or so, I finally conceded that the frosts really would set in before I got round to cutting the peppers, took my knife, hid the book again and set off towards the plants. As I hacked and stabbed, I worked on the first of a little series of problems that I had stored up in my mind for examination later, and calculated the total distance in nautical miles covered by a ship on a voyage of fourteen and three-quarter days if it travelled at 14 nautical miles per hour for six and a half days and then increased the speed by 17 per cent for the remainder.

Several problems later, by the time I had a neat row of peppers and onions lined up before me, I was beginning to understand why Desanka thought school attendance was a waste of time. It was all so easy. You could pick up the basics of mathematics in the blink of an eye and still have time for the milking and the mulching. And the best thing about it was that you didn't need complicated equipment, most of it could go on inside your head. I needed a pencil and paper from time to time, but for the most part, I could do it *while* milking and mulching.

It still didn't make me forget about Eduard, though. I didn't know much about babies, so I imagined him as a smaller version of Hans Albert, neat and blond in a shining white suit with string in his pockets.

I gathered the peppers and onions into my apron and wandered over to the mud and water beside the bank of the ditch. In my pocket was Hans Albert's magic stone. I had worked it out by now. Metal. That was the key. It pulled metal to it. A rusty nail, a coin. It stuck to the side of a milk pail. I didn't know why it did this, but I felt I had mastered part of its secret, just finding its limitations.

After I had worked this much out, I took the stone into school, where Frau Mehanovic had given me a name for it. A magnet. She told me that what I was seeing was magnetism.

Another word. Magnetism. Gravity. Light. I sat for a while, turning the stone over and over in my hands, overwhelmed with the weight of things I did not know. Gravity. Light. I could still see the wreckage of the houses and farms that Hans Albert had smashed, the places where we would all live trampled underfoot. Magnetism. I pushed my shoe into the wreckage and wished I had known that the small white boy had been my brother. I'd have asked him more questions.

Questions. In the kitchen I tipped the peppers and onions into a bowl with a flourish.

'Desanka . . .' I put on my best little girl voice. 'Desanka, where is Zurich?' If they weren't going to come to me, perhaps I could go to them.

'Switzerland.'

That meant nothing, either. 'Is it far away?'

'Very far. Over lots of mountains. Your name is Swiss.'

'Is it?'

'Or German. I think it's German. I think Mileva said . . .' She shrugged. It was another of those things she didn't know, that didn't matter. That didn't matter to her.

'What is physics, Desanka?'

Desanka sighed. 'They do things in . . .' She waved her hand. 'Laboratories, I think.'

I sighed. There was no magic there. We both knew it. Faced with the intractable reality of civil servants' salaries and what might or might not go on in laboratories, whatever they were, we had reached the end of any meaningful conversation.

I smuggled *Practical Mathematics for the Common Man* into the house and fell asleep in the cherrywood nook trying to calculate percentages. If a general has lost two-sevenths of his men in battle, and 6 per cent of the remainder have succumbed to sickness, out of his original 95,884 men how many does he have left?

Desanka fell asleep with the money under her pillow.

26 August 1911

Fräulein Freisler had pearly white teeth that almost smiled of their own accord; they pushed her wily face into a smirk of sociability even against their owner's will. She smoothed the fabric of her blue dress against her thighs as she opened the door to us and couldn't help but smile.

'Yes?' She was about twenty, I guessed, and had the look of a schoolmistress about her, hair scraped back from her forehead, a severe cut to her collar. Good. That would reassure the interested parties.

'The German . . .' said Desanka. 'We saw the card.'

She omitted to mention that I had pointed it out. Driving the ox-cart on the way to market was an undertaking that required all Desanka's concentration. An hour along narrow country lanes into the great conurbation where she could sell her corn and eggs. It was a trial. Not taking her eyes off the road except to check on her cargo, she had no time for frivolities like looking in windows. All she cared about was getting her goods safely to the market.

'Come in.' Fräulein Freisler dimpled at us. 'Second door.' She swished her low-waisted dress away from us and beckoned for us to follow her. Her blond hair, piled up on the top of her head, shone with a light of its own in the dark corridor.

Fräulein Freisler was renting two rooms in Frau Heidel's boarding house in Novi Sad. They were along a passage with polished wooden floorboards and were unremittingly gloomy. We walked the floorboards carefully, the money safe in Desanka's pocket.

The money arrived regularly, though the news was haphazard. The same amount came every month, sometimes with snippets of information which Desanka tossed to me over the bread of the breakfast table. 'Your father has had another paper published. He is working further on the effect of gravity on light . . . Your family is in Prague. Mileva doesn't like it much . . . They are doing a little better, Mileva says, but your father finds it hard to study with the boys constantly about.'

'Does she mention me?'

I asked the first few times, but the question always drew the same answer. My mother hoped we were all well.

I stopped asking.

In *Practical Mathematics for the Common Man*, I had got as far as

algebra. I liked it a great deal. Not only did it make the expression
of powers and negative quantities much easier to deal with, it also
made everything more manageable, too. Instead of huge sprawling
columns of numbers, I could reduce everything to neat algebraic
expressions, which were much easier to keep in my head. But still I
needed the German lessons. It had taken nearly a year of unrelenting
effort on my part to get Desanka to come this far, pointing out the
card in the post-office window, the reasonableness of the rates, how
useful German would be in business dealings with corn traders from
the west. I capitulated on the music. If I had German, I fancied I
could get by well enough without the violin.

Nevertheless, even now, at the threshold of Fräulein Freisler's
rooms, Desanka was still not convinced. There were a hundred
things on the farm . . . I knew she was thinking specifically of a
tractor. We had just been through hay-making time and a tractor
would be infinitely more useful than I ever would. I hated the whole
procedure: the poles at the edge of the fields looked to me, when
dressed with black clover, like nothing more than shrivelled people,
uncannily strange and alive. And shorn of the hay, the poles, set at
the edges of all the fields, looked like crosses in a vast cemetery,
crosses against which no-one would ever put a wreath or a name. I
spent more time moping than working.

Desanka expressed her doubts to the schoolmistress. 'I don't
know that a girl this age needs German.'

Although I had used every power of persuasion to convince
Desanka, my potential linguistic skills were still a feather in the
balance against the weight of a motorized threshing machine.

I turned therefore to Fräulein Freisler, this woman that I did not
know, pleading with her silently to become my saviour. I tried to
put a longing to learn German into my expression.

'Of course she needs German,' exclaimed Fräulein Freisler
opening her eyes wide at Desanka. She proclaimed herself incredulous. 'It is the language of the coming century. The language of the
future. Soon, every European will speak German.'

Desanka humphed.

Fräulein Freisler paused, assessed, saw the lie of the land and adjusted her tone accordingly. 'You are wise, Madam, to take your daughter's education so seriously. Very wise.'

'Fräulein . . .'

'Call me Maja, please. I feel we shall be friends.'

'Fräulein . . .' Desanka drew a blank on first names. And then she asked a question which threw me. 'Fräulein, why are you here?'

I didn't know what Desanka meant. To me, everything in Novi Sad was strange. Desanka rarely brought me there and I was unused to its clatter and noise, the people on the pavements pushing each other, calling, shouting. I couldn't guess then that Fräulein Freisler was strange in her own right, a woman on her own, out of her native land, earning her own income. If the question threw me, however, it did not startle the Fräulein.

'Come here,' Fräulein Freisler gestured. 'Over to the window. Look.' She flung open the window, as if that could let in more light. 'The Athens of the North. That's what they said.'

We stared at the buildings, the heat and the light.

'That's why I came here,' said Maja. 'The culture, art, music . . .'

She gestured over the sill of her window to the noisy streets of the city. In the distance beyond the buildings, the cornfields shone a shimmering yellow. I detected perhaps a certain disappointment in Fräulein Freisler's tone, but thought I might be mistaken as Desanka took the words at face value.

'The Athens of the North,' Desanka said dreamily. 'It is indeed.'

Fräulein Freisler's acknowledgement of the sophisticated heights of culture attained by and encapsulated in Novi Sad, her admission that the whole of the Habsburg Empire had nothing to show more fair, appealed to Desanka's Slav heart. It convinced her – in a way that nothing else could have – that German was, after all, the right course for me to take. If this woman, a native speaker of German, could still appreciate the wonders of Novi Sad, then perhaps there could be no harm in it. And she would still have the music money to put towards the tractor.

Desanka turned away from the cultured panorama beyond the window and smiled back at Fräulein Freisler, careful to show rather less of her teeth, for they could not match the dazzling whiteness of the Fräulein's. But when Desanka smiled, she smiled seriously. She hugged to herself the idea of being wise, of being thought wise by this young woman of the world.

'Then we will do it,' she said.

'For each half-hour, though . . .' said Fräulein Freisler, assessing what we might be worth. But Desanka, wise in this way at least, had already anticipated her. She undid her scarf and tipped a shining coin on the table.

Fräulein Freisler picked it up and held it up to the light. 'A wise woman indeed,' she approved. 'Looking to the future and cherishing the past as well.'

'She must speak it by the end of the year,' said Desanka, unsure of her demand, only knowing with a farmer's sense that she must have something tangible to show for the money, in case Mileva ever made her promised next appearance.

'It?' said Fräulein Freisler, mockingly, lifting a fingernail from the coin. 'All of it?'

'As much as is possible.'

'And what do you think is possible?'

But here, if Fräulein Freisler had intended to outsmart Desanka, to draw a circle around her and declare herself the winner, she was mistaken.

'Enough', Desanka said hoisting her shoulders and fastening her scarf tight again beneath her chin, 'to tell her mother she loves her. And to mean it.'

Maja considered and reflectively bit the rim of the coin in her shining white incisors.

'I think', said Maja, 'that such a declaration would be a bargain in any language.'

Desanka nodded. It was practically the only thing upon which these two women, in the whole of their lives, agreed: the value of motherhood. And neither of them would ever so much as give birth.

19 July 1912

I knocked at the door of Frau Heidel's boarding house in Novi Sad happy. It was a Friday and I was getting out of the threshing. All week we had been at it and I was exhausted. Today was my escape. Every Friday, at a time mutually convenient to Desanka – who dropped me off on the way to market – and Fräulein Freisler – who had time to go to morning church before our lesson – I learned German nouns and gerunds and the past pluperfect and a hundred adjectives.

I had thrown myself into the task with a zeal and application that Fräulein Freisler, even at the first lesson, couldn't mistake.

'You are doing very well,' the Fräulein now declared.

'Good,' I said, 'it's important.'

She paused. 'Just why are you learning German, little one?'

'As Desanka told you. To tell my mother I love her.'

'Desanka, she is not your mother, then?'

Fräulein Freisler had long ago guessed that, I was sure. 'She is for the moment.'

'And your mother is German?'

'She speaks German. In our family, now, we speak German.'

'But you are not with your family.'

'Not yet. One day. That's why it's so important that I get it right.'

'I see.'

'Fräulein Freisler, what's the German for gravity?'

'Gravity? Why on earth do you want to know that?'

Gravity and light. They were the only two clues given to me by my mother and they weren't much to go on.

'It's what my father does. Physics. In a laboratory. I think.'

Fräulein Freisler considered for a moment. 'Have you ever been
to the Reading Room?'

My blank expression was answer enough. 'Then come, I shall
take you.'

The Serbian Reading Room. In the Athens of the North, that
great conurbation of high culture on the Hungarian plain, even a
child such as myself could walk into the building with books on the
shelves and look at them.

'Where do we start?' Fräulein Freisler was as much at sea as I was.

'My mother', I said carefully, 'said I should start with Newton.'

'Come on then,' said the Fräulein, and made for the shelves.

With her help, I found a book which, although it wasn't by
Newton, or even about Newton, did mention him from time to time.
It was a start.

Once I started reading, something happened to the time. The
Fräulein disappeared for her lunch, and it was only when my own
hunger became insistent that I realized I was at least an hour late for
meeting Desanka again at the market. I put the book back on its
shelf, reluctantly, storing up its phrases for later.

Despite the fact that I didn't know a great many of the words it
contained, I decided that this didn't matter. Even the little I had
been able to understand had given me a faint inkling as to what
gravity might be. Something very big. And powerful, that was clear.
And invisible, which didn't help.

'Every particle of a body is attracted by the earth, and the total
force exerted constitutes the weight of the body.' I decided to
concentrate on that. Every particle of a body . . .

I thought, if I can understand gravity first, I can leave the light
for later.

I thought about gravity a great deal and was unusually quiet on
the ox-cart home. By the time the edge of the farm was in sight,
though, I was beginning to get agitated.

'Stop fidgeting,' said Desanka.

'I've worked something out,' I said.

'What?'

'Do you know which is stronger, Desanka, magnetism or gravity?'

'Lieserl . . .'

'When we get home, I'll show you.'

And as soon as she had pulled in the reins, I was away.

'Wait here.'

'Lieserl . . .'

I ran to the lee of the wall where I had hidden Hans Albert's magic stone, ignoring Desanka's protests that the flour needed storing before night fell, and brought it back to show her, complete with the rusty nail.

'Look, Desanka, look. Watch.'

I held out my hand and put the nail on my flat palm. I waved the magnet over it and the nail leaped obligingly, as it always did, to the tug of the magnetic force.

'There is this tiny magnet against the whole earth, Desanka, and the magnet wins.'

I was overwhelmed with delight. Gravity might be big, but magnetism was bigger. And I could hold it in my hands.

I felt the universal forces flowing through me, the gravity that held me to the earth, the magnetism that lifted the metal from my hand. I felt at last that I was on the verge of understanding everything.

'You', said Desanka, 'take after your mother.'

26 July 1912

'So your mother came to visit you, did she?' said Fräulein Freisler, after I had told her the story of the magnet and how every particle of a body was attracted by the earth.

'Once,' I said.

'And you want to tell her you love her.'

'Yes.'

She was in a bad mood. I guessed the evening before had been
rather less successful than most. Even if Desanka was taken in by
the schoolmistress appearance, I, and most of the men of Novi Sad,
were not. I knew that Fräulein Freisler had other cards, cards that
advertised services more strenuous and lucrative than the teaching
of foreign languages. This suspicion had gradually crystallized from
stray remarks and finally hardened into certainty with the discovery
of one of those calling cards between the pages of a German primer.
I could only assume that either Frau Heidel genuinely believed
there was an insatiable need amongst the gentlemen of Novi Sad for
the acquisition of foreign languages, or she was taking a percentage.

I wondered if it was principally for commercial reasons that
Fräulein Freisler had come to Novi Sad, a place where no-one might
recognize her. I still wasn't exactly sure where she did come from.
Whatever had happened last night though, she was taking it out on
me.

'What makes you so sure she loves you?'

I stared at the Fräulein in horror.

'She came all the way to see me,' I said. 'She had another baby
coming. She shouldn't have been travelling, but she travelled to see
me. Just me. Her daughter.'

The Fräulein was not to be satisfied so easily.

'If she shouldn't have been travelling, why didn't your father
come?'

I didn't know what to say. I had never thought about it. It had
always been clear to me that my mother had come because she loved
me, because . . . now I remembered. She had come because she
wanted to say goodbye. Why had she had to say goodbye?

'Why didn't your father come?' said Fräulein Freisler. 'Why?'

'Because . . .' Because he'd been writing a paper about the effect
of gravity on light. I couldn't bring myself to say it. As an excuse it
sounded thin, even to me. 'I don't know,' I said. 'I don't know why.
No-one knows.'

I slammed the door on my way out, in no mood for German, in no mood for anything, and the next week refused to go to my lesson.

Desanka didn't ask why. Perhaps she thought I had come to my senses and realized the futility of the enterprise at last. I agreed with her. I didn't need German to tell my mother I loved her. My mother would know that already. I might just as well spend my time learning the violin.

Over the next few days, I got to the end of *Practical Mathematics for the Common Man* and cast about for something else to occupy my mind. I could calculate the area of any quadrilateral with ease, divide and multiply by logarithms and solve simultaneous equations, but still I wasn't happy.

In the end, I realized I was going to have to ask Desanka about it after all.

'Why didn't my father come to see me?'

Desanka looked up from her mending. In the flickering firelight of the kitchen, she looked older than I had ever seen her before.

'Your father', she said, putting down the needle for a moment, 'is a despicable human being who got your mother in the family way before they were married, forced her to leave her native land, and made her give up her own studies so she could look after him.'

The cherrywood in the grate crackled.

'Why does she stay with him if he treats her so badly?'

Desanka sighed, as if the mysteries of the human heart were beyond her. 'I suppose she loves him. She says she does.'

I watched the flames dance, numb to the end of my fingertips. 'Why didn't you tell me all this before?'

'You never asked.'

Which left the question of why I had never asked before. That, at least, was clear to me. I had been afraid to know.

I realized that she hadn't answered my question, either, but she no longer needed to. I could see it for myself, plain as day. My father hadn't come to see me, hadn't once visited me, had never asked about me because he didn't give two pins for my existence. Against gravity and light, I counted for nothing.

I sat in front of the fire until late, watching the embers glow red. At some point Desanka went off to bed and left me to it, watching the fire, the light.

If I'd understood that physics book correctly, then everything in the world was either a wave, like magnetism or gravity, or a thing made of tiny particles. Even human beings were made of particles. But the light . . . Light sometimes looked like it was all one thing like a wave, but sometimes it looked like tiny sparks, millions of separate packets, like the dust motes in the beams, each with its own energy and glow. What was it, wave or particle?

I thought, looking at the firelight, and the flickering and the flow, that light must be both wave and particle. The tiredness was still going round in my head. Dizzy, I wondered whether we, us poor humans, were really waves and particles also. We could be all one thing, flowing together, or always and for ever separate. I was all wave, flowing everywhere, out to find my family and back to this small room, and I was all particle, separate, in a world unable to be joined together.

Now, in the firelight, I felt even the tiniest particles of my body grow tenuous and thin. Everything I had ever been certain of was disappearing. I was leaching away to nothing. I wasn't even a real person any longer. A ghost. I was becoming a ghost, with no place in the world. A ghost with no home.

My father had never visited me.

My father had never even asked about me.

My father, the father that I had never seen, had abandoned me to a place where I could hope to be nothing but everybody's helping hand at harvest time, a milker of cows and a collector of peppers and onions all my life. There was no-one going to give me a dowry, no-one even to buy me a good milking cow to set up home with. There was nothing in my future, nothing at all, and he didn't care. He neither knew nor cared whether I lived or died.

Only one thing remained solid and real in this sea of nothingness. My mother's tear. She had wanted to take me with her. That was clear, because she had cried. He had made her say goodbye to me because he did not want me, but she had betrayed her love for me in her tear. Her one shining tear.

I thought of my father, the Patent Officer, caught up in his science and solutions, distracted from his daughter in the cold laboratories of Zurich, bothering only about stupid gravity, useless light.

I hated him.

I hated him not only for what he had done to me, but for what he had done to my mother.

I hated him so deeply that I felt the elements in my body begin to come together again, in new and different shapes. I stood up tall in the firelight, feeling the warmth of its last glow on my arms. I was me. All things together. Me.

The old Lieserl, the Lieserl who had hoped to be a princess, that changeling child was melting away, and a new me, one that did not yet have a name, would one day take her revenge. I was red in the firelight. A ghost of light and fire. I was fire, I was light and one day the whole world would be fire and light in endless waves. I danced in the kitchen to think that I was fire and the whole world would be fire one day. I twisted in these dreams, round and round, until I found that the room was cold, the fire dead and I had danced myself wide awake.

There was only one person in the world standing between me and my rightful destiny, my place at the side of my mother, my mother who loved me and couldn't take me with her. One person. One hateful, hateful man, and I would . . . I would . . . What?

I would do what ghosts always do, I decided.

I would haunt him.

CHAPTER THREE

The River

7 March 1913

'I WASN'T SURE YOU'D BE BACK.'

'Neither was I.'

'But you still want to learn German.'

'I do.'

'To tell your mother you love her.'

'I don't need German for that. You knew that anyway.'

'Come in,' said Fräulein Freisler, and swished away down the passage.

I followed her over the polished floorboards which shone in what little spring sun reached the boarding house. Everything still seemed to be shining, full of new resolve and promise. Everything had shone all through the winter, through the deepest snows, days when the ground had set like iron and the water in the well froze solid. My vision of the world as fire and light had burned inside me and with the spring it had hardened into action.

'I wanted to talk to you', I said, putting my books down on the table, 'about vocabulary.'

'Vocabulary?' said Fräulein Freisler. 'Which words did you have in mind?'

As our lessons were on Fridays, and Fräulein Freisler was a

Catholic, some of the first words she had taught me were for fish. Gratifying as this knowledge was, I had become aware that it was not going to be sufficient. I needed a thorough grounding in the physical sciences, not to waste time any longer practising my discourse upon halibut, bream, trout and cod.

All winter I had been mulling over the breakfast snippets of news and the strange phrases in the library textbooks, trying to make sense of them.

What did you fight fire with? Fire. By the same token, I reckoned, what would you fight gravity with? Gravity. And light? You fought it with light.

If they were my father's chosen weapons, I had to know every single thing about them. Instead, Fräulein Freisler had taught me about hake and the signs to look for to indicate its freshness. Even if my German was impeccable, that wasn't going to win any battles.

'I need to know the German for molecule,' I began. We were all made up of molecules, I had discovered. These were the tiny particles of our bodies. It felt very strange to know I was composed of molecules.

'*Molekül*,' said Fräulein Freisler. 'Not so difficult.'

'Also thermodynamics, gravity and electromagnetism.'

'Ah.'

'All the leading physics journals are published in German. If I ever get hold of one, I want to be able to understand it.'

Fräulein Freisler sighed. 'So this is why you're learning German now? To read physics journals?'

'Yes,' I said. 'Partly. I want to be a physicist.'

'You don't need German for that. Just learning. Mathematics, mainly.'

'I've done the mathematics,' I said. 'In fact, I think I've done all the mathematics there is in Novi Sad.'

'But mathematics is the same all over the world, is it not?' said Fräulein Freisler. 'You don't need languages to do sums.'

'It's not just sums,' I said. 'It's ideas. For instance: the way the magnet works.' It was one of the things I'd been puzzling over throughout the long cold season. 'There comes a point at which the tug of the magnet grows too strong for an object to resist. But what determines that point? It varies from object to object, but there is a limit beyond which the magnet won't work, however small the object. Who draws the boundaries? Is the force proportional to the mass?'

The Fräulein shrugged.

'I don't know,' I said, 'because I'm not sure of the words. I need the language to make certain I understand.'

'I fear that even in a dozen languages I would never understand all that,' said Fräulein Freisler. 'Perhaps you will be a physicist after all.'

'I must be,' I said.

'Why?'

I decided it would be easiest simply to tell her the truth.

'Revenge,' I said.

'I think you'd better stay for lunch,' she said. 'Besides, I have a trout today. Enough to share.'

I gave silent thanks. Miles from the sea as we were, anything other than freshwater fish for Fräulein Freisler's Friday lunch could never be top quality. She always said that didn't matter, the fish was a sign of her suffering anyway, so although Desanka had known it before I did, I had soon grown aware of how strange Fräulein Freisler really was.

We picked over the trout. It wasn't a good one and Fräulein Freisler said what else could you expect; it had been a gift, anyway.

'Revenge. Just who does this little one wish for revenge upon?'

'My father.'

She considered a moment, then got up to heat the kettle for tea.

'Revenge is a dish best eaten cold,' she said. 'And you sound very cold to me.'

'I think physicists are,' I said.

'Have you ever met your father?'

'No.'

'Do you know where he is?'

'He is a professor in Prague. No, Berlin. No, Zurich, I think.' My mother's postcards were always vague.

'A professor of what?'

'Theoretical physics.'

'Ah,' she said. 'Things begin to become clear. I must warn you, though, little one, that in your case the dish might have to be eaten very cold. It will take *me* years to learn enough German to cover a discussion of physics, never mind you.'

'I've got years,' I said. 'I'm only eleven.'

'Is that all?' said Fräulein Freisler. 'I had forgotten.'

'They won't let me into the university yet.'

'Probably not. If ever.'

'But I have to get into a university, or something like it, if I am to . . .'

'To what?'

'I'm not sure. If my father's still working on a theory of gravity and light, then I want to beat him to it. If he's already come up with a theory, then I want to be able to pick holes in it and prove him wrong. Either way, I've got to be able to understand what he's doing to fight him.'

'Revenge,' said Fräulein Freisler. 'Now fights. What if he's working on something else entirely?'

'He can't be,' I said. 'He's a physicist. What else is there?'

'Magnetism for a start. You told me so yourself.'

'It's all part of the same thing. You know, if you start thinking about gravity . . .'

She shook her head. 'I don't want to start thinking about gravity, now or ever. It gives me headaches. Tell me, Lieserl, when did these ambitions appear?'

'Oh, Fräulein Freisler, don't worry about all that. Let's make a start. Magnetism. Gravity. These are what I need to concentrate on.' I was anxious to be under way. 'As things stand, I only know how to offer him a halibut.'

'That won't get you very far in the way of revenge,' she agreed. 'Unless it's a very bad halibut.'

'Will you do it?'

'Does Desanka know about any of this?'

'Not unless you tell her.'

'If I am to do it,' she said, 'to take you on, you must be a constant student. It's going to take me an age . . .'

'There is nothing constant,' I said. 'I've learned that much already.'

'But you are truly his daughter?'

'I am.'

'That will never change. See, there are things in this world that physics cannot describe.'

'Can you find out about him?' I asked.

'I think I will have to,' she said, 'to get you the right vocabulary. Is he Swiss?'

'German.'

'What is his name?' Fräulein Freisler took out a sheet of paper from a bureau drawer and a pen.

'Albert. Albert Einstein.'

She wrote it down in violet ink.

'I have not heard of him,' she said. 'Probably neither has anyone else. But I have a friend of a friend in Prussia. I will do my best.'

31 July 1914

When Fräulein Freisler answered the door, I could see that she was happy.

'You're cheerful today,' I said, as she swished down the polished floorboards to her rented rooms. 'I heard you singing before I knocked.'

'I had a pleasant night. There's going to be a war. That's always good for business.'

'Aren't you worried?'

'About the war? No. In fact, it's probably started already. What difference would my worrying make?'

I had to concede the point.

She paused before the second door. 'Before we go in, I must tell you that we have a visitor.'

I was suspicious. 'Who?'

'A friend of another friend. I was telling him about your mathematics and he says he would like to meet you.'

I dragged my feet, making it clear I did not want to meet him.

'Chin up, girl.' Fräulein Freisler took me by the shoulder and pushed me down the corridor. 'You won't get far in life if you don't meet it head on.'

When I was pushed into the room, I relaxed a little. Another schoolteacher, that was plain to see from the shabby suit with the shiny elbows and the way he put his head on one side and smiled to put me at my ease.

'Your little prodigy.' He shook me formally by the hand.

'Herr Grünbaum,' said Fräulein Freisler. 'This is Lieserl.'

I made a sort of grunting noise by way of greeting, but he was not put off.

'The little girl who wants to be a physicist.'

'I've been getting textbooks', I said, 'from the Reading Room.'

'Newton?'

'Some bits,' I said.

'The *Principia*?'

'They haven't got it in the Reading Room,' I said.

'The Fräulein says you're a mathematician.'

'I might be.'

'Here.' He wrote some figures down on a bit of paper. Forty-nine and forty-nine. I stared at him.

'What do you want me to do with them?' I said. 'Add them up?'

'Yes,' he said.

It was almost beneath my dignity, but I did.

'Multiply,' he said.

I gave him the answer.

'How did you do that?'

'Don't you know how to square numbers near fifty?' I said. 'Look, you square fifty – that's two thousand five hundred – and subtract one hundred times the difference of your number from fifty. In this case it's only one, so you take away one hundred and get two thousand four hundred. To get the number exactly, you square the difference and add it on. One squared is still one. So it's two thousand four hundred and one.'

It took me much longer to explain it than it did to do it, but when Herr Grünbaum asked me again *how* I did it, I couldn't explain.

'It's how I do any long string of calculations and multiplications,' I said. 'I just look.'

'You don't work it all out methodically and then arrive at an answer?'

'No. That would take too long. I generally get the answer first. I do the calculations afterwards, if I have to. First of all, I *see*.'

'You *see*?'

'Plain as day.'

We went through square roots, cube roots, logarithms and the main principles of Euclidean geometry to determine exactly how far I could see, before Fräulein Freisler declared the lunch ready. It was an evil-looking carp.

Herr Grünbaum smiled. 'I will get you the *Principia*,' he said. He turned to Fräulein Freisler. 'Is her German up to it?'

'Pretty much,' said Fräulein Freisler. 'She is a hard worker.'

'She is a good mathematician.' He smiled again and patted me on the head. I did not smile back. It wasn't a compliment, it was only the truth.

Herr Grünbaum was true to his word and the next week the book was waiting for me. A modern edition, with clean type, in German. Fräulein Freisler said she'd had a quick glance through and could translate any word with which I was not familiar, but I wasn't to rely on her to explain them, too.

I didn't need her to. I was entranced. I was plunged into a world of ships sailing past each other at constant speeds, sailors waving to observers on the shore, signalling with lamps, sailing upstream, sailing downstream, dropping feathers and cannon balls with abandon and measuring the results.

At home I incurred Desanka's wrath more and more as I forgot the yeast in the bread, the scoopful of yogurt in the stew. I was living in the realm where we go when we do science, the universe where things shine, in the company of my friend Isaac Newton, who made the world such an orderly and logical place.

Calculations, calculations. Long silver threads of them. Measure the rate of this, the speed of that, do it often enough and you could come up with the rules which made things behave in the time-honoured ways.

And there were rules, built in to the very fabric of the universe. Things that were moving kept moving. Things that were standing still stayed still, until you pushed them. Every action had an equal and opposite reaction. Everything moved in an entirely predictable manner. The laws of gravity, of magnetism, of force governed the apple falling from the tree, the ebb and flow of the tides, the swing of the compass. Do enough calculations and you could arrive at the inverse square law that kept the planets in their place.

Up there the celestial mechanics moved the planets through the ether. They moved slowly, like a cosmic clockwork set in motion by God, following the rules, swinging along the paths of their allotted destiny against the fixed, eternal background of the stars.

'Details, Lieserl,' Desanka would say, as we ate another tasteless supper in which I had forgotten all the salt. 'Pay attention to the details. The devil is in the details.'

I knew that, but it didn't help with the cooking, which contained only details in which I couldn't summon up the slightest interest.

If the universe obeyed fixed laws, then I could eventually find them all out. The magnet in my hand was proof of that. Even the largest, most intractable force betrayed itself by behaving in the same way, every time. It was open to measurement, to calculation. It was only a matter of time, I decided, before I learned all the laws and could understand everything.

With this ambition in place, I was happier than I could ever remember being. There was nothing in Newton that jeopardized my plans. The laws of dynamics kept a thing travelling in a straight line until a force was applied to it, and then it would change direction, or its speed, or both. Naturally, therefore, if I kept straight on my path of revenge, I would one day meet my father. Everything had its path, everything had its destiny. I had found mine.

I had a picture of us colliding into one another like cannon balls. An explosion. An equal and opposite reaction. If I met him head on, he couldn't ignore me then.

I was relegated to the egg-collecting again, which suited me as I had more time to think. And Desanka shouted because the hens stopped laying.

There was a long way to go, to be sure, but with every fact I accumulated, my stockpile of weapons grew. With every theory I considered, those weapons were getting sharper. Finally, I was reading Newton, the way my mother had said I should, and it was exactly what I needed to do.

Also, equally comforting, at last I had an explanation of why the stars didn't fall on my head.

26 March 1915

Maja took a rolled-up sheet of paper and unravelled the whole of Europe. 'Look at this,' she said.

I was spending more and more time with Maja – I had gradually stopped calling her Fräulein Freisler. I had missed her severely over the winter months when the snow had blocked the lanes, making travelling almost impossible, and I was confined to the farm with Desanka. Now that the spring had melted the snows, I was hungry to have her back. Maja had had a successful winter, she said, and showed me a fur to prove it.

'Ocelot,' she said, wrapping it around her neck.

I did not know the word and wondered if it had lost something in translation.

'Isn't that a kind of rat?' I said.

We spoke only German now, and I fell into it as easily as if it really were the mother tongue, choosing to ignore the fact that my mother, as Desanka still lost no opportunity to point out, had grown up speaking good Hungarian just like me, and had only switched to German when she went to dubious foreign lands. Nevertheless, when I went back to the farm, where Desanka had invested the money from my music lessons not only in a new set of saucepans, but also a farm hand to do the heavy work of milking and ploughing, I felt strange talking the language of my childhood. Besides, at Maja's I had a proper bed, sharing hers except when I needed to sleep on the sofa during an urgent foreign-language appointment, enjoying the luxury of a pillow, gaslight to read by, and I didn't need to hide the textbooks.

'Ignore all these red lines,' Maja said, sweeping a hand over the map. 'They are the temporary markings of nation states.'

'Am I getting a lesson on the war?'

'Do you need a lesson on the war?'

'I don't think so. Desanka has told me all about the war. One of Mileva's old boyfriends, Karl, has joined up. And the son from the next farm. Desanka's worried she'll lose her farmhand next.'

'Ignore all the roads. Until the invention of the petrol-carbon engine, roads were never more than a way to market with the wagon. Now people have bigger ideas, but . . . Look at that thick blue line that runs across the page – from the mountains of Germany.' She jabbed a finger. 'It was here, at Ulm, where the river is new, that your father was born. And here, in the great Hungarian plain, here at Novi Sad, the Athens of the Habsburg Empire, that your mother was born.'

'And me,' I said. 'You've been doing your homework.'

'And what joins them?'

I read the name on the map. 'The Danube.'

'Yes, the unremitting Danube. If you want to find your father, you must travel the length of the Danube.'

'By boat?'

'Sometimes, Lieserl, you are remarkably stupid.'

'Aren't there any boats?'

'There are plenty of boats, but there is a war on. For a while, we may have to pay some attention to these red lines.'

'Are we really going, then?'

Maja laughed. 'No. You're still too young, there's too much to do and Desanka needs you. Also, there's typhoid in the towns.'

I disagreed with all of those points except the last one, but didn't argue. I thought I had grown up more than Maja had given me credit for. I was not too young any more. I was getting tall. And in a town where most of the people were dark, like gypsies, my skin was more yellow – olive, like my mother's. I was a Slav, I am a Slav, and that fact shone through my dark hair and olive skin and strong cheekbones. I am a Slav like Desanka, and like my mother, but narrower than both those women. My face is not wide, my hips are not wide, and neither are my hands, so the farmhand thought I was frail and carried the milk pails, even without me asking him.

I didn't argue, though, because there was still a great deal I wanted to work on and the war would just get in the way if I started travelling now. My main concern was Newton.

'Did I tell you', I said to Maja, 'that Newton was wrong?'

'Ha. You've been telling me for months he's got everything nailed down.'

'How do the stars stay in place, Maja?'

'They just do, don't they? I know they do. I see them shining every night.'

'According to Mr Newton, the stars are all evenly distributed in the ether, all over the universe, therefore the force of gravity pulling on each star is the same in all directions.'

'So?'

'So they stay put.'

'Sounds very reasonable to me.'

'It doesn't to me.'

I saw no reason at all to trust Newton on this point. He was right about a lot of the universe, to be sure, but he was also mad. He had invented calculus – differential and integral, the application of which was aiding my computations enormously – and then had kept it secret for most of his life. Also, he had spent his latter years reading the Book of Daniel and trying to construct maps of Hell. In the light of these facts, I concluded he was not always a reliable guide.

If Newton had applied himself to the task in hand, as I did, he would have seen that the slightest deviation would pull a star in one direction or another, and then all the stars would start to move. And as one star moved nearer another star, the gravitational force would get stronger. That was the inverse square law. So once they started to move, they'd start to move more quickly, and then more quickly, and it wouldn't be long before the entire universe had collapsed.

As the universe had not collapsed, the stars simply couldn't be standing still. But if they weren't standing still, what were they doing? I thought it might be possible to try to work out what was going on through a series of equations. It would take endless calculations but that had never bothered me before. The shining threads of numbers always led to an answer in the end. I didn't want to go travelling until I had got one.

But I knew I'd want to be on my way after that.

13 August 1915

Despite Maja's warning that foreign travel was not imminent, I
spent the spring and summer at the farm helping Desanka and the
farmhand sow the wheat and milk the cows with a light heart. Not
only had Maja spoken for the first time of my going to find my father
– who was now, according to my mother's most recent postcard, a
leading light in the physics department in Berlin – she hadn't said
no when I said 'we'. I began to harbour the hope that when I left,
she would come with me. I knew no-one outside Hungary besides
my mother and Hans Albert and I couldn't guarantee that either of
them would be pleased to see me if I arrived on a boat from the
Danube.

Herr Grünbaum decided to pay another visit, bringing some salt
cod and a new textbook that he'd only recently acquired himself.
This time he didn't pat me on the head.

'Cod,' he said to Maja, who immediately went into the kitchen to
mash it into fishcakes.

'Maxwell,' he said to me, with an air of benevolence.

I leafed through the pages. Four equations. I could have kissed
Herr Grünbaum. I nearly did. Four equations and the whole world
of electricity and magnetism was laid out at your feet. Think of a
problem and one of those four equations would solve it. No doubt
I'd have got round to working them out myself, eventually, but this
saved an awful lot of time.

Like me, Maxwell had first started trying to explain just one
thing: in my case, gravity; in his case, the behaviour of radio waves.
But every calculation he did showed that radio waves, along with all
the other electromagnetic waves in the spectrum, travelled at one
speed and one speed only – the speed of light.

'So light is a wave, after all,' I said to Herr Grünbaum. 'I did
wonder.'

'What else did you think it could be?' he said, but I decided not
to tell him about my dance in the firelight on the farm where I

thought light could be little particles, too. That idea seemed silly in the brightness of the day, especially now that I had four equations in front of me which proved it was a wave. There was something else odd about the equations, too. Light always travelled at the same speed. There it was in the equations, the little letter c that denoted the speed of light. Light *always* travelled at the same speed.

'That's odd,' I said to Herr Grünbaum.

'What is?'

'Light always travelling at the same speed.'

'What's wrong with that?'

'Well, it's not what you'd expect, is it?'

I could tell from the look on his face that he had expected neither one thing nor another.

'If I throw a ball to you,' I said, 'you could catch it, couldn't you?'

'Most times,' he said.

'But if I'm travelling on an ox-cart,' I said, 'really fast towards you, and then I throw a ball to you, you might not be able to catch it, might you?'

'No,' he said. 'It would be coming too fast.'

'Exactly,' I said. 'The ball would travel at the speed of the ox-cart *plus* the speed of my throw. It would look fast to you, even if it looked slow to me. Speed is relative. That's what you'd expect to happen if I threw the ball, and you'd be ready for it, even if you couldn't catch it.'

'So?'

'This is the point. Light's not like that. Look.' I pointed to the little letter c.

He looked, but I don't think he saw. He may have had the text-book, but that didn't mean he was thinking seriously about what was going on in its pages.

I tried to be patient with Herr Grünbaum. 'If I'm travelling along in my ox-cart and I send a beam of light to you, it will still travel at the same speed it always does. Not the speed of light *plus* the speed of the ox-cart.' I considered. 'Not that the speed of the ox-cart is all

that significant when compared with the speed of light.' Indeed, as
the speed of light was around three hundred thousand kilometres
per second, you could almost call the ox-cart negligible.

Here was something I hadn't been quite prepared for in Newton's
universe. Light didn't behave the same way a ball would when
thrown about. It was a constant. Always a constant. And that was
worrying.

Herr Grünbaum didn't seem worried by it. Neither did Maja.
They ate their salt cod talking about the war, which was well and
truly under way and which Herr Grünbaum thought far more
worrying, though Maja still maintained that when it came to war,
worrying was an irrelevance.

As I was packing my books away, a final thought occurred to me.
'A wave', I said to Herr Grünbaum, 'has to be a wave *in* something,
doesn't it?'

'I suppose so,' he said. 'Like a wave of water in an ocean.'

'Then light must be waves in the ether,' I said.

'I suppose it must,' he said. I had lost him.

I was going to ask him if I could keep the textbook but he seemed
to have forgotten it by the time he and Maja had discussed whether
the fighting would be in the East as well as the West, so I put it in
my bag along with the German books anyway and I don't think he
ever noticed.

As I left, I was thinking about the stars again. I had some
equations now. What was I going to do with them?

10 April 1916

Can people be in two places at once? I sometimes think that
throughout my childhood I grew up with Desanka on the farm
and Maja in Novi Sad simultaneously. Books and farming. German
and Hungarian. Two women who were not related to me in any way
but had my best interests at heart, and in between I could go to the

world in my head where I could think about equations and what they meant and no-one could touch me.

This is a dream that lasted until the morning Desanka and I woke to hear gunfire, distant but unmistakable, beyond the lowing of the oxen.

The storks scattered from the river and fled, leaving the eggs in their nests.

I hitched a lift on an ox-cart and flew, as fast as ox-carts allowed, to Maja. Maja was in tears. She was packing her bags. The ocelot was round her neck and kept getting in the way. I was at a loss. I sat on the formal chair in her tiny parlour and watched her fling belongings around, not knowing what else to do.

'Desanka says the Empire is breaking up.'

'The Empire,' said Maja. 'I spit on the Empire.'

Interested, I sat myself up a bit straighter.

'Remind me,' said Maja. 'If I ever think like this again.'

'Remind you of what?'

'Never to put my faith in men. They are not worth it.'

I didn't know that there had been a man important enough in the world to make Maja cry. It made me realize that her life in between my visits with the textbooks was real, that she did not hold everything in abeyance until I dropped by again to discuss the Doppler effect.

'The priest,' said Maja. 'The priest blessed him in the church before he left. The God of the Trenches. The God of the Righteous Guns. Led to the slaughter like an animal to the abattoir. Where are your bags?'

'My bags?'

'You have packed, haven't you? You have told Desanka you're going?'

She looked at me, sitting uncomfortably on the upholstered chair, and stood up. I noticed for the first time that she was dressed in black from head to foot.

'I haven't brought anything,' I said. 'I didn't know I was meant to.'

'Lieserl. There has been a desecration. Perhaps nothing you ever see again will measure up to the ignorance and obscenity that sent this fine young boy off to die. I want you to go home and pack. I don't want to hear a word about bloody gravity.'

'We heard gunfire this morning,' I said. I was roused sufficiently to pull together my textbooks from under Maja's bed.

'Time is of the essence,' said Maja, and slammed her suitcase shut.

The farm looked strangely quiet. The spring wheat was growing. In the hollow by the river the first green buds of the early summer strawberries would be forming. I would have expected to see chickens running, the farmhand out in the fields. Against the horizon, the low rumble of gunfire continued. Whatever was happening, it was not going away. It was coming closer.

Desanka was waiting for us in the low kitchen, bread and a little butter on the plate before her. She was white-faced and grim but the kitchen was clean.

'Fräulein Freisler,' she said. 'I wondered when you'd get here.'

'It's time,' said Maja. 'You know you have to go.'

'I'm not leaving,' said Desanka. 'This is my home.'

'Lieserl is leaving,' said Maja. She gestured to me. I went into Desanka's bedroom to find a bag to pack. I hesitated but Desanka turned and waved me away, too.

There was a grey holdall the wastrel brother Ferdi had stuffed gold coins into once and I took that. I didn't have much. Clothes. One of the blankets from my bed, a patchwork that had been in Desanka's family long before I arrived. Nothing to rival Maja's ocelot. Maja had all my important books, anyway, in her bag, and I had Hans Albert's magic stone in my pocket.

I lingered, despite having packed. I could hear the women talking in the kitchen.

Maja wanted to know: 'What will you do?'

'Stay here.'

'The fighting is coming. Where's your farmhand?'

'Gone.' Desanka snorted. 'Gone to defend his family.'

'Things are already dangerous,' said Maja. 'They'll only get worse.'

'That's why you have to take her far away. There is nothing to hold her here.'

There was a pause.

'Will you?' Desanka's voice was low.

'I'll take her,' said Maja. 'You know I will.'

And thus, only just within my hearing, Desanka handed me over.

I made Maja wait outside with her brown suitcase and my grey holdall. 'I won't be long,' I said. 'Just wait.' She hopped from one foot to the other in her impatience, but she waited.

In the kitchen, I put my arms round Desanka. 'I have to know', I said, 'before I go.'

Desanka didn't waste any time. She knew one day I would ask and she had been ready. She sat down on the bench and put her hands flat on the wooden table. The story came out like it had been rehearsed.

'There was a scarlet fever epidemic', she said, 'in the spring of 1904. When the snows melted. Infection everywhere. Mileva's brother's wife – they were at the family home . . . Mileva's brother's wife had a baby, a new baby. You were nearly two when you came down with the fever. They didn't expect you to live.'

'But they had to get me out of the house.'

'They had to get you out of the house. They thought you wouldn't live and there was the new baby . . . Your mother was away, with your father. They were married by then, of course. And her family was bringing you up. That was the plan.'

'Why you? Why did they give me to you?'

Desanka shrugged her shoulders, as if these things should have been apparent.

'I asked for you.'

'Why?'

'Mileva and I . . . Mileva and I have known each other since school. She knew Ferdi. She was very clever, your mother. Very clever. Like you at school. Then she went away to study . . . Mileva was my friend and you were her daughter. No matter what mistakes she made, no matter what trouble she got herself into out there in that foreign land, with that stupid good-for-nothing, she was still my friend. And you were part of her. If you were going to die, I wanted it to be with me.'

'But I didn't die.'

She laughed. 'No. You nearly did, but you were a strong girl. You came through that fever even stronger in the end.'

'Then why didn't you send me back?'

I thought Desanka wasn't going to answer the question. And then I thought that whatever answer she gave – that they didn't want me back, that my mother's family had forgotten about me by the time I was strong enough to learn to walk again – I would not want to hear it. But she did answer.

'I didn't tell them you'd got better.'

'No-one?'

'Only Mileva. She sent money when she could. And I asked her to tell the rest of your family you were dead.'

'And she did?'

'She did.'

'Where are my family, Desanka?'

'Over the other side of Novi Sad. They have a big house. You've seen them sometimes in town. Your uncle. Leopold Marič. Your grandfather. Your cousins. You've walked past them in the street. They don't know you.'

All this time I had been looking so far away, to the ends of the Danube, and I had a family here, in Novi Sad.

'Why? Why didn't you tell them I was alive? Why didn't you take me home when I got better?'

It was so simple.

'Because, little one, by then I loved you.'

How could I blame her? My own family had packed me off without qualm, an incident, an anomaly, glad to see the back of me. No doubt it was easier for Mileva, too, able to go home and visit her family with her new legitimate sons, without having me sitting waiting there like an embarrassing parcel in the left-luggage room. Desanka had made a bed for me in a cherrywood nook and told me stories of princesses. She had loved me all these years, waiting for the day when she knew I would go.

In the circumstances, I decided not to worry her with my ideas of revenge, and simply kissed her.

'Goodbye, Desanka.' I hesitated. 'If I can, I'll be back.'

She turned away.

'No, you won't.'

I kissed her again. Very hard, as if I could pack into one kiss ten years of thanks.

In the cart, I noticed that Maja had a newly acquired wedding ring on her hand.

'You are too young for full black,' she said, 'but here . . .'

She placed a band of black material around my upper arm and pinned it into place.

'I don't know anyone who has died,' I said.

'That's not the point,' she said, 'we want people to think we do.'

'Why?'

'It does away with questions,' she said, 'and petty inconveniences at borders.'

We drove towards the north-west. In field after field, the grapes were ripening on the vines, tied against poles 4 or 5 metres high. We passed their orderly rows over and over, ticking like a metronome. Not ripe yet. Not ripe yet. They would be ripe. Anything and everything grows in that soil, it is like a breadbasket. Everything grew on the sun-drenched plain while the war washed the Empire away.

To stop myself thinking about Desanka, to stop myself from running back to her and certain death, I kept Maxwell's equations

at the front of my brain. I held them there like a shield and didn't
let myself look behind.

Here on earth, all speeds were relative. But what if you took a wider
point of view: the entire universe? If you measured the speed of light
against some fundamental reference frame of absolute space – the
ether – then light could be a constant, after all. Its speed was simply
relative to the ether.

What was particularly interesting about the equations, though, as
far as I was concerned, was that when you looked at them properly,
there was no need for ether at all. The mathematics worked perfectly
well without it. In fact, I just didn't see how ether *could* work,
despite the fact that every textbook I had read kept banging on about
it. It just got in the way.

If the earth was moving through the ether, like a swimmer in a
river, then sometimes we ought to be going with the flow of the
ether, sometimes against it, like swimming against the current. And
if light always travelled at a constant relative to the ether, then sometimes we'd see differences in the speed of light depending on
whether we were moving quickly with the current or more slowly
against it.

I bet there was no difference. I bet the speed of light was always
the same. Here, I was up against a brick wall. So far, everything I'd
thought about the universe, I'd been able to do in my head. It didn't
need any special equipment – just thinking was enough. But to find
out whether light looked to be moving slower or faster depending
on our position in the ether needed someone to go out there and
look. I'd have to wait for them to do that.

Meanwhile, the mathematics said there was no need for ether.
And if there was no ether . . . then the whole universe was up for
grabs.

Then I remembered Desanka saying, 'Serbs don't curtsy,' and
burst into tears.

*   *   *

At every line we were borne to the front on a wave of sympathy for our sad loss.

Maja was gracious. 'My daughter is so tired,' she said. 'It is such a help to us.' Inclining her head. 'Thank you very much. Thank you so very much.'

Some time in the middle of the night, the second night, the third night, a man in a uniform spoke to me.

'Lieserl Marić?'

I raised my head in sleep from Maja's shoulder, the only soft part of her I had managed to find above her whalebone corset, surprised to find I was standing up. 'Here.'

'Sign.'

And I signed the piece of paper, whatever it was, whatever it promised, using my given name for the last time. And so I left for ever the country where I did not even have a bed of my own, just some blankets in the nook between the chimney breast and the outside wall, cold in the winter, hot in the summer, and went wherever Maja was taking me.

'Where shall we go?' she said at the station.

I looked back over that flat plain of wheat and oxen, and for a moment almost allowed myself to be seduced by a breeze from the south, laden with lemon and magnolia, the softness of ripe peaches. But that was not where my father was.

'North,' I said. And so she bought tickets and we crossed mountains to where the air was ever colder, and we began our random walk across the continent.

I was going to get there first, I had decided. Devise an explanation for things that would take the place of ether. I'd beat my father to an explanation of the universe if it killed me.

In the fields, all the wild flowers were out.

CHAPTER FOUR

The Forest

26 January 1918

I HAD MY SIXTEENTH BIRTHDAY IN VIENNA. EVERYWHERE WE
went, everything was rationed or restricted. Nothing was to be had
without a high price. Nevertheless, Maja made me a cake with chantilly cream and meringue, out of God knows what black-market
sugar. I think she arranged things deliberately on our travels so that
I would have my birthday in Vienna, so that I would always remember the chantilly cream and sugar against the squares and rococo curls
of the buildings, the churches with their cupolas and white spires.

I had been thinking about it for a long while, but it was on the night
of my sixteenth birthday, after the cake and the walk in the curlicued
squares, that I decided that, once you acknowledged that light was a
maximum and a constant, then time itself was the problem.

Then Maja kissed me full on the mouth and told me I was grown
up now.

13 October 1918

We were living in a dour set of rooms under the watchful eye of Frau
Goldberg who owned the house where we rented. She was pleased

to have a schoolteacher and her daughter for company. No-one was renting rooms these days. Scarcely anyone. On the very steps of the house was a peasant woman who came every day to sell turnips and firewood. Maja still wore full black and myself the black cotton armband. Frau Goldberg was so sorry for our loss.

By now we had invented a dead husband for Maja called Wolfgang. Along the way, we had acquired a black-edged photograph in an ebony frame which took pride of place on the rented bureau. Someone suitably fine and strong, firm-jawed, resplendent in the uniform of the Kaiser. Maja dusted the picture daily, to Frau Goldberg's approval. She was so glad to have us that she put up with the inconvenience of science students trailing up and down the stairs of an evening.

'Ah, yes, science has always been my subject,' said Maja. 'Gravity, magnetism. You know.' She racked her brains for something else she had heard me say. 'Thermodynamics.'

Frau Goldberg was suspicious.

'Don't you find it inspirational', continued Maja, warming to her theme, 'that our young men still wish to better themselves, to advance their scientific knowledge, even under the hardship of war?'

Frau Goldberg took a sideways glance at me. Nothing improper could be going on, surely, with me as chaperone.

'With our atoms and molecules we shall defeat them! Scientific endeavour shows the true spirit of the German people! And if you should ever wish for lessons yourself,' said Maja, infused with the German spirit, 'well, my motto is, it's never too late to learn something new.'

Frau Goldberg backed away.

Luckily, the boarding house, twice as clean as Frau Heidel's in Novi Sad, had two beds in the room, so I never had to move my growing collection of textbooks to make room for her when I fell asleep at nights, and I never had to sleep in the detritus of Maja's customers, though I sometimes had to lie very still and be quiet.

Lying very still and quiet was an ideal way to work on the mathematics. I carried my equations round in my head and twisted and worried at them at every opportunity. Why could no speeds added together add up to more than the speed of light? Why? Just because there was chaos all around me didn't mean I had to stop asking questions.

I could go no further. I needed more to work on. I decided, therefore, that I now knew enough German vocabulary and enough basic physics not to be daunted by the journals. By the time scientific theories had become accepted as largely correct, by the time they were published in textbooks, they were already years old. The world was moving on too quickly for me to wait for books. In the journals you got the raw material, the stuff of experiment and premise. Half of it might be entirely wrong, but . . . I had never been in a place where I might get hold of any journals before, so now was an ideal opportunity to find out exactly what they contained.

However, I met unexpected opposition.

The library in Vienna was much less enlightened than the Serbian Reading Room, although better equipped. There were technical journals in there, in a special section, but I couldn't take them out. And I wasn't allowed in there to see them because I was (a) a foreign national (b) a girl.

Getting to those journals was important. I knew my father had his theories in print – my mother had said so. If I could read them, I could find out exactly what his conclusions were on gravity and light. But short of inveigling a decent, honest, upright Viennese male citizen to go in there, look through all the volumes of *Annalen der Physik* and copy out by hand anything that might have been written by one Albert Einstein, I was stumped.

Frau Goldberg had a son, Josef, who had escaped almost certain death in the war by having a weak heart, thus being excused to stay home and look after his mother. In those frenetic weeks, when all the reserves left were daily being summoned to the Eastern front, Josef lived on tenterhooks, and so did his mother. Josef had pale skin spotted with freckles and ran a business from the back of a truck, selling butter and eggs and army vodka.

At weekends, Josef Goldberg and I would wander to the slopes of the hills and the lakes. We walked for miles. The autumn had been mild so far and we gathered berries for jam and nuts for the birds that Frau Goldberg liked to feed as they hovered, twittering, in the trees surrounding the backyard, tempting them down with some beech nuts. The pine needles of the lower slopes of the hills lay thick and green like blankets on the ground, almost hiding the mushrooms that pushed up through the dark like white fists.

One Sunday evening, I made love to Josef Goldberg on the green blankets and white fists, just in case he was called to the Eastern front, or in case he had to face the barbed wire and the mustard gas, scattering the beech nuts in the fury of our limbs, and all the time I fretted about Maja, at home doing the mending, finding out.

Josef Goldberg, on the other hand, was entranced.

'How old are you?' he kept saying.

'Sixteen. I am sixteen.'

'Sixteen.'

His arms and legs rested heavy on the earth. Pine needles still have a smell today that I can never associate with anyone other than Josef Goldberg and that Sunday evening on the slopes of the hills above Vienna.

'Josef,' I said afterwards, a few mushrooms gathered in my lap for good measure against Maja's discreet enquiries. 'Could you get me something?'

'What?'

'Magazines.'

'Of course.' He was easy. He knew the sort of thing I would want. Pictures. Fashion plates. The new collection from the house of Worth. 'Which ones?' His pale skin was white in the dark of the forest.

'The *Annalen der Physik* from Leipzig and as many recent copies
as you can get of the *Jahrbuch der Radioaktivität und Elektronik*.'

Josef Goldberg rolled over onto his elbows, propped himself up
on the floor of the forest and looked at me. 'Sure,' he said, unwilling
to be defeated by a girl.

'It's very kind of you,' I said, brushing pine needles off my skirt.

'Think nothing of it. Nothing of it at all.'

12 November 1918

Through all the rest of that autumn, I brought Maja mushrooms
and Frau Goldberg beech nuts. I told Maja I got the mushrooms
early in the morning, walking in the forests. I decided not to
mention Josef Goldberg. Certainly when I brought the gifts of my
guilt into Maja's kitchen, the dew of the forest was still fresh in their
secret gills; Maja would wipe their shining white heads and slice
them neatly into thin slivers, brown and white together in a wedge.
Then she would melt a few drops of oil in a pan, stir in flour, add
milk and slide my mushrooms into the liquid. In moments, the
white milk would be softened. No longer hard-edged, uncompro-
mising. It changed. Without there ever being one point when it
changed, the milk stopped being white and became beige, the colour
from the mushrooms leaching into the liquid, swishing and lapping
as it thickened against the sides of the pan, gentle waves from Maja's
wooden spoon sending it up, almost to the edge where it could over-
flow, overspill and burn on the stove. I watched her do it, over and
over, in the calm of the morning.

When they were cooked, the creamed mushrooms, we ate them
with thin toast. Toast but no butter. For breakfast in our rented
rooms.

No butter because this was in the days when the bread was made
out of turnips. The meat Maja brought home from the market was
half bone, half gristle. There was no milk to be had on the open

market – we had to rely on Josef for that. You could buy butter – for two marks a pound. Under the counter, you could get as much as you liked for ten times that price. But most people had to go without. We got one egg a fortnight and sometimes I just wanted to stare at it, to prolong the moment when I knew I had food to eat. I was so hungry, the numbers fell away in my head. I couldn't concentrate on equations or logarithms; all I could think of was egg dumplings and stuffed peppers, smoked sausages and spice cake. I couldn't keep my head straight about time and light and gravity, it kept straying to trout with dill and cucumber, and strawberry pancakes arrayed under a muslin cover on a wooden kitchen table.

There was a tin bath on the third floor, with temperamental plumbing and iron claws, which was free for our use on Tuesday afternoons. I was so despondent about the intractable equations and lack of strawberry pancakes that this Tuesday, while Maja was at the market, I decided to take my mind off things by having a bath, something I had not attempted since the autumn, when the temperature began to fall.

As there was no heating in the bathroom, I became colder and colder waiting for the hot water to fill the tub, and by the time there was enough water to get into, my feet were so blue, I couldn't put them in the water without them feeling like they were being scalded.

I gave up and got into bed, only marginally cleaner.

I got Hans Albert's magic stone out of the holdall, held it in my hands and watched it perform its tricks. Always and for ever the same. I reminded myself that even universal forces could be reduced to this: small biddable elements.

Sometimes the science students Maja brought back to the boarding house left a newspaper. I now picked up an old copy of one of these. I was cold and hungry, looking for distraction and comfort, and so it was, almost by accident, that I discovered that the war was nearly over.

I discovered something else, too. In the process of the war, Desanka's beloved breadbasket of Hungary had been trodden

underfoot. Towards the end, I surmised, gangrene, cold and
diarrhoea destroyed anything the Serbs and the Croats hadn't.

I crumpled the newspaper and used it to light the fire. Pulling the
blankets tight around my body – Frau Goldberg's and the patchwork one I had brought with me – I fell asleep thinking of Desanka,
thinking of my mother's family in Novi Sad, thinking of Desanka
and her one shotgun.

Maja came back from the market with a squirrel. The next week,
a crow. I pleaded and pleaded with her, picking over bits of wings
and feathers, not to try to make a stew out of a sparrow, as others
were doing.

15 December 1918

The trick about staying warm is to get warm before you go out and
then keep moving. Maja stood by the oil fire to put on boots, coat,
overcoat, scarf, hat and mitts, but there wasn't much scope for
moving about in the hour-long religious services she still insisted on
attending. It was one of the most bitterly cold winters that I had ever
seen, and I had seen plenty of them on the farm. I had therefore
decided that the most efficient way of keeping warm and conserving
energy was to stay in bed. I could not persuade Maja of my wisdom.
Out she went, trailing scarves. She had recently, and triumphantly,
come up with a recipe that utilized tree bark. I found it not very
sustaining. Our clothes hung on us like sacks.

In bed, I could think. And thinking was what I liked doing.
Wrapped up warm in my Sunday solitude while Maja was out
worshipping, straightforward thinking was the only way I knew to
try to forget the fact that I was ravenous.

I decided that there was no reason to ditch Newton completely.
He gave a good enough description of the everyday world. That
suited me. It supported my plans. If I kept on my path slowly but
surely, I would get my revenge on my father one day. Like trains

along a track, like cannon balls across a battlefield, we would meet.
Tick, tick, tick. You could almost hear the cosmic clockwork
moving.

It was only at speeds approaching the velocity of light itself that
the calculations became strange and the numbers didn't lead where
you would expect them to. And this was because space and time
were linked.

That constant, c, is a speed. And what is a speed, after all? It is a
measure that relates space and time. One is meaningless without the
other. A speed tells you how fast something is moving in the form
of kilometres (space) over time (per hour). You can't have the space
without the time, so the fact that the fundamental constant linked
space and time was telling me something significant about the
universe. But what?

I wished Josef Goldberg would hurry up with the journals.

After Mass that Sunday, Maja began to cough. The next day, so did
Frau Goldberg. It went on and on.

Maja being so indisposed, we could not pay the rent. I told Frau
Goldberg that Maja would be well in time, but Frau Goldberg,
herself awash with medicines and having taken to her bed, already
did not care. Josef did not care, either. He said as much over the
lemon syrups that he had made a special order for from Holland.

Before we realized what was happening, illness lay over the land
like a veil. The streets became quiet. In Maja's church, people had
been praying for so long for an end to the war, it came as a surprise
that they had to switch tactics and start praying for the good health
of their near and dear ones instead. But they couldn't ignore what
was going on. People around us were dying from the influenza like
flies. Nevertheless, people, Maja included, battling on against her
cough, said the same old prayers with the same old words.

In all those days when she had just a cough, Maja did not miss
going to church: the Christmas Eve service, the Christmas Day
service, the Feast of Saint Stephen service, the Massacre of the Holy

Innocents service. At the end of the proceedings, the words of the hymn came tumbling over themselves, hurrying in their eagerness to be done with, as if the singers were anxious to pass on to other, more practical endeavours: to feed themselves, to keep themselves warm, to get out of the range of the sneezed germs. I boiled endless kettles and took hot tea to Maja and Frau Goldberg and told Josef to try to get hold of some linctus.

One evening in that interlude between Christmas and the new year, Josef Goldberg called by with the first issues of the *Annalen der Physik*. They were heavy and bulky, and he had great difficulty getting them up the stairs. Some were torn, all were full of dust. The others, he said, would take a little longer and God only knew these had been difficult to get. Just how difficult, I was to surmise from the lengthy and varied nature of the payment required. Maja, in the next bed, didn't even wake up, so I knew she was more ill than she had admitted and the cough was worse than it seemed.

Late that night, through all the hours of darkness, I sat in my bed, after Josef Goldberg had gone to tend his mother with lemon syrup in the rooms below, fetching Maja, at intervals, anything she required: cool flannels and contradictory warm blankets, pouring the newly acquired linctus into her mouth whenever she opened it. And in that night I read for the first time the three papers my father had published in Volume 17 way back in 1905. One in particular, 'On the Electrodynamics of Moving Bodies', was interesting, and I guessed it must have been the one my mother had said, on the day that she had come to visit me, would make them famous. It hadn't made them famous yet. Perhaps, I hoped, that was because it was entirely wrong. I read with grim determination.

The paper contained a special theory that at last reconciled the behaviour of light with the familiar rules of Newtonian mechanics. I checked the figures and saw that they were right. At one point it looked like my father had been using a co-variant form of the electromagnetic equation and I harboured a hope that he just might be on treacherous ground. But no. Like me, he had come to the inescapable conclusion that if light was a constant then time itself was relative. The faster you travelled, the slower time went.

It was against common sense. Given the right circumstances, according to those equations, time would go backwards.

Maja had had a good night. I watched the sun come up feeling that there was still hope.

Not long after dawn, Josef Goldberg came up the backstairs and told me his mother showed no signs of getting better and asked me what I was doing.

'I'm worrying about whether space and time are different in moving and stationary systems.'

'I've got breakfast.'

'Tree bark?'

'Butter. Eggs.' He whispered. 'Cream.'

'Oh good,' I said. 'That'll keep Maja's strength up.'

'I was thinking about yours,' he said.

'It's the same thing,' I said.

12 February 1919

Just when I thought we had come safely into the new year with Maja's cough being only a cough and a bit of fever, and the worst thing I would have to worry about was Lorentz's transformation equations because Frau Goldberg was on the mend, Maja got worse. Her brow burned. The gold of her hair was dull. The blue of her eyes was almost black. Through the cold and the night, she was hot, soaking the sheets of her bed with sweat, and all the time she shivered.

Perhaps if she had been less pious, I told her, Maja's cough wouldn't have developed into influenza. Unholy creature that I was, and grubby, I didn't even get a sniffle. Neither did Josef Goldberg. We were conspicuously and suspiciously healthy.

With Maja sick, we had no money coming in. Although we didn't

have to worry about the rent – Josef told his mother, who was still
frail, that we had paid for the next two months in advance, which I
considered I had – when Josef was away we couldn't eat. We had
nothing except for what I gleaned from him, no money to buy even
a sparrow. Most people by now were starving. Josef was doing a
roaring trade in illicit basic foodstuffs and patent influenza medicines. The mushrooms on toast of the previous autumn seemed like
a dream. I did dream about them. I dreamed of Maja stirring the
creamy liquid and me eating the turnip toast, and in the mornings I
would wake up still hungry. If I was thin, though, the bones in
Maja's wrists threatened to snap, her skin was pitted with sores.
When I put the flannel to her forehead through the days that melted
into one another, I listened to her chest rattle.

Josef came to visit and turned grey at the sound of this gruesome
breathing.

'Good God,' he said. 'This is dreadful.'

'I know,' I said.

'I knew those medicines were sugar and water.'

'Then why did you give them to me?'

'They worked on my mother,' he said.

This aside, Josef Goldberg was quite cheerful. The Allied
blockade was good for business. His prices were becoming more
and more extortionate. As well as the medicines, he brought me
more *Annalen der Physik*, some cans of corned beef, looted from
some defeated British army trench in France, and packets of
foreign cigarettes. I took three cans of the corned beef and the
cigarettes, though I wasn't sure what to do with them, and paid
him, because I was busy in my worry about Maja, with only half an
hour in bed and a string of costume jewellery from Maja's brown
suitcase before he went off to Munich to chase up a consignment
of cheese.

I unwound a can of corned beef and sniffed it, then persuaded
Frau Heimlich on the second-floor landing to swap me a potato for
one of the other cans. I sold the cigarettes for more money than I

would have dreamed possible and hid the notes under my pillow. I boiled Frau Heimlich's potato, mashed the beef into it and spooned the resultant mess into Maja's mouth. It is one of the few times I have undertaken any serious cooking and I like to think it was one of my most successful as Maja immediately revived enough to sit up and spit it out.

I ate the rest myself, going over my father's papers in the *Annalen der Physik*. The most surprising thing I found was something that was not there. I had expected to see my mother's name on those papers, too, not just my father's. Why wasn't she there, if she did his mathematics? They were very beautiful mathematics, I thought. Precise, elegant, devoid of unnecessary complications. Just like Mileva. Just like I remembered her.

There was that little c over and again, the one I had first encountered in Maxwell's equations: the speed of light, but this time in a different set of figures. The precise, elegant set.

If you multiply a speed by a time, you get a length. If you travel 3 kilometres per hour for two hours, the length you get is 6 kilometres, obviously. If you go about things properly, you can link these measures of length (space) with measures of time all in the same set of equations. In its simplest terms, this is what my father had done.

Pushed to their limits, though, the equations showed that time wasn't what we thought it was. We are so used to travelling in it in one direction only, unlike space, in which we can move about more or less at will, that it is hard to think of time as anything else but a one-way arrow. Looking at those equations, I realized it couldn't be. Space and time were just aspects of one single unified whole. Spacetime.

Quite what I was going to do with this discovery, I didn't know.

I sighed. I couldn't get Maja to eat, and travelling at the speed of light was not something I was likely to accomplish in the next few days. I didn't think the corned beef tasted half bad, though.

*   *   *

Josef Goldberg came back again three days later and, with the air of one casting a few pearls before swine, said, 'They say there's real medicine in Munich.'

Munich was a day and half away at best. More if Maja couldn't walk. I knew it would be a waste of time to make the journey. There would be no medicine, most likely. Or there would be medicine, and it would cost more than the cigarette money, which was all I had. Or, if the medicine was real, and I could afford it, it wouldn't work. In those days before antibiotics, there was no telling. Worse, the journey itself could possibly kill her.

'If you don't do something soon,' said Josef, listening to the rattle in Maja's chest like a medical expert, 'she'll die.'

I couldn't not go. Equally, I couldn't leave Maja behind. No doubt I might have drafted in an unwilling Frau Goldberg to look after her, but I couldn't bear to leave her. I couldn't bear to leave her knowing she might die when I wasn't there. Like Desanka. If Maja was going to die, it would be with me by her side.

'Come on, Maja,' I said, stirring her from her bed. 'It'll be worth it. Josef says he'll take us in his truck.'

I looked hard at Josef and he nodded.

14 February 1919

We rattled along with a new consignment of corned beef, journals and foreign cigarettes to the outskirts of Munich, Maja under the patchwork blanket I had brought from Novi Sad and her head on the mysterious brown suitcase that had always been with her.

I said to her, 'Don't worry, Maja. There'll be medicine in Munich. And I'll tell you something else, too: why should gravity only concern uniform motion? Nothing else in the universe is uniform. It's a real flaw, Maja. I'm surprised nobody's seen it. Uniform motion, Maja, uniform motion. Hush now, hush.' I cradled her head in my hands, against the bouncing of the truck.

It was freezing. The temperature had long ago dropped well below zero. What I had never known before was how much cold could make you hurt. In my fingers there was pain. In my toes there was pain. It burned and it insisted.

I kept rubbing Maja's nose and chin so she wouldn't get frostbite. It hurt to touch her. My toes turned to ice.

Josef dropped us at the outskirts of the town to avoid the checkpoints, so it was only in the morning, when I had dragged Maja the last painful mile, that we found out the truth.

The medicine in Munich was chloroform, and it was being given to the dying to ease them into death.

28 March 1919

The children had woken me up, crying. tiny faces, large blank eyes, small arms just skin and bones, rickety foreheads, crooked legs. They never stopped crying, until they became too weak to continue.

I turned to Maja. I thought she might live one more day. It wasn't just the influenza, there was something else wrong, too, and at first I couldn't work out what it was. It wasn't just the phlegm she coughed up, the racking rattle of her chest in the night, the way her fever burned and she muttered in her half-sleep. That had gone on for days and I was used to it.

It was as if she had become infected with torpor itself, or some sluggish fluid that coursed through what was left of her thin veins and weighed her down. She still didn't want any corned beef. She didn't want the sausages Josef Goldberg had obtained at no little expense from an Allied depot in Brussels. More than that, she no longer cared whether she lived or died.

I had been trying to cheer her up by telling her about my problems grappling with gravity in order to formulate a more general theory of space and time, one that would reach wider than the specialized theory in my father's paper.

The principle of equivalence, which I had discovered in back issues of the *Jahrbuch der Radioaktivität und Elektronik* had been a great help in this endeavour. I had been pestering Josef Goldberg for more journals and more, the ideas in them feeding my own, sending my brain in new directions every time I opened their pages.

'There has recently been a war, Lieserl,' he reminded me tersely. 'Scientific papers are in short supply. People have been using them to light fires with.'

'Please,' I said. 'Get me what you can.'

'You know I will,' he said.

To describe what was going on in the universe, I needed the right field equations. But I was almost there. I tried to convey to Maja some of my excitement.

'It doesn't matter if you're accelerating *or* in a gravitational field. Things work the same. If you were in a lift, say, and the cable snapped, you'd fall, wouldn't you?'

Maja mumbled something indistinct, too tired to argue.

'Now, if I was in that lift and you were in that lift, and I shone a beam of light across to you while we were falling, it would look to you, and to me, that the light was moving across the lift in a straight line. Wouldn't it?'

Maja groaned.

'But Josef, say. Say if Josef was outside the lift, on the ground somewhere, watching us fall, he'd see the light curve. In the time it's taken the light to cross from one side of the lift to the other, the lift would have moved downwards and the light would have moved downwards with it. In other words, Maja, a light beam must be bent by the effects of gravity.' I considered a moment, thinking about light beams. 'Maja, why don't you have a sausage?'

'I don't want to.'

In 1919, I didn't recognize this for what it was. It was the first time I had seen it. Over the years this inertia would become familiar.

Lethargy. Despair. The twentieth-century disease. In its famili-
arity, I would hold it in contempt. In Maja, that first time, it was an
unknown quantity.

I wondered what there was in her past that was bearing in on
her now. I knew nothing of where she had come from, nothing of
her family, her parents, her homeland, nothing of the young man
she had briefly cried over when he had met his death at the Eastern
front, nothing of why she had rescued me.

We were in a shelter, run by people with a mission from God,
who once a day provided meagre amounts of a grey gruel they called
turnip soup, greenish rolls and dubious mussel puddings. They laid
Maja out on a pallet on the floor in the gymnasium of the school they
had taken over, and I thought, This is really it. Wherever she has
come from, this is where she will die. The people from God had told
us the armistice was holding and we should all rejoice. I thought,
The war might be over but Maja never cared about the war anyway,
the temporary red lines of nation states, so that isn't going to help.
She hardly breathed any more.

Nobody in that gymnasium passed five minutes without
scratching. In the daylight, when the sun was strong, we picked
through one another's heads, parting the hair close to the scalp,
examining it strand by strand for tell-tale signs – sticky eggs that
held fast close to the hair root, tiny crawling things. We would sift
through each other's hair, squeeze between fingertips the minute
white eggs, the tiny black specks roaming over the skin, and pull
them to the end of each strand and away. Under our hair, our skin
was bleeding from bites. I had a family of fleas living in the patchwork blanket I had brought from Novi Sad. No matter how many
times I shook it against the sun, those insects stuck, with their
patented familial flea glue, and came back to torture Maja.

Whatever the weight of her past, every day in that gymnasium was
a struggle. Every morning she had to make the decision simply to carry
on living. In the mornings the people from God would come with a
cauldron of a thin dark liquid they described as coffee, and every

morning I went and stood in the queue with two metal cups, one for me and one for Maja. Each morning so far she had decided to live, raised her head enough to drink some of the bitter gritty liquid, and I was glad. But the simple exhaustion of that repeated decision was wearing her down. If I didn't do something it would overwhelm her completely, and one morning she would say no, refuse life, refuse us all. I had seen it happen to others there, the homeless, the dispossessed, the refugees, the ones who had lost every relative, the ones who had nothing to hold them to the earth any more.

I talked to her incessantly, all through the day, my stomach gnawing with hunger, my limbs cold through lack of food. I talked about gravity, about time, about the best way to make goulash, about preparing the meat beforehand, soaking it and cutting it and seasoning it. I talked to her about the vegetables that would accompany it, about the wine that would go best with it, the pastries that would follow. I talked until the short day closed and it was time for the ration of turnip soup again.

'Maja,' I said, holding her thin wrist in mine, a cool flannel to her forehead, 'if you go, what will I do?'

'You'll get by without me,' she said, the words painful in her dry mouth.

I wasn't at all sure that I would.

If she died, I could still continue my journey along the Danube, along my slow and certain path towards my father. I could extract my revenge, claim my rightful inheritance – no-one had taken away *that* reason for living, certainly, even if I wasn't yet exactly sure of the details of all of this – but that wasn't the point. Nearly everyone I knew in the world had disappeared. If Maja went, too, the whole world would be just too . . . cold. Hard. Lonely. And this was Maja, Maja who had rescued me. I wasn't going to let Maja simply slip away without a fight. I had to come up with something that would become her reason for living, but so far I had failed.

I let go of her hand and let her fall into sleep, certain she would never wake again.

In the absence of anything else I could do, I stayed up late and let my mind slide completely into the one place where I couldn't feel pain, the world where the numbers shone like shining threads and I could lose myself in following them to their end. I grappled with the field equations, thought a lot about light beams and had a good go at working out a more generalized theory of relativity.

Objects – anything, planets, apples, people – distort the space-time around themselves, so that other objects moving through this spacetime are deflected, tugged by the gravitational forces. Newton's laws still apply – the force will be inversely proportional to the square of the distance.

It was quite a simple idea, but the equations needed to describe its ramifications were pretty complicated, though I say so myself. It took me most of the night to write it all down, with paper and pencils Josef had supplied. On the whole, though, I was pleased, as it looked as if I had now explained everything.

I wasn't sure it would impress Maja, but it was the best I could do at short notice. It was certainly the best theory I had seen so far of how gravity really worked.

When I had finished, I wrote 'A General Theory for the Universe' at the top of the page, underlined it twice, went to sleep and dreamed of cheese and chocolate.

29 March 1919

The next morning, a cold saturday morning, still bone-achingly cold even though it was so late in the year, I woke to find that I had lost all sensation in my feet. Maja was still, but still breathing. I got up and hobbled out to the school playground, hoping the exercise would bring back some feeling. The bird bath in the play-ground had frozen to a perfect oval. Nothing marred the edges of the ellipse, not even the tentative feet of birds. It was whole, perfect. A complete band of ice. I stood for a moment, watching its edges, holding on to its perfection in an unfamiliar universe. Although what I had written down the night before was quite simple, really, nothing more than a description of gravity, it did depend on the idea of a curved spacetime.

If my calculations were right, if you followed them through to their logical conclusions, then the world as we had known it had disappeared. In my new world, straight lines weren't straight at all, and time was infinitely fluid. I felt that this made sense but, as a reason for deciding to go on living, it was a bit tenuous.

The only thing that was missing was proof. Equations were all very well on paper, but how was I ever going to prove they were right?

My only consolation was that, if my father had been working along these lines as well, and for all I knew he had even reached the same point in his calculations as I had, then he wasn't going to be able to prove it either. People would just have to take it on trust. Spacetime was curved, and that was that.

I watched the bird bath for a while, that perfect ellipse, gradually realizing that I could feel only some of my toes, and then, all of a sudden, the brightness of the day darkened. Up in the sky, the sun had been blotted out.

'Oh, ' I said, and ran in to tell Maja. I shook her awake.

'No, I don't want any more of that wretched mussel pudding,' she moaned. 'Or cabbage water. Go away.'

'Wake up, Maja. Listen. What about an eclipse?'

'Ah,' she said and sank back on her blankets, looking at the darkness of the gymnasium. 'Now?'

'No,' I said hastily, worried that she was taking the darkness for a suitable stellar omen that she had reached the right time to die, and hauled her up again. 'This is only a cloud.'

'You've woken me up for a cloud?'

It began to rain, spattering hard on the gymnasium roof. I explained, briefly, in the interests of saving time, about my General Theory for the Universe.

'I think you're going to have to tell me that again,' she said.

I would always have this problem. What was so clear and shining to me in my own head just couldn't be put into plain words. I only made things more muddled the more I tried to explain them. Nevertheless, heartened by the fact that she was taking an interest, I had another go.

'Don't you see, Maja? An eclipse would be make-or-break time for me.'

'Why, for Heaven's sake?'

'If light passes through a curved spacetime', I said, 'it will be bent. Now, what if a beam of light from a very distant star passes close by the sun on its way to reach us?'

She didn't answer.

Undaunted, I pressed on. 'It will be bent as it moves through the spacetime that is distorted by the sun's huge gravitational mass. Now, how can you *tell* if light from a distant star is being bent by the sun?'

'I give up,' said Maja.

'It is difficult,' I acknowledged, 'because generally the sun is in the way. So, what do you do? You look at the stars behind the sun when the light of the sun has gone. Simple. If the light's been bent, there will be a shift in their apparent position.'

'Go on, then,' said Maja. 'Pop out into the playground and have a quick peek.'

'Rain clouds aren't enough. You need an eclipse. Something really solid like the moon in the way. Maybe I should ask Josef Goldberg for a telescope.'

'How long have you got?' Maja was perking up. Ever practical, she liked practical problems to solve. 'When's the next eclipse?'

'I don't know,' I said, 'but I can find out.'

If I had worked out the theory of relativity in any other era of human history, I reckon I'd have had to wait a good few hundred years, possibly a thousand, before the right kind of eclipse came along to prove me right. However, after consulting the various ephemera that I ordered from Josef Goldberg, I discovered that the next eclipse was in May.

May. Weeks away. I felt as if the universe was demonstrating that it was on my side.

I like to think that it was the news of this forthcoming eclipse that gave Maja enough reason to go on living, at least for another couple of months, gave her enough curiosity to see what would be the eventual outcome. It put an unmistakable pep into *my* daily routine.

Maja, on the other hand, maintains that she only really began to feel herself again when I told her I had obtained the nourishing corned beef by selling her costume jewellery. Certainly she woke right up and told me that I was the stupid one, that any fool could have seen those pearls were real.

I didn't believe her I said, or, if she was telling the truth, look at her sitting up and arguing. Even if those pearls *were* real, the price was worth it.

I hugged her, over and over, my Maja, back to life.

I wondered if Josef Goldberg had known the pearls were real and decided he did because of the willingness with which he furnished not only the ephemera, but promised to look out for a suitable present for Maja. I wished our ex-landlady's son well in his undreamed-of riches. When he went away, on his endless economic travels, I felt his absence.

20 April 1919

Every time I thought of the situation we were in, I scratched my head. I was alternately damp, in which case I scratched because I was itchy; or hot, in which case I scratched because I was sweating. One of the children had shrieked, at the beginning of the year, about finding a flea in his blanket. By now, when we had dealt with nests of them, the children were used to squashing them between thumb and forefinger, slowly, so that the soft insides oozed out with an audible pop.

The children that hadn't succumbed to the influenza and starvation, that is. And as most of them in that shelter were without mothers, we never knew precisely how many there were. Most of them no longer knew their own names.

It was time to move on. Maja was strong enough, well enough, had had enough turnip soup and I told her so.

She said, 'But where shall we go?'

I wasn't sure. I wasn't even entirely sure where we were.

'Do you still want to follow the river?'

I wiggled my feet. It had become a habit with me to check that they were still there after I had lost four toes on my right foot when they had first frozen then turned gangrenous. The doctors at the shelter had chopped them off with nary a qualm and I had watched them drop white on the floor. The nurse had brushed them up into a pan. I still missed them.

Maja flung her hand wide in the same gesture she had used to indicate the total lack of art, culture and music in the outpost of Novi Sad. 'It's up to you.'

Josef Goldberg had told me things were pretty much the same everywhere. Not enough food. Not enough money. Too much illness and sorrow.

'Let's go to Berlin,' I said.

'Why?'

'My father's there. He's been there the whole time the war was on, I don't imagine he's moved now.'

Maja was reluctant. I gathered from this that she had been to Berlin, once, and didn't particularly want to go back there.

'Also,' she said, 'it's full of communists.'

Either that, or there was simply something in Maja's nature that didn't let her travel backwards. It was only when I brought out Josef Goldberg's present that I was able to persuade her otherwise.

'I've got something for you, Maja,' I said.

She was suspicious. I think she thought I'd brought her some-thing outlandish to cook, like an eel or a flatfish, in the quest to restore her good health.

I handed her the tissue-wrapped box. She weighed it in her hand. A minute more and she'd have raised it to her nose to sniff it before risking a look inside.

'Open it, Maja. It's a present.'

She unfolded the tissue, reached inside and held the little gold pot in the palm of her hand. I didn't have to tell her what it was.

'Where did you get this?'

'Josef Goldberg. In the wreckage.'

She couldn't take her eyes off it.

'There's a mirror.'

'Where?'

'Inside.'

Maja opened the tiny pot, looked in the small mirror in the lid and put a little of the rouge on her lips. She breathed deep. She put a tentative amount on her cheeks and glanced at me.

'More,' I said.

She applied more. And more. Her mouth was as red as roses.

'Perfect,' I said.

I had India ink, too, but the India ink had to wait till the next day when we were sitting by the side of the road, Maja laced tight into her corset on the brown suitcase, me more askew on Ferdi's grey holdall. But, when she stained her eyelashes with it, I began to see what Maja would be, what Maja would become. Thin as she was, tired as she was, my Maja was beautiful. And looking into the mirror that was my eyes, Maja saw this, too. Even Josef Goldberg saw it when he came to pick us up in the truck. The colours on her skin made her into someone else.

Josef had a consignment of schnapps and we poured a little into a scoured-out tin and shared it between the three of us.

'Survivors,' said Maja, fluttering her eyelashes.

'Survivors,' I said, drinking as fast as I could to warm me up, and declining to flutter mine.

Josef Goldberg laughed.

29 May 1919

It was raining. We were possibly somewhere in northern Austria or southern Germany judging by the height of the mountains and the lingering chill in the air, but I was fairly certain of the date.

Maja was huddled on a hillside under the patchwork blanket, using it to protect her head and shoulders. 'Do you think anyone will be doing the observations?'

I considered. 'There's probably hundreds of them out there now, armed with measuring instruments.' I stared across the mountain slopes, expecting battalions of astronomers to appear at any minute.

'Don't despair,' said Maja. 'It's still only a theory, and theories can be wrong. Perhaps if it's wrong, you can come up with a better theory.'

'Oh my theory's right,' I said. I had no doubt that Nature would prove me correct. 'But if they *are* out there looking for star displacement, it can only mean one thing.'

'What?' The clouds cleared but the sky did not brighten. There, in the middle of the afternoon, was the make-or-break darkness. The eclipse had begun.

'He's told them to look. Not me. I haven't told anyone. If they are looking, that means he's beaten me. That means he'll get all the glory.'

Slowly, imperceptibly, the moon moved across the sun. The last lip of brightness lingered a moment and then was gone. The day turned grey and Maja huddled further under her blanket.

Together we stared gloomily at the prematurely darkened sky.

9 October 1919

As the autumn wore on and there was no news from anywhere
about the eclipse, I began to think I had got away with it. If no-one
had reported on it, that meant no-one had been looking at it in
the particular way necessary to prove my theory. And if no-one had
been looking at it in that particular way – to see if the light from the
stars was bent or not – it meant that no-one had yet written a paper
telling them to look. More to the point, my father hadn't yet written
a paper telling them where to look. So I still had time. I could still
beat him. I hadn't lost my share of the rightful inheritance yet.

I was copying out in neat handwriting my general theory for the
universe, double-checking the calculations as I went, in between
helping Maja to haul home from the market the sacks of potatoes we
would need to get us through the winter.

We were finally in Berlin, in a Prussian set of rooms off the
Mohrenstrasse. For the first time, I was in the same city as my
father. The streets were straight, long, grey and uniform, full of
orderly buildings. I woke up snug in my bed in the mornings, revel-
ling in the unaccustomed softness of a mattress and blankets, and
breathed the air in deeply, as if it were somehow different,
containing more of the atoms and molecules of oxygen and carbon
dioxide that had recently been breathed in by my father. I could
almost smell his presence on the autumn winds, a chemical smell of
musty papers and sharp lead in pencils. I was getting closer. And as
I breathed, I plotted ways to get myself inside, right inside the
Kaiser-Wilhelm Gesellschaft, and into the university where my
father had his sanctum.

Once we had set ourselves up in our two rooms, once Maja had
sewn a pair of curtains and installed Wolfgang on the bureau, I told
her that the time had come for me to do some serious study.

'If I'm not at an academic institution, no-one will publish this.
Ever.' I waved my papers at her. The equations really were quite
charming.

Maja was looking very modern. Her dress had a tight bodice, a low waist and a full skirt that shockingly came to only just above her ankles. This fashion plate was also embarked on some serious pickling and bottling against the day fresh vegetables would disappear from the market. She put water into the kettle, set it on the stove, picked up her knife, began slicing carrots and said, 'What do you want to study?'

'Descriptive and analytical geometry, astrophysics, astronomy, gnomic projection and matrices. And the theory of the definite integral.'

'I think you should go to the secretarial school,' said Maja, starting on a turnip.

'What?'

'Learn to type.'

'But . . .'

'Bookkeeping, too.'

'Yes, Maja, I know that's the sort of thing they teach you at secretarial school but I want to go to the university. You can go if you . . .'

'I know how to type,' said Maja, 'you don't.'

'I know I don't know how to type,' I said, 'but . . .'

'Then you need to learn,' said Maja.

'You don't need to type to be a physicist,' I said.

'Can you earn your own living?' said Maja. 'You're seventeen. Most girls are working at your age. I wouldn't be doing right by Desanka if I didn't teach you how to make your own way in the world.'

'But who's ever going to give me a job as a physicist when I don't have any qualifications?'

'Then, off you go to the secretarial school and get some.'

'I don't think shorthand and typing will impress the physics department,' I said.

'The only alternative is to work in a shop,' said Maja, 'and in a shop you stand up all day. If you type . . .'

'I don't think you're being fair,' I said.

'I will pay the fees for a good all-round foundation course', said Maja, 'from my current earnings. We will need to live frugally for a few weeks, but this we can do. You can pay me back from the earnings from your first job.' The kettle boiled. She poured water over the carrots and turnips and watched the steam rise with satisfaction. The twin concerns of Maja's life – her physical appearance and her housekeeping – were blossoming.

'This is a waste of my true talents,' I said.

'If you enrol now, you could be earning by July and we would be able to afford more than boiled beans for supper.'

Thus also neatly pre-empting any criticism of the supper menu planned for that evening, Maja finished the bottling, lined the two jars up in the neat row growing in the larder and settled to a leisurely file of her nails. They were still brittle, showing how the influenza and the unremitting cold had taken their toll, but getting stronger.

'You will need some papers,' she said, almost as an afterthought. This was true. Any identification papers I had ever had were long gone. Probably still in the school gymnasium or in a bureau in one of the many rented rooms. 'You will need to think of a new name. A good German name.'

'Helga,' I said sullenly. 'Helga Hansbach.' Perhaps if I hadn't been so cross, I would have come up with something a little more mellifluous, perhaps even something a bit more princess-like. I spooned grey sugar into a cup and made some tea. It was neither refreshing nor reviving, nor even very nutritious. For nutrition, I could look forward to the boiled beans. Suddenly life, a whole future of boiled beans and Helga Hansbach, just didn't seem exciting.

I decided to wheedle.

'Maja, if I enrol at the secretarial school, will you promise me something?' I put a cup of the grey tea at her side.

'Of course, little one.'

'If my theory of relativity is right, and I send my paper about it to the university and they accept me . . .'

Maja laughed.

'Yes, I know it's not likely. Especially if my only qualifications are in words per minute. Not a speed to impress them, either. But if I could sit an examination, show them what I could do . . .'

'Then . . . ?'

'Then you would let me study physics?'

Maja considered. 'Yes,' she said. 'On those two conditions. That you are right and they let you in.'

I spent the evening honing my formulae.

When it was very late, Maja went out. In Berlin, there were hundreds of places where you could dance until dawn, and Maja loved to dance. I had long ago stopped wondering how anyone whose greatest satisfaction in life seemed to be the bottling of vegetables and dusting could also be hell-bent on pleasure. Hedonism and housekeeping were not irreconcilable differences, just differences people usually compartmentalized. In Maja, they existed together.

I went to sleep without her and even though I tried to stay awake listening for her key in the lock, I did not hear it.

She woke me herself, when she returned in the early light. She pulled me to her, pressed her cheek against mine, bringing with her the scent of cosmetics and whisky and dark lights in dance halls and said, 'Physics doesn't matter, Helga. Life does.'

7 November 1919

'Where have you been?'

Maja was not usually so long at the market and I had begun to worry. There had been strikes, once an uprising. She could even have been in an accident, and there was definitely something going on. I had tried to make my way to the secretarial school as usual that morning, but the Wilhelmstrasse was barricaded. All the traffic had been stopped. While I lingered, wondering what to do, someone had handed me a leaflet. 'Here, read.' It was from the

Citizens' Defence Force, warning us to stay at home.

I had dutifully gone home, quite pleased not to have to spend another day listening to Fräulein Hirsch and her infernal marching band music while my fingers pounded the leaden keys of the type-writer.

'There's hold-ups out there,' said Maja.

'I know. I couldn't get to school. What's it all about?'

'It's the second anniversary of the Russian Revolution.'

'Oh.' I lost interest.

'Here.'

She put the afternoon edition of the *Berliner Tageblatt* on the table, then took a red cabbage, a white cabbage and a beetroot from her string bag.

Under the headline, THE FABRIC OF THE UNIVERSE, was a smiling picture of my father. The article announced that our whole conception of the way the universe worked had been changed overnight by the scientific genius, Albert Einstein.

I felt the fabric of the universe fall away from under my feet.

'Blast and damnation,' I said.

A British expedition had measured the eclipse of 29 May and found star displacement at the rim of the sun. Proof that my father's general theory of relativity was correct. He had published it years ago, in a journal that Josef Goldberg had never been able to supply from the ravaged libraries of Europe. I glanced over at the neat handwritten papers on the bureau. They were worthless now. I had been wasting my time.

My father came striding through the barbed wire of the Great War leaving bloody footprints in the snow, the wreckage of the familiar universe dripping from his hands, and the world fell at his feet.

Now we wonder at nothing. The fact that the moon does not fall on our heads. The fact that the seas ebb and flow. That the needle finds true north. None of these in any way moves or excites wonder.

But we were in a mood to wonder in 1919. It was as if my father had climbed up the mountain of bodies and waved a triumphant equation at the crowds and all the crowds could see was the equation. It didn't matter that only my father, Max Planck, Hendrik Lorentz, Helga Hansbach and about four other people in the world could truly understand relativity. That was part of its appeal. You didn't need to understand it all to be awed by some of the things the newspaper said it meant: that time was relative, that clocks could run backwards.

The theory offered hope for things to come. The world we had become used to over the last few years wasn't so much a dream as a nightmare. My father's new theory promised to take the human race beyond the three-dimensional misery we were used to calling everyday life and set us at the shores of a glittering lake where we could sail into a four-dimensional future. The glory was all his. I had lost the battle.

I hated him more than ever.

I stared at the picture that accompanied the article: a kindly faced man with a shock of brown hair, a high forehead like mine, a wide moustache and eyes that were deep pools of black. He looked very gentle and very caring. You wouldn't have thought such a man would have been capable of abandoning his first-born, but he was. You wouldn't have thought that this clear-eyed genius would have left a little baby to the mercy of history and chance and never once enquired after her well-being, but he did.

In the newspaper picture, under his veneer of profound thought, my father seemed to hug himself with pride, pat himself on the back and put a feather in his cap simultaneously. I spat on him.

For the next three days – until Fräulein Hirsch called and told Maja how well Helga was doing in her typing and how she hoped, peering round the door, that Helga wasn't ill; until Maja cast a stern look in my direction and told Fräulein Hirsch that Helga was on the mend and would be back at the school tomorrow – I took the advice of the Citizens' Defence Force and stayed at home, sulking.

I was no further on than I had been at Novi Sad. My haunting wasn't efficient, and my revenge was only a few worthless lines on paper – a theory that no-one would ever read now without thinking I'd copied it from my father. I had thought I was set on a clear path, but somehow, without my even noticing, I had been deflected from it. I wasn't even close to being a physicist, I was much closer to being a typist.

There was little comfort in the fact that my theory had been right, because he had got there before me. The world looked to him as a genius, not me. After that dramatic showdown between theory and proof, that successful eclipse, my father was in every newspaper in the world.

Back at the secretarial school, the teachers brought in all sorts of newspapers. Not only the *Tageblatt* but the *Frankfurter Zeitung*, and all the little papers from Bavaria. Day after day the whole world tried to come to terms with relativity, and in between my typing to music, I watched them do it.

Maja said she'd passed people on the street talking about negatively charged electrons. She seemed quite pleased.

I said, 'I wonder how they'd feel if I pointed out that my father knows nothing of the electrodynamics of the moving body that is his illegitimate daughter.'

The difference between here and there is relative. The difference between then and now is relative. But the difference between my father and myself was staggering. My father, I learned, was selling signed photographs of himself for the benefit of the starving children of Vienna while I improved my shorthand.

My father, the saint, the scientist, had taken people's gaze from the earth and made them look at the stars. And they were grateful. Yet while I was profoundly disgruntled, I couldn't exactly blame people. We *wanted* to look at the stars. We'd all seen a lot of bodies.

Maja said, 'Bide your time. Your day will come. There's a whole reconstruction ahead.'

*   *   *

A couple of weeks later, Josef Goldberg tracked us down. I was glad to see him. I needed comfort and he was very comforting. In my soft bed on the night of his return, with my head against Josef's freckled white shoulder, looking through the square window at the night sky, I realized that if he went away this time and never came back, I would miss him very much indeed. He was something to hold on to in a world where nothing stayed the same for very long. I felt him fall asleep against me and put my arms around him, as if I could hold him there, in just that way, for ever.

With Josef in my arms, I stared and stared at the stars. There was still something not quite right.

CHAPTER FIVE

The Republic

24 December 1919

THE WHOLE TOWN WAS ALIVE. IN FRIEDRICHSTRASSE, BARREL organs played, street peddlers were selling indoor fireworks and tinsel, the smell of cinnamon cakes hung over every market stall. The jewellers on Unter den Linden were all open, the windows brightly lit. Frost sparkled on the branches of the lime trees, and the Christmas crowds were milling through Wertheim's and Kayser's. Berlin was full of people who came from somewhere else, so I felt right at home. In houses all along our narrow street, Christmas trees and candles glimmered.

Over the stove in what was designated as the 'living' of our two rooms, Maja was making preparations for our Christmas Eve meal as the snow began to fall.

'Look,' I said, gesturing to the window. 'Perfection.'

'I like Christmas,' said Maja, busy at the table.

'I know you do,' I said, watching her chop and slice. 'What is that?'

'Carp,' said Maja, neatly bisecting a fish head.

'You know I hate carp.' I looked at it. Its eye stared back at me, cold and accusing. 'Carp, carp, carp. My whole life has been fresh-water fish.'

'Carp on Christmas Eve is a Berlin tradition.'

'Ah.'

'Even if the fabric of the universe has changed', Maja chopped away, refusing to be put out by my petulance, 'that doesn't mean I have to stop upholding tradition. Nor do you. I imagine you'll want a Christmas present, for example.'

I did. 'Some traditions I can firmly believe in,' I said piously.

I left Maja singing Christmas songs to the carp and went and gazed at my early Christmas present from Josef. Volume 49 of the *Annalen der Physik*, at last, where, on pages 769 to 822, my father described 'Grundlage der Allgemeinen Relativitäts- theorie'. As a title – 'The Foundation of the General Theory of Relativity' – it had a certain loftiness, but I did not feel it com- pared with the simplicity of my own 'A General Theory for the Universe'. Although it was doubly galling to hold before me the evidence not only that my father had got to the theory on his own, but also that he had got it into print before me, I was quite pleased to note from the date of the article that it had taken him ten years to move from the special to the general theory. It had taken me three months.

I figured, looking at the pages, that he'd have got there quicker if he'd paid more attention to geometry. Some of his equations were quite beautiful, though, and many – more than mine – had the symmetry of that familiar c at the centre of the equation. I suspected, however, that there might be something more in them, something I hadn't seen yet, and puzzled over them looking for it.

Although I didn't find anything that particular evening, just the sheer joy of having pencil and paper in my hand and a problem to solve meant that I was content enough for the moment. Now that I had had time to study my father's equations of relativity more closely, I found a strange comfort in them. Everything changes, they sang. Nothing is absolute. This applied to everything, from the farthest reaches of the universe to the tiniest particles. I had names for all those particles now, from my reading: inside the molecule were atoms, protons, electrons. The particles just kept getting smaller and smaller.

Between the largest and the smallest of those calculations, the reality of the external world disintegrated. What we were left with was no better than a dream. And in a dream, anything was possible. Freed from the mechanics of a Newtonian universe, any path was possible, including my own. Revenge, therefore, was still possible. It might be revenge in a way I hadn't thought of yet, but it would still be revenge, perhaps an even better revenge than the one I had been working on before. Now that I thought about it, in fact, that revenge seemed decidedly skimpy. Publishing a paper. Was that really enough? Next time I would do it better, and bigger.

By the time the carp was steaming in the kitchen, I had cheered up enough to take a closer look at one of the newspapers on the kitchen table. They still came winging in merrily chattering about space and time and the rest of the gossip about my father's role in it, and I generally stuffed them straight under the sink for Maja to peel her carrots onto.

'Hey,' I said to Maja, pointing to the *Berliner Tageblatt*, 'that's not my mother.'

'I was wondering when you'd notice that,' she said.

The woman in the pictures named as Albert Einstein's wife was definitely not Mileva. This new woman was fair, and, I thought, did not have nearly such fine features as my mother, though she had a motherly look.

'Who is it?' I took it for granted Maja would know. She read the newspapers daily and, when it came to anything they had omitted, her friends of friends could keep her well up-to-date.

'It's his cousin, Elsa.'

'Oh, my goodness.'

I scrabbled under the sink and retrieved whatever hadn't done duty for the vegetables.

On the third page of a recent copy of the *Vossische Zeitung*, only slightly damp, I saw Elsa again, standing proudly with her arms on my father's shoulders. Elsa had two daughters, Ilsa and Margot.

'She and Albert together; they won't risk more,' said Maja authoritatively, 'being cousins.'

I read aloud from the newspaper: 'The father of modern science is father to two girls and two boys . . .'

'That only works if they don't include you in the equation,' said Maja.

'Don't make jokes. This is serious.'

'Still, it explains why the theory took him so long.' Maja stuck a fork into the carp and with a satisfied nod declared it done.

'How do you figure that?'

'Your mother probably wasn't doing his maths for him any more. Dish up the potatoes, Helga.'

I reached for my allotted pan. 'Where is my mother, then?'

'Back in Zurich with the boys. She left your father last year.'

'Why didn't you tell me?'

'What's the point?' The water from the potatoes drained away into the sink and gurgled into nothingness.

I put butter on them, dished up the ubiquitous turnips and sat down at the table. At my place, wrapped in brown paper, was my promised Christmas present. It was a dictionary.

'What's this for?' I said. 'Why did you get me a dictionary?' I looked closer. 'A foreign dictionary, at that.'

'You said yourself that half the interesting articles about relativity were being published in *Nature*. I think the time has come for you to learn English.'

'Maja, you've only just got me started on shorthand. I've got enough to do. And the universe isn't going to wait.'

While I put a few potatoes on my plate and a little extra basil on the turnips, I explained. An odd feature of the equations was that they insisted that the spacetime in which our universe had its being could not be static. It must either be expanding or contracting. Rather than admit Newton was right and concede that the gravitational pull on the stars was such that they were gradually pulling closer and closer to one another until they did literally fall on our heads, my father had inserted a little term into the equations – the cosmological constant – for the sole purpose of holding spacetime still. I shook my head. A cosmological constant, for Heaven's sake. He was wrong. It was never going to hold up.

'You had two conditions', I said to Maja, 'if I was going to go to the university and study physics. One, that my theory was right. And it was. My father might have put it slightly differently, but the ideas and conclusions are exactly the same.'

'I know,' said Maja. 'Congratulations. You're halfway there.'

'Two, that they let me in.'

'Right.'

'Well, how am I going to know if they will let me in or not if I don't try?'

She admitted the point.

'There's a university examination in June. I've still got a few months. I could go to the library, begin to read again, really probe the edges of the universe . . . Either it's expanding or contracting, one or the other. It's not standing still. My father's wrong. If I can prove it, I'm sure they'll let me in. So you can see, I don't have time to learn another language.'

'Hmm, it will be difficult, especially as you'll need to finish Fräulein Hirsch's foundation course as well.'

Nevertheless, while we ate the fish, which was done to perfection, Maja introduced me to the first of many irregular verbs.

Just before midnight, when I had got to grips with the past imperfect of being, just before Maja went off to church, and because I wouldn't be awake when she got back, I gave her her own Christmas gift: a black block of mascara from Bourjois in Paris. A large block. Josef Goldberg's import/export business was doing well.

It was Maja to perfection.

7 March 1920

On a rare Sunday afternoon in Berlin, Josef Goldberg took me for a walk by the lakes. I decided I could spare a few hours from the typing, research into relativity and irregular English verbs to let him lead me by the hand around the shore.

One of the best things about Josef Goldberg was that, even if he did not understand the first thing about relativity, and would have been hard-pressed to explain what a molecule was, he was content to let me talk about them without telling me I'd be better off practising my shorthand.

We sat on the grass and looked over the blue water. 'If you pursue the equations right to the end . . .' I said.

Josef looked towards me expectantly. 'Yes?'

Most people, including my father, including the entire physics department of the Prussian Academy of Sciences, still thought along the lines that Newton had, that we all had until recently: that the universe was fixed, eternal, unchanging. The stars were static, with the ether flowing past them. I had now done the calculations to prove that this could not be the case.

'If you pursue the equations right to the end, then you will see that the universe can't be standing still, after all. It just won't work. The stars have to be moving.'

Josef considered a moment. 'In which direction?'

At that point I felt unutterably depressed. 'I'd take a good guess, my darling, that the universe is expanding.'

I found this depressing because, if it was expanding, it meant that at some point the universe had all been together in one place, and had begun. And if the universe had begun, it would one day end. If I pondered on the implications of this for too long, then it seemed like every human endeavour was pointless. I tried to convey some of the pointlessness of everything to Josef, but he said I should look on the bright side.

'How can there be a bright side?'

'Well, Helga, the universe isn't expanding so fast that it will end and we'll all die tomorrow, is it?'

And he blotted out any further conversation on the subject by asking me to marry him.

When I told Maja that evening, when Josef had left again without an answer, Maja stopped for a moment while putting on her coat and considered this. 'I think it is time,' she said.

'What for?'

'For you to get married.'

'How am I supposed to fit in being married with all the other things I've got to do?'

She eyed me critically.

'I'm not going to give up trying to get into the university, if that's what you're thinking. I've already told Josef that.'

'That's not what I was thinking. I was thinking that if you delay much longer, you will be an old maid, like me.'

I laughed. She looked lovely. 'You're not an old maid.'

'Of course I am. Think about it.'

I decided Maja must be older than me, because she always had been, but she certainly didn't look it. If I ever thought about it, I didn't think anything concrete, just that she was beautiful.

'And think about Josef Goldberg seriously,' she said. 'You won't get many better offers.'

The door slammed behind her.

I sighed and spent three hours on English adjectives.

30 June 1920

I had answered two questions on the examination paper: one on the general theory of relativity, the second on the nature of light. With the first question, I had taken care not to be too controversial – this was, after all, a conservative institution and I didn't want to depress them with the idea of an expanding universe as well.

I had become rather too engrossed in pursuing the implications of the second topic. I had discoursed on the nature of light at some length, without, I suspect, necessarily being required to do so, as it meant I ran out of time for a third question. Nevertheless, a week and a half later, on the last day of June, I was called in for an interview with a member of the physical sciences department, a short excitable man with a beard. I brought along my neatly handwritten copy of 'A General Theory of the Universe' just in case I got the chance to impress the professor with how my own equations differed ever so slightly from what was fast becoming accepted as the norm.

After he had got over the fact that I was a girl – I had put only H. Hansbach at the top of the paper – the short excitable man was interested in one thing only: my beloved idea that light could be both wave and particle. I regretted ever having mentioned it.

'Don't you want to talk about relativity?' I asked desperately.

He waved his hand, as if relativity was neither here nor there.

'Light is electromagnetic radiation, is it not?' he insisted.

'Yes.'

'And all electromagnetic radiation behaves as waves, does it not?'

'Yes.'

'Light behaves as a wave, does it not?'

'We've known that for a long time,' I said.

There were old experiments which proved it conclusively. If you drop a pebble into a still pond, you can watch the waves spread out from it. If you drop two pebbles in, you know what happens, you don't get the perfect circles any more, the waves interfere with each other and produce a more complicated pattern. If you shine a light through two holes in a board, the pattern you get on the screen behind is exactly this same sort of interference pattern we're familiar with from the pond. Shine the light. See the pattern. Light was therefore a wave. No argument.

'But . . .' I said.

'So how can light come in little lumps as well? Do any of the experiments show light behaving as little lumps?' The tone of his voice was rising.

I was right. I could *see* that I was right. In my head, light behaved perfectly well as little lumps all the time. But how was I going to be able to explain that to him?

I knew that the head of the department, Max Planck, had done some tentative experiments which showed that objects emitted or absorbed light only in definite amounts, as if it did indeed come in little packets, which he called light quanta. So I felt I was on fairly safe ground at least mentioning these.

'Max Planck . . .' I said.

The Herr Professor's voice reached new heights of rage. I was shown the door before I had a chance to dazzle him with the only copy in existence of 'A General Theory of the Universe'.

In the corridor, I danced with frustration and anger. Although I might be simply an innocent victim of inter-departmental squabbling, caught between the particle camp and the wave camp, the university was not going to let me haunt its corridors now or in the foreseeable future.

I had been going to fight my father with the only two weapons I had, gravity and light. The gravity was fine, it was the light that had let me down.

The next time Josef Goldberg was in Berlin, I curled up against him and sobbed and sobbed. Even if he didn't understand quite why I was crying, he was comforting. In the face of the pointlessness of all human endeavour, I was comforted, and promised that I would marry him, after all.

27 August 1920

'I wish you wouldn't disappear like this,' I said to Maja. 'I do worry, you know. Plus I've had a hard day at work.'

In fact, I never had a hard day at work. The shorthand and typing demanded by the law offices where I was one of five junior typists were scarcely exacting. The worst thing was the jolting tram ride there and back, but Maja wasn't to know that and it meant that on grounds of extreme tiredness I could reasonably expect a cooked dinner every evening before we embarked upon the tortuosities of English grammar.

'I've been to a very interesting meeting,' she said.

'You don't go to meetings.'

'The Anti-Relativity Company,' she said. 'Quite a good turn out. They hired the Philharmonic Hall.'

'You're joking,' I said.

'Oh, the science isn't very serious,' she said, 'but they are.'

'Serious about what?'

'The Jewish nature of relativity. Hence, the suspect nature of relativity.'

'I can see that,' I said. 'The notion of absolute relativity does not fit in very well with the good German liking for order, does it?'

I looked at her more closely. It wasn't just the mascara. Her eyes seemed to be completely outlined in black.

'What's that?' I said.

'Kohl,' she said. 'It's all the fashion.'

I hadn't realized Josef was supplying her with fashion accessories outside my knowledge. Last time I saw him, he had been knee-deep in Havana cigars and making a killing, planning for a lavish wedding reception.

'I don't see how you have time for fashion,' I said, 'attending all these interesting meetings.'

'The most interesting thing, though,' said Maja, 'is that your father turned up. I saw him sitting in one of the boxes.'

All this time we had been in Berlin, I had hovered like an electron in orbit round my father but had never actually come into contact with him. Maja's expedition reminded me it was possible. After all, in the new universe, anything was possible. Even so, we had never met.

My absence was partially deliberate. I knew why I had chosen not to go to any of his lectures, for example. I had been waiting until I was a member of the university, too, so I could meet him as an equal. Without that seal of authority, there was no way he would take me seriously if I tried to engage him in conversation about physics. Any hopes of this happening in the immediate future, however, had been dashed after my disastrous interview in June.

Although I had tried to get over my disappointment that I had let my personal feelings about light get in between me and a university career, I was still bitterly angry. Josef kept reminding me, as did Maja, that perhaps it was for the best. I didn't say anything. I was preoccupied with finding a new form of revenge but hadn't yet come up with anything remotely promising

Nevertheless, perhaps just out of interest, I might go to one of the lectures my father was holding. To meet the great public demand, he was doing at least one a week. I could sit at the back and glower.

No, I wouldn't go. I might give myself away.

17 October 1921

I was speechless.

I came home from work, found her downstairs in the laundry room and didn't know what to say.

The blond hair that Maja had been so proud of, with its shiny gold in the curls, Maja's beautiful hair that I had known and depended on since I was eight years old and having German lessons in Frau Heidel's boarding house, had disappeared. Maja's hair was now blue-black and a good 6 inches shorter. It came to just below her ears, where it turned under, coyly, in what Maja assured me was a bob.

'A bob?'

'What do you think?'

'I think it's . . . lovely,' I said, 'if a little unusual.'

'Times are changing,' said Maja. 'We have to change with them.'

'Josef says they're changing, too,' I said. I had seen rather less of him lately than usual as business was booming and we had postponed any wedding until things settled down. The mark was worth nothing in international exchanges, Josef had informed me, but what bothered *me* was that my tram fare was becoming more and more out of reach and I had to walk. 'Things are getting more and more disordered throughout the universe,' I said. 'Disorder in tram fares is only the least of it.'

Maja was folding a blouse and looked at me as if I were insane.

'This isn't new,' I said. 'This is the second law of thermo-dynamics. People have known about this since Newton.'

'That's as may be,' said Maja, 'but that doesn't make it true.'

'Are you arguing with Newton?' I said.

'Newton only has to look at me to realize I spend *my* life making things more ordered.'

'You need to get away from the purely personal,' I said, gesturing at the pile of folded laundry. 'Look at things on a larger level.'

'The personal level is just fine for me,' said Maja. 'If a theory's going to work, it will work in the kitchen as well as the universe.' She whipped a teacloth from under me and went upstairs. In the kitchen there was a delicious smell of bread rising. I often wondered how she managed to do so much cooking without damaging her nail polish.

I followed her, not to be daunted. 'Think about scrambled eggs,' I said. 'Once you've scrambled an egg, you can't unscramble it. You go from one neat egg in one nice tidy eggshell to a mess in a pan. An increase in entropy.'

'That's only true', said Maja, 'if you didn't *want* a scrambled egg.

If a scrambled egg is what you want, then you've increased the total order in the universe, surely.'

I'd lost my ground. 'Let me think about that,' I said.

'While you're thinking,' said Maja, 'think about Leiden. There's a good library there, you'd have no trouble in studying while you found a job. Or Göttingen. I've had enough of Berlin.'

Göttingen was very appealing. It had three separate Institutes for Physics. Franck was there, and Pohl and Born. All good scientists and mathematicians in their own right. But I still felt pulled into my father's orbit.

'Start afresh,' said Maja. 'Get a new outlook on the universe.'

'My universe is perfectly fine, thank you.' In fact, my universe was getting quite intriguing. If the universe was expanding, as I believed it was, even if no-one else did, then at one time all the galaxies must have been close together. Just how close could they have been? What had happened when all the galaxies, all the stars were *touching* one another? And what had happened *before* that?

'Then get yourself a new haircut,' said Maja. 'It'll make you feel like a new person.'

'I'm not at all sure a bob is ever going to suit me.'

'It's the fashion.'

'You mean there are women in Europe who actually *want* to look like that?'

Maja opened the oven door and wafted out the bread. 'There are hundreds of women in Europe who want to look like this. *I* want to look like this.'

'I'll never want to look anything remotely like it.'

'Trust me,' said Maja. 'You will.'

6 February 1922

One evening, not long after I had undergone the transmutation into Helga Goldberg, which had involved a wedding reception for hundreds of relatives from Vienna I didn't even know Josef had, Maja called round. Although Josef and I had moved into two rooms off the Kirchenstrasse – a state I was still getting used to and to which I had only agreed on the stipulation that Josef employ a cook – I still saw her most days. I still missed her most days, though she said she didn't miss me, but I thought she only said this to be kind.

'Come on,' she said, and pulled me by the hand away from my reading. I did not want to go. The branches of the trees were bare. The room with its oil stove was warm and the streets were full of snow. Even now, I was uncomfortable going out in the cold. I pined for my toes. The gap where they used to be always ached in the winter. I informed Maja of this, more than once, in high dudgeon, on our walk through the snow-covered streets.

As my pursuit of my father to the furthest reaches of the universe had ended in such miserable failure, I had decided to go back to the point at which I had stumbled: light. Despite having been promoted to Head Typist, now that I was married I'd had to leave the law firm, so I had plenty of time for thinking.

The last time I'd thought seriously about light, apart from deciding it could be bent, was when I'd asked Herr Grünbaum in Novi Sad about whether it was a wave. It undoubtedly behaved like a wave – the short excitable man with the beard at the university was *convinced* it was a wave – yet the work for which my father had recently received his Nobel Prize supported the opposite view. If you shone light of a high enough frequency on a metal surface, it knocked electrons out of the atoms in the metal. What else could it be but the absorption of the *particles* of light, the quanta, which was doing the knocking?

'Do you know what, Maja? I don't see how it can be either/or. Either light's a wave or it's a particle. If I do the calculations one way, it's a wave. If I do them the other way, it's a particle. It's both, I know. But how am I going to prove it?'

I had begun to contemplate giving in to Josef Goldberg's desire to have children instead.

'Buck up,' said Maja, pulling my wool hat on my head more firmly over my ears against the cold. 'Forget waves. Forget particles. This is important. It may be the only time you ever see your father.'

We were not invited, naturally; we did not have a ticket and could not have got in under false pretences, either. Even Maja, with her talent for blending in, admitted that if we had managed to secure a place in the audience at the lecture theatre by less than conventional means – she had considered bribery – it would have been clear from our gender alone that we were not physicists.

No, we stalked him, after the lecture was over, followed his trail through the slush and snow to the formal reception at the physics laboratory and stared through the window to where they were handing round glasses of moselle and little things on plates. We weren't the only ones staring. There were a dozen or more of us desperate hangers on, driven or foolhardy enough to risk the ice round the ankles, the threat of frostbite.

I knew why I was there, and Maja was there for me, but at first I couldn't figure out why all the others thought it was vital. Relativity was still fashionable. My father was still a celebrity. There were autograph hunters and memento seekers and anxious young men with manuscripts of their own, theses which they tried to press into this eminent scientist's hands. But it was well known that he would have none of them. There wasn't much reward in being there, all in all. Why were they doing it, then? It must be, I thought, that people were still waiting for the promised keys to the universe.

At that moment my father walked by, not 2 feet away from me. His hair reminded me of my mother's, thick and black, and on top of it was a grey felt hat which he kept pushing back at intervals, rendering the felt even more shapeless. But he walked quickly, sure of himself, full of energy. He reminded me of a rock that hurtles along, its rough corners getting smoothed only at the expense of damage to whatever dares to get too close. He had brown eyes, I noticed, which I had inherited, not the grey of my mother's. His brown eyes never touched me once, although I almost held out my hand, almost said something.

The man next to me was more persistent. He pushed his way to the front of the crowd as the party was breaking up and my father was being shown to the car. He shouted something about an equation, about the consequences of an equation, and my father's interest was momentarily captured.

'Here,' said the young man, pushing forward, shoving his sheaf of papers into my arms. 'Mind this. I just need this one.' And he took the topmost sheet, which was scribbled with figures, and held it so my father could see. I could not follow all he said – he spoke with an Austrian accent and the words were long – but some drifted through. 'Energy. Mass. Your work proves it. Now see what you have done, what has become possible.'

'Stuff and nonsense,' said my father.

'Let me show to you . . .' said the young man.

My father glanced at the figures then tore the paper in half. 'You are a fool,' he said. 'The work is nonsense.'

'I can prove . . .'

My father tore the paper in half again and dropped the pieces on the frozen snow. 'Moonshine. Poppycock.'

'No,' said the young man, dropping to his knees and scrambling against the ice for the scraps of paper. 'You must listen . . .'

My father got into the car and the driver started the engine.

'Arrogant bastard,' shouted the man. 'Jewish scum.'

I got down onto the ice with him and picked up some scraps myself. Some elementary mathematics, familiar formulae . . . but the way the young man had arranged them was very interesting. I had never seen things worked in quite that order before.

'Do you know what you have done?' screamed the young man as the car faded from view. 'You have destroyed us. You have destroyed us all.'

'This looks very interesting,' I said to the young man as he gave up shouting. He had hardly noticed me. I was a girl, after all.

'I'll have those back.'

Perhaps if he had been nicer, I would have given him all of his papers back. I had memorized most of the important steps anyway. Perhaps if he had been willing to talk to me, to discuss his methods and procedures – and I longed for someone with whom to discuss methods and procedures – I wouldn't have simply given him back the most unimportant papers of all, including the one right at the front that held his name and his qualifications, and perhaps I wouldn't have folded the rest of the papers into my left hand behind my back and stuffed them into my pocket.

30 August 1923

In her kitchen, Maja was busy. She had propped a mirror on the window sill to catch the clearest light and was going at her eyebrows with such savagery that her skin was turning red, flinching from touch. I knew what this was about. Maja had seen Louise Brooks in a movie at the Rollkrug and had embarked upon a quest to become her identical twin. The bob had only been the first phase. Now it was the eyebrows and the lipstick. Like most other women, I still wore my hair in sensible plaits wound round my head.

Maja had also taken to wearing dresses that nearly revealed her knees.

'We've *got* to get out of Germany,' said Maja.

I was inclined to agree with her. I was thoroughly fed up with the Weimar Republic. Except for the small opposition of lunatic groups like the Anti-Relativity Company, for the most part my father was a true German hero and everywhere I went I met his image. In the shops, they were selling Einstein cigars and Einstein candy. Every baby boy you passed in the street was called Albert. Every newspaper brought a different snapshot: my father in the United States espousing the cause of Zionism, founding the League of Nations, proclaiming pacifism, shaking hands with the Archbishop of

Canterbury, hobnobbing with the Emperor of Japan, in Japan.

'Your father won't be able to stay in Berlin much longer, anyway,' said Maja. 'Things will turn violent.'

'I can't go just yet,' I said.

'Why?'

'Two reasons. One: I still haven't had my revenge. If I move away from where my father is, how am I ever going to be able to do it?'

'You don't know how you're going to do it yet, do you?'

'No.'

'Then how do you know you won't be able to wreak revenge just as well at a distance instead of up close?'

'I don't. I just feel that I should be near him. Keeping an eye on him. Seeing what he does next.'

'You've never even got near him except that once when I forced you. What does distance matter? Especially if we're safer somewhere else.'

I couldn't explain. It was just that I didn't want to move on without a purpose, without knowing where I was going and why. I wasn't like Maja, who could flit from town to town with no more thought than a butterfly.

'I'll think about it,' I promised, though she knew I wouldn't. 'Is there anything for breakfast?' The cook was visiting her aunt.

'I wondered why you were here so early. Eggs. Hard-boiled. In the pan. If you want to scramble one, do it yourself. Be responsible for your own disorder in the universe.'

'If you could go back far enough,' I said, lifting an egg out of the water and cracking it, 'right to the beginning of the universe, you'd know everything.'

'Would you know why?' asked Maja. Her mouth was no longer red. She was making it a deep plum, arched by a confident pencil into an unnatural expression of pain.

'Why what?'

'Why the universe was made.'

'Maja, that's not even a proper question.'

'It's the question I'm most interested in. Not *when* the universe was made. *Why* it was.'

'And by whom?'

'I'd presume that would be self-evident.'

'To you, maybe.'

'And to God. And that's all that matters, really, isn't it?'

'I'm not sure I'll ever find the mathematics for that,' I said.

Maja was done and cast a critical eye over herself in the mirror on the window sill.

'Have you got used to my hair yet?'

I kissed her. 'I am sure, out of all of the ladies of Europe, my dear, none of them looks more like Louise Brooks than you do.'

'You mean none looks as good as I do.'

'You know what I mean.'

She kissed me back, the plum of her mouth leaving a kiss like a bruise against my cheek.

'I'm off out. What's the second reason?'

'For what?'

'For not leaving Germany yet.'

'Josef's just bought a house.'

31 August 1923

The house was in Oberlandstrasse and Josef had bought it from a nice middle-class family for $200. Peanuts. The dollar was now worth over a million marks and Josef had plenty of dollars. He paid the two secretaries who worked in his offices at midday and they immediately rushed out to buy food, or goods which could one day be bartered for food, before the prices went up later in the day. And they were going up alarmingly. In July my tram ticket to Maja's cost 3,000 marks, at the start of August 10,000, on 20 August 100,000. After the house, Josef bought a car.

Between them, Maja and Josef were making a fortune. Sex and

dollars were the two commodities most in demand. Everything we bought on the black market we bought for a song. We weren't the only ones. The smart shops were still all open, while in Neukölln and Wedding, stale bread and cabbage soup changed hands for colossal prices. In the house at Oberlandstrasse, I bought carpets, curtains and plenty of furniture from people who were practically giving it away.

In between the acquisition of household goods, I had plenty of time to keep up with the journals. Gravity and light. Gravity and light were still my best weapons, I was sure of it. It was for gravity and light that my father had turned his back on me, and it was with gravity and light that I would get back at him. I read the pages avidly, looking for something glimmering through, something that would show me a way to my revenge. But, as if mirroring the looking-glass world that Germany had become, something equally strange was happening in the land of physics. Until now, that realm had always been the lovely familiar one I knew. The sailors passing each other on ships at constant velocities might have been replaced in the papers in the *Zeitschrift für Physik* by spacefolk going about their business of sending messages to each other and blinking lamps at each other in free fall, but it was still essentially a warm, orderly, predictable world.

But Heisenberg, among others, was changing all that – far more, I thought, than my father had ever done. The foundation of the world was even more shaky than any relativity theories had heretofore allowed. Relativity explained only how gravity worked; these new theories, the quantum theories, explained how everything else in the material world worked. And when you came right down to it, down at the level of the tiny, at the level of the quantum, things behaved in a determinedly strange way.

Electrons did *not* behave like tiny little cannon balls bouncing around off each other in accordance with Newton's laws. The old rules still worked fine when things behaved like particles, but when things behaved like waves, everything went awry. And suddenly electrons were behaving like waves all over the place. The universe didn't run like clockwork any more. It went about its business, on the quantum level, in an utterly unpredictable way. Even if you did the same experiment twice, by making one single electron interact with another single electron, for example, there was no guarantee that the results of the second experiment would be the same as the results of the first. Uncertainty was built in.

The uncertainty principle. It sounds like nothing more than a description of life as we live it, the way things appear to most of us most of the time, shifting and unpredictable. But in physics it is even stranger than that. By their very nature, waves are spread-out things. So we cannot, at any one point in time, be entirely certain where an electron, say, is. We can only hazard a guess as to where it might be. Some places are more likely than others, but none of them are certain.

'So?' said Maja.

'We're left without any real picture of the atom,' I said. 'Indeed, one of the key components of quantum theories is that you *shouldn't* be able to visualize an atom.'

'So?' said Maja. 'Does it matter? Have you ever seen an atom, anyway?'

I admitted I had not. In fact, I couldn't immediately think of any practical repercussions except that I'd always liked visualizing atoms. Little clusters of sub-atomic particles: the protons in the centre, the nucleus, with electrons whizzing around them in neat orbits. A comforting picture. Apparently, however, this picture was at best a fiction, at worst, a complete lie.

'I'm made of atoms,' I said. 'So are you. Don't you find it disconcerting to think that your electrons could take it into their heads to wander off somewhere else in the universe at any moment, and you couldn't be sure where they'd gone?'

'I find life itself disconcerting,' said Maja. 'I always have.'

'At the moment,' I said, 'so do I.'

I sought refuge from the chaos that was physics and the chaos that was life in Berlin in the organization and maintenance of my house. Also, although it wasn't quite the done thing for a married woman to work, it was acceptable enough for me to go into the office with Josef and keep an eye on the books. I could at least make my own part of the universe as predictable and as comfortable as possible.

Maja moved in on the top floor, where Josef had made an attic flat, which was the most comfortable thing of all.

12 August 1924

Although Josef's import/export business suffered greatly through-out the whole of 1923, we pulled ourselves away from the brink of ruin, I like to think, by dint of my efficient office administration. There was only so much satisfaction to be gained from buying upholstery at knock-down prices and resolutely not visualizing the structure of the atom. I concentrated instead on keeping the balance sheet in order. Even if exchange rates varied hourly rather than daily, there was still a need abroad for German goods, German chemicals, German machine-tooled parts. It was only a question of keeping the mathematics under control and the potato soup well watered when necessary.

Despite the fact that I came so near to leaving the place, and despite the unrest that flared up over and again during the next few years, I have only good memories of Berlin in those days. The cobbles of the old city before it was bombed. The department stores around Alexanderplatz. The fine old houses made of stone and blocks. Between them, Maja and Josef, in the places they knew where to look, could find all the food you could wish to eat: sausage, fried potatoes, dumplings with hot vanilla sauce, even Swiss chocolate.

On the street where we lived, there were carved door panels, plate glass, meretricious railings. The steps of the house on the Ober-landstrasse shone bright red. My house with the parquet floors and linen-coloured walls, my house where, in 1924, my daughter Tina was born.

On the afternoon of Monday 11 August, too heavy and too slow by then in the summer heat to help Josef in the office, I was stretched out on the bed reading an interesting article in the *Zeitschrift für Physik* about particles, when I began to get very excited. I could see that you didn't just have to stop with electrons, you could go further, *inside* the electron, and then . . .

Whatever it was that I had been about to see was swept away with a sudden and massive contraction that heralded twenty hours of labour. I never forgave Maja for not being there, but Josef was a staunch supporter, telephoning at regular intervals for an interim report from the maternity nurse whose hand I wouldn't let go of, once even leaving the office for an hour or two. The pain was intense, rolling over and over, lifting me off the earth.

She was born in the early hours of the following morning, without a cry, as if the stresses and waves of labour had meant nothing to her, and she was content to come into the world in her own sweet time. When the maternity nurse insisted on going off for her specified lunch break, I was left alone for the first occasion with her. I lay in almost exactly the same position as the day before, but this time with a baby.

I had fed her, and now cuddled her in my arms against me on the bed. She was a strong girl. Straight away, right at the beginning, she lifted her heavy head against the downward pull of gravity – all babies do this, of course, but most when they are a few days old, not a few minutes – and I was pleased. My baby was only thirty minutes old, light against my twenty-two years, and already she was testing the limitations and restrictions that the earth put upon her body. I hugged her to me and laughed. It betokened a participation, a taking part, a joining in. These were qualities which, although I had never possessed them, I knew were valuable.

I was even more pleased when I saw her place her head back on the sheet, without a grimace of frustration. I thought it was a good sign that she accepted the limitations of the earth.

Together, as the light got stronger, we drifted into sleep.

My father rejected utterly the quantum theories. It is one of the few things that people actually know he has said: 'God does not play dice with the universe.'

At the heart of the quantum world was not only the idea that outcomes were uncertain, but also that two objects – say, two electrons – could have an influence upon each other, instantaneously, beyond the known laws of space and time. My father denied any possibility that this could be the case.

He was lying.

I knew he was lying that morning, falling asleep in my bed with Tina in her doll-sized nightdress in the crook of my arm. I heard her heart beating, fast, strong but in a slightly irregular rhythm, almost matching my own. At once I knew that whatever she did, wherever she did it, it would affect me for the rest of my life.

It is a commonplace miracle. Objects much bigger and a hundred times more discernible than protons and electrons have influences over each other every day of the week. It is something we all know. Who hasn't heard of a mother crying out in anguish at the instant the bullet pierces her son's heart? Who hasn't listened to stories of a daughter seeing the clock stop at the moment her mother dies?

For the first time in years I thought of Mileva, Mileva my own mother, who had cried for me as she drove away with Hans Albert in the carriage. In a strange way I felt I understood a bit better now how she could have left me with Desanka. She could drive away and not look back because she knew that whatever happened, we were linked together, no matter the distance, the countries between us, the years, outside the laws of space and time.

She had done what she thought best for me, so it wasn't a question of forgiving her, for there was nothing to forgive. She would always be my mother, as I would always be Tina's mother, and it was enough to know that.

Most fathers know that bond, too – if they allow themselves to feel it. But my father did not allow himself to feel it. He had sent me away, refused ever to feel the link which might draw us together, snapped any bonds which might endure beyond space, beyond time.

No wonder my father rejected quantum physics. It was in my father's interests to deny it. To deny me.

I had dealt with the large, I thought that day as I held my new baby in my arms, I had looked as far as the edge of the universe. And I had begun to deal with the small, the hazy world of waves and uncertainty that lay at the heart of all things. I considered the possibility of combining these two extremes into one mathematical package. Would that be revenge enough, to stitch together quantum theory and relativity, and thus show my father that the universe he had helped create was intolerable for him to live in? I decided, until I could describe in mathematical terms exactly what was going on, to keep my head down and think about it.

I held Tina close all that afternoon when I woke and all that evening and all that night because I never wanted to deny her.

16 August 1924

Maja was away in Franzensbad in the Sudetenland for a mud cure when Tina was born. She spent a great part of each day buried up to her neck in a bath of hot peat, she said, which she claimed had a beneficial effect on the skin. When she came back, she refused to wash with soap as the minerals were still soaking into her pores and she did not want to sluice them away. I said she was going to have to wash her hands, if she wanted to hold Tina and, after great fussing, she did. Of course she did. She wanted to hold Tina. This was my first baby, a precious bundle, an absolute sweetheart. Maja cooed and kissed and cuddled Tina and Tina cooed and made dribbling noises back. Maja exclaimed upon the beauty of her eyes, the fineness of her hair, the graceful curlicues of her ears. I did not disagree.

Maja didn't like the name. Nor did Josef.

I did point out to Josef that the name was doubly appropriate. Not only had his daughter been named in honour of the great German scientist who had been awarded the Nobel Prize only recently, this scientist had also, in his recent espousal of the Zionist cause, done much good for the Jews in Germany amongst whom Tina would now be taking her place.

Josef was not swayed. 'I don't think talk of Zionism will do us any good at all.'

As it was unusual for him to venture an opinion on anything but the current state of the market place, I was interested. 'Why not?'

'Too much talk of a national home for the Jews and people will start demanding that we go and live there.'

I could see his point. Nevertheless, even though he made a last-ditch protestation that Albertina was too much of a mouthful for a tiny baby, I had my way. The abbreviation was a compromise.

9 October 1924

Tina, not two months old and still tiny, wouldn't sleep. It was dark, past midnight. I walked her back and forth over the parquet floor as if I had been born to do nothing but walk. Tina treated sleep like some dark deep pool into which she was afraid to fall. She had to be coaxed over the edge with songs and rhythms and rocking, her eyelids fluttering open once, twice, perhaps three or four times in a last defence, her hands clutching desperately at my hair before she gave up entirely and let the water close over her head.

And when she did sleep, it was without hope of return. The silence was total, all movement stilled. She barely breathed. Each morning it was hard to haul her back again, as if she had sunk so far into lightless depths she might never be able to struggle upwards through that dead weight and return. I would have to call and kiss, and watch her turn restlessly, pulling her head against gravity, blinking against the light.

I walked over and over the floor, thinking about the nucleus of the atom and gravity, and then suddenly, that night, dark, past midnight, walking over the floor with Tina fast against me, I felt fingers on my arm.

There was no-one there. I stopped, looked round, and it came again. It felt like fingers, like someone was running their finger along my arm from my shoulder to my wrist and back again, the next finger, up and down, up and down. A light touch, but there really was no-one there. I looked. I was not frightened because I knew the fingers weren't real.

I wondered if it was Mileva, my mother, thinking about me. Perhaps she was thinking about me because I now had a daughter of my own and knew how she had felt. I touched Tina's sleeping head against my shoulder and thought that perhaps Mileva had never felt this way. If she had, how could she have let me go?

13 December 1930

Over the next few years, I had time for nothing except dolls and toys. Without me, physics departments all over the world finally decided light did come in little lumps after all, and even gave these lumps a name, photons. I felt somewhat vindicated though it was little comfort. And, hardly pausing for breath, people kept digging away at the structure of the atom; they discovered neutrons in there in the nucleus with the protons, and kept on going until the atom contained a whole flora and fauna of particles, most of which were very odd indeed. I kept leafing through the last remaining shreds of atomic structure, but there was hardly anything certain left, certainly nothing that could be used as a weapon.

In comparison, my life was slow. I sang to the children, I polished the floors, in the afternoons I came up the basement steps to chat with the other Berliner Müttchens, all the little mothers, while the sun still shone.

In the living rooms, I acquired tea glasses, fruit bowls, cabinets. In the cellar, Josef accumulated bottles of Rhine wine which fetched a good price, Black & White whisky and cognac. Trade was steady. All in dollars. I learned, slowly and painfully, to drive Josef's car so I could take Tina across town on Tuesday and Thursday afternoons to a kindergarten where they didn't mind that she didn't talk.

By the time Josef and I were expecting our second child, we knew that Tina lived at a different rate to the rest of us: slow. A much, much slower rate than even me. She grew into a tall girl with plaits on either side of her head like her mother, but she didn't say a word. She didn't even gurgle. She smiled, but there was no sense behind the smile. Behind her brown eyes that she had inherited from me, that she had inherited from her grandfather, there was nothing.

Maja had tried to be comforting.

'It's all in the scheme of things, Helga.'

'Don't tell me, God knows best.'

'Well, yes.'

'I have to tell you that that isn't much comfort.'

I walked quicker. I spent, I think, almost all of the 1920s walking over that polished parquet flooring lulling Tina to sleep in my arms. I was exhausted now, and hopeless, and Tina was growing heavier.

'I don't know why you place so much faith in God,' I said to Maja crossly. 'I see no reason to. I think you're completely misguided.'

'It's because He provides answers.'

'You're wrong there. Science is what provides answers. Clear answers. Clean answers. No-one can agree on the answers they think God's given. Why do you think there are so many different religions?'

'What about physics?' said Maja. 'In physics does everyone agree on the answers?'

'Not straight away, no. But after a couple of years, usually, yes.'

'That's good.'

'Why?'

'Because it means people might stop calling your father's theories Jewish hallucinations.'

'Ah, that. That'll pass.'

'I hope so. I hope so for your sake. And Tina's sake.'

Tina. My precious girl. Nothing that happened in science, very little that happened in the real world would ever matter to her.

By the time our second baby was born, during the feast of Hanukkah in December 1930, by the time I had read the work of Schrödinger and Dirac, and come to terms with the reality of the uncertainty principle – and even though the matrix algebra is complicated, I'd worked out that Heisenberg was right – Tina had already taught me in my heart, the only place it mattered, that there are no certainties. With Tina, the rules that governed our everyday world, and the stranger rules that governed the world of the tiny, crossed over and met.

Tina taught me that there are no certainties and Paul taught me everything I needed to know about hope.

The moment I gave birth to Paul, I screamed. The back of his head was angular, distorted, out of shape. I thought he was deformed. The slope of the forehead, the curve of the skull was large and overemphasized.

Maja thought I screamed because there was something wrong with him as well – she had doubts herself, at first – but I only screamed because I tore. Paul's sloping head forced its way into the world in a rush, with no patience.

Josef was pleased to have a boy. He held the new baby high in the light of the candles.

I had seven stitches with the finest catgut. The boy in Josef's arms whimpered quietly in the candlelight.

I knew that the best we could hope for was a probability that something good might happen to Paul, a possibility that something bad might not, and to hope that we might be able to influence things one way or another.

But then, hope doesn't have a place in physics.

CHAPTER SIX

The Beach

10 December 1932

MY FATHER AND ELSA, HIS COUSIN, HIS SECOND WIFE, LEFT
Germany just before the turn of the dark, at the turn of the tide. I
woke at dawn, even before the children, and felt the wave that held
us together ebb out, stretch thin and break.

I often wonder that my father stayed in Berlin as long as he did,
when attacks on Jews were becoming commonplace.

But then, we stayed, and Josef was a Jew.

But then, Josef was pretending not to be a Jew any longer.

In the kitchen I made coffee and told Maja that I felt strange,
knowing my father had gone and would never come back, even
though he had said he would come back.

'You're running a risk,' said Maja, her breakfast efficiently over,
cutting two slices of cucumber to put on her eyes.

'We've got new papers,' I said.

We had indeed. After the first boycott of Jewish shops and busi-
nesses, Josef, Paul, Tina and I, we had all melted overnight into
fully-fledged Hansbachs. Paul was too young to know he had ever
been anything else, and Tina never told anyone her name anyway.
The business had moved offices and opened under a new name.

Josef had employed a new secretary who was happy to be working for the nice, successful, German Hansbachs. If anyone knew what was going on, they could easily be persuaded to turn a blind eye. Josef's extensive legal and illegal import and export channels, in place since the Great War, provided all manner of bribes. As long as people wanted butter and sugar and bread and chocolate, I reasoned, we were in no danger.

Other mothers I met at the kindergarten, at Tina's school, were even jubilant. There was an air of joy, that the old past of defeat had been erased and the bright future of prosperity was beckoning for the German people. The other mothers were all for self-sacrifice, hard work, patriotism. The excitement in the air was tangible.

'We'll be fine,' I said.

'Don't say I didn't warn you,' said Maja. 'Now I think I'll have a quick lie-down.'

The children tumbled into the kitchen and I shushed them. Josef was still in bed. His mother had died and he had, until late last night, been away clearing the apartment in Vienna. I had held his head in my hands when he got back and couldn't sleep.

30 January 1933

I was upstairs playing with Tina and the doll's house in Tina's room when Maja came home.

Tina's room was pink with the promise of perfection. Tina liked pink. Pink toffees, pink dresses, pink sheets, pink ice cream. Josef denied her nothing. Pink ribbons at the ends of her plaits. Tina used to pull Josef's gifts of toffee between her teeth, lift the skeins out and examine the spun sugar turned white.

By this time, Tina had begun to collect the dolls that travelled around with her everywhere she went. She didn't like to let go of anything she had ever owned – a bear, a shoe, a skipping rope. When

she went downstairs to the courtyard where the girls played skipping under the linden trees, she took her own rope and held onto it,
resolutely turning the end for hours with one arm, her doll tucked
under the other, while the others bounced and sang. Tina was
always welcome at the skipping games for her resoluteness, and I
was pleased to see her there, although she was already taller than
most of the others around her.

'I'm here,' I called to Maja. 'Come on up.'

'I have a visitor for you, Helga. Someone I'd like you to meet.'

'Oh,' I said. 'Fine. Come on, Tina,' I said. Ever tractable, Tina
began choosing a selection of dolls to bring down the stairs with her.

'Has anything come through?' I shouted.

'Helga,' called Maja, rather too cheerfully. 'I'm sure you hardly
need hear the radio news to know the result.'

'What?'

What I wanted to know was whether there'd been a reply to my
letter to Schrödinger at Göttingen. People had been writing endless
papers exploring crystal lattices in all the physics journals lately.
On a couple of occasions, after checking the mathematics, I had
written to people and put them straight over an integral or two.
Anonymously of course. I felt it was no more than my duty. But to
Schrödinger I'd written as H. Hansbach. His equations were that
seriously flawed.

I shouted again, 'What are you saying?'

'If you want to know whether Adolf Hitler was voted into power,
then yes.'

'What is your aunt talking about?' I said to Tina, who smiled a
wide smile.

'Isn't this good news?' Maja's voice was joyous, even over the
expanse of stairs.

'Your aunt', I said to Tina, 'has gone seriously mad.'

'Mmmm,' said Tina.

'I'll tell you what it does mean,' I shouted. Tina was picking up the last of the chosen dolls. 'It means my father will never set foot in this country again.'

'Come down, Helga,' said Maja, urgently. 'Come downstairs.'

At the foot of the wide stairs, Maja was standing next to a short man in a brown uniform with a red swastika armband and slicked-down hair. The short man greeted me with a click of the heels, a raise of the arm and an earnest, 'Heil Hitler.'

'Herr Weiss,' said Maja, unable to stay still in her agitation. 'Herr Weiss, my good friend Frau Hansbach, about whom I have told you so much.'

'I am pleased to meet you, Herr Weiss.' I held out my hand graciously and smiled, a Berlin hausfrau in perfect working order.

Herr Weiss had the devil's eyebrows: the sort that arch naturally and threaten to come to a point somewhere just above the bridge of the nose.

'Frau Hansbach,' he smiled. 'It can never be anything but a pleasure.' Herr Weiss kissed my hand. He also had the devil's charm, I decided. But when I needed to, so did I.

Herr Weiss clicked his heels again with my hand in his. I suppressed the urge to laugh and gave him a gracious smile. Tina held up her first doll for his inspection.

'Shall we have tea?' I said, hoping to make some sense of this, and we did have tea, China tea, a consignment that Josef had ordered specially, around Frau Goldberg's deep-brown walnut table that Josef had brought back with him from Vienna, and Herr Weiss drank three cups and was endlessly polite.

In the evening, when Herr Weiss and Maja had gone again, and Josef was going over the books in the study, I lowered the blinds in the children's bedrooms and watched the torchlight of the distant SA parades flickering against the walls. I hadn't told Josef of Herr Weiss's visit. I would, but not yet. There was shouting and singing out there in our street, and I hoped it wouldn't wake the children.

14 April 1933

Maja was cross with me for being angry, although she was trying not to show it, refusing to let the smooth planes of her forehead be ruffled for the sake of anything so temporary. I had come up to her top-floor sanctuary to berate her.

'I don't know why you keep on seeing him,' I said. 'He's a horrible vile little man. I don't know why you had to bring him to our house.'

'Insurance,' said Maja. 'If you're not going to leave, my girl, you need all the insurance you can get.'

'Herr Weiss is not insurance. Herr Weiss is a joke.'

'You shouldn't let these things upset you so much,' Maja said. 'You know the absolute best way not to get wrinkles, don't you?'

'What?'

'Not to wrinkle up your face yourself. Not to fret about unnecessary things.'

'But Maja, I can't go through life not wrinkling. That would mean I couldn't smile, either. Or frown, or shout, or get angry.'

'That's why philosophers always look so young,' said Maja, 'because they don't do those things.'

'You,' I said accusingly. 'You smile. You smile at Herr Weiss all the time.'

'That's because I have to,' said Maja complacently. 'If you had any sense, so would you.'

'It won't make the slightest bit of difference.'

'Here,' said Maja. 'Herr Weiss gave me this. Take a look.'

It was a small book, glossy like a shopping catalogue, only in this case the Nazis had produced a catalogue of state enemies. My father's picture was on the first page. Underneath were the words, 'Discovered a much-contested theory of relativity. Was greatly honoured by the Jewish press and the unsuspecting German people. Showed his gratitude by lying atrocity propaganda against Adolf Hitler.'

In brackets, as an afterthought, were the words '*Noch ungehängt*'. Not yet hanged.

Well, well, I thought. Even though I disliked my father intensely, I didn't want the State getting its revenge on him before I did.

'Does Herr Weiss know who my father is?'

'Not yet,' said Maja. 'Herr Weiss doesn't know anything about you yet. Or about Josef. So I'm going to keep on smiling and smiling in the hope that they'll invent wrinkle-reducing ointment by the time I need it.'

'If you'll be able to afford it.'

'Oh, money,' said Maja, refusing to frown even slightly. 'Money is the best skincare lotion of all. You never have to wrinkle your brow and worry over the price of things if there's more money than you need. You never have to settle for second best, to agonize over whether you've got enough to get through the week. Money is the ultimate emollient.'

'Herr Weiss, I presume, has lots of money.'

'Lots,' said Maja. 'Lots and lots. No end of emollient.'

'By the way,' I said. 'What happened to the trees?'

'Which trees?'

'The limes on Unter den Linden.' I remembered them from our first Christmas in Berlin, sparkling with frost.

'They were cut down to make more room for military parades,' said Maja.

'Oh,' I said. 'It seems a waste.'

'*Solang noch Untern Linden die alten Bäume blüh'n kann nichts uns überwinden – Berlin bleibt doch Berlin*,' sang Maja.

As long as the old trees bloom on Unter den Linden, nothing can defeat us, Berlin will be Berlin.

'Where did you learn that?' I said.

'Oh, a long time ago,' she said. 'Before you were born, I should think.'

Then she shook herself and was off, before I could ask her anything further, with her nail polish red and her hair blue-black, off in pursuit of emollient.

6 June 1934

In the first days that promised summer, Herr Weiss suggested a holiday. We drove north, all of us, to the Baltic coast. The whole Hansbach family: me, Maja, Josef, Paul, Tina . . . and Herr Weiss. Herr Weiss had a new Adler and patted the gleaming bonnet. Despite having to sit in the same car as Herr Weiss for endless hours, I was entranced. The further north we went, the flatter the land became. I felt quite at home. The hills became smaller then disappeared until you could see the horizon on every side. And suddenly before us the sea, grey and glittering. In all my life, I had never seen the sea.

On the first day, when the holiday was still young, we found a beach to the north of the main resort, a fold tucked in to make a bay, where a pebbly strand led down to a flat stretch of sand and then the timid sea. The sand was white and grey. The seaweed was bright green fingers and frilly grey laces upon the chilly pebbles. Herr Weiss took off his shirt, refusing to believe that the good German breezes of summer could be cold. Josef manfully followed his example.

Paul collected shells, lining them up in neat rows on a space of sand, sorting them out into cockles and mussels, whorled little fragments, ready for decoration on the neat ramparts of the castle his father and Herr Weiss were busy constructing. I thought of the name labels we had ready for him at home for the following week, when he started at kindergarten, his name set in black and white, in stitched cotton, in stone. They seemed appropriate.

I walked down to the water and dipped the children's feet in the waves and the wind blew against us, raising goose bumps on our pale skin. Tina shrieked and smiled, splashing against the apparently biddable small sea. It held no evidence of the turn of the tide.

I turned. Up near safety I could see Josef building and building, shovelling deep in the sand, Herr Weiss leaning on a spade, watching. Our insurance, Maja said. As long as we had Herr Weiss's approval, we were safe. No-one would point the finger, put us under a cloud of suspicion. I wondered just how dangerous Herr Weiss could be. What would he do if he found out he was fraternizing with Jewish scum?

For the first time in years I thought of the young man who had scrambled against the ice, pressing his papers upon my father who had ripped them into shreds as moonshine. Arrogant bastard. Jewish scum. 'You will destroy us all,' the young man had said in such ringing tones of certainty.

What had he been talking about? I thought back. It seemed very distant, but he had been so sure of himself. All the figures he had written down were to do with the structure of the atom. The structure of the atom. I thought, if you took the atom . . . Did it matter that its structure had become so uncertain lately?

Then somewhere a dog was barking and the sea against my ankles had grown cold and Josef was shouting for me to come up the shore and get dry again.

'The castle,' shouted Herr Weiss. 'The castle is ready.'

Paul shrieked with delight and ran up the beach. I held Tina fast against my hip and clutched her hand all the long walk back up the shore. Tina had no idea that the sea would ever come in.

The castle was magnificent. Wings and ramparts and little bridges over a moat. Turrets. It could have been the Patent Office itself.

Paul flew to his sorted mounds of shells, whooping with pleasure, and began adorning. Blue-black mussels on this wing, fluted cockles on that. An arpeggio of shiny shale above the drawbridge.

After the sandcastling, Josef and Herr Weiss put on their shirts and went to get lemonade. They went to get lemonade but they came back having drunk beer. I knew this because Josef was eating a pickled onion.

'Josef,' I called. 'Remember your heart.'

Maja lay on grey rocks in warm sun, copies of the as yet unread Berlin papers lavishly arrayed before us, my two children within earshot and eyesight, but absorbed in pursuits that they normally only associated with story books – the exploration of crab claws, the collection of pebbles, the defence of the castle. Tina was dipping her doll's feet into a rock pool.

'In his element,' Herr Weiss said on his return, watching Paul test his feet against the mauve and violet stones.

'Good,' I said. Tina had her dolls but Paul . . . He was the youngest and the least transparent of my children. I never knew what Paul had or didn't have, wanted or didn't want, and he was only three. Paul was born with his tears too close to the surface. The tiniest scratch, a harsh word, and out they would leak, an endless reservoir. You could try pushing things in the other direction – a moving piece of music, a kindness, a stray sentimental act, even a sunset that seemed impossibly fine and orange – all could make the tears well up, usually silently. It took cruelty for the sobs to seep out.

We left before the heat of the day had lessened, before the water had come washing back.

Practically from the moment we left, Paul agitated to go back to that beach. Maybe, I thought, he understands something of power, something of solitude, something of the endless variety and fascination of the water. Maybe he does, even if he is young. Maybe this is what he has been looking for.

But on the Tuesday we went into town so Maja and I could see something of the shops and sights. Seaside sweets. Holiday hats. Paul wanted only a red bucket and spade. When he slept in the night, his head was hot, like his father's, and the sheets were wet with his sweat. I held his hand between mine and wondered what country he was in, away, where I could not reach. I had no knowledge of what went on behind his eyes. No matter how long I waited, he did not stir. I let his hand go and left him to his dreams.

Paul woke early on the Wednesday morning and rushed in to Josef and me in our borrowed wide white bed, bucket and spade in hand, demanding to know when we would leave for the nice beach again. But we had woken to rain. It spattered against the windows like rain always does, inexorable and wet.

It was the last full day of the holiday. Paul was distraught. After lunch, when I had tidied most of the farm cottage, packed most of the bags in preparation for our drive back after an early start the next morning, and had reined in my temper – admirably so far, I felt – against Paul's incessant demands, I gave in. The rain was still pouring down steadily, the windows were awash in streams.

'All right,' I said, giving up on retrieving Tina's bedtime picture book from where it had fallen into the gap between her bed and the wall. 'All right.'

I went downstairs and looked round the door into the sitting room, past the oak-beamed timbers, the stone-inlaid fireplace. Josef was asleep in a wide chair. Herr Weiss's eyes were half closed. Tina and Maja half sat, half lay, one each side of the rug, in a nirvana of dolls' concerns.

'Anyone want to come with Paul and me to the beach?' I said, feeling heroic.

On the sofa, Herr Weiss opened one eye a little further and said, 'You've given in, then?'

'It's his holiday as well,' I said. 'I don't want him to go home with cabin fever.'

'It's pouring with rain,' said Herr Weiss.

'What does that matter?' I said. 'He's a strong boy.'

'He is,' said Herr Weiss approvingly.

'I'm taking your car,' I said.

I made Paul put on his wellingtons and duffle coat, and took a scarf for good measure. Although it was nearly summer, the last whip of winter was in the wind. The rain was worse because of the cold mixed in with it and Paul, despite what I had said to Herr Weiss, was not used to cold.

Paul sat on the back seat of the car with his red bucket in one hand and his red spade in the other. By the time we reached the beach, the rain had slowed to a drizzle. I was overcome by a last-minute unwillingness to get out of the car. It was warm in there, but my breath was already beginning to fog the windows and soon we would be hemmed in, invisible. I got out, put on my coat and lifted Paul from his seat. He ran off towards the sea, bucket and spade poised at the ready. I watched him go.

It was spinning in my head like a merry-go-round. If you took the atom . . . If you took the atom, what would happen? I had grown used to thinking of the atom in no very constructive way at all, just as a series of waves and uncertainties, of no practical value but deeply disturbing, which was largely why I had stopped thinking about it and concentrated on the children instead.

I followed Paul slowly. There was nothing for me here on this beach, this day. There was no chance of reading, the rain put paid to that. I walked a little way down the shore, beyond the wavering line of seaweed that marked the high tide. Over in the west, there was a glimmering of lightness, as if we might have sun before the day was completely over. I could see Paul turning over pebbles with his foot. I walked a little further, watching him, then stopped and sat, not bothering about the damp.

It didn't get you anywhere if you took the atom and it was just waves and uncertainties. But an atom was particles, too. The young man who had scrambled against the ice had known this. And particles could be split into smaller particles.

The waves were higher than they had been on our previous visit. Even at this distance, I could hear them as they broke. Paul was busy. Digging in the sand with his bucket and spade as if this had been his only intention ever. Too close to the water for my peace of mind, but not too close for me to haul him back. Just close enough for me to sit there, watching.

Particles could be split into smaller particles . . . And then I realized, all of a sudden, what this meant. I thought back quickly over the calculations. There was no doubt that the young man was right. I was so astonished that I laughed out loud. For all his important equations, my father was so stupid that he couldn't see what they *meant*. I gazed open-mouthed at the sea. I had it, I had it now.

Why had it taken me so long? It had been right there before me in the one equation that was important and I hadn't seen it. $E = mc^2$. The very essence of it had been right in front of my eyes and I had missed it. Desanka had been right; I needed to pay more attention to the details.

The point was this: if the nucleus of an atom was split into two pieces, the mass of those two fragments would be slightly less than the original nucleus. This tiny difference in mass would be transformed into energy. Simple. But the key equation would hold: the energy released (E) would be this tiny, tiny, tiny amount of mass (m) multiplied by the square of the speed of light (c^2). And as the speed of light was 300,000 kilometres per second, that was a very large number indeed.

Tiny amounts of mass, but vast amounts of energy. It fitted with all the observable facts. It had been right there in the special theory of 1905 and I simply hadn't bothered to look at it closely enough.

Paul brought the bucket back to me full of stones. He had ransacked the beach to give up its secrets. Purple, black, flints, chalk and granite overspilled the edge. We looked through them together. A tiny black pebble, small and thin. A purple lozenge. A grey oval with a white line that went all the way round. It was one of the things I had always meant to do, I thought, to find out about stones. To be able to walk along a beach and think confidently, This is quartz, this is anthracite, this is diamond.

How many times had I heard that one equation, the one that everybody knows, muttered like a revelation, breathed like a solution, and with as little thought or comprehension as a prayer?

How had I missed it?

'I'm taking them all home', said Paul, 'for my collection.'

'You don't have a collection,' I said.

'Yes, I do,' said Paul. 'This is it.'

'No,' I said. 'Not everything. Don't take everything.'

'I'll carry them,' said Paul.

'It's not that,' I said. 'It's just that . . .'

'What?' said Paul, rubbing the purple lozenge between his fingers.

'It's just that you mustn't always take all the time.'

'Share,' said Paul, well drilled.

'More than that,' I said. 'As you get older, it's . . . it's giving something back.'

He was my last baby. Part of me wanted to keep giving and not ask for anything in return. The instant he started giving something back was the instant he didn't need me any more. I decided he could keep them, keep them all.

I helped him arrange his collection in a line on a sand dune and then took him down to the water. He took his bucket with him, in case of buried treasure, unexpected booty from the high tide.

Beyond the dryness, the sand was grey and dark. Where you put your foot against it, it left a lighter surface, a betrayal of the moisture within. The seaweed beneath our feet was brown bladders and black fingers. The shells crunched underfoot. The tide was very far out in the estuary. It had ebbed away from the massy rocks and seaweed whose natural home was under the water, unhappy to be so exposed. In an hour or so, the sea would come washing back again, swift and savage, swallowing up bits of balsa wood, the paper from the sandwiches of holidaymakers, any stray morsels that had been left in its path.

Even so, someone had been here before us. There in the flat sand was a pattern of shells. When you looked harder, you saw it was a face, open-eyed and smiling, hair adrift in the wind, with writing below, two names and the date, written with a stick, perhaps salvaged from elsewhere in the flotsam of the beach, scraped in the sand and underlined with a flourish.

Paul fell to in delight and I screamed at him, 'No!'

'What's wrong, Mutti?'

How could I explain in terms that made sense to the boy?

'It is a gift to the sea, Paul. Not yours. Not yours to take.'

I thought of talking about drowned sailors, about appeasement, about how taking something that belonged to the sea would mean that you owed something in turn to the sea, but I knew he wouldn't understand these legends, these half-baked peasant superstitions.

'It's your choice, Paul. You decide.'

The wind from the sea, from the ocean beyond the mouth of the bay, was becoming stronger. The sea had a glittering hard light now, like a mirror, and the black shapes just visible in the water beyond were rocks that would harm shipping.

Paul looked at me for a moment then took the eyes, which fell with a clank in his tin bucket.

I thought, I'll only have to turn my back now, and he'll be taken. The water will come washing in faster than he can run. He won't even see it coming, Paul collecting his shells. He won't even have to turn his head and it will be upon him, the fast tides, the currents.

'Come on,' I said. 'It's time to go.'

We walked back up the beach, the wind cold, past the remnants of the ruined castle from our earlier visit, safe above the high tide. Paul walked ahead of me, his collection spilling from his bucket, all the way back to Herr Weiss's car. Paul's dark hair glinted white in the light of a half-hidden sun. His father's son.

Back in Berlin, back home, I ransacked the oak desk in the study until I found what I was looking for. I studied the old papers the young man had written very carefully, to see if there was something vital I had missed, something lost in the ink that had run in the water from the melting ice.

No. There was nothing missing. I saw that day the devil in the details that I was meant to see, the devil that was the greatest revelation of my life.

I had been looking in the wrong direction. I had been looking out, to the edges of the universe, when I needed to look within, smaller and smaller, to the very inside of the atom. It didn't matter, for my purposes, whether light was waves or particles. It didn't matter that you couldn't tell whether an electron was here or there with any certainty. All that mattered was that if you held the atom in one place, still enough, for long enough, you could smash it apart.

It didn't matter if my father had the wreckage of the familiar universe in his hands. I would have the wreckage of the atom, that smallest pivot on which the entire universe, familiar or not, depended.

If I took just this one equation, I could build a weapon so powerful just the light of the detonation would blind. I thought of the explosion, how it would deafen. I shouted with joy to think of it. Here, without me even looking for it, was the best revenge of all.

I had the way to do it here in my hands.

It would be like holding a piece of the sun.

My shrinking, despicable father – the man who hated all weapons – wouldn't be able to ignore me then.

That night, after tucking Tina and her dolls and Paul with his hot head and his itemized shells neatly away in their safe beds, I slept well and without dreams, in a country of my own, with the whole dreaming house in order under my fingertips. Things were working out better than I could have hoped. To take my pacifist father's theories and make their practical application the greatest destructive force the world had ever seen seemed to be a highly appropriate form of revenge. I couldn't think of anything better. I felt certain he would agree.

When I woke, with the first light of the morning coming through the thin curtains, I started thinking more seriously about practicalities. Nuclear fission, I had to admit, was going to pose a bit of a problem. Where was I going to get a laboratory big enough to split anything?

Something would turn up, I thought. It always did.

24 June 1935

I was feeling lonely.

Hitler's purge of the civil service, whose laws automatically applied to the universities, was well under way. Anyone of Jewish descent was removed from office. Nearly everyone of any importance had left. Born and Franck had gone from Göttingen – I would never get an answer to my letters now – Szilard had moved out of reach. I had no-one to talk about fission with. I'd nearly finished my mathematical model of the core structure of the atom. I was just having a bit of difficulty with my half-integral quantum numbers.

Josef, over a dinner of chicken and dumplings, was telling me about the day's work, about the import and export of sodium and wood pulp. Facts, figures. Statistics.

'Oh, yes?' I said, already not listening, leafing through the newspaper. From time to time there were still items about my father, but fewer and fewer as we got used to the new universe he had introduced, hardly any at all once he had become a traitor to the German people. I liked to read them though. They contained such passionate hatred I admired them.

Josef was on to cement and groundnut oil by the time I found something of interest.

'Hey, listen to this.' I read aloud from the paper. '"Max Planck..."' he's the director, you know, of course you know, I've told you often enough, "has delivered the following message to the chancellor:

'"The Kaiser Wilhelm Gesellschaft for the Advancement of Science begs leave to tender reverential greetings to the chancellor, and its solemn pledge that German science is also ready to co-operate joyously in the reconstruction of the new national state."

'There. What do you think about that?'

'What's that got to do with groundnut oil?' said Josef.

'Groundnut oil?' I said. 'I'm talking about revenge.'

Here was an opportunity. Here, finally, was a definite path to retribution opening up before me, not just in theory, but in practice.

'Do you know what, Josef?' I said, interrupting his résumé of groundnut-oil reports. 'I think it is my duty to joyously co-operate.'

My husband raised his head. 'In what way?'

'By going to help German science in its hour of need.'

Josef drew a line under the groundnuts and I kissed him.

CHAPTER SEVEN

The Laboratory

15 July 1935

A REPLY TO MY LETTER TO MAX PLANCK CAME WITHIN DAYS, though not from Max Planck himself. A 'Research Officer' with an illegible signature invited me to the Berlin Technical College on Hardenburgstrasse, just across from Army Ordnance, for an informal discussion about scientific matters of great importance to the state. This time I was prepared, and I planned things carefully. They weren't going to let me near enough to joyously co-operate with anyone if I started talking about atoms, light or particles, but they might well let me join in if I claimed to be able to discredit Jewish science. And that was what relativity was, after all – Jewish science. I was going to talk about relativity and not say a word about quantum mechanics, expanding universes or depression.

The short excitable man with a beard was nowhere in evidence. Now I had a blond beast in front of me, who purred like a panther.

'Fräulein Hansbach. Do sit down.'

I had decided to leave the encumbrances of husband and children out of my letter. In this new Germany, married women stayed patriotically at home, preferably in the kitchen. They didn't get involved in matters above their little heads.

'You have a scientific view on the relativity theory you wish to share with us.' He looked sceptical, as if I wouldn't even be able to pronounce it, never mind understand it.

I smoothed my grey wool skirt down a touch more over my knees. 'I feel, Herr Professor,' – I wasn't sure he was a professor, but I didn't know what else to call him – 'that the theory of relativity is just one more example of the dangerous influence of Jewish thought on the questions of nature.'

'Do go on, Fräulein Hansbach. Do go on.' This was just the sort of joyous co-operation the Reich wanted to hear.

'Herr Einstein', I said confidently, 'has produced nothing more than a botched-up ragbag of ancient ideas and unsound mathematics. Even now, already, it is gradually falling to pieces.'

The panther purred. This was music to the Reich ears. Even so, I tried not to underestimate him. It was perfectly possible that he knew in his heart, as I did, that relativity was, well . . . nearly right.

'Is your sole objection to the theory on patriotic grounds?' The panther leaned forward, over the desk, as if he really wanted to know.

'Of course not,' I said. 'For a start, quite aside from the fact that the theory is an affront to German science, it does not explain inertia.'

The panther sat back at inertia.

'Really it is quite simple. We've known since Newton that if you give an object a push, it will keep on moving in the direction you've pushed it – ignoring the effects of friction, of course – until you give it another push. If we had an almost empty universe, containing only one particle, motion would be meaningless – there wouldn't be anything for the particle to measure its motion against. And if it has no motion, it can hardly be said to have inertia, can it? But if you add a second particle, does the first particle have inertia then? And what if you then add more and more particles, does inertia increase? If you look at it like that, you see that a particle, before it could determine its inertial response to being pushed or pulled, would have to determine its position relative to every other single particle in the entire universe before it could move. And moreover, it would have to do it instantaneously. Patent nonsense. There's never an appreciable delay when *you* push a particle, is there?'

The Herr Professor conceded that there wasn't. 'I'd like to see some calculations on that, though.'

'Fine,' I said. 'Have you got a piece of paper?'

Within ten minutes I had taken him through enough mathematics on inertia to give him a headache.

'Stop,' he said. 'I can see you know what you're doing.'

The figures I'd written down were patent nonsense, I knew that. But it is amazing with what little twists of statistics you can seem to prove the impossible.

I said quite a lot more about it being my patriotic duty to smash the theory of relativity simply on the pure grounds of its untenability, never mind its Jewishness, and my scheme worked. In a letter a week later, I was invited to the college to pursue my ideas in a research capacity. A word from the blond beast had given the clearance. There was a shortage of physicists – those who hadn't been dismissed had largely left the country. They were probably glad to have me.

I didn't care two pins about relativity any more. I certainly didn't care about inertia. I wasn't even much bothered with gravity or light. They had been my way in, a childhood obsession, old weapons. Now I was on to more grown-up pursuits. And what better weapon could there be than my father's own work, turned against him? Here, with money and equipment at my disposal, I would have the facilities to smash the atom.

I would smash it. I would smash him.

I danced round the house, the joyous letter in my hand, as elegantly as my four missing toes would allow. Josef watched. Tina watched. Paul watched, uncomprehending. 'It is my duty,' I sang, waving the letter, my voice gleeful above the remains of the nursery tea on the walnut table. 'My duty, my duty, my duty.'

Paul went off to sort his toy soldiers. Tina retired to her room to tuck in her dolls for the night. Josef watched and watched while I danced and danced.

'Bombardment,' I said to him. 'That's the best way.'

In the middle of the celebrations, Maja arrived.

'You're looking more and more like your mother,' she said, when I told her the good news. This wasn't the reaction I had been hoping for.

'You've never met my mother,' I said.

'You limp like her,' she said. 'Now. You never used to.'

'I'm going to do physics,' I said. 'Now. The way she did. The way I was never able to before.'

'Perhaps that's it,' she said. 'Perhaps that's all it is.'

'That's all it is,' I said. 'I don't want to hear you say any more.'

So she spent the rest of the evening telling me and Josef about the first experiments that were being done with electricity and muscles. She was particularly fond of these because all she had to do was lie down on a pampered sofa and relax while tiny currents caused her muscles to contract and expand at alarming rates.

'Does it hurt?' said Josef.

'The wonder of it is', she said, 'it's completely painless.'

'Maja,' I said, 'it carries the risk of short-circuit and electro-cution.'

If she wasn't going to be nice about my experiments, I wasn't going to be nice about hers. Not that my warnings about possible annihilation were going to put her off.

24 September 1935

I reported for my first day of work in a state of great anticipation. If I was to smash the Jewish relativity theory, after all, and advance the cause of Aryan physics, I needed access to the finest instruments the Reich could offer.

The two men in the room, there for my formal welcome, glanced at each other. Up to a point. I could have access to the finest instruments at a distance, as it were.

'You see how it is.' As a woman, I was not to be allowed inside the laboratory itself. That was unthinkable. The director of the Kaiser Wilhelm Institute for Physics, who controlled all access to the lab, shrugged his shoulders. 'You do understand, don't you?'

'Perfectly, Herr Debye.' I smiled.

He was telling me that I might rock the established order of the universe but I wasn't going to be allowed to transgress against the social niceties in *his* department. I smiled again, to show just how understanding I could be.

In fact, I smiled at every opportunity. In particular, I smiled a great deal at Herr Vahlen, who, I discovered on that first morning, was my official supervisor from the Reich Educational Ministry. If he was going to be my supervisor, then I was going to be charm itself.

So Debye and Vahlen shook hands with me on that formal morning, said they were pleased to meet me, and then I was taken to a dusty basement office where I could work. It smelled of bleach and there were scattered rags on the floor where it looked like mops and buckets had only recently been removed. There wasn't even a proper desk, only what looked like a trestle-table someone might use for pasting wallpaper and a rickety chair.

I sighed. Still, it didn't matter. All I needed was pencils and paper, when you got down to it, and someone to carry out my instructions.

Dieter Habbel, my assigned lab assistant, was pleased to make my acquaintance, also.

'So you're here to work on relativity?' he said.

'After a fashion.'

He looked about him. 'I don't think I've ever completely understood relativity,' he said.

I smiled. 'Not many people do.'

'Do you?'

It never occurred to me to be less than honest. 'Oh, yes.'

'Then explain it to me.'

I frowned. I'd never been able to explain it to Maja or Josef, who knew me best of all, and I'd had several attempts. The words just kept going round and round every time I tried to pin things down and in the end I confused myself.

'I don't think I can,' I said.

'Why? Is it because you think I'm too stupid to understand it?'

'No, Herr Habbel. It's because I'm too stupid to explain it properly.'

He was less than satisfied, but after pressing me to give it a try, conceded my point after two or three sentences.

I was pleased we could dispense with relativity so easily. Out of all of my father's writings, I was concerned with only that one equation now, and I was going to try to push it, push it to its furthest limits until it broke apart and unlocked more energy than the world had ever seen.

After a day and a half, I judged Herr Debye and I had charmed each other sufficiently for me to broach the idea.

Against my expectations, he wasn't very interested. 'Heavy atoms? Equations?' He couldn't care less. 'There's more likely things you could work on, Fräulein Hansbach, rather than wasting your time with this nonsense.'

Habbel couldn't see the point. 'It looks like a lot of work for very little result. Let's face it, it's never going to have a practical application, is it?'

So, to keep everybody happy, I started work on a project to investigate the penetrative power of electrons, which involved the preparation of very thin metallic films. Habbel prepared about twenty to my every botched one. I had been a theoretical physicist all my life. I wasn't, I decided, cut out for experimental work.

After another week or so, throwing the electron films up in the air, I pressed the matter again.

'Rutherford's doing work on it', I said, 'in the Cavendish. You don't want the British to get there first, do you?'

'You're supposed to be working on relativity,' said Debye. 'Go away and let me eat my sandwich.'

I left him to his pastrami and pickle, went back to the basement where the smell of bleach was slowly dissipating and did some perfunctory calculations on inertia, just for show.

The following week I tried: 'Are you content to let the rest of the world move ahead in its knowledge of the subnuclear world?'

'Yes,' said Debye, nodding, obviously infinitely content for the subnuclear world to be left in the jumble that it was. 'You have real work to do. Inertia, Fräulein Hansbach. Relativity. You're supposed to be writing a paper on it, remember?'

I tracked down some dusters and gave the trestle-table a good polish. I had been a Berlin housewife for too long to let my standards slide.

The following week I said, 'If the fatherland thought that you had deliberately held up research on a weapon that could convince the world of the superiority of German science, that wouldn't go down well, would it?'

Debye looked up from his calculations and said, 'Weapon?'

'I think so, sir.'

'A weapon.' He thought a moment. 'Possibly. If it works.'

'If it works, we will have a weapon. If it doesn't work, we will have proved the basic equation wrong: energy does not equate with mass. Either way there's glory.' I put as much earnest patriotism as I could into my voice.

'If we accept that in theory at least the lab might start work on this, what sort of timescale are you talking about?'

'Four years? Five?'

I had no idea. I was faced with my astonishing lack of any real knowledge about the process in practicality. It wasn't just a matter of splitting one nucleus apart and releasing the energy, this splitting had to be done thousands of times, and at roughly the same moment, so that enough material would release its energy and explode.

'You said Rutherford was working on this. What were his results?'

'He tried shooting particles at hydrogen . . .'

'And?'

'About one in a million of the particles got through.'

Debye considered.

'You and Herr Habbel can have one year.'

'But . . .'

'One year. And remember that this is a weapon you're working on, Fräulein Hansbach. One that we may need one day.'

I skipped out of his office and down the hall, eager to impart the good news.

'Herr Habbel, Herr Habbel, we must start work immediately on a project that is of vital importance to the German struggle. Get me some lithium.' Habbel sighed. He'd been enjoying the electron films.

At home I sang over the laundry, smiled at the children throughout breakfast, danced and danced through the days and in the dark when Tina cried. We had a girl in for the afternoons when the children came home from school – Kätzchen, a semi-distant cousin of Josef's, only seventeen and therefore content to be with children.

Josef was glad to see me happy. He had always known that inside I wasn't happy. I thought I was happier now than I had ever been and kissed him several times to prove it.

29 November 1935

My practical skills did not improve. something similar to Rutherford happened to Habbel and me. After a great deal of fuss and bother, we shot particles at lithium and found that at the end of the experiment, we'd put more energy into the shooting than we got out. A negative expenditure. I knew all about the drawbacks of that from keeping Josef's books.

'It's like shooting birds in the dark,' said Habbel.

'In a region where there aren't even many birds,' I said.

Habbel was disappointed. He could see that any glory for our potential weapon was going to be a long way down the road. I was optimistic. At last I had all the help I needed. And Habbel was a good co-worker. He was in no doubt that the work we were doing was vital for the German cause.

If I had stopped to think about it, I might have said the same. But, of course, I didn't stop to think.

7 February 1936

It was a Friday afternoon and I had stolen an afternoon away from the dusty basement for Maja and I to go shopping. She for nylons and a fresh turbot for supper, me for shoes. I always had difficulty finding a pair that would fit my odd-shaped feet. I had been complaining the whole time we were out about the way she still cooked fish on Fridays.

'Do you think God cares, Maja, whether we eat a fish or a ham? Do you think it makes the slightest bit of difference to the universe?'

'Did no-one ever tell you', said Maja, 'that God's ways are not our ways?'

'You're all the same, you believers,' I said. 'There's nothing we scientists can say that will ever change your mind.'

'And aren't I glad about that,' Maja said. 'Scientists talk the most immense amount of twaddle.'

We stopped, along with the people around us in the haberdashery department of Kayser's. It wasn't the first time we'd been ordered to listen to one of these events and it wouldn't be the last. All the factories, offices and shops were under compulsion to broadcast the speech. Loudspeakers had gone up in stations, streets and squares. Even if you didn't want to listen to this proclamation from Hitler, and I couldn't have cared less either way, you could scarcely avoid it.

I used the opportunity of the enforced break in the shopping excursion to take off my shoes and rub my feet against the backs of my legs. I was tired. We still didn't have enough accuracy in our lab instruments and so had precious little to show for our efforts. The voice ranted on. I looked at the ribbon counter in front of me and saw some scarlet that would look just right against Tina's hair. The bits of the speech I didn't manage to avoid hearing were astonishing, claiming largely, in that unmistakable rolling Bavarian accent, that Hitler was the saviour of the nation.

'Honestly,' I said to Maja, running the scarlet ribbon between my fingers to check its quality, 'and you said that scientists talked twaddle.'

She kicked me on the leg.

At the end of the broadcast, when people had applauded – my 'Why are they clapping? Don't they know Hitler can't hear them?' was lost in the groundswell of approval – tall Maja had put her arm affectionately round my shoulders and said, rather too loudly I felt, considering how close her mouth now was to my ear, 'What a great speech, hey, Helga? Thanks to our leader and his personal courage, Germany has been preserved from chaos and revolution.'

'What?'

Maja's voice was even louder now. 'All loyalty to the great and glorious leader of all the Germans.' She smiled at all around her.

She continued to beam while I had the scarlet ribbon measured and cut, and only stopped when we waited on Unter den Linden for the tram.

The flags on the hotel balconies fluttered above our heads: the bright red slash of the silk, the clarity of the swastika, the black against the white. All the officers that early season had red lapels and fine wool coats to protect them from the spring chills and in the Berlin streets their breath turned to mist.

'Honestly, Helga,' Maja said when we had got on the tram and paid for the ticket. 'Sometimes you can be so stupid.'

I sat down next to the window. 'I don't see how everyone else can be so stupid.'

Maja sighed, as if reluctant to speak, with the air of one who has had a difficult decision to make and is unhappy at the outcome.

'I'm going to do something that you won't like.'

'That's nothing new.'

'I'm going to join the NSDAP.'

'For God's sake, Maja, why?'

'For the sake of appearances. Herr Weiss . . .'

'I don't trust that man.'

'Neither do I. That's why I'm doing this. You're in a difficult position, you know. A Jewish family . . .'

'None of that will come to anything, Maja.'

'Herr Weiss has been asking questions. I think I need to make it very clear where my loyalties lie. Where our loyalties lie. This is one of the best ways I can think of to protect you all. You and Josef can't apply in case they make enquiries and discover your tainted inheritance. Me joining is the next best thing.'

'Oh, Maja,' I said.

'Of course', she said, 'you would be even safer if you all left Germany.'

'You know I can't do that,' I said. 'Not right now.'

In the lab, I had a chance. Where else could I come so close to destroying my father? To leave now would take away my chance for revenge and that revenge was still the driving force in my life.

'I know,' she said. 'So that's why I'm joining the party. Come on, it's our stop.'

When we arrived home, we found Kätzchen at a loss. Paul was crying, oblivious of the noise he was making, the tears running hot and wet down his cheeks, his fingers clutching at nothing. There had been some incident at school, some friend had left suddenly and wasn't coming back. Paul was inconsolable. I dropped the shopping and held out my arms.

'Would you like to sit on my lap?'

To my surprise, he nodded.

I lifted him and held him close against me. The tears lingered a few moments more and then, putting his head against my blouse, he announced, 'I might sleep now.'

Kätzchen was busy slicing apples. Maja got out her turbot and began instructing Tina in the art of making a sauce. Tina liked to think she was learning to cook. I sat and held Paul.

To prevent him slipping off my lap, I held him tight. He became heavy as his head lolled, but I did not let him go. This was the first time for months that I had held my son on my lap, the first time for over a year he had fallen asleep against me, already claiming he was much too grown-up for that sort of thing. Now he was small again, made small by his tears. I felt like a thief, taking such joy in my son's sorrow.

I would have liked to stay there all evening but when, an hour later, my legs dead and complaining, Josef came home and took him from my lap and carried him upstairs to his bed, Paul didn't wake.

He never saw his friend again and, after a few weeks, stopped asking where he had gone.

13 March 1936

One morning, when I was in the bath, with Tina splashing down the other end, intent on making bubbles between her fingertips – although she was nearly twelve, she was too frightened of the bath to get in it by herself – it suddenly occurred to me that if we could find an element which emitted two neutrons when it was shot with only one neutron, then we'd be on the right lines.

'Hey, Tina,' I said, 'Mutti's got something.'

I wrapped her in the towel and kissed the top of her head. I dressed her and Paul for school racking my brains for all the elements I knew of that could possibly perform such a trick. I left a note for Kätzchen to make sure the children had some fresh fruit for tea as I was concerned about their vitamin intake and Josef was expecting a shipment of oranges, and put on my make-up for work. When I got to the lab and mentioned the problem with the elements to Habbel, he immediately said, 'Uranium.'

'Why?' I said. Chemistry was never my strong point.

'It's the heaviest known element. It's one that stands the best chance.'

'Then let's find some. Come on, don't waste time.'

We looked all through the basement of the institute, all the musty-smelling storerooms, down underground in the chemical stores where the drums of sodium and potassium were mouldering away, but there was hardly any.

This was a blow. I thought uranium might be a bit beyond Josef's import and export channels and, when I asked him, he agreed.

Habbel was detailed to find uranium. I did some serious sums.

7 May 1936

When I arrived at work, late one morning, I spotted through the doorway a familiar figure leafing through the papers I had left scattered over the trestle-table.

I ducked back down the basement corridor. 'What's he doing here?' I said to Habbel.

Habbel glanced up at the stranger. 'Oh, he's just looking over some papers. Filling in forms. You know what these chaps are like.'

'I do indeed,' I said, and made my way over to greet him.

'Good morning, Herr Weiss.'

'Frau Hansbach. I beg your pardon. *Fräulein* Hansbach.' He gave the salute. I watched him do it and didn't respond. He gave me a moment and then turned to the papers again.

'Some very interesting work, here, Fräulein Hansbach. Measuring atoms. Measuring the atoms within the atoms?'

'The particles,' I said.

'That's right. Measuring the particles.'

'You can't. That's the problem.'

'Why so?'

'You can't know momentum *and* position of a particle at the same time.' This was the uncertainty principle itself, fundamental and glorious in its simplicity. 'By the time you've measured the momentum of an electron, for example, so that you know where it's going and roughly how fast, its position has changed. You don't know where it actually is any more. And if you measure its position, you change its momentum. You change everything just by the measuring.'

Herr Weiss's face was impassive. I did not know how much or how little he could understand. I certainly didn't want him getting an idea of what I was really doing with my atoms.

'That doesn't sound very logical,' he said.

'It is', I said, 'if you think about it. It's the same with Maja. If you know where she's going, you don't know where she is. If you know where she is, you don't know where she's going. If you try to gauge, roughly, by asking her if she'll be home for dinner, you've changed her. If she was going to come home, now she won't. If she wasn't – and generally you know her well enough to think that she won't – now she will.'

Herr Weiss laughed. 'I will tell Maja that,' he said, 'that she behaves like an atomic particle.'

'I think Maja already knows,' I said.

'And you,' said Herr Weiss. 'What is the momentum of your project to . . .' He tipped his head back, as if trying to remember something. 'Your project to, what was it, "smash the Jewish theory of relativity"?'

'Oh,' I said, dismissively. 'Herr Habbel and I,' I waved a hand at my ever-helpful lab assistant, 'Herr Habbel and I are not quite there yet.'

'But you will not give up in this patriotic duty?'

'Not for a moment,' I said.

'I'm glad to hear it,' said Herr Weiss. He put on his hat and coat. 'I shall keep in touch. I should like to know about the momentum of your project. Or the position. One or the other if I can't have both.'

'It will be an honour,' I said, watching as he gave his flourishing salute goodbye.

When he left, I spent an hour going through the papers, trying to see how much he could have worked out from the notes I had scribbled. Plenty, I thought, if he was a mathematician.

And I suspected that he was.

'I saw Herr Weiss today,' I told Maja when Paul was safe in his bed and Tina was in the drawing room staring, as she often did in the evenings, into a mirror at her own reflection.

'I know,' she said.

Maja was in the kitchen, cutting Kätzchen's hair and listening to sentimental love songs on the radio. You could get hardly anything on our box radio in those days except stirring music or sentimental love songs and none of us could abide the stirring music. She wasn't allowed to go and have her hair cut any more, Kätzchen said, because Herr Hitler had announced that Jewish hair was infectious. Maja was cross. Kätzchen was just getting to the age, she said, where a good, carefully designed cut was vital. She did not say vital for what. Kätzchen also wanted shoulder pads.

'Just shoulder pads?' I said.

'And lipstick.'

Maja said she knew a man who would get Kätzchen some from Paris. The black block of mascara that Josef had brought from there about eight years ago was almost gone, she was eking it out to its last oily flourish, so she would ask the man to get more of that, too, but mainly the lipstick as she could see it was important.

'Red lipstick, I think,' said Maja. 'That would suit you, Kätzchen. Somewhere in Germany, Herr Weiss tells me, there are people making a bomb that will fly by itself.'

'I wonder what sort of bomb,' I said.

'Scarlet,' said Maja, looking closely at Kätzchen's mouth.
'Scarlet, I think, by Guerlain.'

'I wonder how far it will fly,' I said.

Maja sighed. 'Bright scarlet red. As red as the German flag.'

'Maja,' I said.

'I'll find out,' she said. 'If you think it's important.'

'It might be important,' I said. 'I might have competition.'

'I'll find out. Flying bombs. Don't worry for a moment.'

She went into the drawing room, took the mirror away from Tina
to Tina's disgust, brought it back into the kitchen and showed
Kätzchen the back of her head.

While I took Tina upstairs and put her in her nightclothes, Maja
caught the Number 5 tram, that night, the one which took her
straight to Alexanderplatz, where she could have a good time, where
she could find out.

Maja had stockings made of silk and lipstick made of glycerine.
Her eyelashes under their black mascara would steal anyone's heart,
extract any information you desired.

14 September 1936

We had a tiny amount of uranium and Habbel and I disagreed on
the best way to deal with it.

'If we manage to knock two neutrons out of the nucleus and they
go on to hit two more nuclei, and then those four . . . well . . .' He
shrugged his shoulders. 'In fact, we just need to know whether we
can keep this process going.'

'Oh, we don't need more uranium just to prove that,' I said. 'Of
course it will keep going.'

'How do you know?'

It was simple – I could see it in my head. It was as clear to me as
nature: we don't have to think about whether apples fall down, we
don't waste a minute on idle speculation as to whether we will let

our hearts beat another beat. The fact that the process would continue was just *there* and I could see it.

'Take my word for it, Herr Habbel, it will work. It will.'

'I'd rather see it written down on paper.'

So I spent the rest of the afternoon sitting at the trestle-table writing down equations on bits of paper – some of them hard, even for me. Think how many words it might take you to write down your feelings for your husband, your child. You could write paper after paper, reams of words defining, describing . . . and even then you would fret that you had left something out, not explained all the parameters, every assumption, all the circumstances. But you do not need to explain this feeling to *yourself*; it is just there. It modifies and shifts at will, but you can feel it at every moment.

Sometimes it takes a lot of paper to write down something that is very simple.

By the end of the afternoon I had enough paper to convince Habbel that if we had a large enough mass of material, we could sustain a nuclear chain reaction and I went back to the lab to tell him so.

I found him ashen-faced, leaning against one of the benches, a curious expression in his eyes.

'What's the matter with you?'

'That man's been here again.'

He didn't have to tell me who he meant.

'What did he want this time?'

'My signature.'

'On what?'

'A piece of paper testifying that the work you are doing here is vital to the cause of the fatherland, and that you are completely loyal to the Führer.'

I considered a moment. 'Did you sign it?'

'Of course I did, Fräulein Hansbach. It is true, isn't it?'

'Of course it is, Herr Habbel. How could you think for a moment otherwise? Here, look. The uranium. I wrote it all down for you.'

Habbel looked over the paper, the endless equations, the clarity
of the process.

'Are you going to show this to Herr Debye?'

That had been my intention. Now I wasn't so sure. I wasn't sure I
wanted anyone to know about this. Except Habbel, who needed to know.

'Not yet,' I told him. 'Let's see how far we get first, shall we? And
then we can surprise him.'

I made a mental note that I was going to have to salute Herr Weiss,
after all, the next time I saw him.

24 September 1936

Our year was up. We hadn't got very far at all. We had done some
dazzling demonstrations on paper but practically, even I had to
admit, things were disappointing.

Debye had a formal meeting with Habbel and me where he looked
over the reports, checked our calculations and sighed.

'In the end it doesn't matter what I think – although in my judgement you ought to stop this nonsense as soon as possible and get
back to some real work – you are to carry on anyway.'

'Why?' I said.

'Orders from higher up. Someone thinks that whatever it is
you're working on here could be very valuable to the fatherland.'

'It could be,' said Habbel, 'if . . .'

'If it ever works,' I said, not wanting to give anything away. I
didn't know who might be watching or listening.

'Report on a regular basis,' said Debye. 'Keep me informed.'

Somehow, the knowledge that I was free to do what I wanted to do
– work on nuclear fission for as long as it took – didn't make me so
happy any more. I felt as if something else was going on, something
big that I had overlooked. But I couldn't think what.

I was having trouble with two crucial measurements – the

diffusion of neutrons in the lattice and the number of neutrons that might be freed during fission. No matter how I did the calculations, things just didn't work out. Perhaps this was the reason for my unease, that the mathematics was failing us.

Still, I thought, we've got no real reason to hurry. Hitler had just proclaimed that the Reich would last for a thousand years. I thought that ought to give us plenty of time.

13 October 1937

I spent the next year and a bit in this state between happiness and unease and never seemed to move forward.

I was not getting enough sleep. All through the day in the lab I was tired, at night I was tired, but my brain wouldn't stop thinking, ticking over.

Elsewhere, Fermi had bombarded uranium with neutrons and reported the production of several different radioactive elements as a result. I read his papers in the journals and thought that he was wrong, but I couldn't yet prove it. I worried that atomic fission, for me, for anyone, was never going to be more than a dream. But it was a powerful dream. When I thought about it, when I let myself think about it, I felt the light of the atomic sun in my mind warm my whole body. I would hold the power in my hands, as easily as I had once held Hans Albert's magic stone, and make those elemental forces do their tricks at my bidding.

I didn't sleep, I decided, because my days were so full of dreams there was no room for any more of them at night.

21 March 1938

We knew war was coming but we didn't know when.

Josef wanted to leave, he wanted us all to leave but he knew I wouldn't go. I no longer had the excuse that I wanted to stay in Berlin to be near my father, he had long ago gone to America. The only thing keeping me there was my work.

At the very least, then, Josef explained, we should send both Tina and Paul away. He had relatives in England, somewhere near Ealing. People who would give them a good home till everything blew over. If they went, they wouldn't be the first. Children were beginning to disappear from the streets, whisked away and transported to distant lands. Josef wanted Tina and Paul to go somewhere they would be safe, before the fighting started.

'Tina,' he said. 'You know Tina hasn't a hope if . . .'

But I put him straight. There wasn't a hope in Hades of him getting her out of my arms.

'She needs her mother,' I said. 'Look at her. Don't you ever think differently.'

'But Helga, you can't protect her.'

'I work in a laboratory doing science for the fatherland,' I said. 'How much safer do you want her to get?'

I held on to her fast. As soon as she was born I had said I would never let her go and I saw no reason to change my mind now. In the garden where she still played, the girls didn't taunt her, call her names, and they were well used to calling names by now. The Jewish families in our neighbourhood had been called every name under the sun. I considered the fact that Tina escaped this taunting a good sign. I thought Oberlandstrasse was a place where she could be safe. It was her home. She needed to be at home, near her mother.

Besides, Tina and Paul would be safe, we would all be safe, because Herr Weiss was counting on me to deliver a weapon to the fatherland.

'And when I've finished my work,' I said to Josef, 'don't worry, we'll go.'

'When will that be?'

'Soon, soon. I'm nearly there.'

20 April 1938

'We have a holiday,' Herr Weiss explained to the children. 'At the invitation of the Führer. It is his birthday.'

I had given Kätzchen the day off and done breakfast without her. We were gathered in the hallway, ready for the outing. Josef was away in Hamburg, and had been for over a week, in negotiations with a factory for sheet metal. Maja had relayed the invitation to me from Herr Weiss. In the absence of their father, she said, he begged to offer his own services as a chaperone in order that we could enjoy this holiday in the way our dear leader had intended.

Maja hadn't exactly said the outing was compulsory but I knew it would not be a good idea not to go. I didn't know where we were going, or for how long, but I had arrayed the children in their best clothes, just in case. Tina was a dream in a pink dress and jacket, Paul a little soldier in a brown suit. I had recently allowed Maja to cut Tina's hair – Tina had been asking for this ever since Kätzchen had had hers done – and I could tell Tina thought that she looked like a grown-up. She almost did. Until you noticed the two dolls she had tucked under her arm. Until you spoke to her and realized just how little there was behind those blank eyes. You would have expected such a beautiful creature to start telling you about boys, her schoolwork, her folk-singing classes. But she never said a word.

We walked down the steps to Herr Weiss's car. There were picnic hampers ready and I began to relax, to think that the children might enjoy this day after all. We drove to the shores of one of the Berlin lakes and I installed the children on the grass with instructions to play nicely. Above our heads, the cherry blossoms were just coming out. In another week, they would be thick on the branches like a white cloud. All along the shore, there were daffodils, tulips, white waves on the blue water reflecting the blue sky like a bowl.

'How is your project going?' said Herr Weiss, just when I had begun to think this was nothing but a picnic after all. 'How is the measuring in the particles?'

I thought, I'll leave now, now before the clouds come over the blue sky and turn everything grey.

'We don't have enough uranium,' I said, 'and the measurements are uncertain.'

'Look,' said Maja, bringing Paul over to me, 'he has a new collection.'

In his hands, Paul held out a bundle of snails, gathered from the underside of the leaves of the flowers.

'Look at that,' said Herr Weiss. 'Quite a little scientist in his own right.' He smiled benevolently at the child who, flattered, smiled back.

The snails were giving me the creeps. Already they were beginning to inch their way over each other and over Paul's palms. I didn't know how he could bear to touch them.

'He'll grow up into a fine young man, your son,' said Herr Weiss. 'How I envy you, to have a boy you can give to the service of the Führer.'

'I am very lucky,' I said.

Now was the time to go. I wanted Paul to have a memory of the lake and the flowers intact, not smashed to nothing.

Maja gazed without speaking at the snails. One made its way to the edge of Paul's hand and he pushed it off, so it dropped with a bump into the lush grass in its bright spring green.

I stood up, went over to Tina and took her by the hand, holding her close against my hip.

'I'm taking her up to the tea shop,' I said, to no-one in particular. 'She is cold. She needs a warm drink.'

Herr Weiss nodded. Paul never looked up, intent on the journey of the snails, busy with his creatures, tilting his hands so he would lose no more. I fastened Tina into the coat I had brought, a long coat that buttoned up to her neck, walked up the shore, past the tea shop to the station and caught the train home.

Maja brought Paul home much later, asleep, in the back of Herr Weiss's car, and together we lifted him into his bed. After that, we argued late into the night and the shouting woke Paul, who cried.

No matter what happened, no matter how much I had tried to harden his heart, to toughen him up, in the end I admitted defeat. The tears were there, inside him, and nothing I could ever do would make them come to an end. I tucked him back into his bed and told Maja I'd compromise.

'Paul can go,' I said. 'I'm going to tell Josef that Paul can go.'

When Josef got home with his sheet-metal contracts, I told him to write to Ealing. Then we waited for a reply.

9 November 1938

Just before lunch, Habbel split the nucleus of the uranium atom into two. There was no doubt about it. We had done it. This was the first real step on the way.

The quantitative calculations had too great a margin of error to be certain we could ever make this thing into anything more than a laboratory curiosity, but the results were promising. When the nuclei had flown apart, they had released 200 million electron volts. That 200 million was enough to keep Herr Weiss happy for at least another year, I reckoned.

I breathed a sigh of relief and hugged Habbel, who was as pleased as I was that we finally had something to show for all our calculations and pieces of paper. Then I came home early to tell them the good news and found they had gone. Josef, Tina, Paul, Kätzchen.

The shops opposite the house were in disarray, their windows were smashed, goods were littered on the pavements outside. On the walls one word had been daubed in white paint with a rough brush: *Jude*.

On the steps of the house, in a neat suit, Maja was waiting. I sat down beside her, hollow in my stomach and my knees, my hands shaking. She took my hand in hers, as if to steady it.

'As I am such a good friend of Herr Weiss,' said Maja, 'and such a loyal member of the NSDAP, he has agreed not to take you, too.'

In the street four or five girls were skipping. The rope, I noticed, was Tina's. One of them held Tina's pink doll in her hands. The rope turned, over and over, kicking up red dust. I watched them for a while, not letting myself think or feel anything because the minute I let myself feel anything, it would overwhelm me so much I thought I might go mad.

The girls sang, 'Raspberry, gooseberry, apple jam tart, tell me the name of your sweetheart.' They came into the rope and out again, one after the other, repeating the rhyme.

'That's not right,' I shouted to them. 'That's not what I sang when I was a girl.'

The children were suspicious, not wanting to know. The rope lay flat in their hostility.

I sang to the children, to Maja, 'Apple, peaches, lemon pie, who's the one you'll love till you die?'

The Hungarian felt strange on my tongue. Then I stood up, came down the steps and started walking.

The rope started turning again. The girls began singing, in good German, unfamiliar words, strange phrases, unutterably wrong.

Their voices rang clear and high, swooping like birds over the flat earth.

CHAPTER EIGHT

The Office

10 November 1938

THE CHIEF OF POLICE WAS VERY POLITE AND MADE AN APPOINT-
ment for me with the Gestapo. There were children on the
pavement outside the headquarters building – boys, mostly, lunging
at each other with two pieces of wood tied together. I almost didn't
go up the steps.

I gave my name and appointment time to the porter on duty and
he opened the iron-railed gate to let me in. It was all so orderly.

The iron gate clanged shut behind me.

An armed sentry took me down a long straight corridor. On each
side was closed door after closed door. Our shoes clattered on the
stone floor.

At the end of the corridor, I was shown into a little waiting room.
There were several armchairs and a low table covered with periodicals. A man was also waiting, twisting his hands, and we waited in
close silence. Neither of us looked at the periodicals. Neither of us
spoke. If we said anything, it would make the world real and we did
not want the world to be real

At exactly the appointed time, as indicated by the clock on the
wall, I was led by a smiling secretary into a small office. It was like

offices everywhere, a filing cabinet in the corner, a telephone on the desk, papers filed neatly into a tray.

'Sit down, please,' said Herr Weiss.

He gave me a broad smile and indicated where I was to sit. His uniform was freshly pressed, his boots newly polished. In this neat small office he looked bigger than ever. His eyes were bluer than ever.

'Herr Weiss,' I said. 'I've come to ask you to change your mind.'

Herr Weiss did not get angry and he did not get agitated. He simply remained unmoved. He was not even going to confirm that he had given the order to have my children, my family, taken away. However, he felt that I should know that he was outside anyone else's jurisdiction, and, if he *had* given such an order, there was no power on earth that could have it overturned. None.

Was I allowed to know where they were?

No.

Was I allowed to send a message to them?

No.

Could I go and see them?

No.

Was there anything else that I could do to help the situation?

There was. For the next ten minutes, Herr Weiss elaborated.

It hadn't really been Maja who saved me. It hadn't even been the piece of paper that Habbel had signed that day, testifying that the work I did in the lab was vital to the cause of the fatherland, and that I was loyal to the Führer. Herr Weiss waved his hand, to indicate the ultimate worthlessness of these frivolities. If that was all I had going for me, I would have been taken to the KZ along with the rest of them.

No, what had saved me was Herr Weiss's belief that some day soon I would come up with more tangible proof of my loyalty to the fatherland. A weapon of destruction – a new kind of bomb, say – that he could deliver to the Führer like a proud parent.

'Debye says you and Habbel are working on such a weapon. Is it going to be possible?'

For a moment I considered playing Herr Weiss at his own game. I could issue my own ultimatum: if he didn't return my children to me immediately, then I wouldn't set foot inside that lab or any other ever again. But he held all the bargaining power. What did I really have to threaten him with? If I didn't do the work, Habbel would, Debye would – thousands of others prepared to joyously co-operate with the Third Reich would – and Herr Weiss could afford to take a chance that they would eventually manufacture a bomb perfectly well without me. Theories are only theories, after all, but Tina and Paul were my children.

'Yes,' I said. 'Such a weapon is possible.'

If I managed to bring this new kind of bomb into reality – a proto-type even – Herr Weiss implied, he could arrange that I saw my children again.

'And Josef? And Kätzchen?'

He shrugged his shoulders. 'That matter is already out of my hands.'

I bit my tongue hard to stop myself crying, wailing out loud. If I hadn't been sitting down, on Herr Weiss's neat office chair, I would have fallen. Josef was gone. He was gone. All these years he had been with me, and I had taken him so much on trust that I hardly had the words to express how much he meant to me. I had never thought I would need the words. I had always taken it for granted he knew. And now I would never have the chance to tell him.

I stumbled and hesitated, tasting blood in my mouth, looking for the words I needed now, the right words.

'Success is not guaranteed, Herr Weiss. This is theoretical physics. These are early days.'

Herr Weiss granted me that. But it wasn't really his problem. If I didn't come up with the goods, then not only would I end up in the KZ, I would certainly never see Paul and Tina again.

'Herr Weiss,' I said, standing up and shaking him by the hand, 'I will do everything I can.'

Thanking him for his time, I shut the door carefully behind me.

I imagined his brains bruised out over concrete, the red blood and grey matter sluicing over the paving stones of the street. I would do it myself. I would kill him myself, with my bare hands, if only they gave me the opportunity.

I was out of the corridor, through the iron gate and into the air. I waited until I had turned the corner by the finely wrought railings before I took out my handkerchief and wiped the tears from my eyes. If Herr Weiss was watching, I didn't want him to see the extent of his victory. The handkerchief didn't actually smell of sulphur but I thought it might as well have done.

In all, my pact with the devil had taken less than fifteen minutes.

I was right where Herr Weiss wanted me. All I cared about was getting the children back. I'd have done anything. Anything. If I could have got them back only on the condition that I *stopped* this work, that I abandon physics for ever, I would have done it without a moment's hesitation. I never wanted to go inside a lab again. Getting revenge no longer mattered. Smashing my father to pieces no longer mattered. All that mattered was Tina and Paul. Getting them back to me.

And to get them back, I had to keep on working. Keep on doing the one thing Herr Weiss wanted me to do.

Back at the house, the empty house, on Oberlandstrasse, she was waiting for me.

'You warned me, Maja, didn't you?' I said. 'You told me we'd have to get out and I wouldn't listen to you.'

She stroked my head against her shoulder.

'How could I have been so blind? How could I have been so stupid?'

'Hush, baby.'

'Josef, what had he done to them?'
'Nothing, sweetheart, you know that.'
'Kätzchen, what harm did she ever do to anybody?'
'None.'
'Then it really is all my fault, isn't it? Isn't it?'
She stayed until I had cried myself to sleep.

I slept in the children's beds. One after the other. Paul's, then Tina's. While the scent of them was still warm in the blankets and pillows, I stayed with that closeness, revelled in it, drank it in. The pink candyfloss of my daughter, the harsh sea-smell of my son. In the night I hugged the pillows close to me, loving them, stuffed the blankets against my face and smelled them, drew them back to me, my children, my lost loves, the only things that mattered.

11 November 1938

I wouldn't get out of their beds. first one, then the other.
'Go away,' I said to Maja, when she came into Tina's room in the morning. 'Go away.'
I turned my back on the light, Tina's dolls all around me on the bed.
You hear people say that so-and-so has a good sense of direction. Generally when they say this, they are talking about the amazing fact that this lucky person will know whether the turning for the market is on the right or the left, whether they need to turn east or west at an unmarked country crossroads, but there are invisible forces governing the universe that we do not make use of, and this is one of them. Sometimes people know which way is south if they have been driven 30 miles blindfold and dropped off in a dark forest. 'Find your way home,' the callous experimenter says and, astonishingly, they do. Hansel and Gretel could have done with their infallibility.

But whatever this gift is, it applies to finding people, too.

As sure as the needle is swung to the pole, as the compass finds magnetic north, just as ineluctably I could swing towards them. I lay there in one bed after the other all that day and found my children with the ends of my fingertips.

I knew that, somewhere, they were still alive.

In the evening, Maja brought up some tea on a tray. The buttered toast looked sour and flat.

'If I co-operate,' I said to Maja, 'I'm co-operating on the wrong side, aren't I?'

'Yes,' she said.

'But if I don't co-operate, I'll never see them again.'

'Yes,' she said.

'Then what choice do I have?'

9 December 1938

We were designing an atomic pile – just one way amongst others of putting uranium together – using carbon as a moderator. Size and shape were crucial. We needed to put together just enough uranium and carbon in just the right way to start the fission process. My over-riding concern was whether this process would continue into a chain reaction. The measurements Habbel and I did showed that we got somewhere between three and four neutrons with every fission, so I thought it was possible. And if it worked, the sums showed the chain reaction would take a fraction of a second.

Enough uranium, though – that was the difficulty.

'We need a lot more than this,' I said, looking over the calculations.

'Definitely,' said Habbel. He sat down on the edge of the trestle-table, in the one space not covered with papers.

'Where are we likely to get some more?' I said.

'The mines in Czechoslovakia,' said Habbel. 'The Belgian Congo.'

I thought that in many ways my education had been remarkably limited.

'There must be some closer to home,' I said.

'Who do you know who's going to give Germany uranium now?' he said.

'No-one.' I sounded as despondent as I felt. Everyone was betraying me, including the fatherland. 'Unless we overrun Belgium.'

I hadn't told anyone at the lab about Josef and the children. I thought, if I told them why I needed this so badly, it would only make things worse. They would fret and worry and sympathize, and the calculations would go awry. I thought that if they just concentrated on doing their sums correctly that would be enough. We only had to get this right and I would get my children back.

I thought, If the worst comes to the worst, I'll overrun Belgium myself.

9 January 1939

I wasn't the only one on the trail. Hahn's paper describing the process of nuclear fission in an atomic pile had been published just before Christmas. The news had reached even us. And if we had seen it in black and white, then by now the whole world knew fission was possible, in theory.

My secret was out.

I looked over the paper carefully. It didn't say whether, in an atomic pile, or even in a weapon, a chain reaction was possible.

I *knew* it was. I could see it, there in the numbers. Never mind the fact that it might take 1,000 kilograms of pure carbon, 600 litres of heavy water and 3,000 kilograms of pure uranium oxide, none of which I had. I knew it was possible, so I was still ahead of them.

So, in the days, immersed in the calculations that estimated the optimum configurations and the endless mathematics that blotted out the pain, frantic to keep ahead, I worked.

In the nights, immersed in the warmth of their beds, I reached out for my children.

7 February 1939

Time ran slow, then slower. The days dragged by as if I had weights attached to my limbs.

The worst thing was not knowing what had happened to them. I didn't know if they were well or ill, whether they had been sent to live with a fine upstanding Aryan family who were unfortunately childless, who knew nothing of their origins, or whether they were shut in one of the camps to the north.

In the lab, they'd gathered together every atom of uranium we could muster and it still wasn't as much as I wanted. The element, unfortunately, does not occur naturally as pure uranium, but has to be refined, like iron from iron ore, to reach a fissionable state, and it was this refining that was slow. We didn't have the resources to go to full industrial production and I didn't have any alternatives.

But something worse was happening, too. The beds were getting colder.

'Do not let your heart be troubled,' said Maja. 'Trust in the Lord.'

'Out of all the Biblical advice you could have given me, Maja, I think that's the most inane.'

'It's the truest.'

'It's not the Lord I want to trust in. It's Herr Weiss. Can I trust him, Maja, when he says he'll give them back to me?'

She wouldn't look at me. I couldn't remember a time when Maja hadn't looked me straight in the eye.

'Herr Weiss just says that the sooner you complete the work to his satisfaction, the sooner things will be back to normal.'

I spat at her. And then I put my head on her shoulder to cry, because there was no-one else I could turn to.

I had to trust her. I had to trust him.

I missed Josef so much, it was intolerable. Things could never get back to normal because I would never have Josef again. I knew that and Maja knew that, no matter how many prayers she said. Even Herr Weiss knew that.

13 March 1939

The results continued to be patchy. The design of the uranium pile was quite impractical and I blamed Debye. He was ultimately in charge and I wasn't allowed near the thing. Under his direction, the design of the pile was becoming rounder and more compact. I tried to stretch it out, as I stretched in the night to the ends of my fingertips, as if at the ends of the beds I could still find my children. But if you stretched the material out too far, the whole thing fell apart.

I couldn't see how to put it right, even on paper. I certainly couldn't see how to put it right in practice. Neither could Debye: when it came down to it, he was even more of a theoretical physicist than I was. He couldn't tie his own shoelaces.

Late in the day Herr Weiss made one of his periodic visits at which we all smiled and said that things were progressing as well as could be expected. I did decide, however, to point out that the continuing shortage of uranium was becoming a major obstacle.

'I think it will be possible to get more,' Herr Weiss said. He inspected his fingernails. 'The Joachimsthal mines in Czechoslovakia. Yes, that should be possible.'

'I hope it will be,' I said.

'All things are possible,' said Herr Weiss.

In the universe as a whole, I knew this was true. In the Third Reich, I knew it was true only in so far as Herr Weiss allowed it to be true, in so far as Herr Weiss could make it true.

When I explained the problems that evening to Maja, she was more intrigued by the way things had turned out than anything else, that the structure of certain isotopes could cause explosions in the right circumstances.

'Did you really think, Helga,' she said, putting on her lipstick, 'that the universe would be made this way? I didn't.'

'I think the universe is a lot stranger than you're giving it credit for,' I said, thinking of the way electrons could disappear into a haze of uncertainties in quantum mechanics. 'It's certainly a lot more difficult than I ever gave it credit for.'

'Difficulty', she said, 'I know all about. What did you say you needed?'

I watched Maja closely. The shining beads at her neck, a glass of Eiswein in her hand, the silk of her dress. Her beauty. It wasn't much of a practical tool against the *Wehrmacht*, but she was doing her best.

29 April 1939

Two crucial measurements – the diffusion of neutrons in the lattice and the number of neutrons freed during fission – had been botched. Looking back over the filed reports, I could see this now, clearly, and moreover, could see that this had happened at an early stage. I was furious. No-one else seemed a bit surprised. Debye shrugged his shoulders. Habbel was apologetic.

No-one mentioned the botched measurements to Herr Weiss in any report, written or verbal. It was in absolutely no-one's interests to admit that we'd made mistakes.

But there was a mistake, somewhere.

I looked over my papers, over and over endlessly until my eyes could no longer focus and another night was gone and another day was about to begin. Whenever I thought about Josef, I felt physical pain. Whenever I thought about the children, the pain spilled over into tears. And tears would do them no good, no good at all.

To keep from crying, I went over and over the equations, looking for answers. Over and over the equations, staving off the dreams. Over and over the equations, because there was nothing else I could do.

The next day in the lab, we started again.

14 July 1939

Things were going from bad to worse. We had worked out that only one form of the metal – Uranium-235 – was going to be capable of sustaining a chain reaction. Only the U-235 nuclei were easily split, but they formed only one part in 300 of the metal. The U-238 nuclei, which formed the overwhelming bulk of the uranium, usually just absorbed anything that hit them. That was one of the reasons my calculations had been so awry.

One step forward but two steps back. The notion of making a block of U-235 big enough to sustain a chain reaction was even more outlandish than just getting enough ordinary, common or garden uranium to experiment on.

I would need about 100 kilograms of U-235, I reckoned from the figures, to make a critical mass. Anything less than that and there wouldn't be enough neutron collisions to start the chain reaction, most would simply fly off into the space beyond the metal. And there was a sudden worldwide shortage of uranium, despite what Herr Weiss had promised.

That in itself, if nothing else, told me that we weren't the only ones working on this particular problem, trying to put the theory into practice. The important thing now was to get there first. If I didn't, Herr Weiss would have no reason ever to be nice to Maja and me again.

'Herr Habbel,' I wheedled. 'What do you know about isotope separation?'

'I think, Fräulein Hansbach, that to produce enough on the scale we'll need is beyond industrial capacity at present. Given the situation.'

I knew what he meant. Factories had their hands full producing tanks and weapons, not separating out rare isotopes.

'Gaseous diffusion?' I said.

'Using what?'

I had not overlooked the fact that uranium was a metal and not, in fact, a gas, so I had my answer ready. 'Uranium fluoride?'

Habbel sighed. 'You're talking about something that's so corrosive that no-one's yet designed a pipe or a pump, let alone a diffusion barrier, that would even stand up to it.'

'Ah.' I was a physicist. Chemistry was still beyond me.

'Everything would have to be redesigned from scratch and even then the size of the plant you'd need to produce just a few pounds of uranium would be gigantic.'

'Just how gigantic?'

'Tens of thousands of skilled workers.'

I sighed. Most of the skilled workers were out fighting the war.

'No chance of making enough here in the lab, then?'

'None.'

Of course I dimly realized that even if I did get enough Uranium-235, I couldn't just assemble a critical mass and leave it lying around – for one thing, it would explode – but I'd think about the problem of making the equivalent of several thousand tons of TNT explode in the right place and at the right time later. Availability was the problem at the moment and that's what I was worrying about.

I tried one more tack: 'What about a cyclotron?'

'None of those have ever been more than experimental.'

It was the confirmation I needed. If I had thought that industrial production of my isotope of uranium was possible, I'd have asked them to get straight on with it. I wouldn't have wasted time asking silly questions, I'd have launched straight in to trying to persuade Habbel it was a good idea. And Habbel thought that anything done for the good of the fatherland was a good idea.

But industrial production wasn't possible. And without industrial production, there was no way on earth I was ever going to get enough U-235. And if I didn't have enough U-235, my much-vaunted chain reaction would fizzle into nothing.

My whole life was falling apart in my hands.

1 September 1939

I woke up and their beds were cold.

I had lost them.

After that morning, I never went back to the house on Oberlandstrasse again. I gave Maja the keys and she locked the door. She took some money, some clothes and some things for the children, and we let the house fall to whatever fate was in store for it.

We went back to rented rooms, in a different part of town, which weren't nearly so comfortable, but it was all I could bear. I knew if I walked back up those red steps once more, saw the pink perfection of Tina's room or Paul's shell collection, I would break down in tears so hard and bitter I would never focus on a single piece of atomic structure again.

And somewhere in there, in the structure of the atom, was the key. All I had to do was find it.

19 September 1939

Within days of the outbreak of war, Debye disappeared. Habbel and I shrugged our shoulders. We had learned not to ask questions. Then Herr Vahlen disappeared, to be replaced by a brisk man from the Weapons Research Office, who gave us a brief inspection and an enthusiastic salute. We asked him for isotopes and he went away again.

Apart from that we were left undisturbed.

21 November 1939

The isotopes began to come through. Small amounts, but enough to continue work.

'Even though we're at war,' I said to Habbel. 'It's astonishing.'

'Helga,' he said. 'It's *because* we're at war.'

I thought I was probably the only person in Europe who was pleased war had started.

The practical problems of assembly were going to be immense. I was still working largely in theory as we had too little to practise on, but I had realized that when we finally did bring two subcritical pieces of uranium together to form the critical mass, it would have to be done very quickly. Too slowly and a stray neutron from one could trigger a localized nuclear reaction in the other piece, which would blow the whole thing apart and prevent the major reaction from taking place.

'If only . . .' Habbel began.

I knew what he was going to say and I wouldn't let him say it. He was going to say, 'If only all the Jewish scientists hadn't disappeared. We could do with their expertise now.'

He was right, of course. Most of the people who could have helped us had long since left for America. But we were good Germans. We were supposed to be able to do it on our own. To admit otherwise would be treason.

I was in no mood for treason, I was in pain. The thumb and forefinger on my right hand were fat and swollen, pushing the skin taut at the edges of the nails, already white and curling, like paper about to tear, to split. The pressure was hard and the pain intense.

Obviously, where I had been biting the skin around my fingernails, I had let an infection in. Nothing but an infection. An ordinary disease of an ordinary war. The fever was beginning to kick in, there was sweat around the back of my neck and along my forehead.

I had lived a whole year now, without my children, and to admit possible defeat would be to betray them. I wasn't going to let that happen. I had to concentrate. I had to live through these moments. Here. Now. Not live the future over and over in its various ways, torturing myself with what might happen. Not even live the past again and again, though that would have brought a certain comfort, letting the wheel roll out the low chances and the high winnings. One after another, second to second, this work was what I needed to do to keep us all alive. Not for one fraction of a second could I take my eyes off the goal.

I pulled back some of the skin next to the nail on my thumb and watched the pus leak out, white and slow. If I didn't act soon, there was no telling how far this infection might spread. It would stop my work completely if I let it.

I took Habbel's scissors, pulled back my thumbnail and then, before I could think too much about it, stabbed down as hard as I could, then went on to the forefinger. I did it so quickly, the pain in my thumb had only just begun to dawn in the conscious part of my brain by the time the forefinger was over.

And then time started again. The pain almost took away my sanity. Blood and hot fluid ran over my hand in streams. The weight of it dropped away as the poison ran out, but the pain went on.

Then Habbel took my hand, plunged it into hot salt water, and the poison leached out of me, cell by cell, for the rest of the day.

24 December 1939

By Christmas, my hands had healed sufficiently to hold a pencil again. Even that didn't give me cause to be any more optimistic than usual. As a weapon, anything I had was next to useless.

But while Maja went off to church, I worked on my calculations. They were the only things that mattered. If I let my mind slip away from them for just one moment, I would realize all over again that this was Christmas and the children weren't here.

'Why didn't I let them go?' I asked Maja, when she came in late and cold, long after the midnight Mass, with her cheeks bright red from the frost. 'Why didn't I listen to Josef and just let them go?'

All my life I had been asking questions, and this was the worst one of all.

1 February 1940

We'd been noticed. Habbel and I were summoned without warning early one morning to the research office of Army Ordnance. We were met by a man in a suit and tie with a dreamy expression on his face.

'I've been told to assess the possibility of the technical exploitation of atomic energy,' he said. 'Think there's anything in that, do you?'

'Perhaps,' I said.

'Possibly,' said Habbel.

The dreamy man took from his desk some papers I recognized as mine.

'Tried carbon as a moderator, have you?'

'Yes.'

'Paraffin?'

'No.'

'Heavy water?'

'There's not enough,' I said.

'There will be,' said the man. 'I've just recommended the construction of a heavy-water plant.'

Curiosity finally got the better of me. 'Who are you, exactly?' I said.

'Heisenberg,' said the man, standing up and offering me his hand. 'I'm in charge now.'

'I'm pleased to meet you,' I said, and smiled. I knew all about smiling. Also I was genuinely pleased to meet him. I recognized him now. I had seen him from a distance once before, at a lecture he had given on relativity. It had been a fascinating experience as he was allowed to talk about the topic on the proviso that he did not mention my father's name. It had been a sterling performance. I had written to him afterwards – anonymously, of course, as I did not need an answer – congratulating him on his lecture and pointing out a small fault in his mathematics. When it came to relativity, I still had the edge.

Heisenberg knew more about electrons than even I did. Not only in theory – I flattered him about his seminal 1927 paper on the wave properties of the electron until even I thought I was going too far – but also in practice. He had drawn closer to their real nature than anyone before.

If I could get him on my side, then things might begin to move a little faster.

'You've had some interesting results,' he said, looking over the papers.

'Fairly,' I said. And I explained about the design of the pile and the lack of uranium and the endless calculations. I didn't say a word about a chain reaction.

'We're building a dedicated lab for all the fission experiments,' he said.

I looked surprised.

'Oh yes, there are others,' he said. 'Here, and in Leipzig. And Hamburg. We call you the "uranium club".' We were all so cut off from each other, it was hard to know what anyone else was doing. 'I realized what you might be up to when we had three separate requests in a week for 1,000 tons of uranium oxide.'

'Why?'

'Because at that time there were only 150 tons of the stuff in the whole of Germany. Someone was bound to ask questions.'

I blamed Habbel. He should have known that.

'You do understand, Fräulein Hansbach, now that the fatherland is at war, we must work together?'

'Perfectly,' I said.

Habbel managed a nod.

'Then we'll keep in touch, won't we?'

As I left, I saw him stamp the word '*Geheim*' at the top of my stolen papers.

We walked back across the road to our basement. 'If we're all working together,' I said to Habbel, 'why is he stamping everything "Secret"?'

'A dedicated lab,' said Habbel. 'An industrial heavy-water plant.' He was beside himself with excitement. I had my suspicions. They weren't entirely dissolved when we discovered that the dedicated lab was being built in the grounds of the Institute for Biology and, to keep out the curious, it had a sign above the door saying 'Virus House'.

19 November 1940

In the virus house, our prototype atomic pile was finally providing useful information. The length of time in which the fissionable material for the bomb would have to be assembled and detonated was becoming clearer from my calculations. Habbel looked over them appraisingly.

'One millionth of a second,' he said.

'That's right.'

'The specifications are going to have to be very precise indeed.'

'German engineering is renowned the whole world over,' I said.

Habbel looked at me. 'I didn't mean to imply that our workers would be unable . . .'

'No, I know you didn't. But be careful. Don't say anything about German workers when we tell Heisenberg.'

I suspected that Herr Weiss kept tabs on the project through Heisenberg as well as through Maja, but I was never sure just how much information was passed on. I kept feeding these little nuggets of progress, my small successes, into the system, but nothing ever came back. I would have liked something: a letter, a lock of hair, anything to prove they were alive. Although I still believed Paul and Tina were out there somewhere, I had nothing more to go on than a mother's belief.

Most days when I thought about them, and I thought about them every single day, I imagined them with another family somewhere. I saw them at breakfast, Paul dressed in a neat brown school uniform, Tina with her hair tied back, possibly wearing an apron, happily helping the Frau of the house sweep the kitchen floor, scattering crumbs in the garden for the birds the way her grandmother, Josef's mother in Vienna, always used to. It wasn't an unhappy picture. In this picture, both children had long forgotten me.

It was a mother's belief. And we all know how beliefs can delude us.

22 December 1940

Maja had discovered facial exercises and spent five minutes on alternate days staring at herself in the mirror while screwing up her nose and lifting her eyebrows individually. She had a gruesome chart on the wall disclosing what the human face would look like without its protective layer of skin, every muscle marked in medical script.

'*Obicularis oculi*,' I said, reading out loud and grimacing. '*Sterno cleido mastoid*.'

'Facial wrinkles disappear,' Maja said confidently, lifting her right *obicularis oculi* a millimetre or so higher than the left. 'Ditto double chins and jowls.'

'Don't be ridiculous,' I said.

'Think about it,' she said. 'If you don't move your muscles about, they just sit there, getting longer and longer, until they collapse.'

'But if you look at things rationally, my dear, the laws of physics . . .'

'The laws of physics.' Maja laughed. 'That's exactly what I'm dealing with here. Gravity. And the way eventually your face drops into your neck.'

Getting through the time with Maja made my whole life with Josef and the children seem like a dream. If I closed my eyes and listened to the sounds of her cooking, heard her humming over her mending in the rooms we rented, watched her putting on her face powder and snapping shut her black patent handbag in preparation for an evening out, I could almost imagine things were back the way they always used to be when I'd had nothing worse to worry about than a theory of time and space and revenge upon my father.

That seemed so far away now. The only person I wanted revenge on was Herr Weiss. I wanted to smash his face under my feet into the ground. He was the only person I wanted revenge upon and he was the only person I couldn't touch.

8 December 1941

My children had been missing for three years. Maja, through sources of her own, had long been looking for them, but they had disappeared without trace. Not a story, a hint of gossip, gave any clue to their whereabouts.

If I passed Paul in the street now, I calculated, I might not recognize him. He would have grown through those quick childhood years that make so many changes. His hair would have darkened, he would have lost that rounded body as he lengthened out, and his talk would be beyond my recognition. Tina, I imagined, would still be the same as I had always known her, but I was only guessing.

In the lab, we were on the second prototype, but there was something in these new figures that bothered me.

I showed Habbel. In the millionth of a second it would take, the core of the bomb would go from metal to liquid to gas. I had been trying to work out how well the fission reaction might continue under such conditions, but it now seemed as if the heat build-up might cause a consequent fusion reaction. Instead of things splitting apart, they would come together.

'So?' said Habbel.

'If this fusion reaction is with nitrogen, we're in trouble.'

'Ah.'

I didn't need to tell Habbel that nitrogen made up 80 per cent of the atmosphere. I didn't need to tell him that there was therefore a chance that any atomic explosion might ignite the entire air of the earth. I could see from the whiteness in his face that he had already worked this out for himself.

'What are you going to do?' he said, his face pale.

'Not tell Heisenberg,' I said. 'He'll stop us in our tracks.'

'We'll be stopped in our tracks if we set the earth on fire.'

'That's not certain,' I said. 'I have to go over the figures for heat loss through radiation. That might rule it out.'

'Might?'

'Yes, it might.'

'Let me know, won't you?'

I thought, If they are dead, then I don't care if the whole earth burns. I don't care.

8 January 1942

The fourth atomic pile – LIV – was bigger than the others. Encased in two hemispheres of aluminium, it was lowered slowly into a large tank of water. Then they introduced the neutron source, which we hoped would initiate the fission within the uranium in the pile, through a shaft into the centre.

Then we began the measurements.

A short while later it was clear that the pile was producing more neutrons than were being injected. I allowed myself a small smile. For the first time in the world, the beginnings of a chain reaction could be seen.

As I scribbled in my notes, I reckoned that if we increased the size of the experiment by a factor of approximately fifteen, we would be able to sustain that reaction.

I presented the conclusions to Heisenberg, thinking that here was a nugget of success that must surely elicit some response, some word. I hoped that perhaps I had even done enough now to warrant their return, though I knew that nothing less than the weapon itself would satisfy Herr Weiss. Spurred on by success, though, I began to calculate the size of the basic structure I would need if I was ever going to turn this thing into a weapon. I had a rough estimate of the average theoretical distance a neutron would have to travel before colliding with another atom, and from this I reckoned that a sphere 20 centimetres in diameter should contain enough neutrons for the reaction to occur. This project, that for so long had been nothing but theory, was beginning to turn into fact after all, definite, quantifiable facts.

Heisenberg's reaction, however, was less than I had hoped for.

'How do you know', he said, 'when the reaction will stop?'

'Ah,' I said. 'That I haven't worked out yet.'

'Even if we found a proper detonator, it is possible that this experiment would set up a wave of disintegration through matter that would make Berlin and a greater part of the Reich disappear in smoke.'

'That's not my intention,' I said, trying to be reassuring.

'Intention or not,' said Heisenberg, 'it's possible.'

'But not likely.' I was guessing.

'Nevertheless, we have to face facts,' said Heisenberg. 'We're not going to do it.'

I was aghast. 'But . . .' I said. The words fell away. I couldn't believe what I was hearing. He was supposed to be on *my* side.

'All we've done here is demonstrate the theoretical possibility of a weapon. We haven't been able to move on to serious industrial production. And if we tried to do that, Fräulein Hansbach, do you know what would happen? Before this weapon worked, it would bring about Germany's defeat.'

'How?'

'Think of the manpower we would need. Think of the materials. If we start draining resources like that, the fatherland won't be able to produce tanks and aeroplanes.'

'If we succeed, the fatherland won't need those tanks.'

'We can't wait. Germany needs those tanks now.'

Until now Germany had been doing so well in the war that nobody apart from Herr Weiss seriously believed the fatherland would one day have need of such a weapon. The fatherland was doing very well with the weapons it had already got. Victory was almost assured. But now the balance had started to swing the other way.

'I know the situation is bad, Herr Heisenberg.' This was treasonable talk and I hesitated before continuing.

Heisenberg interrupted. 'The situation is too tense for technical projects. Let's just say that.'

'All right, but . . .'

'There's no point in arguing, Fräulein Hansbach. I've just received an order preventing any technical experiments that will take more than half a year for completion. And how long will yours take?'

'If I could have just a bit more time . . .'

'You've had several years, Fräulein Hansbach, and you're scarcely any further forward.'

'But the results today . . .'

'They are the results from one small experiment. Inconclusive. The Allies are pulling ahead. It will be more cost-effective for us all to concentrate on rocketry. That promises quicker returns. And we need quick returns now. Think about rockets, Fräulein Hansbach, or go back to work on the Jewish theory of relativity. That's what you originally came here to do, isn't it?'

The words were like something from another century. I had long since left relativity behind. In the scheme of things, relativity seemed like the least important theory ever invented.

20 May 1942

We were being disbanded. It was a direct order from the Führer. All that work – our new lab, the endless calculations – all for nothing. I was numb to the ends of my fingertips. When I pressed my hands together, as I did when I heard the news, the scars from the infection in my hands shone clear as thin silver lines.

Habbel was reassigned. Heisenberg suggested that I go along, too, to the obscure backwater of Germany that would give birth to Hitler's vengeance weapons.

Habbel was very excited. 'Just think, Fräulein Hansbach. A jet-propelled flying bomb.'

The fact that an engine-propelled bomb would need to travel further and faster than anything of the kind before and was just as theoretical as *my* weapon passed him by. He had all the enthusiasm of a child with a new toy. For the next two weeks, until his transit papers came through, Habbel talked about nothing but tolerance levels, guidance systems that would take into account the curvature of the earth and the still-new science of electronics.

For two weeks I pretended to be interested, even pretended I was coming with him. I was waiting for Herr Weiss to call, to tell me what he was going to do. There had been nothing but silence from that quarter. Even Maja hadn't seen him.

'Don't you want to take your papers, Fräulein Hansbach?' Habbel was watching me stuff them in the incinerator.

'No,' I said. I was too busy pushing them in to explain why I didn't need them, that what was written on them was as clear and obvious and as unforgettable to me as my own name. 'I'll have some tea, though, if you're making it.'

Habbel smiled, the good and faithful servant, and disappeared to do some science in the kitchen.

I watched another set of papers turn brown at the edges and disintegrate. Those papers had only ever been written for the benefit of others, to try to explain what I saw. To me, what those papers contained existed as a clear and shining thread within my head. They contained nothing I couldn't take with me. For good measure, I had cleared Heisenberg's desk, too, and taken some key papers from Habbel. If this project was being disbanded, I didn't want anyone else getting their hands on this information. If I wasn't going to be allowed to make an atom bomb, I didn't want anyone else to make one, either.

Sheets and sheets of numbers, every one of them beautiful, went into the flames. The numbers themselves were free from human uncertainties, devoid of the capacity for betrayal, shining pure like frost under a dark sky. But they were meaningless now. Geometry, calculus: how beautiful and complicated it was and how useless. What did it matter to Tina whether the angles of a triangle occasionally added up to less or more than the Euclidean norm? What did Paul care when the patterns went awry and parallel lines met? Lucidity and the most elegant of equations couldn't bring them back to me. Only Herr Weiss could do that.

Something caught my eye.

The figures weren't quite right. A quick glance showed me that.

Because of all the work I'd done with radioactivity, the mean life and the half-life, I knew that the log of 2 to the base *e* was 0.69315. Heisenberg had written it down with two digits interchanged.

I laughed for a moment, to think of the author of the uncertainty principle himself, always so calm and assured, typing figures incorrectly. It was reassuring to think that even the most perfect of us can make mistakes, and it made me laugh without enjoyment to think that even at a moment like this I could catch mathematical errors.

I looked idly through the paperwork still in my hands, the next batch for the burner. Surprised, I found more errors. Not just isolated ones, either. I looked further. Figure after figure, report after report. It gradually dawned on me that this was no one-off human mistake. This was systematic, persistent fabrication.

My knees turned to water. My sense of balance left me and I sat down on the floor, burning my hand on the hot metal of the incinerator. Experiments I had done had been filed with the wrong results. Calculations had been completed with vital elements missing.

There, beside the heat from the burning papers, I went cold. I knew what this meant. I knew the only thing it could possibly mean. Heisenberg was not the good German I thought he was. He had been suppressing the news of how successful our project had been, feeding back erroneous information to Herr Weiss, to whomever else he was paid to report to, those dark and shadowy figures of whom I had only the vaguest sense. Heisenberg had been filing reports that were complete lies. He had been telling them we were no further forward and they had believed him. No wonder we were being disbanded. He had lied and lied and now my children were further away than ever.

I shrieked in rage, uselessly, searing and long, banging the hot metal of the incinerator so loudly that Habbel came running back from the kitchen.

'It's over,' I said to him. 'All over.'

Whatever Heisenberg had done was done and I was helpless.

'Oh, Fräulein,' said Habbel, bewildered.

'You don't understand,' I said. 'We've been betrayed. You can't know just how much we've been betrayed.'

I slammed the incinerator door shut and, a few minutes later the door of the lab shut, too, not caring who heard it, not caring who came looking.

I had stuffed the rest of the papers into my briefcase and took them away with me, thinking they might be the last chance, the absolute last chance.

'It says in the cabbala', said Maja, 'that God counts the tears of women.'

I had sobbed by then for an hour and a half, shivering uncontrollably on the bed in our rooms, despite being wrapped in the blanket I had brought from Novi Sad.

'He can't count mine,' I said. 'I have too many. And I don't believe in Him.'

Maja sighed. There was nothing she could do to comfort me. We had been drawn into the systole and the diastole of the twentieth century – it sucked in children and gave us back soldiers and bones. I didn't know yet what had happened to Tina and Paul but, if I left these papers uncorrected, I knew they would be bones, bones and dust.

'What do you want to do now?' said Maja. She stared at the papers I had spread over the floor, the deliberate errors marked in angry red, a grammar of lies spelled clear for all to see.

'I'm going to tell Herr Weiss,' I said.

'You could,' said Maja quietly. 'And then what would happen?'

I knew that. The moment Heisenberg was found out, it would mean execution.

'Tell me why', I said, 'I should let that bastard live.'

'He didn't know about Tina, did he?' said Maja, calm, the voice of reason. 'He didn't know about Paul.'

'No. No-one does except you and Herr Weiss.'

'So don't blame him for something he knew nothing about.'

'What I want to know is why,' I said. 'Why would he do this anyway? Why would he risk it? It makes no sense.'

'It makes perfect sense to me,' said Maja.

I stared at her.

'He did it because he knew it was right.'

'Maja, no.'

But I was denying it because I knew it was true.

Heisenberg had risked death to keep Germany from gaining the advantage in the war. He wasn't going to let the wrong side win. I stared at the red sentence of guilt on the floor.

He had acted from the highest of motives. What higher motive could there be? But in his attempts to prevent the fatherland from obtaining the ultimate weapon, my calm and assured director had condemned Paul and Tina to death.

'He did it', said Maja, looking at the papers, 'because he had to. He knew the risks but he took them. No-one would try to pull the wool over the eyes of the Third Reich unless it meant more to him than life itself.'

'But that isn't his life down there in red,' I said. 'Or mine. Those red lines are my children's.'

Maja sighed. 'Oh, Helga.'

I looked up sharply. 'Do you know something?'

'No, I don't know a thing. That's the trouble. Not a thing.'

'Listen, Maja,' I said. 'I could have been found when I was a child. I was there. I could have been found if the right people had come looking for me. But they didn't come and look for me, Maja. He didn't come. My father. I know what that feels like. And I won't do it to Paul and Tina. I have to go on looking for them and I have to keep on looking for them no matter how long it takes, and no matter what it takes.'

'I need to speak to Herr Weiss,' said Maja. 'Leave it to me.'

*   *   *

But whatever plan she had in mind, she didn't carry it out. That same night, although it wasn't late but it was after we had gone to bed, Herr Weiss came to us.

'Stay here,' said Maja, listening to the harsh buzz of the bell. 'It'll be better if I do this on my own.'

When she got out of bed and walked across the floor, pulling her white bathrobe over her shoulders, to let Herr Weiss into our flat, her blue-black hair shining, I thought she had never looked so beautiful.

'Where is Frau Hansbach?' His voice, slighty drunk and slightly loud, echoed through the room.

'Asleep,' said Maja. 'Don't wake her, she's been crying all day and needs to sleep now.'

'She's told you what has happened?'

'That the project's over? Yes.'

'It's a direct order. From the Führer himself. There's nothing I can do to change that.'

'I know that,' said Maja soothingly. 'Helga knows that, too. Here, let me get you a drink.' I heard the noises and imagined her opening a bottle of Riesling, Herr Weiss taking off his hat and sitting down on the creaky sofa.

I got out of bed and fixed my eye to the keyhole. I couldn't see much but I could hear.

I knew Maja well enough to know that it might be several hours and much of the wine later before she asked him the only question she wanted to ask him, and I was right. I pulled my nightdress about me to keep out the cold and settled in. Maja sat on the sofa, poured the wine and found out about Herr Weiss's excursion to occupied Paris, his trip to occupied Denmark, the state of his ingrowing toenail, and how well, or not so well, the rocketry was coming along in Peenemünde, before she brought up the topic of the children. Ice clinked in a glass.

'Who?' said Herr Weiss. He was sleepy and I got the impression he had forgotten who he was talking to.

'Tina,' said Maja, stroking him softly across the forehead. 'Paul.'

'Oh,' said Herr Weiss. 'Dead by now, I should imagine. The camps are full.'

I felt something tear in my brain. The picture that had brought me solace, kept me going, the picture of Paul and Tina in a happy house, was torn into shreds. It was ripped apart and I felt the pieces fall across everything I had known. I clutched at the falling pieces with my hands. It was all I could do to stop Herr Weiss hearing me cry aloud, hearing me mourn.

'And Helga,' said Maja, without a pause in the same soothing voice. 'What shall I tell her?'

I buried my head in my hands. My children had died long ago and I hadn't even known it. My hands felt numb, then my face, then the whole of my body. I was slammed into utter defeat next to the door and no-one would ever be able to move me again.

'You won't have to tell her anything,' said Herr Weiss easily. 'She's a Jew, as well, isn't she?'

There was only darkness, darkness while I bit back a shout. I wasn't going to cry, not yet. This hurt went too deep for that. At the moment, there was only anger, red, red anger, and a blackness deep inside.

Maja stood up and fetched her black patent handbag. She took out the gold Guerlain powder compact that Josef had given her eight or nine Christmases ago, and said to Herr Weiss, 'Next time you're in Paris, do you think you could get me a refill for this?'

He sat up and looked for something, perhaps his glasses to see what she was showing him.

'The right shade, mind,' said Maja. 'Guerlain Number 42. You have to check the label. Look.'

Herr Weiss leaned forward just enough to look at the faint label, just enough not to notice that Maja was reaching into her patent handbag again, which is when she took out the Mauser .98 and shot him.

In the silence that followed the shot, I could hear nothing but my heart beating.

'Helga,' Maja shouted. 'Come here.'

I opened the door and came through. I had been cold before, so cold in an Austrian winter that my body had frozen solid, but that was nothing to the cold I felt now.

She gave the gun to me to hold while she snapped the Guerlain compact shut and briskly put it away, back in her handbag. The muzzle was still hot and burned my fingers.

'Ow,' I said.

'I should sew up something to keep that in,' said Maja.

I couldn't take my eyes off the hole in Herr Weiss's skull. It was neat and red. The silence was terrifying. I knew that people above and below us had heard that shot, that people were listening. I also knew that no-one would come asking questions. Not till dawn. It was too dangerous. Although I was frightened, for the moment, I guessed, we were safe.

Maja went through Herr Weiss's pockets, extracting every paper she could find and placing them carefully in her handbag. Then she took the gun back from me. 'Still too hot. A little pouch in red velvet, I think,' she said. 'If I put it back in my handbag before it's cooled, it burns the lining.'

So she placed it carefully on the bureau while we mopped up the worst of the blood so that it wouldn't seep through the floorboards, and by the time this was done Maja deemed her precious gun cool enough not to sully the lining and snapped it away again.

'There,' she said.

I stared at her. I didn't know what to think or feel any more, what to do.

'What do you suggest now?' I said.

'Running, I think,' said Maja.

'I'm a long way from running,' I said. 'And I'm too old.'

'Forty's not old,' said Maja.

'It's much too old. I get pains in my left knee when the winters come. Could be rheumatism, could be arthritis – I have no history so how should I know?' I shrugged my shoulders. I didn't care what happened any more. 'I'm a long way from running, Maja, and in the wrong direction.'

'We're a short time being here,' said Maja, 'and a long time being gone. I don't see the point in hanging about.' She swept up a cushion from the sofa and noted the small bloodstain in the corner, red, already turning brown.

'Paul . . .' I said. I was swimming in a fog. I was trying to cling on to a hopeless belief that Herr Weiss had been lying, and I could still find my children if only I looked hard enough, if only I knew how to look, where to look . . .

'What about him?' Maja's voice was sharp and to the point.

'He is my son,' I said.

'And Tina is your daughter,' she said. Her voice, if I hadn't known it better, was brutal. 'That won't ever change.'

'Then how can I leave?' I said. 'How can I even think of leaving them behind?'

We are all tied by blood. I have seen it. I have felt it. Always, always, we feel that blood tie in our bones. Wherever we go, over any part of the earth, after no matter how many years, home really is the place where your family is. I knew that better than anyone. And my children were here. Here. They would never leave Germany now, so neither would I.

'Listen to me, Helga. Sit down.' Maja sat herself on a part of the sofa not occupied by Herr Weiss.

I was too sad and disinclined, but did as I was bidden, as I had always been bidden, to sit still and keep clean. It was a habit too ingrained to let go now.

'There's nothing you can do for your children by staying here,' said Maja.

'I know something,' I said. 'I know how to make the bomb.'

'And if you tell a single soul, then you'll be handing it to Hitler on a plate.'

'You're telling me it's time to go,' I said.

'You know it's time,' she said. 'In your heart you already know it. And we don't have much time left.'

I had to trust her on this last point, having little knowledge of what was going on in the outside world, but knowing, as I had only let myself know today, that it was bad.

'If you say so,' I said, beginning to let go of the last shreds of the happy picture of Paul and Tina in my mind. They fell away like leaves on a gentle breeze.

'I say so,' said Maja. 'Besides, if we stay here, they'll kill us.'

'I'm ready,' I said, opening my hands and letting my fingers feel the air. The pieces of the picture settled themselves across the scattered papers still on the floor with their red annotations in a chaos that meant nothing.

I was going to go. I was going to go with her because I had nothing else left to lose.

CHAPTER NINE

The Library

21 May 1942

IN SCIENCE, THE ONLY THING THAT DISTINGUISHES THE PAST from the future is the accumulation of disorder. The more we go on, the more, despite our best efforts, things become disordered. Cups break, cars smash, rockets explode. It is this entropy that gives time its direction. As we go forward, it seems, we are condemned to a world that is more and more chaotic.

It is this chaos that Maja fought against every minute of her waking life.

Maja spent a great deal of the evening after shooting Herr Weiss putting a new red rinse on her hair, which shone bright in the dim light of the room.

'Auburn, I think you'll find, Helga,' fluffing it over her brush with a preen like a peacock's, 'is the word for it.'

'If you say.'

Whatever word she chose for it, she was unrecognizable as Herr Weiss's one-time blue-black bobbed paramour. Herr Weiss still lay dead on the sponged-down sofa. I still could not take my eyes off the hole in his forehead. I sat in the chair with Maja's black patent handbag tucked into my lap and looked at him.

In preparation for our removal to somewhere not yet specified, but not Berlin, Maja stayed awake the whole of that night with her blue-black hair and washed every item of clothing we owned between us, in shifts, and all the blankets and the pillows, every mat and cushion and duster, and now, in the first light of morning, they were all drying in the one room, the sweet smell of fresh laundry suffusing the flat, a sanctum of cleanliness, almost disguising what lay beneath.

There is a particular smell that dead bodies have. Once you have known it, not only can you not forget it, you can never mistake it for anything else. I knew it from before, in the gymnasium. So I was in no doubt that Herr Weiss was dead, and in that smell I sensed the deaths of Tina and Paul as well. Fresh deaths, still raw, even if they had truly died long ago, perhaps only days or weeks after Herr Weiss had them taken out of my hands.

Somewhere in the early hours I got up from my chair and broke Herr Weiss's dead fingers one by one in my own.

There was a faint yellow bloom to the sky, even in the blackout dark, as if there were thunderstorms coming.

The mats and cushions would stay behind, Maja decided. The pillows would also stay behind, and most of the bedding. We would take Ferdi's grey holdall and Maja's brown suitcase and black patent leather handbag with the gun inside it, and be on our travels as if we were simply being practical and leaving Desanka all over again, as if there was nothing in the intervening years that could stand in our way.

There was of course. As well as all the usual possessions, like the blanket from Novi Sad and Hans Albert's magic stone, I had one of Tina's dolls, Paul's shells, and an ebony frame that had once housed the picture of Maja's fictitious husband Wolfgang and now housed a picture of Josef in his office – not his best, but the only one I liked.

In the course of packing I came across the neat handwritten pages of 'A General Theory for the Universe'. Maja had kept them. My great work, still unpublished. My great work that would never be published now.

Maja took the papers with Heisenberg's death warrant written in red upon them and burned them. I didn't need to keep them, and everything I needed to know about bombs and detonations was still written clear in that shining thread that criss-crossed my mind, that shining thread of numbers that refused to be dimmed, even when obscured and overlaid with the torn shreds of the happy picture of my children, the happy picture I had comforted myself with for so long.

Once Maja had covered Herr Weiss with a clean sheet and declared the room tidy to her satisfaction, she made some sandwiches for the journey. She dressed herself in a good wool coat for travelling, a new pair of leather gloves and made me put on my stoutest shoes. We went out of the flat and posted the keys back through the letter box. The sun was just coming up.

I felt that I was leaving the greater part of myself behind. With every step I took down that narrow flight of stairs, I was denying Paul, with every step down that narrow hallway to the door, I was denying Tina. I could never find them now, and if they ever came looking for me, they would not be able to find me, either. I would be gone.

Maja and I would have no home but each other from that day forward, I knew, and I hated her for it all the time I loved and needed her for it.

'Where shall we go?' said Maja.

She set down her suitcase to beckon me out into the street, so that she could lean back and quietly pull the door to, softly so as to wake no-one else in the block. Then she beckoned, with that turn of her hand, as she had done once before, and she indicated the whole of Europe spread out at our feet, everything and beyond.

I thought one last time about staying, but I knew it was pointless. They were all dead, Josef was dead, and upstairs on a sheet to stop his blood seeping through and alarming the neighbours, Herr Weiss was dead. The lab was disbanded, the papers were burned. Habbel was in Peenemünde and Heisenberg was off in Dahlen testing ridiculous detonators for rockets that would never work.

Where else? I cast the net of my fingertips wide, as if I could sense the right direction.

My mother was in Zurich nursing my schizophrenic brother Eduard. Wider, wider. Desanka's farm was overrun. Wider. My father and his cousin were on the eastern seaboard of the United States in a clapboard house on a tree-lined avenue. Hans Albert and his family were also in America, having fled from the war. But even that wasn't it, even that wasn't the place where I needed to go. Wherever it was, wherever was the right place for me, it just wasn't clear.

'I'm not sure,' I said to Maja. 'Let's just walk and see where we get.'

'We have to get out of the country as quickly as possible, you know that,' said Maja. 'They'll come looking for us as soon as he doesn't report for work.'

'England then,' I said. It was the only part of Europe not occupied by Germany. We needed to place ourselves firmly on the other side. 'We'll have to go much further than that in the end, I think. I'm just not entirely certain where.'

'You worry about that later,' said Maja. 'For the moment I'm going to about getting us out of here in one piece. And I think we'll have to progress a little faster than walking speed, dear one. Trains, not footpower.'

So she led and I followed, and we did walk at first, in a walk we had taken many times on a Sunday, with the children, across the Tiergarten to the Brandenburg Gate, and every time I stopped and looked at the grass or the trees or the neat paths, she turned and said, 'Come on.'

We were standing at the Zoological Gardens station waiting to catch the train when Maja had a last-minute panic. 'The documents, the documents.' She began a frantic search through handbags, Ferdi's holdall and the brown suitcase – then remembered them. She patted them, these precious documents, through her new leather gloves. This was so unlike her that I had to ask.

'What is it that's so important?'

'Money. Herr Weiss's money. I have the papers to his Swiss bank account.'

Such had been her panic that I began to realize how much money there might be hidden away in that bank.

Our travelling money amounted to 10 marks, all that anyone was allowed to take out of the country at the time, and once we reached the borders, Maja knew, it would be practically worthless. Even the extra 10-mark notes that she had packed into our sandwiches would buy us next to nothing. The Swiss money was vital.

The engine huffed and puffed its way over miles and through frontiers, into tunnels and back into sunlight, without us in our cosy carriage being conscious of the journey, apart from brief interludes at forsaken stations where soldiers and train conductors of one sort or another opened people's cases, asked them to empty their pockets, and constantly and ferociously demanded passports. A dozen times, perhaps, they inspected our impeccable papers.

It was our good luck to leave Germany just before the *Luftwaffe* began to falter and the Allied bombing began in earnest. Maja knew this was a danger. I didn't.

I knew little of what had been happening in the rest of Europe. Invasion of Belgium, France. There were skirmishes I was aware of, a war, but, as far as I knew, it was almost over. Europe would settle down again with the borders rearranged, and things would go on just as they always had before. Maja now told me different.

In her stories, people died. There were flames and screaming. A percentage of each bombing attack, she said, was always reserved for the sheer terror factor. A few on the houses, a few on the fields, even, well away from the main targets. It helped to highlight the random nature of the event, reminded people that whether they lived or died had nothing to do with their intrinsic goodness or worthiness or even evil, it was to do with chance. It was unfair, but that was the way the world worked. So everyone became that little bit less certain, that little bit less confident that as they sowed so should they reap. So they were sowing carelessly. And did not necessarily suffer for it. It was a dangerous land indeed.

In the last of Germany, we bought a loaf and some red cabbage at a station and ate it in small bites.

As we crossed the border, somewhere into Denmark, I saw a light beyond the clouds. It was pale and diffuse – it could have been missed. It was only a guess that I said it was the moon. I no longer knew whether it was day or night, and I no longer cared.

The turn in the dark again, just before the sky grows light with dawn, just before the familiar arms in an unfamiliar borrowed bed put themselves in their accustomed place around me. The time in which the world shifts. The crook of her elbow under my head, my hair spilling across her body. We were in an unfamiliar city, in unfamiliar streets, but a world away already with a shiny new identity laid out in all the requisite papers on the dresser. She tore my German passport into pieces.

'Who are you?' I said, turning with the morning to kiss her.

'I am Luitgarde. Your aunt.'

'Who am I?'

'You are Greta. My Gretchen. My niece. We are going home to Sweden because your mother, my sister, is ill.'

'Pleased to meet you, Luitgarde.' I kissed her again and folded myself further into her supple, soft, comfortable body.

'Behave, Gretchen. This is a dangerous country.'

The station was milling with soldiers in brown and grey, and their lady friends in tight boots and furs. Many were drinking, many were drunk.

Those left behind on the platform waved through the billows of steam.

We shared a carriage with a soldier who slept throughout the journey, his head on Luitgarde's shoulder. She did not remove it, then slept, too.

However frightening it might be to have to tumble into that dark deep water, I envied Luitgarde her sojourn in it. After I left Berlin, sleep was never anything more for me than a turbulent noisy shallow in which I paddled sometimes without enjoyment, more as a duty, and careful never to lose sight of the shore.

Deprived thus of my comfort and solace, with Luitgarde and the soldier deep in each other's dreams, I unpacked an item from the suitcase. I leaned out of the train window. In the cold dark air, I let trail from my hands the neat handwritten pages of 'A General Theory for the Universe', one after the other into the night. I wouldn't be needing them any more. I sat down in the crowded compartment and rested my head against the rattling window of the train.

Inside our carriage was a weak yellow light from one overhead bulb. Outside, there were large masses in the dark – hills, slopes, with no colour, only a looming darkness that you felt was there by its very weight. I was travelling through a land which could not be written on a map, inside my head, featureless and indistinct.

In Stockholm, we changed again. I went with her to see how she did it. I was installed in a corner of the bar with instructions to sit still, be quiet, and refuse if anyone offered to buy me a drink. She put her scarlet lipstick on fresh and combed her auburn hair till it shone.

It was a matter of moments before she found the right knot of men at the bar, a matter of minutes before she was buying them drinks, a matter of an hour only before she took me to a boarding house where no questions would be asked.

It was two days before the papers came through, and in the meantime more money had to be paid over, and three more before we could get on a boat. I didn't see her again for all the nights we were there, but I didn't fret. She had her own ways, and she would take her time, but she would always come back.

We showed our passports in the harbour in a night lit by orange lights. We showed the new passports with our new names.

'Helene Krauss?'

She stepped forward, unafraid, her good wool coat and her leather gloves immaculate.

'Elisabeth Krauss?'

'She is here. My sister.'

I was losing track of who I was or how I might be related to anyone. I had to hope no-one asked questions.

The night passage over the North Sea, as we had been warned to expect, was vicious. So a green Helene Krauss said the next morning. I had vomited immediately, the first time I felt the swell of the sea. I couldn't credit that lurching, that dizziness, the way my body turned to waves underneath me out of sympathy for the sea. Helene washed me and changed my clothes, though once I had an empty stomach I had to admit that I felt much better. I lay in the lessening dark of the bunk she tucked me into and, out of habit, tried to find my children, stretching out my arms.

As always, there was nothing. The trail was cold.

In that narrow bunk, with nothing more to vomit out, nothing more to hope for, I slept over the whole expanse of water. Thus I missed the momentous occasion of my leaving the mainland of Europe.

It was almost dawn when we came in sight of land. At first the world had no colour. Everything was rough shapes, no discernible lines on the coast. In the east the sky lightened to chalk and the light showed a bright sparkle of damp in the weather. England was grey. I had expected white cliffs, shining bright in sunshine, but there was only rain and flat land and damp. Helene had decided against going through standard immigration procedures on the grounds that we might simply end up in an internment camp somewhere as undesirable aliens. Therefore, at no little expense, we ended up being rowed to a flat expanse of beach on the Norfolk coast, while I was violently sick again, and Helene shouted that the waves were getting the luggage wet.

We sat on the beach just long enough to dry out and comb our hair and put on new make-up, and then we found the train station. Everyone was friendly enough, kind enough, but slow. Before issuing us with tickets, the stationmaster asked for our papers. Helene showed him our alien registration booklets, indicating that we were refugees from Nazi oppression. He smiled in sympathy. The stamp admitting us to England was placed just so, in the centre of the documents.

In London, bombed-out houses punctuated every street and there were piles of rubble on street corners, but they didn't give the place a derelict air, the streets were too busy for that. There were people walking here, walking there, travelling on the buses, on the trains, on the underground, all the time, always with business to get on with. Helene sighed with pleasure.

The correspondent bank for Herr Weiss's Swiss bank was the first item on her agenda. She was anxious. This, after all, was the sticking point. If we failed here, life would be difficult indeed. As it turned out, she needn't have worried. They must have been used to it, people putting money in and taking money out of numbered accounts, and weren't going to ask the reasons. The National Provincial Bank in Piccadilly let her retrieve the money without a flutter or a murmur. She presented a British passport, pressed an unfamiliar signature against one or two forms, and took possession of an amount which would see us safely through more than a year. Herr Weiss had been unduly, if unwittingly, generous.

'There's more,' said Helene. 'How much, you wouldn't believe. They're all doing it, all the officers, salting stolen money away just in case Germany doesn't win the war. I consider it no more than my patriotic duty to claim some of the money back.'

We went to the Lyons Corner House in Coventry Street and ordered chicory coffee and fresh orange juice and soft white bread and butter, small amounts as everything was rationed, but the richness of the food meant I was almost sick again.

Over breakfast, Helene brought in the English papers. I could read English well enough as she had drilled it into my head so sharply all those years ago, even though I was having trouble understanding what the people around me were saying.

There was only one topic which really interested me. It wasn't the first time I'd read reports in the newspaper of fighting in my homeland, and it wouldn't be the last. Reports that, by the fact of their existence, their beginning, middle and end, implied that the world was susceptible to order, could become clear through reasoning. It never worked. I got to the end of every report and was none the wiser, still enveloped in the same fog of muddle and disbelief that I'd had when I started, still sighing that these things, well, I just couldn't believe them, couldn't understand them.

And I was content to leave it at that, for I knew that if I delved much further beneath the reassuring thick skin of the beginning, the middle and the end, I would find that the words themselves dissolved into chaos and insanity. For proof of that, I only had to look around us. And, worse, I suspected that even if I did understand, I could not change anything. Desanka would still be lost. The farm would still be destroyed, and in the end that was the only sense I needed.

'Is everything as bad as this?' I asked Helene.

'Worse,' she said. 'You don't know the half of it.'

'Tell me.'

'No. I saw back there, Elisabeth, things so dreadful I can hardly believe they were done. But they were done. I am not going to catalogue them now.'

'Why didn't you tell me this before?'

'You had your work. You were working for something. And if I tell you now, what good can come of it?'

'I might understand. I might understand what happened to my family.' I sighed. 'I might even understand why Paul and Tina were taken away.'

'If you do not know what has happened, then for me to tell you would hurt your mind. If you do know what has happened, then you will want to forget, as I do. There is only one thing worth saying now – that it should not happen again.'

But even as we fell silent we knew that it would happen again one day, somewhere, without protest.

22 June 1942

Helene found two rooms in Marylebone that had the benefit of hot water and a gas meter that needed a constant supply of shillings.

I settled in London easily. London was a series of bright fanlights over locked, glossy-painted doors above high steps. If you wake in the country and it is the middle of the night, there is almost absolute silence. Yes, if you go into your garden and it is overrun with moss and helxine, you might hear the chomping of snails, the squirming of slugs over fresh green leaves, but there is nothing companionable about that.

But it is not like that in cities. In London there was always something to listen to in the nights when I was awake. Traffic, sirens, shouting. Explosions. At any point, we could be hit head on by a bomb, but we were already past the point of letting that worry us. Helene refused to be squashed up with others in a bomb shelter and I concurred. Whatever we did, the arbitrary death could not be avoided.

So we lay in bed, listening to whatever the night brought us. There was nothing in front of our eyes – utter blackness, blackness and darkness so thick it was tangible. No lights anywhere. We couldn't even see each other.

In that blackness, though, I began to see something else. Something in my mind, some path forward. I didn't see it clearly yet, and its edges were indistinct, but I groped towards it blindly. I remembered that young man, scrabbling to collect the fragments of his papers from the ice where my father had thrown them. He had been so passionate, so alive. Once I had felt like that, too, when I was doing physics. It had been the only thing that mattered. The only thing that gave my life meaning. And then it had taken all the meaning away.

With the deaths of Tina and Paul, I had thought I would never see again. I had no reason to see again. But here it was, this strange gift of sight, coming back slowly in the darkness.

I wondered, not for the first time, if this gift was something I had inherited. If my father could see like I could see, what was he seeing now? There had been nothing from him for years except some tentative leaps into quantum mechanics, from which he had withdrawn, baffled. Maybe his gift of sight was failing. Mine wasn't. It was coming back, just as strong as before. Perhaps this time the seeing would take me into the heart of the grey zone, the zone at the centre of the ordinary world, where mathematics and molecules became strange. I hoped it would, because that was where I wanted to go. It was the only place strange enough to suit me any more.

I also wondered, possibly for the first time, if I actually had something to thank my father for. Without that gift of sight, life would have been bleak indeed. But now, in the blackness, with Helene's arms about me, it occurred to me that this gift gave me a chance to salvage something from the wreckage. Someone, somewhere could still be made to pay.

9 July 1942

In our second month in London, I got a job for £3 a week in an insurance company just off Baker Street run by a man too pleasant to be good at business. I needed to practise my English, though it was difficult to find anyone willing to employ a refugee from Nazi oppression. He had taken me on because he had had dealings with the Germans before the war and regretted what had happened to the country.

We stopped every afternoon for tea and a cake. He liked to chat.

'Were you ever in Berlin?' My boss was interested.

'Oh, before the war. I passed through.'

Berlin meant nothing more to me now than an empty lab. There was nothing there for me, not even the hope of my children.

I steered him onto the topic of the weather, which he found inexhaustibly fascinating.

The days were filled with typing. Whole hours passed by while I filed insurance schedules. I ate cakes and talked about the cricket scores, the state of the war and the weather every afternoon, my vowels becoming rounder, my accent softening and slipping away. In the evenings, I looked forward to Helene cooking me warm pies. It was almost as if I had never done anything else.

But the Library gave me away. I couldn't keep away from it. In the British Library, there were journals from all over the world. Right until the last minute, they had been freely exchanged throughout Europe and they made for endless reading. Many, naturally, I had not been able to get hold of in Berlin.

Now I learned there were other teams working on atomic fission all over the world. The team in Chicago looked like they were furthest ahead.

I wondered how far they had got, what sort of lab they had to work in, what measurements they had done. I wondered how they were getting on with the experimental assembly, if they were thinking along the lines of a gun to fire the first piece of subcritical uranium into the second piece of subcritical uranium. That was a mechanism I'd lately come to see was possible, after all. In the Library, the silver thread in my mind began to shine more clearly and I hugged it to me. My thread of hope.

13 September 1942

There was a strong smell of ammonia wafting down the Marylebone stairs, more interesting than the boiled cabbage that was coming from the ground floor but not nearly as appetizing. When I opened the door to the sitting room, I found Helene mixing two powders together in a blue china saucer.

'What's going on?'

'I made the first mixture too strong,' she said, 'and it took the enamel off the plate.'

It was true. The plate was in the sink, the blue glaze stripped away and offending brown baked clay showing through.

'You still haven't said what's going on.'

'A surprise,' said Helene and, whipping her saucer away with her, banged into the bathroom.

It was a Saturday. She was often skittish on Saturdays.

I took out the notes I had made that afternoon from a recent issue of *Nature* and set them out on the table by the window, brushing away the last remnants of Helene's powders. It would be a good hour before she emerged, I estimated, and there was no point in scrabbling through the cupboards to see if she had a potato or a carrot laid away from the ration cards somewhere for soup – on the days when she undertook an overhaul of her appearance, she had neither the time nor the inclination to prepare a meal, but would want, instead, to go out, where she could dazzle a new set of followers, a new set of airmen on leave.

A little later I heard her singing, so I guessed that the ammonia mixture must have worked this time. A while after that there was a faint burning smell, a smell of an experiment gone slightly wrong, but without an accompanying shriek.

Then she knocked from the inside of the bathroom door.

'Come in,' I said.

'Be prepared for a transformation,' said Helene through the door.

I took a deep breath. 'I'm ready,' I said.

I was prepared not to recognize her.

Even so.

She wafted into the sitting room in a cloud of steam, bringing with her more of the singeing aroma.

My mouth stayed open.

Her auburn hair, the red, red hair that she had cultivated with such assiduousness for the days of our transit, had been bleached out of existence.

'Helene,' I said.

'Wait,' she said. 'You haven't got the full effect yet. I haven't put my lipstick on. Or my eyebrows.'

The lipstick had been acquired a couple of days previously and had been the topic of much conversation. Helene was particularly pleased because it was French and she believed that the cosmetics of the highest quality came from France. As to the eyebrows – I had noticed that they had been making a comeback of late – more and more of her own singly solicited hairs creeping back into the arch she generally pencilled in – an arch which had now become some-what flattened at the centre.

She swept her French lipstick across her mouth, dusted the arti-ficial pallor of her skin a little more into whiteness, then asked for my opinion.

'What do you call it?' I said, gesturing at the hair, which I had so far not been able to take my eyes off. It was almost completely white, parted at the side, and curved down from her forehead in small marcelled waves. She wasn't an expert at this procedure and I could see that some of the hair ends were singed, which accounted for the burning smell.

She mumbled something indistinct.

'Plutonium?'

'Platinum.'

'Lovely.'

She shook a little more powder across her cheeks, which now looked so like marble you would swear she had been sculpted.

She turned her marble cheek to me, this ethereal vision. 'Do you know where to go yet?'

'Almost.'

'Where?'

'The New World.'

In Chicago, I had gleaned from the latest reports, Fermi had produced the first self-sustaining chain reaction. If that was the case, then that was where I wanted to go. But there was activity elsewhere, too, out on the sidelines, little flurries. Prominent members of research projects were suddenly disappearing, shining lights of scientific establishments were going absent without leave. I needed to know where they were going. I had to bide my time and see where the project was going to be.

'The New World's a tall order.'

'Start working on it. I don't have the details yet, but soon.'

'Fine,' said Maja, lifting one eyebrow, then the other, individually, in the mirror. 'It's Saturday night. Let's go out.'

2 December 1942

As I was typing, it suddenly became clear. It was the only place possible. Geographically, it was a winner for a bomb project – miles from anywhere and not a place you would visit by choice out in the desert. It would also explain where everybody was disappearing to.

There was nothing in this world that was not susceptible to calculation. The shining thread shone clear and strong.

I could salvage something from the wreckage of my life, after all. I could salvage the one thing I had started out with: revenge.

My father had a Nobel Prize and a secure place in the eternal hall of fame. And what did I have? No-one had ever heard of me. I didn't have a home. My children and my husband had been taken away from me. I didn't even have my own name any more. My father had everything he had ever wanted and I had nothing. How could I let him rest easy in his bed?

There was only one way I could hurt him. If I could make sure that his work led ultimately to the one thing he hated above all else, then, surely, that would be vengeance of the best kind. My father, the pacifist, responsible for the worst weapon mankind had ever created. His equation. This weapon. One led to the other. The young man with his moonshine papers in the snow had first shown me that. I was going to prove him right. My father had laid the pathway, I would make sure it was followed to its conclusion. And when I did that, he would hate himself. Most other people, I thought, would hate him too, if not as deeply as I did.

It was his own fault. He should never have abandoned me. Who would do that to a child? He would have to pay. And I would make sure he did pay. It was possible. The Americans weren't up against it like the Europeans were; they had the time, the resources and the money. In fact, I thought, they were probably building several atomic piles right now. I envisaged nuclear reactors springing up all over the continent, breeding all the uranium I could want.

I'd said I would haunt him, and this was the best way to haunt him I knew.

I stayed until the dot of five, filed the last schedule, blew a kiss to the man too nice to be good at business, came home on a bus through the damp foggy streets and danced up the stairs. They were eating boiled cabbage again below.

'I know where everyone's going to,' I said to Helene, the words spilling out in my excitement. 'And we've got to go there, too.'

'Where?'

'The Land of Enchantment.'

She frowned. 'Do we need passports?'

I said, 'Helene, we need more than bloody passports, we need letters of commendation from General Eisenhower himself.'

Helene smiled. 'That may be beyond me,' she said, 'but I'll work on it.'

'And I'll tell you something else', I said, 'while I think of it. I'm glad you made me take shorthand in 1919.'

'Yes?'

'Because, more than anything, what do you need when you're building a bomb?'

'Shorthand,' said Helene.
'Typing,' I said. 'Filing.'
'Good ear for dictation,' said Helene.

Two months later, she packed paint, powder, liquid mascara, untwisted her bullets of scarlet lipstick to check they were still potent – all her most sophisticated weapons in the war of seduction and secretarial qualifications.

'Are you ready to go?' She put the last of my shoes in the suitcase and sat on it.

There was no hesitation. Everything and beyond, where we could travel, weighed down with no obligations at all.

'I've been ready a long time.'

'Then come on.'

I would take only Helene and the shining thread of mathematics from Europe. The shining thread that would lead to my vengeance. Everything else, I would leave behind.

And so, in the spring of 1943, although the Atlantic was not safe, we crossed, in the company of a hundred other refugees who were also willing to risk possible death against certain death, from Europe, to the New World.

We paused in New York long enough for Helene to acquire some relevant papers and some up-to-the-wartime-minute, fabric-saving American outfits, and for me to establish beyond doubt that the main military base was being set up in New Mexico – it wasn't hard as that was the one place everyone took care not to mention – then took a train to Santa Fe.

We had left the London flat owing two weeks' rent. The velocity was breathtaking.

CHAPTER TEN

The Land of Enchantment

14 May 1943

HELENE FOUND A MOTEL ROOM ON THE OUTSKIRTS OF SANTA Fe and bought the ingredients for a copper rinse. I was hopping up and down with excitement and didn't see why we had to stop, much less stop for another change of hair colour.

'It's not for me,' said Helene. 'It's for you.'

'No.' But my protests were useless.

'We are none of us getting any younger,' remarked Helene, squeezing unguents onto my hair.

No matter how I tried to persuade her that quantum physics harboured uncertainties on this matter, it was a topic on which she retained a definite view. Still, that was no reason why she should not try to defy the ageing process. Or why I shouldn't, either. She picked up a strand and held it out for my inspection. 'There's grey in there, definitely.' She pulled a face.

'So?'

'Secretaries can't have grey hair.'

She tossed her own, that recently retouched blond, contentedly over her shoulder.

An hour later, I perused the results in the mirror and had to admit they made a difference.

'Five years,' said Helene. 'Seven. Yes, you look at least seven years younger.'

She sent me out for nail polish and a corset in the hopes of demolishing an extra few years so that I would pass for someone still in my late twenties – the appropriate age, Helene informed me, for an American personal secretary.

In the supermarket, puzzling over the strange items on the shelves, I widened my vocabulary. When I held out the collection of notes to pay, I smiled, hoping that the clerk wouldn't ask me anything. I knew my accent would betray me for a few days longer. I needed a bit more practice until I had mastered the art of American vowels.

In the bakery, where I branched out to buy cookies, and the bookstore where I called in to see if they stocked any journals – yes, but only those that would appeal to Helene, dealing with hemlines and soda bread – I was polite but no more. In the clothes shop, I was daring, risking exchanging a few words with the sales clerk about the colours this season. I smiled at endless amounts of people who would have been astounded to know what was happening in their home state. Even if Helene and I knew a great deal, they knew nothing. Los Alamos was one of the best kept secrets of the war.

I listened to the radio, all day every day, parroting the phrases from the mysteries and comedy serials and advertisements back at the motel room walls, working instalment by instalment until I could get every pitch, every transatlantic nuance just right.

I also decided, while waiting for the denouement, to take up smoking. It earned Helene's disapproval, but it passed the time.

I was in the motel room practising out loud my 'hello theres' and 'pleased to meet y'alls' and waving my cigarette in the air, and wondering if you could eat the thing that Helene called corn on the cob raw when she came back with the stamped and sealed papers. Our qualifications and proficiencies were outstanding.

'I had to travel as far as the Mexican border', she told me, 'to find people who are used to forging papers. They're not used to it here the way we are in Europe.'

'The ink's not quite dry,' I said, seeing it catch the light.

'I reckon overnight will do it.'

It did.

The next day she drove out with our astonishing papers in a rented Ford to the Hill, and the day after that she came back to fetch me in a car borrowed from the Co-ordinator of Rapid Rupture himself.

'I was given the passes in half an hour,' she said. 'Piece of cake.'

'How did you do it so easily?'

'Fortunately', she said, 'it takes a bit more than a lump of radio-active metal to make an atomic bomb.'

'I know,' I said. 'You need explosive devices, electronic com-ponents . . .'

'You need cups of coffee,' she said. 'You need pieces of paper, doughnuts for breakfast, typewriters, typists, water-coolers, and everyone needs somewhere to sleep, so you need buildings and bedding and people to clean the rooms.'

'But security's tight.'

'Oh, security's tight, but not tight enough. They're looking in the wrong places. Sure, they're checking all the scientists within an inch of their lives, but we're secretaries. *Secretaries.* They're taking on hundreds. What threat could we be?'

We packed the flotsam of our motel room and drove out beyond the town, our neat cases safely stored in the trunk, our bright plati-num and copper hair glinting on our shoulders, up a donkey track in the Jemez mountains to Los Alamos. At the last bend she paused, pulled in the car to the side of the road and stopped. That last bend high on the mesa where the sky goes further, where the sky is bluer than you could ever dream, and where, against that wide horizon, the Manhattan Project was growing, was where Helene decided to let me know who we had become.

'What are we stopping for, Helene?'

'Clare,' she said. 'Please. Clare Walker.'

'Sounds nice,' I said. 'Nice and plain.'

She handed me a green card and a brown certificate. I looked at them uncertainly. 'Mary-Jo?' I said. 'Is that the best you could do?'

'It is the very best I could do. We were on a limited budget and this name was available.'

'Well, hello there, Clare,' I said. 'I'm Mary-Jo Forrest. Pleased to meet you.'

'Look at this, Mary-Jo.'

The woman in the car waved her hand and in that moment she became Clare. All the Helene and the Luitgarde and the Maja fell away from her, and Clare waved with her arm to indicate the high ridges, the sky that went on being blue, the fragility of the thin air.

'Oh, Mary-Jo, isn't part of you just glad to be alive?'

The air was warm against my hands, I felt the sun against my forehead.

'I'm not here for the scenery,' I said. 'I don't count myself as alive yet.'

The horizon went further than I would ever have dreamed possible. From edge to edge, it left you alone and abandoned. In that impossible landscape, I felt as if I was walking on water, as if I had left any balance behind me. I remembered the smell of my children's pillows and this anchored me, solid, against the distance of those horizons.

We drove past barbed wire and soldiers with guns into a ramshackle collection of buildings. The Hill. The place was growing quickly. New staff were arriving every day. The sign above the main gate said, 'Please show passes', so I got out of the car to show mine.

'Hello there,' I said to the guard.

The pass was naturally impeccable, despite thorough scrutiny, because it was actually genuine.

The barrier banged shut behind us, but, once inside, I felt freer than I had in those empty spaces. In here was fission and uranium and neutrons. All the things I was familiar with. In those things I could lose myself. It was only in those things that I could forget my children, in here where they might have enough Uranium-235.

9 June 1943

Beyond the hastily erected army gate, Los Alamos was like a city – a dusty new town sprung up on the high stone with prefabricated buildings and boards for sidewalks. In those first months, trucks and bulldozers were still hard at it, shifting, temporary. The air was full of dust and noise.

Despite the size of the place, the wonder is not that it was kept secret. The wonder is that even within it many people were kept in the dark. Everything was compartmentalized: not once in the whole time I was there would I set eyes on the plutonium piles. But I knew they were there. And I could do the maths. That was the important thing.

A physicist called Feynman drafted me in to work on one of the endless calculations that were going on in series. They were numbers, just numbers, but I guessed from the figures that the main work they were engaged in was a careful determination of the fission-neutron yields obtained from uranium bombarded with neutrons. They still didn't know the critical mass.

Although the work was scrambling on at breakneck pace, all the calculations had to be done on mechanical gadgets, which kept breaking down, and to speed things up they'd broken every sum down into a series of simple steps. The first girl added two numbers together, passed them on to the next girl, who subtracted something, passed it on to the next who cubed the result, to the next who added something else . . . All I did all day was take a yellow card off the girl to my left, cube the number and send it on. As a process, it might have been efficient but it was not very fulfilling.

In nearly every conversation there was speculation as to how far along the Nazis might be in their development of atomic energy. Of course, I could have told them that Europe was way behind on this one – largely due to the fact that neither Heisenberg nor I could construct a decent experiment – but I felt this would have taken some of the panic out of the proceedings and complacency was the last thing I wanted at this stage. I had waited too many years for this, I didn't want the big day delayed while the eggheads sat around and congratulated themselves on how far ahead of the Germans they were. If they knew they weren't in imminent danger, why, they might not even bother with Los Alamos at all, and then I would really be in trouble.

Besides, it was clear from conversations in the mess that they were in some trouble anyway. The Manhattan Project was currently two projects really, because they hadn't yet decided which path to take. There were two teams up and running, working on the uranium bomb and the plutonium bomb separately. This was interesting. Until the last few weeks, it had still not been proved for certain that plutonium existed. To hamper things further, plutonium does not occur in nature at all, in any form. You have to make it from uranium in a controlled reaction, changing the structure of the atoms so that they are transformed into this new metal. Even worse, from everyone's point of view, this transformation could only take place in one carefully controlled environment: the inside of an atomic pile.

If plutonium was a denser element, I reckoned, you'd need less of it. Which was useful because the Project was plagued by the same problem I'd had – no-one could get enough of any fissionable material. There were reactors scattered over the country, and there were hundreds of gaseous-diffusion and electromagnetic-separation experiments. But that was all they were: experiments. Not one of them was producing the real goods, the pure isotope in its radiant form.

I mused over the papers left on someone's desk as I oiled the type-writer. No-one ever looked twice at a secretary. They left their papers all over the place and I could take as many notes as I liked. Occasionally I had to open one of the trickier safes they'd had installed after some bright guy decided the filing cabinets weren't secure enough, but that was easy to figure out. Most of the time the secretaries would write down the combination in their diary or address book, not wanting to run the risk of losing it, and carry it around with them in their pocketbooks. And it was easy enough to steal a glance at those in the ladies' room.

I knew to look for a sequence of six numbers, which was what the combination lock on the safes needed, and most of these people, these scientists, they were so predictable, they would use a six-figure number they would be sure not to forget, like a mathematical constant. More safes opened with the decimal places of pi – 31 41 59 – than you would bet on, and those that didn't opened with 27 18 28, the base of the natural logarithms.

I could have got every secret I wanted about the atomic bomb just because I knew pi, but everyone assumed I wouldn't know pi. And I got most of the secrets without even opening a safe because they didn't think a woman could understand equations and left the papers around just anyhow. Although this assessment of my innate abilities was depressing, I was cheered somewhat when I jotted down my notes because I knew for a fact that not one of them could understand shorthand.

Mind you, shorthand was practically the only language it was wise to use. Half the scientists on the Hill had fled from Eastern Europe. Hans Bethe was German, Fermi was Italian, Kistiakowsky, who came later, was Russian. I might have got away with using Hungarian but I didn't want to take chances.

In passing once, out of interest, I asked Fermi if there were any Hungarians on the project.

'You mean the Magyars?'

'Yes.'

'An Asiatic people of obscure origins who do not speak an Indo-European language?'

'That's right.' Trust a Nobel prizewinner to be pedantic.

'No,' he said. 'They'd be too depressing. I have never met a single Hungarian who wasn't unremittingly gloomy.'

Was I so gloomy? I poured a stream of oil savagely into the insides of the typewriter.

Probably I was.

The oil spilled on the papers and I didn't care. I went back to reading them anyway.

I was right about the plutonium – the experiments made it clear you'd get away with a lot less of it and there was an industrial plant in Hanford manufacturing it in a helter-skelter of impatience. The trouble with plutonium, though, would be bringing the subcritical pieces together quickly enough. It would probably be an alpha-emitter, sending out so many stray neutrons that these would initiate just enough fission to blow the bomb itself apart and no more. Not very useful. A gun mechanism was never going to work with plutonium, it just wouldn't be fast enough. What were they going to do?

In desperation, I opened the personnel filing cabinet and assigned myself to T Division under Bethe. That was where the theoretical physics was going on and that was where I wanted to be. I didn't want to waste time mouldering in the engineering sub-committee and cubing numbers.

When I got home, pleased with this accomplishment, I found Clare struggling as usual with the cumbersome wood-burning stove in our utilitarian rooms. Every day I met people who had won the Nobel Prize, and none of them could light it, either. We had them round in series. They all came willingly. There were two shortages on the Hill, water – the supply was erratic and in the winter the pipes froze completely – and women. It was only because women were in such short supply, I reckoned, that they were willing to spend any time with mere secretaries at all. Nine times out of ten, no-one could make the stove work and we ate a cold dinner.

Clare was happy enough. After the cold dinner, she would put on a New York outfit and red lipstick and head for the Leisure Center or a party. As we weren't allowed off the base, people held a lot of parties.

In T Division, they were having the same problem I'd come up against: how to kick-start the chain reaction safely. They were working on implosion. I could see its advantages. Instead of firing two bits of metal at one another, you shaped the fissionable material into a hollow sphere surrounded by explosive. The hollow sphere would be subcritical. When you detonated the explosive, it forced this sphere to implode, collapsing into a critical mass, at which point the nuclear explosion took place. Certainly, I thought, looking over the figures, the act of going critical would be almost instantaneous, certainly quicker than anything using the gun method. Getting the shock wave even would be a problem, though. Shock waves, pressure gradients, edge effects . . .

I knew, however, that my mathematics was up to it.

27 July 1943

As the geometry of spheres was too complicated to handle, we were doing small-scale experiments on cylinders. They were. Of course. I was taking notes. In shorthand. The experiments mainly consisted of taking thick lengths of metal piping and surrounding them with explosive and a tamping material. When the explosive was detonated, they retrieved the battered piece of pipe from wherever it had been flung by the blast and looked at it intently. It reminded me of a schoolboy's laboratory.

Of course the hope was that the pipe would collapse evenly, but every single one of them came out twisted and deformed, not neat in the slightest.

'More explosive,' said Seth, currently in charge.

I pointed out that this was ridiculous. Actually what I said was,

'Gee, won't more explosive simply blow the pipe into smithereens?' And I batted my eyelashes for good measure.

If the pipe was destroyed, we would lose the only evidence of whether the test had been successful or not. As Seth realized this, he glared at me all the harder.

So they began thinking of ways in which the moment of explosion could be recorded automatically, and then we wouldn't need the pipe, we would have the measurements, instead.

He never acknowledged I'd put him on the right track. People wouldn't have believed him anyway.

Clare had invited people over for martinis and owing to the lack of space we were sitting on the bed.

'Doesn't it sometimes bother you, Mary-Jo?' Joe said, huddled up politely next to my pillow. I liked Joe. He was one of the few scientists there who bothered to ask me serious questions.

'What?'

'These things we're working on here, a bomb like this, it wouldn't discriminate between who it killed: military or civilians. Anything where it happens to fall.' He waved his glass and a little of the drink sprinkled on the bare wooden floor.

'They'll never use it,' I said. 'It's only ever going to be a deterrent. One great big explosion in the desert. That's all. That's all we'll need. People won't want to risk this thing dropping on them. They'll soon surrender.'

'But it's possible, isn't it, that it could be used?'

'So?' I said.

'It's not right,' he said.

'There's lots of things in this world that aren't right, either,' I said. 'So why are you still here?'

'I am working on this because I hope that when we've won and the war is over, mankind will never have to fight again.'

'Joe,' I said, 'that's a pretty high-minded attitude. Plus, I never want to hear you talk like that again. It's sedition.'

And I knew how to deal with sedition. I'd learned my lesson. I wouldn't let anybody do to me again what Heisenberg had done. This time, they were going to get all the information they needed, and they were going to get it right.

24 November 1943

They were still having trouble with where, exactly, the explosives should go: the plutonium would be in two hemispheres in the middle, obviously, but what about the Baraton, the stuff they were using to ensure an even shock wave? After a gap? No gap? Should the thing be solid or not? And, more interestingly – once the explosion had been kick-started, would it ever stop? That was a fascinating cul-de-sac, that the first atomic blast would trigger the end of the universe, but I had dismissed it, long ago, like Bethe, as counter-intuitive.

This was the land of theory, where we were all as happy as sand-boys. I knew from Clare's trawl through the filing cabinets and the gossip at the parties, however, that getting the actual stuff that would be used in the bomb was still a difficulty. The product of the plant at Oak Ridge was so impure that all it could be used for was to feed one of the other separation processes. In the land of reality, this was the biggest hurdle.

And, more worryingly, if the explosive did not produce an entirely even shock wave around the hollow sphere, that sphere would be blown apart before it went critical. This wasn't so much a problem of stray neutrons and pre-detonation, but simply that the sphere would be subject to such amazing forces that only a tiny imbalance would be needed to tear the sphere apart. It was all very well constructing perfect equations to show how an idealized wave passed through a uniform field. Here we were dealing with the flawed landscape of stubbornly imperfect reality. An even and totally symmetrical shock wave was going to be very difficult to achieve. In fact, I thought, impossible.

But I was working on it.

16 December 1943

The team Clare worked for were all advocates of the gun method. It was where the main effort of the laboratory was directed and all the experiments *she* wrote up were going well. The U-235 neutrons, she told me, were nearly all emitted in less than a thousand millionth of a second.

'Quite fast enough, if you ask me,' she said, 'for a reaction to take place before the gun blows itself apart.'

'I wasn't asking you. Since when did you take an interest in science?'

'I've never had the chance to take an interest in science before.'

'I talked to you all the time about relativity. You just ignored me.'

'That's because relativity wasn't very practical, was it? This is.'

'I wish you'd leave me to worry about the physics.'

'I just don't want to see you get this far and then fail, that's all. Reassign yourself, Mary-Jo. A uranium bomb is feasible. A plutonium one isn't. Your experiments are simply going nowhere.'

'That's only because we don't have enough plutonium to work on.'

'There isn't enough uranium, either. You told me yourself that the plant at Oak Ridge employs what? Ten thousand?'

'Thirteen thousand.'

'Thirteen thousand people and what have they got to show for it? A few grams of black powder.' She sniffed.

'In Hanford', I said, 'they've got forty-five thousand men working on producing plutonium.'

'And what have *they* got to show for it?'

I didn't answer because she knew the answer as well as I did. Nothing.

But she was suddenly interested in science not only because she didn't want to see me set off down the wrong track, but because above all what we had here was a practical problem. A problem that needed solving. And she always liked a challenge.

'I have no doubt', she sighed, 'that God's designed things in such a way that He can understand them, even if the rest of us can't.'

'You don't need God to explain the world,' I said. 'Just the laws of physics. And we'll understand them all eventually.'

'Not necessarily,' said Clare. She shrugged her shoulders in the complacent way of one who could notch up a whole lifetime of church attendance. 'God made those laws. Don't you think He could have made them any way He chose?'

'I don't want to think about God,' I said. 'Even if I believed in him, I still wouldn't forgive him.'

I wasn't the only one in amongst the scientists taking notes, I realized. There was a runaway German in Bethe's theoretical physics gang, defected to the British years before and sent by them to the project. I found him looking over the safes more often than was natural.

'*Kann ich Ihnen helfen, Klaus?*'

'I do not speak German any more, Mary-Jo.'

'Easy as pie, Klaus,' I said. 'Can I help you with something?'

'No.'

He'd already passed the theory about the critical mass for the plutonium to the Russians faster than I could type it. I didn't care. That was none of my business. In fact, the more people who knew about this the better. I didn't want to keep it secret any more, although the Americans did. In fact, I wanted everyone in the world to know. I wanted everyone to be in on it when we finally succeeded. I wanted them to know just what we had done and who was ultimately responsible. My father. Without his equation, none of this would have got started. The more people who knew, the better, because then there was no way my father could escape from the consequences of what he had done, could pretend it was nothing to do with him.

I waved Klaus away. I was busy. I'd done some calculations on the implosion experiments so far and these showed that there could only be a 5 per cent variation in the symmetry of the shock wave. I had more calculations to do to be certain. And what would happen in the fractions of a second before the plutonium became a nuclear blast? The temperature would reach 50 million degrees centigrade. The pressure would be more intense than at the centre of the earth. I was calculating blind, but so was everyone else. Mostly, I just fed my results back into the reports and summaries and everyone thought someone else had done them. No-one asked. No-one noticed me. Secretaries benefit from invisibility. And that suited me fine. This wasn't personal glory I was after. Just payback.

6 March 1944

Small samples of plutonium had arrived from Oak Ridge. They were kept behind a screen and moved about with grab handles. Tests showed that they contained much more of the isotope Pu-240, which was a source of background neutrons, than the early amounts. Any more we could expect would be even more heavily contaminated. As I had predicted, it produced so many stray background neutrons that the only hope of using it was making the implosion method work.

I thought of the battered and twisted pipes, hurtling through the dust bowl of the desert air, and almost laughed with the sheer hopelessness of it. There was a general air of despondency over the Hill.

We now had an explosives chamber in which we had been developing various high-speed photographic techniques for measuring the results of the experiments. Not that we had done very many experiments. We'd modified the shape of the explosive, the kind of explosive, and the position and number of the detonators, but we still hadn't overcome the essential problem: the shock waves that move out from a point detonator move out through the surrounding explosive like a wave, like a wave sent through water from a pebble. So it is always a curved wavefront that hits the surface of the core, and, to produce an even symmetry, the wave needed to be flat. And things got worse: when several detonators were fired, the waves met and interfered with each other, in those old familiar interference patterns, destroying any possibility of symmetry.

Not that we had even done any experiments with spheres yet. And we all knew that a sphere was what we were going to have to have.

'Progress?' I said to Clare when she asked on her way to the 12-cent movie. 'Progress is minimal. And there's nothing I can do till they get on to spheres.'

'Or you have enough plutonium,' she remarked. 'I still think you should switch teams. You've worked hard to get this far, don't throw it away.'

I made sure I didn't have any difficulty falling asleep at nights by staying up so late juggling with the configurations of detonators and explosives, the diffusions, the geometry and the probabilities that when I crawled in between the sheets, nothing could keep me from the dark.

15 June 1944

A lens. An explosive lens. The same principle as an optical lens. The shock waves passing through the thick centre of the lens would be slowed down most, those through the thin edge would be slowed down least. If we surrounded the spherical core with a series of lenses, all of which were detonated simultaneously, it should be possible to produce the symmetrical shock wave we had been searching for – so far in vain. Through the lens, all the waves would arrive at the core at the same time.

The idea had come to me in the middle of one night. I knew straight away it would work and made sure everyone else knew, too. I typed it into the minutes.

To make this happen, though, the calculations would have to be exact to several decimal places. Absolute detonation timings. A perfect specification for an initiator, a neutron source to start the reaction. Precision moulding and machining of the explosive material. There was no room for error.

In the centre of my feet, and along the ridge where my toes had been, there was pain. I had a cold feeling in my spine that came from low blood pressure. I looked at my fingertips, disorientated, and expected to find them distant from me.

The more time I spent lost in theory, the less real I seemed to be becoming. I wondered if, in this process of haunting, I might become invisible and fade completely, without me even noticing.

19 October 1944

The initial tests on the development of the lens were encouraging. In principle, it would work. To convert this principle into a fully practical reality was going to require a lot of experimentation and a stream of calculations to analyse the results.

That didn't worry me, either. I liked calculations. In the days, the canyons around the mesa reverberated to one explosion after another. In the freezing nights, I sat at a desk wrapped in woollens and thermal underwear and lost myself, forgot even the cold, forgot everything in one number after another as I analysed the test results. When they brought in a prototype computer from IBM to do the number crunching, I liked the calculations even more. Here was a chance to do some spin, a twist to the standard differential equations, a creative balancing of the mathematics. Here was the time and space to make the guess that all scientists make when they take the next step forward. Here was the chance to smooth everything out, from the infinitesimal to the inifinite, to make sure perfect symmetry was achieved. I felt as if I were on a quest for something clean and pure, without flaw.

Although it wasn't a pleasant image, it came into my head more and more often. My children were like leeches, the sort that carry their own dose of anaesthetic, so that you never feel the bite; you remain blissful while they attach themselves to you and you sustain them, and the pain only starts when they are torn away.

Between them, the cold and the calculations numbed some of that pain. Not enough, but some.

27 December 1944

For Christmas I ordered Clare a set of professional make-up brushes from one of the Hollywood studios and she got me a paper lampshade that had a hand-drawn map of the world on it. We took two days off and when I got back I found the group had been reorganized into G Division, to concentrate on the nuclear physics. I made sure I stayed with them. It wasn't going to be long before we had to run a real test, and I didn't want to miss it.

Before Christmas we had made great strides, and by now the symmetrical shock wave was a possibility. A practical possibility, not just a theory, even though the geometry of imperfect spheres still caused mathematical complications. Even so, far from being jubilant, I was worried. People were beginning to talk, now that the possibility was becoming closer, of just what it was they were creating. I took precious time away from the calculations to do emergency work comforting the conscience-ridden over very dry martinis in the gap between Christmas and New Year.

'You have no responsibility for how it might be used,' I cooed to ambivalent scientists.

'Yes we do,' said Joe.

I filled his glass. 'That's for politicians.'

'They can never understand one tenth of what I know. I know just how powerful this thing could be.'

I know, too, I thought, but I won't tell you so.

'It may never be used,' I said. 'Remember that. You can't hold back progress just because you're worried about what the world might do with your invention. We'd still be living in trees if we all took that attitude.'

'You understand nothing, Mary-Jo, do you? If we've got it, then we'll use it. Some day. Soon. On someone.'

I couldn't see it. 'Nobody would ever be stupid enough to use this thing. It would damage those who dropped it just as much as those it was dropped on. Not at first, sure, but eventually.'

One of the scientists working under Frisch had already received a lethal dose of radiation. Some were talking about this as retribution. I was more pragmatic. It simply confirmed that a detonation in the desert was all that was required. Knowing what we now knew about the effects of the radioactive fallout, we couldn't ever seriously contemplate using this weapon on people.

A spectacular shattering and shimmering in the desert air. That was what I wanted. That was *all* I wanted. It was all I needed to drive my father to his knees.

But I wasn't even nearly there yet. My calculations showed that the implosion weapon might only yield the equivalent of 850 tons of TNT. Spectacular, but not spectacular enough. This was supposed to be my revenge, after all, not a damp squib.

30 January 1945

Just when we thought it couldn't happen again, the world changed.

On the newsreels in the Leisure Center we watched as the

Russian troops discovered Treblinka. At last, the secret was out. Was this what Clare had known and refused to hurt my mind with? I stopped breathing. If she had known even one tenth of what was going on, how could she not have told me? I watched the black and white images of the children of Auschwitz who had survived, a series of twins, perfect sets of them against the mountain of limbs.

Clare, along with most of the other women in the hall that night, sobbed and sobbed. I didn't. Tears were worthless, meaningless. I had already sobbed rivers over all the wounded orphans and childless mothers of the war and it had got me nowhere.

'What good?' I said, walking her home over the duckboards laid down over the snow. 'What good is all this weeping, this wailing? You might as well cry over every sparrow that has lost a wing, every daisy that doesn't open for all the difference it will make.'

'It helps me,' said Clare. 'It is all I can do.'

'Tears have never mended an arm or a leg. Crying won't put together anything that is broken.'

'What is the matter with you?' She looked up at me as I found the keys to the room. 'What is the *matter* with you?'

My face was hard. There was no evidence of sorrow there. Even inside, I thought the well had run dry.

'All your tears,' I said. 'They can heal nothing that has ever hurt.' I opened the door and pushed her in.

'I cry for my own good,' she said. 'My heart would break without the tears to glue it together.'

I thought of Tina, pushing her pink doll along in its pram, of Paul building a sandcastle that would resist the oncoming tide.

'Nothing you can say will help them now,' I said. 'Nothing you can say can ever mend this.'

I was cruel to Clare because she deserved it. Because she hadn't saved my children. Because she had seen what was coming and hadn't put a stop to my self-centred obsession to make me see it, too.

She should have made sure they were taken safely out of Germany before it was too late. But she hadn't.

I said, 'There's nothing you know about fixing things together.' And I slammed the door and went out into the night to drink enough vodka until I could sleep somewhere else.

26 February 1945

In my dreams, children walked. I tried to sleep less and less so I would dream less and less. I worked every waking hour. It was all I had left.

It looked like there was only going to be enough uranium from Oak Ridge to make one uranium bomb before the year was out. And getting implosion right was the only way to make a plutonium bomb work.

The current odds were a hundred to one against either ever working. The Project was going to need all the help I could give it. Late every night I pored over figures and printouts and readings, the sum of innumerable random collisions, and weeks went by when I didn't see Clare. I was still too angry with her to talk civilly.

And then, as the winter wore on and the cold bit in harder, though I still didn't see her at all in the daytime, at nights, to keep warm and to anchor myself to the earth, I crept into the narrow bed beside her and wrapped my chilled limbs against her warm ones. What did it matter now that she had been trying to protect me? At least she knew there was something to protect me from. Her only fault was that she had protected me too well, so that I had never known the real danger. I tried to forgive her.

It was out of the question that I would ever forgive myself.

I had lost weight lately, forgetting to eat, and my arms always felt thin and cold despite layers of knitwear. I smoked all the time, even when I didn't need to. I looked older, too. Every morning as I filed through the narrow gate to TA1, the main tech area, I thought that without the thick layer of make-up I plastered on, I might become noticeable. And I had to stay invisible a while longer yet. I had to make this thing work, or everything meant nothing.

23 March 1945

Two pieces of good news emerged. The critical mass was only going to be around 5 kilos, less than we had expected when we only had theoretical calculations to go on. And someone had come up with a detonator that could fire with the accuracy that implosion demanded. Also, as it was now clear that the Germans were going to lose, the consciences of those around me became less anxious. We weren't going to need to use this weapon ever, because by the time it was ready, the war would be over.

Clare, who went to the service that was organized daily, put these developments down to the power of prayer.

'I think that praying is possibly even more useless than crying,' I said. 'At least crying would make you feel better. Praying has only ever made you worse. As you kneel there, your guilt racks up until it becomes unavoidable.'

'It's unavoidable anyway,' she said.

I didn't disagree with her, for I was in the same position myself.

13 April 1945

The flags were flying at half mast all over the hill because their president was dead.

I was in a better mood, though, because there had been some progress. We were planning a dress rehearsal involving 100 tons of TNT. The balancing act with the geometry of the explosive lenses was coming to an end as we got ever nearer perfection and T Division had come up with an initiator which looked promising. Things were becoming more and more symmetrical, I felt, more on an equilibrium.

I typed a telegram telling Truman that the bomb would be ready for testing by July. It probably came as a shock to him.

7 May 1945

Clare had been typing summary reports for a week solid, she said. Harry Truman had to be told every single thing that was going on under the mountains – he hadn't known a thing about it.

'Truman's a hick,' she said. 'He must be. He can't understand at all what's been going on here. I'm typing in words like, "This is a BIG explosive".'

'It doesn't matter,' I said. 'Nothing matters now. The war in Europe's over.'

'The war in the Pacific isn't,' said Clare.

'That's nothing to do with us,' I said.

But it was insofar as this enterprise high in the mesas wasn't simply a life or death race any longer. The ending of the war made it even clearer to me that what we were working on was for interest's sake only. Nothing more. No-one could risk anything else. The radioactive waste packed in with the 100 tons of TNT had provided a harmless simulation of fallout and, after the initial crash and bang and general hurrah, the results were disturbing. The cloud that resulted from the explosion had been swept by high-altitude winds further than we had dreamed, hundreds of miles.

And a blast from a real bomb would carry even further. The rain it would scatter wouldn't care whose side the people were on.

12 June 1945

I was sleeping even less because I could feel it getting closer. The team I was taking shorthand for drove out to the Trinity site to see the tower that was being built at Point Zero for the test and I went with them. The design of the plutonium bomb was still so unstable that Oppenheimer insisted on testing it in secret. Then, if it was a failure, no-one need know.

The place was a nightmare. Trinity was packed with GIs, physicists, weathermen, telephonemen and scorpions, all milling about and shouting at each other. There were poisonous spiders, snakes and reptiles on the desert floor. Although we set off around 5 a.m. to make as much of the cooler hours as possible, by the time we got there the heat was baking the top of your head off.

Everyone was in radio contact with everyone else and, despite the fact that this was supposed to be a secure frequency, we were on the same channel as a railway yard 600 miles away in San Antonio, and comments about prevailing weather conditions were punctuated by railmen shunting their rolling stock.

Dust and sand blew into the measuring instruments and made everybody cross. Indeed, there were so many measuring devices out there it's a wonder they measured anything meaningful and not just each other. There were wooden boxes littering the ground: beta-gamma monitors, dials, meters, readouts, printouts – endless things to count other things. I laughed. We were hoping for a blast the like of which we had never seen before and we were measuring it with pieces of paper. One of the scientists had opened a book on just what the yield of the bomb might be. The official prediction was 5,000 tons of TNT. Bethe put his bet in at 8,000, Kistiakowsky 1,000, Teller 45,000. Good money was being placed and anyone had a chance of winning, the situation was so uncertain.

The dust stuck to our faces. The water to wash it off with was heavily alkaline and left an irritant scaling on the skin. Irritated, people's tempers were running high.

My temper was precarious but I never once let that show. I was bad-tempered because the detonators, so perfect in theory, simply weren't reliable. It needed only one out of the dozens round the bomb to fail and the symmetry would be lost. The yield would be minimal. And the detonators, lately presented with much pride by the engineering division, failed regularly and inexplicably, without warning. I wished the team working on them had been better. I wished I had been able to drop in and give them the benefit of a few calculations of my own, but I couldn't be in two places at once. And as well as working late into the night on all the little corrections I'd been putting into the reports when I typed them up, I had the regular shorthand and filing to do, too.

I looked up at the tower. I knew the idea behind putting the bomb up there at the top of it was to reduce the size of the dust cloud and its lethal consequences. But none of us knew what would really happen, whether this precautionary measure would have the slightest effect. It was just another one of those guesses, and we would be taking chances anyway. Never mind the prevailing wind direction, we still had not entirely ruled out the possibility that the detonation would set light to the earth's atmosphere.

Under the shadow of that high tower, there was an air of panic. No-one wanted to acknowledge it, there was still much bluster and bravado, but it was there underneath. Sometimes the panic shaded off into despair. No matter if anyone had second thoughts now. There was no going back. It was too late.

In the nights, Clare hugged me to keep me from shivering, something that still happened to my body despite the advent of the warm weather. She didn't say anything and I didn't say anything.

1 July 1945

By the beginning of July, everyone had perked up immensely. We had a definitive figure for the critical mass. We had better detonators. Even more cheering was the fact that the defeat of Japan was now inevitable. The Navy was destroyed, most of the major cities razed. The war was almost over, the tower was built and we were ready to go.

We even had a new initiator unit. I had awarded myself a temporary assignment over in the lab and after a couple of days could see what their problem was. I could see it shining like stars, naturally, a simple flaw in the basic geometry, but they couldn't. I wrote out pages and pages of equations so they could see, finally, that my modifications made sense. And I presented them in the form of an old report, pushed to the back of a dusty filing cabinet, which my efficient filing processes had unearthed. When they looked over it, they could see what the report was getting at. They had to do the algebra over again for themselves to be sure, but they had done it, now, the team, and congratulated themselves on their insight.

With the installation of the new initiator unit, I had finally pushed the last cog into place; everything was now out of my hands. In the past few days, the final assembly of the core had gone on surreptitiously. The explosive material had been driven down from Los Alamos. The core had been placed deep inside the explosive. It was ready.

There was nothing more I could do. I felt like a theatre director who, after the last dress rehearsal, has to hand over the work to the cast and crew and can only sit back helpless and watch the first night. I'd waited for this day for the best part of my life, but it was up to others now to make a success of it.

I was almost asleep, lying shivering under a desert sky, when I felt something that I hadn't felt for years, had almost forgotten about. Fingertips on my arm, up – all the way to my shoulder, down – all the way to my wrist. It was a familiar touch, light and soft, not threatening, not frightening, just strange.

I lay awake all night just thinking about it, about who it might be, long after it had stopped.

15 July 1945

The weather had broken. After months of skin-scorching heat in that enchanted summer, the sky was troubled. Storms were forecast. All through the night we had watched weather balloons floating up over the site and all morning clouds scudding across the sky.

Clare came up from South Station to tell me of a memo she'd just seen. She couldn't tell me over the radio as that would run the risk of informing not only the entire crew but also the railmen of San Antonio.

'They did a dummy run back at base to test the symmetrical explosive.'

'And?'

'Not only was it not symmetrical, it was complete chaos.'

'Why are you telling me this?'

'I don't want you to get your hopes up too high, Mary-Jo. I think you should be ready to face the fact that this may never work.'

We watched as they began winding the bomb slowly up the tower. It looked brutish, a mess of tangled wires and leads connecting the sixty-four detonators to the assembly. They'd put about 20 feet of mattresses on the ground underneath. If it fell, it wouldn't make the slightest bit of difference whether it had something soft to land on. If it worked. Which seemed increasingly unlikely.

The wind was getting stronger and blew dust hard against us. I needed this to work. What had my whole life been for if it didn't work?

'Let's just wait and see,' I said.

'I've got to get back,' said Clare. 'I've got cameras to check. How's my lipstick?'

I kissed her.

'Perfect.'

16 July 1945

I hadn't been to bed. Neither had my superior officer but that didn't stop him ordering a round of maple syrup pancakes in the early morning hours. As he poured the syrup, he was fretting.

'What's the matter, sir?' I said. 'Are you worried we won't be able to go ahead?'

'No,' he said. 'I'm worried that we will.'

There had been new additions to the book. Some of the scientists had been inviting bets on how far the reaction would spread, whether it would lead to the destruction of all human life on the planet, or just all human life in New Mexico.

'Is there anything I can do to help, sir?'

He turned and looked at me narrowly. 'If it goes ahead, you can get out there along with the rest of them and take photographs. If it works, we'll need them. If it doesn't work, we'll still need them.'

I got myself issued with equipment and stood with the rest of the crowd waiting for the news. Unless the wind shifted, we would have to postpone. Rain spattered on the roof. A lull in the storm would be useless: detonating just before rain would mean that we ourselves would be deluged with fallout. The sky had to clear.

Dawn was only three hours away. We had to test the bomb in darkness to be able to see it properly, so if we didn't get a decision soon, we'd have to cancel anyway because of the light.

At 4 a.m., the rain stopped. Forty-five minutes later, we heard the final report: 'Winds aloft very light. Conditions holding for next two hours. Sky now broken.' A small army went out to the tower to arm the mechanisms. The time was set for 5.30 a.m. There was no going back now.

And so I went on one of the buses out into the desert, out to White Sands.

I got into a hole with another photographer named Mike. He was one of several that the military had, as usual, drafted in and given as little information as possible, just in case everything went wrong. If the whole experiment had to be covered up, the less anyone knew, the better. But if by some fluke the thing worked, we were necessary for documentation.

'Hi, Mike,' I said.

'Do you know anything about what film speed I'm likely to need?' he said.

I put on dark glasses. 'Normal,' I said. I didn't think that talk of the light of a million suns would go down well.

Zero minus twenty minutes. We had been issued no protective clothing apart from a surgical mask of thin gauze. I told Mike this was perfectly safe but I covered my face with sun cream and wound a scarf around my throat as well. We were 8 miles away from the blast but I was taking no chances.

I listened to the countdown over the radio and didn't know what to expect. Mostly I thought nothing would happen, or we would have a partial explosion, no more spectacular than the firestorms we had all seen in the war. But nothing less than the full effect itself could satisfy me now. Total revenge. I had been abandoned, and this was at last the moment when I could pay him back.

Minus one minute. Minus fifty-five seconds.

It had to work.

At minus forty-five seconds they threw the switch to set the automatic timing mechanism. At minus five seconds, they threw the manual switch.

Zero.

Without a sound, all darkness and colour disappeared. Nothing but dazzling white, no matter which direction I looked. Intense white light. I felt its glow on my face, searing the skin. Slowly the light became tinged with yellow. It was everywhere. It was very bright but I kept on looking and blinking; I didn't want to miss a thing. The only radiation that could hurt your eyes was ultraviolet, I reckoned, and I had the sunglasses on to protect me against that. I kept on looking as the light began to move along the spectrum into orange. I was beginning to feel nervous in the deep silence. A small sun began to rise from the ground over a column of swirling dust.

It was utterly silent. In films made since, the sound and the image are always cut together so that they seem simultaneous and, of course, they were not, not from any human vantage point. The

world was quiet and went on being quiet. Mike began photographing the light, which lessened the tension. At least thirty
seconds passed. This wasn't what I thought would happen.

I said to Mike, 'It hasn't worked.' There was a blue glow of
ionized air around the column now. In the pit of my stomach I felt
a deep black ball of depression forming.

'What hasn't worked?'

I waited another ten seconds, then I opened my mouth. I might
as well tell him. There was nothing more to lose.

At that moment, the ground shook and we heard the sudden crash
and bang of the blast wave, very sharp and loud, hurting the ears,
followed by a low rumble, like thunder.

'What *was* that?' said Mike.

'That', I said, 'was . . .'

And then I felt a pressure, sufficiently intense to hurt, like a
hundred hands against me. But this was the opposite of force, something like the dip between the swells of a tide, the antithesis of every
blast wave. And with the tangible reduction in pressure came a
strange sensation in my ears. The only thing I have ever experienced
like it, and that was not until many years later, was in an aircraft
when it suddenly lost height rapidly. The experience had the same
air of imminent death about it, too.

The fireball grew. I whooped with delight.

'I've done it,' I said to Mike. 'I've done it. Twenty thousand tons
of TNT at least. Teller was probably closest.'

Mike climbed out of the trench and started photographing. The
desert sand looked like a cake baked a fraction too long in the oven,
sticky and shiny, but dry and unappetizing. I climbed out, too, and
jumped up and down in my excitement. I waved my arms over my
head and danced backwards and forwards, feeling the heat burn over
my arms and legs and the back of my neck. The shock wave rumbled
on under my feet and I danced on, shouting for joy, looking at the
flames and the fire. Thousands of tiny desert creatures ran towards
us from the undergrowth, crazed, haring away from the blast.

Then everything seemed to go quieter again and we risked looking up at the sky. I hadn't taken a single picture yet and couldn't even begin. I could only stare at the cloud gathering above our heads.

'What *was* that?' said Mike again.

'That', I said, 'was a practical demonstration that Einstein's mass-energy equation was right. Tiny amounts of mass. Vast amounts of energy.'

Mike looked at me as if I had gone mad.

'It's a nuclear bomb,' I continued. 'When he finds out about this, he's going to regret ever publishing anything in the *Annalen der Physik*, I can tell you.'

Once, everything was miracle and worship. People could only gaze, amazed, content, unable to explain any phenomenon of nature. But in our time we have only science and no miracles.

I knew science was all there was, but nevertheless, that day I looked at the desert before me with something approaching worship. It was 16 July 1945. I was 8 miles south-east of Ground Zero, and I watched as the sands vaporized and the rocks beneath turned in the heat and the light to green glass.

I had done it, and I was full of wonder. Wonder and a deep, deep pleasure.

He had been right all along, that young man with his equations in the frozen snow, and my father had wanted to deny it. I wouldn't let him. He couldn't deny it now. He couldn't deny me. It had taken twenty years, but I had done it.

It was only a matter of time, now, before my father found out what I'd done. Only a matter of time before my vengeance was complete. I just wished I could be there in front of him to see his face when he heard the news. I wished I could deliver the news myself, in person.

'You,' I would say. 'Look at what you have created. Look at what you have brought about. Everything you've touched has turned to destruction. And do you know who is telling you this? Me. Your daughter. The one you left behind. The one you abandoned. The one you tried to forget.'

I had fought him with gravity and light, after all. And I had won. The light I made that day, the light that shone over Trinity, was so bright, it blinded.

The shadow this new light cast across the sand was suddenly ominous, demonic. I didn't feel proud of myself, all of an instant. I felt very tired.

A stunned fly buzzed along into the trench. It was only a fly but it held us in thrall. By now Mike had finished all his film and we were waiting for someone to come with the bus and take us away. The fly droned along, lethal and low, a killer bluebottle like a dive-bomber, dying in the hot season of the year. Mike took off his shoe and swatted it.

Twenty minutes later, our area was declared 'dirty' and we were evacuated. By this stage the cloud was an ugly blot against the blue day, reducing the light. We took off our clothes – but not our underwear, of course, concern for safety did not extend to indecency – showered, showered again, got ourselves a drink and some salt tablets and got dressed again.

'There,' I said to Mike, handing him my radioactive scarf and glasses. 'Put them in the designated containers.'

We drove back to base. I felt excited but exhausted. I was suffering from lack of sleep and the typing that was going to have to be done didn't bear thinking about. The bus rattled and my head jolted against the window.

Throughout the bus, people were talking. We were alive, that was one topic of conversation. We had seen the sun on earth, that was another thing people said. This was something I was to hear over and over again. Many people, in their writings about this most sacred of the sites of twentieth-century science, have said that what we saw was like the sun, but now that I had more of a chance to think about it, it wasn't. The power I had created that day was unlimited, endless, ready to tap into, but it wasn't a life-giving force, it wouldn't make things grow. It reduced us all to shadows. My bomb was the sun turned to opposite ends: unlimited destruction, not unlimited life.

But even a new sun wasn't enough for them. Straight away, in the bus, I could see the looks on their faces. They wanted to know only one thing: 'When can we use this for real?'

They were already dreaming the dream that was the real gift I had created that day: the dream of power beyond imagining. Not since Zeus had unleashed his lightning or Thor the hammer to smash the earth had mankind come so close to the mythological dream of universal destruction. And I had given them the means to do it.

With a sickening feeling, I thought everything might have gone horribly wrong.

1 August 1945

I told Clare to tell me everything she knew. Everything. 'The truth,' I said. 'The truth makes you free, don't forget.'

'We told the President in Potsdam that the Trinity test was successful.'

'How?'

'Telegram.'

'Saying?'

'The baby is born.'

I almost laughed. Baby was not a word I would have chosen. In any event, Truman now knew he had Manhattan. He had it and no-one else.

'What's he going to do with it?'

'Japanese citizens are being taught to sharpen bamboo sticks and die defending their homeland for the sake of the Emperor.'

'Will they ever surrender?'

'The Army will fight to the last man for the preservation of the Emperor. He is god, after all.'

'Is there no hope?'

'The Japanese leadership has been trying to end the war through the offices of the Soviet Union.'

'You're remarkably well informed,' I said.

'I've been promoted,' she said. 'Personal assistant.'

'Do people know the Japanese want the war to be over?'

'Truman has decided that news of the Japanese desire for peace should remain secret.'

'Show me the files.'

'Mary-Jo . . .'

'Show me.'

She showed me. In a dusty office, in a filing cabinet with a combination lock it took me five seconds to crack.

'First file,' said Clare. 'They can propose "no technical demonstration likely to bring an end to the war. There is no acceptable alternative to military use." There. Now you have it.'

'That's not the end of it,' I said. 'There's more.'

'Hardly . . .'

'There's more, I know it. I want to see it.'

We hunted through the filing cabinets and found the minutes of the Interim Committee. This select body made three crucial recommendations:

* That the bomb be used against Japan.
* That the target should be a military one but surrounded by a civilian population.
* That the bomb be dropped without any prior warning.

'This is not what I wanted,' I said. 'This is *not* what I wanted.'

'You mean you've let them spend all these billions of dollars developing your new weapon and now you're telling me you didn't think they'd use it?'

Clare turned towards me, expectant, incredulous, hardly able to believe what she knew she was going to hear.

It sounded weak, even to me.

'No,' I said. 'I never thought they would.'

Two days later, they asked Oppenheimer the same question. He drew in his breath, as if giving this proposal serious thought, then spoke. It was the first time I heard the words that came to dominate the latter half of the twentieth century: 'No comment.'

What could he say? What could I have said? Even if we had said, no, we didn't think they'd use it, said it a hundred times over, no-one would believe us.

In the newspapers they started talking about Oppenheimer as the father of the atom bomb. This was before he started talking about being the destroyer of worlds, before he talked about sin, when he was still happy to take the blame.

But I knew he was going to talk about sin eventually because, after the initial euphoria, I knew that was what came next. I had delighted in my vengeance for only a few instants, it seemed, before my eyes were opened to the reality of what I had done. I had done something wrong. I knew that, now, and this was a knowledge I could not lose. And despite that knowledge and that guilt, I didn't see that there was any way of making atonement.

I felt a sudden longing for those times of which Desanka had told me tales, the olden days, when everything was dependable, when farmers tended their cows and princesses lived in remote castles and burned witches. The days before we knew that molecules danced. The Dark Ages, when I might have danced for joy in wonder and ignorance, and never had to stop for sorrow.

'You really didn't think they'd *use* it?'

Clare's words reverberated in that dusty office.

I could only think of mothers and husbands and children with no prior warning.

'No.'

No matter where I went now, no matter how much time passed in the world, I was guilty and would always be guilty.

'Sometimes, Mary-Jo, you are incredibly stupid.'

Clare slammed the cabinet shut. She was off to take the minutes of the Target Committee from the teletype.

By the time she came back to tell me they had chosen Hiroshima, I had gone.

CHAPTER ELEVEN

The Valley

6 August 1945

THE BOMB EXPLODED AT 8.14 A.M., OVER THE BRIDGE AT Hiroshima, 1,800 feet above the ground.

Up on the Hill, I'd been isolated. I'd cut myself off, the way I had in the Berlin lab, though I hadn't noticed it, hadn't had time to realize it, hadn't let myself see it. Now, on the other side of the gates, the world began again.

At the time of the blast, I worked out later, I was standing on the platform of the station at Santa Fe, my leave pass safe in my pocketbook in case any member of the military should choose to be extra-vigilant. Still no-one was allowed on or off the Hill without suspicious scrutiny. The green trees on the opposite side of the railway line were cool and tall and undisturbed. There was space between their trunks that had not been disturbed by human breath since the line was built a century ago.

They had delivered the baby to the Atomic Strike Force on the island of Tinian. They wanted unconditional surrender. No promises. No assurances. No guarantees.

I chose a seat by a window and put my holdall in the space by the door. I sat opposite a businessman with a briefcase full of papers that he spread all over the table between us.

They chose Hiroshima because it was unscathed by air strikes and thus the full impact of the bomb could be measured. It was a bomb against civilians.

I made room amongst the businessman's papers for a cup of hot coffee and some magazines. I looked forward to drinking the coffee while it was still hot – for the last few years, by the time I remembered I had a cup at my elbow, it was at best lukewarm. I'd had work to do. Now I had nothing. I knew I wouldn't read the magazines, but they were something to mark my place.

Later, I saw in the newsreels the flat desolation of the town. One or two steel-framed buildings remained, the rest was rubble, and it stretched far away into the distance.

I watched the desert outside the train window roll by. By the time the sun had moved out of my eyes, we were in another state and the coffee was cold.

7 August 1945

People at the station where I chose to get out were very excited.

'The Commies'll die from envy,' said the man who checked my ticket with a flourish. 'The Russkies haven't got anything near like this.'

There was an air of jubilation on the station forecourt that I hadn't felt so pervasively since Vienna. People kissed one another, smiling, and patted babies on their heads. Ribbons fluttered. Mothers rejoiced, children breathed a sigh of relief. There would be no reason to invade Japan, now. All their boys would be safe.

'We'll be able to dictate our own terms from now on,' said the taxi driver. 'You just see if we don't.'

The talk was on the streets, inescapable. It was in all the papers. The news was on everyone's lips.

I was good at choosing boarding houses. I knew to look for clean sheets, hot water and a landlady who didn't ask for lights out at eleven. Even so, I was taken aback when the woman showed me to my room and announced with an air of satisfaction after stating the terms in dollars per week, 'We don't hesitate to use the big stuff. We play hardball.'

No matter where I went, I couldn't get away from what I had done.

The papers were full of endless column inches of it. Over 100,000 died straight away. Over the next few years, tens of thousands more died from the radiation.

I couldn't have done it all on my own, I knew that. But, equally, they couldn't have done it without me.

If I hadn't corrected their calculations as they went along, if I hadn't put the right equations in as I typed up the reports, even if I hadn't solved the problem of the initiator unit right there at the end, they'd have still been out in the desert figuring out if they would ever make the damn thing work. If I hadn't been there, a bomb might have been three or four more years down the line.

The worst thing was that I still couldn't see, even after reading the newspapers over and over, that there was any reason for it. The test alone would have been enough, ample deterrent.

Freedom. Justice. Tolerance. These were the things people all around me said we were protecting. I listened, along with everyone else, to the broadcast as the emperor god spoke on the radio – the first time his people had heard his voice – signed the instrument of surrender and admitted defeat.

Victory over Japan. To everyone else, a nuclear bomb seemed a price worth paying, but I knew what I had unleashed into the world. Beyond the bright light and the blast, the plutonium leaked into the groundwater, the fallout leached into every cloud. Even under the New Mexico earth there were barrels and barrels of radioactive waste. Who was going to clean it up?

You can't see it, you can't feel it, there is no taste, there is no colour. 'So why worry?' my landlady said.

'Well,' I said. 'Where there's no sense, there's no feeling.'

The test alone would have been enough. That bright light would have been enough. It would have been enough for me. It should have been enough for everyone.

And as for revenge?

In the series of reports in the newspapers that were published just after the war, when everyone was cock-a-hoop with the power of it all, I learned that Leo Szilard had told my father that fission had been achieved as long ago as July 1939. Further, my father had been informed in detail about the military potential of the nuclear chain-reaction process, about its destructive capability.

Szilard asked my father to write to Roosevelt, which he did in August, asking for a team to start work on the bomb.

Whether it was down to my father's letter or not, the team, which I had joined, had shortly afterwards started work. So not only had my father known all about nuclear fission the whole time I was out there working in the desert, plotting secretly to astonish him with my big surprise, he had actively campaigned for the work on the bomb to begin.

What had happened to his cherished pacifism? What had happened to his utter hatred of weapons?

Perhaps my father, the man who had always said he would never fight, had seen that there were some things you had to fight for. Not only that, he had seen it long before I did.

Of course, if he had encouraged the atomic bomb, then he was as guilty as I was when it was finally dropped. So I had no triumph, no joy, no revenge. All we had in common now was a shared guilt. But to know that he shared my guilt was no comfort at all.

29 September 1945

What did I do when the war was finally over? I slept. Days and nights in one boarding house then another, the odd motel, one room after another in different towns on the strength of unspent and hoarded salary payments dating back years. I tunnelled deep into that darkness, pausing only to turn over a pillow, visit the bathroom in a bright midday or a dim half-light that I couldn't distinguish as the end of one day or the beginning of another and, with another drink of vodka or two, it didn't matter to me which it was so I didn't ask. And I moved on often enough so no-one would get to know me, get to know me well enough to knock on the door, enquire how I was keeping. That was how I liked it, when no-one bothered to knock on the door.

All the bad feelings I had been trying to push away came back and made a burrow in my stomach, where they nestled, like a little black creature, like the rabbit Desanka and I had kept in that hutch on our farm outside Novi Sad which Hans Albert had told me I should think of as a pet. So I had begun to think of that rabbit as a pet and called him Sami, and when Desanka had cooked Sami for Christmas dinner, the way she had always said she would, he had lain in my stomach for days, head on his paws, trembling. I could imagine him worrying at bits of grass and leaves the way he always used to in his hutch, and I had felt sick instead of healthy and happy, the way any farm girl should.

I moved from one room to another wondering, when I stepped into each one, whether this would be it, would be the last one, whether I should just end it all here, whether I would finally gather together the courage to end it all here. I would run my hands over the off-white sinks, the chipped wood of the bedside tables and think for a while how I could do it, and then I would crawl into the wide beds with their motley collections of mismatched sheets and fall asleep.

A line from a poem one of the technicians in the camp had told me, late one night when the coffee was cold and the figures wouldn't come out right and he was sentimental with tiredness, came back to me. 'Home is the place where, when you have to go there, they have to take you in.'

Where could I go? My father was snug in his university with his cousin-wife. My brothers were scattered. They were like faces from a family album that was not my own family, interesting in their frozen black-and-white attitudes, but not familiar. A slight likeness about the slope of the forehead, perhaps, but no more. Josef was dead. The house on Oberlandstrasse was bombed to smithereens. My children . . .

For most of my life the woman I had first known as Fräulein Freisler had been my family. She had been my one constant. And I couldn't ask *her* to take me in. I couldn't bear to live with a person who had the blood of untold thousands of people on her hands, so why should she? I didn't even want to make her try.

There was one person who would take me, I thought. My mother. She was still alive, still living in Zurich. More than anything I wanted to feel her hands over mine once again, to hear her voice, to lay my head on her shoulder. But she had told me to be a good girl. Her last words to me. And what had I been all my life but bad?

We had all once been intact and now we were torn apart. It's something that happens to everyone. Sometimes it happens suddenly, with sharp weapons. Sometimes slowly, with radiation. Sometimes accidentally, in the cut and thrust of living. Sometimes deliberately, insidiously, in secret. A person might think they had come through life intact, but deep within their bones the cell divisions that would kill them were beginning. Deep within my bones, ever since childhood, I had been harbouring a jealousy and hatred that had now spilled out and spread over the whole world. It was only meant to harm one person. How had I let things get so out of control?

I slept because it was the only place I could go where I could get away from the pain. I had no dreams, only blackness and insensibility, and that was just fine by me.

And then, all of a sudden, the sleeping stopped.

When I found myself lying in the light one day, looking at the ceiling with eyes that stayed open, I gave some room to the possi-

bility that whatever it was I had been going through might finally
be over. Here I was, and I was still. For a brief few days, I simply
stayed awake. I tried not to think so much about killing myself. I
even stopped drinking quite so much vodka. And then I started
washing. The grime went to the bottom of every pore.

The consequences were like bruises. When you first harm yourself, the skin is pale, unmarked. Only later does the swelling begin,
the purple striations start and the smoothness of swollen skin
betrays the hurt. Only a long time after the blow does the true
damage become apparent. Now I was going to have to wake up and
face the consequences.

My body was in that state they call 'run down', which means
there's nothing wrong with you that you can't get up and solve yourself, if only you've got the energy and the purpose. I had little energy
but I felt the beginnings of purpose and I directed it at the just-
noticed dirt. Under my fingernails there were infections. When I
swept the plugs of detritus away, every space in my body seemed to
fill at a moment's notice with the accumulated pus of disasters
waged and lost by my immune system. The toes on my right foot
swelled so much I thought they would split. I stabbed at them
repeatedly with the compasses I had stolen from Dieter's maths set
and let the fluid drain away. Eventually the rock-hard red columns
that were my toes subsided and I could walk again, with more of a
limp than ever, the skin peeling and yellowing as the flesh sank back,
white at the edges where I pulled it away. I was anxious for the
flotsam and jetsam to be borne away by the tide, so that I could start
clean and afresh and new, shining and normal, the way I was always
meant to be.

I looked in the mirror and saw that the copper rinse was long
gone, and without the corset my waist was thicker. I looked my age,
no more no less, long past my best, but I decided I could live with
that, I had had enough of lies.

And then I started wanting to eat things I didn't even know I
could eat. I would wake in the morning smelling fresh pineapple, so

fresh it was falling into shreds, sliced bananas ripening in the bowl, orange juice in crystal glasses, as much chocolate – milk or plain – as I could eat.

While I ate, examining my newly filed fingernails around the spoon, I tried to rationalize: I did in the war what most people did in the war – I looked after myself, and I got on with my own life and the things I wanted to do. I didn't look any further than that. Who did? That's what most people would say.

But that was where I knew I'd gone wrong. Of course I've seen the pictures so often now, in black and white and later in colour, the jumble of bones, the lines of sycamore and alders, the chimneys, the grass growing peacefully all the way down to the river, the wire, that I can't believe I didn't think about what was going on in those camps, that Maja didn't. I didn't let myself notice, let myself *look*. All the perfect bodies, violated, violated.

Josef died in Dachau, one of the rags of the winter of 1943. He was the first person I tried to find through the Red Cross when I arrived in California with my holdall and my shining post-war skin. I registered with the agency in the name of Helga Hansbach, took a room downtown, and waited three weeks for the news to come through.

I parried the kindly hand on my arm of the woman behind the desk and set my mouth in a straight line, as if Josef Hansbach had been no more than a distant relative, instead of my husband. I didn't want her sympathy. Herr Weiss had been right when he had told me the matter of Josef was out of his hands. I knew Josef was dead long ago. It was only a matter of knowing when.

I was too frightened to ask about the children. As long as I didn't know for sure what had become of them, there was always a possibility that, in their case at least, Herr Weiss had been lying.

There would probably be no difficulty finding out, I knew. Records were kept, names were noted, statistics were filed. The whole scheme was very orderly, very efficient. But I didn't ask. I didn't want to look for them over in Europe because I still looked for their shadows behind me, still hoped to catch a glimpse of them in the mirror. While they were still undocumented, still unofficial, I could still believe that, somewhere, they lived.

And without that hope, I couldn't have gone on. The damage would have been fatal.

16 November 1945

My voice was going.

I had a job filling shelves at the local supermarket in the small town where I had ended up and when customers asked me questions about the grapefruit and oranges, my accent and the occasional *sie* and *ja* crept into my vocabulary. My syntax betrayed me.

It was when I got that official notification of Josef's death, in that Red Cross office with lists of names tacked to the wall, that I first began to realize just how high the bodies mounted up, how deep was the guilt I had to share. I thought at first it was going to be a collective guilt, a universal examination of the blood on our hands, the guilt that came simply from being human, of the same race as the perpetrators of the horrors. Perhaps I could narrow it a bit. Yes, I was more guilty because I had lived on the same continent, if not within earshot of the screams. Worse, I spoke German.

In those days, to be European was to be identified with the enemy. I came from Europe. No matter which country I claimed – Hungary, Yugoslavia – as my birthplace, it was all the same place, surely, people could tell, for any purposes that mattered. It was all the same place in their minds, every town within sight of the smoke from the chimneys, every neighbour a collaborator.

Yes, it is my fault, I wanted to say. If you need a scapegoat for the twentieth century, make it me.

After all, where had my plans for revenge ever got me? Where had Newton, the laws of thermodynamics, Maxwell's field equations, special theories, general theories and gravity taken me? It wasn't just nowhere, it was somewhere a long way behind the place I had started out from. Once I had been a little girl dancing. What was I now?

I spent the days doing nothing but hiding from chattering customers, filling shelves with peanut butter and sliced peaches and canned ham. I lived in two rooms and listened to the radio in the evenings. The comedy serials were endless. They didn't make me laugh. I spent the nights doing nothing but dream.

4 August 1948

It was early evening and I was dozing after my supper in the day's late light. The radio was on in the corner, a dim and distant noise. A touch of light fingers on my arm. Up, down. Up, down.

A memory, more than a memory, for I could smell my mother's warm skin and the scent of milk, hear her voice, her lovely voice, singing to me as she wrapped me in a soft blanket and lifted me to her shoulder, where I curled a baby arm around her neck.

I looked at the clock on the wall. It had stopped.

I began to cry. My mother's pain was over. The lingering chance of finding her again had gone.

What sort of lives could we have lived if we hadn't been so overshadowed by my father? What would have happened if Mileva had ignored his dictates and kept me?

What would have happened if, instead of hatching a plot for revenge in the firelight of Desanka's kitchen, I had set on a simpler course instead: that of simply finding my mother?

I had spent all my life looking for the wrong person and now it was too late even to tell her so.

I kept on crying, for all that might have been and for all that might have been avoided, if only my mother and I had loved each other enough. And I kept on crying as I heard the knock on the door, the banging on the door, and it was only with difficulty, when Clare kept on knocking, made me get up, made me let her in, when she found me, when she found me crying and wanted to know why, that I could explain to her that my mother was dead.

'Oh, honey, I am so sorry,' she said, putting her head against mine and rocking me in her arms.

'I wish you had met her. I wish you had met her just once.'

'That doesn't matter now.'

'Yes it does. The losses go on and on. There will be no end to them. There is nothing more in life than this for me now, nothing to look forward to except people dying.'

'I'm here,' said Clare. 'You've got me, and I've got you.'

I looked at her closely. She didn't seem to have aged a day since I last saw her, still the same shiny blond hair, the same white skin, the eyelashes that looked as if they had been stained by India ink.

'How did you find me?'

'You're not hard to find.'

'If you know where to look.'

'I knew where to look. It just took a while, that's all. But it's up to you. I've found you. Now you have to decide whether you want me to stay.'

She had come home to me, the place where she belonged.

There was only one last argument, early in the morning when the new sun was coming up and we had watched all night for the memory of my mother.

'I still can't believe I found you crying for your mother. You hadn't thought of her in years. You don't even know if she ever thought of you. Why cry for her and not for Josef and the children?'

'I was crying because I was sad, that's all. She was my mother, always, even if I only met her once. Even if I can only remember meeting her once.' That day she came to the farm was burned clear on my brain but I would never know if the memory of the warm skin and the milk and the singing was real memory or just a dream. 'I'll never know if she thought about me as often as I thought about her,' I said. 'I'll never even know if she forgot about me completely. So sadness, that's all, for what might have been.'

'And you're not sad for the children? For Josef any more?'

'What do you want me to say?' I said, brushing her soothing hand aside. 'I'm not sad. That's not the right word. Even now I can't find the right words for what I feel: pain and guilt and grief, that's just the start. Their loss is like . . . like nothingness.'

I stared at the empty sky brightening outside the window. I kept on talking. It seemed important to explain what I felt, even if I wasn't sure I was right. 'But what do you want me to do, Clare? If I shed tears for them now, I would be doing nothing but being sentimental. That's all I would be doing. I cannot help them now. I could have once, and I didn't. Their pain is over. Their pain is *over*, remember that. It is our responsibility to make sure that their pain does not happen again to someone else.'

'That's our responsibility is it?'

'All of us. All of us who survived. Who else can take it on?'

'Someone else.' She shook her head, as if unwilling to take any responsibility any more, ever. 'We have enough pain.'

'There'll be other Herr Weisses one day, you know, Clare. It'll be up to people like us to recognize them.'

I remembered breaking Herr Weiss's fingers, slowly, one by one. I remembered the sound of his bones breaking. If I had had the chance, I would have liked to do that while he was still alive.

I turned my head against my shoulder and felt the crystals in my muscles crack and grate. The day was almost upon us. Time was catching up with me.

12 September 1948

Everything that had been part of my life since before the war now seemed like relics from a lost civilization. Even the physics I had helped to create was now just a surreal survival of old-fashioned notions. Relativity was neither here nor there. Atoms were neither one thing nor another, just a hazy cloud of probabilities, but that didn't matter. It certainly didn't matter that I'd taken one single atom and split it. Quantum physics was all that mattered, Heisenberg's matrix mechanics and Schrödinger's wave theories. Who cared now that one had been on one side and the other had been on the other in the war? Who cared now that the accepted form of Schrödinger's equations incorporated the tiny improvement I'd suggested to him in 1933?

To admit that you were interested in the way the world was ordered was not only quaint but quite frankly, in this country, dangerously communist. Intellectualism was suspect and I was too tired of being a suspect to want to be part of it. I read less and less.

I felt it was not such a loss. The world where I had always gone when I did physics had changed. In the journals, no longer did I read about industrious spacefolk signalling cheerfully to each other from their craft. Instead, I read about devilish devices with diabolical consequences.

Imagine a box. A small box. It contains one electron. Remember, electrons can be both wave and particle, but we can never see them as both at any one time. If you measure for waves you get waves. If you measure for particles, you get particles.

This was old news. I'd started reading about this in 1930, but then the war intervened and atomic fission took over my brain. I'd forgotten about probability theory, being too concerned with actuality.

But now, take your box and slide a partition across it. In which half of the box is the electron? We can't tell. The probability wave of where it might be is evenly distributed across the whole of the box; there is a 50:50 chance that it will be in either side. The probability wave only collapses into an actual electron when somebody looks inside and notices where that electron is. The observer changes everything.

The person looking changes everything.

It is as if, until that point, there were two electron 'ghosts' in either half of the box, waiting for an observer to make one of them real. When one is looked at and made real, at that moment the other ghost vanishes.

Now the diabolical device comes in.

Take your box again, and the electron and the sliding partition, and put them on a table in a closed, windowless room. The partition slides across. The probability wave spreads. In one corner of this closed room, there is a cat, minding her own business, licking her paws. Next to this poor cat is a container of poisonous gas. This container is wired to an electron detector. If the detector spots the presence of a single electron in the room, it will release the deadly gas.

The lid on one half of the box opens. Was the electron in that side of the box or not? The chances, as always, are 50:50. If it was in that half of the box, the detector has been alerted, the gas has been released, and the cat is dead. If it wasn't, the cat is still safely licking her paws.

But we can't tell until we look, until we observe. Remember, the room had no windows, and until we observe, the cat is neither alive, nor is it dead. Everything in that room is only a probability. We don't make it real until we *look*.

'This is a ridiculous story,' said Clare. 'Of course the cat's either dead or alive.'

'Under quantum rules, no,' I said. 'Not until you look.'

This was why my father disliked quantum mechanics so much. He had spent his life attempting to perfect a description of the universe that was unbiased, independent of human observation. He imagined the universe ticking its way towards its end, the galaxies and gravities performing in accordance with the allotted laws, whether the human race was there or not to witness it. Now it began to seem that the universe was not like this in the least. Observers affect what they observe, and observation itself changes things. Familiar stuff: if you know the position, you can't know the momentum. And the act of looking at an electron's position changes its momentum, and vice versa. For heaven's sake, I'd known that since Heisenberg's uncertainty principle, but now the stakes were higher. Hell, without us looking at it, the universe might not have happened at all.

But then again, we don't know that.

Still, as the physics journals were now full of rather sad cats, shut in boxes, neither dead nor alive till someone looked at them, I decided it was not in my best interests to look very hard at all.

It reminded me too much of my children, who had been neither dead nor alive for years now, because I refused to look, wouldn't look, didn't want to look.

1 January 1949

Clare was having sclerotherapy of her own invention. She persuaded a doctor to inject glycerine into the blood vessels in her cheeks that had broken during the freezing winter of 1918. He was reluctant, mainly because he couldn't see that it would do any good. When Clare pointed out that it was unlikely to do any harm either, he gave it a go.

The inflammation brought on by the glycerine caused the walls of the capillaries to collapse, as Clare had predicted they would, with the result that the blood could no longer circulate and the vein lost its redness. Clare was jubilant. There were some temporary red marks, some puffiness, and only an occasional scar. Clare thought that the price was so small as to be scarcely worth considering and the risk of scarring, while more serious, was also more than worth it. Her skin was being restored to a perfection it hadn't known since the early days of the century. She patted powder onto her cheeks with pride and got out her curling tongs.

When it was clear that the war had truly ended, women's hair-styles had become, almost immediately, astoundingly frivolous. Clare was delighted. She found their complexity a challenge and practised assiduously. Little kiss curls here, little twinkles of a chestnut rinse there. It was an affront. I told her so.

'Try.' She proffered a curling tong.

'Why should I spend my life perched before a mirror trying to coax my locks into the approved pattern?'

'Unheard of delights, pumpkin,' she said, casting a disapproving eye over the grey in my locks. 'Give it a go.' She waved a hot iron in my direction. I declined the offer and looked at my hands instead.

The hands are the first place that show you're getting old. A certain looseness around the knuckles, a dryness around the fingernails. Looking at my hands and biting off a stray cuticle, I realized I was much older than I used to be.

Clare took me out, kiss curls in place, on a miasma of peroxide and leg wax to a New Year's Day party. There were chicken legs to eat, and corn cakes, and chilli relish, and comforting martinis to drink. I drank several.

Towards the middle of the evening, someone took the dance records off as the daughter of the house was being brought into the company to show off her musical skills. She was a tall girl, with the wide smile that Americans have, and the good teeth and the smooth hair, and she smiled at us all before beginning.

The daughter sat in the centre of the floor on a small stool and played the cello. Lovely at first, then more sorrowful – deep sad sounds of strings and reverberating bass – and Clare went very pale and I knew she was grieving. She mourned all over again, as she did from time to time, as if the crying inside would never wholly leave her. For Paul, for Josef, for Kätzchen, for the young man she had lost in the war. Which war? The Great War, The Last War, The War to End All Wars, The War of Serbian Aggression, The War to Preserve All That Is Worth Preserving or The War to Save Civilization. Does it matter which war? Against so many wars, all of them just, all of them decreed, all absolutely essential at the time even though few now remember their reasons or causes beyond a vague frisson of patriotism – what could stand? And she grieved for Tina. In the bows and the arches of that mournful music, she grieved most of all for Tina. She had always loved Tina.

I had nothing to fix my grief against, nothing to hold on to. I didn't know if Tina and Paul were dead. I had no grave to go to for Josef, nowhere to send flowers. I had nothing I could let myself mourn for.

As the music ended and the daughter of the house received her congratulations like a shy star, I thought I would spend the rest of my life drifting like this, untethered, refusing to look in one direction or another, always a ghost, condemning my children to a half-life in which they were ghosts because I couldn't bear to look to see if they were dead or alive. And I was sad because of this and sad because I did not know what else I could do.

But it was not long afterwards, in that American suburb with the cello music still in my ears, that the news came that Tina was still alive.

Someone had found her and made her alive.

'No,' I said. 'No.'

'Yes,' Clare said, raising an arm against my anger. 'I asked them to find out. I asked. I couldn't bear not knowing.'

For the first and only time in my life, I hit her.

9 June 1949

I went to New York to meet Tina off the boat, where she was handed over into my care by an officious-looking harridan in a nurse's hat and scarf.

I knew her immediately. My daughter was a young woman now, in regulation-issue grey clothing, but she still had the same blank eyes and golden hair, with her features possibly becoming more and more rounded like Josef – the same curlicue of the ears, the same determination in the chin. When I held her close against me, I heard the same irregular beat to her heart that there had always been and I knew she was mine.

For breakfast we had orange juice, champagne and oysters in the best hotel I could find. Tina had brought one doll with her, a tired old thing with half its hair pulled away at the roots and one leg missing. Over the next few days, as I took her round the New York department stores, kitting her out with American outfits, she acquired around eight more dolls all done out with blond curls and pink floral frocks, and she tucked them into bed every night, individually. Some had their own beds. At least one came with its own bottle. Bedtime took hours.

I brushed her hair as she brushed the dolls' hair, wondering who had brushed her hair all these years. I wiped her face wondering if she had gone to bed dirty or clean. In the world without language that was the world where my daughter lived, there were no answers because she could not ask any questions. I could wonder all I liked, but she would never tell me.

Tina turned all the dolls' faces away from the light, kissed them and never let them lie in uncomfortable positions. Influenced by her investment of them with life, I apologized to a particularly supercilious creation with hard blue eyes and a knowing tweak to her rosebud mouth when I squashed her uncomfortably into the suitcase when I was packing our things to go home. Home, where Clare was waiting for us.

Tina had come to a world where everything was new. New Jersey, New York, New Hampshire. On the trainride over the country, back to Clare, we stopped in New Falls, Ohio, where we ate *Schnecken* – snails like in the old country: fat butter pastries curled into the spiral of shells – so rich and full of dairy, like along the pastures of the Rhineland, that our tongues grew as smooth at the tasting of them as the grass grows green after rain. Soft grass, warm grass, northern European grass. It was the last taste, and then we were into the prairie.

Between us, Clare and I had decided, we would give Tina the endless childhood she wanted: no weapons, no Europe, no Nazis, no memories. Tina never spoke, or betrayed with even a sigh or a dream what had happened to her in those lost years. The Displaced Persons' Office could give me no more information than that she had been found in Berlin, her birth certificate and 10 marks pinned to her shoulder.

Perhaps my happy picture of my children hadn't been so far wrong, after all, I thought. She kissed her dolls still. Perhaps this meant that someone had kissed her. Perhaps.

But it was as if the act of finding Tina had made the probability wave collapse completely. At the same moment. When I got back and Clare put her arms around Tina, I saw the telegram on the bureau. Black and white. No escape. When Clare had asked them to find Tina, she had asked them to find Paul, too. And they had found out everything.

Paul had died five years ago.

Clare took Tina and hugged her and hugged her, washing her face, changing her into one of her new nightdresses, tucking in her dolls, while I fell down into darkness. It was because she had risked this that I had hit Clare. Hit her hard, on the side of her head. If she had not found out about Tina, then I could have gone on the rest of my life hoping Paul, somewhere, was alive. She had found Tina, but not Paul. My son was dead. My son with his shell collection and his fine brown hair, so fine it fell like silk between your fingers. Always and for ever now, he was lost to me.

17 November 1952

After Tina arrived, we moved to a town laid out in squares, where the north-south streets were allocated numbers and the east-west streets letters. A town in a flat land where nobody talked about anything but corn and grapes and the weather and its effect upon the first two items.

In the course of this move, Clare became Terri, which she felt was suitable, and I had to agree with her, and I became Lisa. It was as close as I wanted to get for the moment to my own given name. Tina was Tina and would always be Tina, and as Tina never spoke, she didn't call us anything.

The flat we bought on D Street had windows on three sides and a kitchen in which the linoleum was shiny and the Formica was white and smooth – all of the things that I liked about America. Easy to clean, too, said Terri.

I ran my fingers over the bright white porcelain in the bathroom. I stood in the hallway and switched the lights on and off a few times. I'd reached the age of fifty and I finally had electric light in my own home. We could afford it. The money in Herr Weiss's Swiss bank account had earned generous interest while we had been in New Mexico. It was more than enough to provide. Terri said she still wondered sometimes what Herr Weiss had been planning to do with it after the war. I didn't. His plans must have been grandiose indeed, judging by the size of the sum he had stowed, and he would have seen himself safe, I had no doubt, no matter which side won. I stopped filling shelves in supermarkets. I had Tina to look after.

I didn't do any science while we lived on D Street. I didn't even do very much thinking because I was out of the habit. I hadn't done science for years except at Los Alamos and that wasn't so much science as engineering. And thinking had never got me anywhere.

The sun would begin the day by shining into our bedroom, and it was there Terri would linger first, sipping morning coffee in bed, wallowing in the warmth between the cotton sheets. Tina would wake when I woke her, needing breakfast immediately.

Later in the morning, her bath completed, Terri would move to the main room, where the midday rays were brightest, following the heat and the light, painting her toenails, leafing through the fashion magazines, exclaiming over the collections.

I would do the marketing, following Terri's lists exactly, taking Tina with me to check off one item after another, and bring home the fresh ingredients for our lunch. In the afternoons Terri would play a little bridge, meet the girls for a round of golf. She really did look extraordinarily well.

I didn't enjoy bridge or golf but I didn't mind knitting, I discovered, though it took me a while to get the hang of it. And as the girls in the bridge parties had grandchildren, there was an inexhaustible need for blankets and mittens and bonnets. I knitted sets at a time, in blue and pink, while Tina dressed her dolls, and we watched the daytime programmes on TV.

By late afternoon, Terri would be in the kitchen, which looked to the west, putting fish or meat or butter and eggs together for our evening meal. It was here that I would find her, like a flower turning to the sun, at the end of the day. Even in the winter when the days darkened early, she would forestall me if I tried to switch on the lamps when there was still light in the sky, a few streaks of orange or red sunset visible between the locust trees. We would wait until the day was gone and only then, when there was nothing more to lose, when the lights in other buildings made beacons outside and we could see our own reflections in the darkened window glass, did Terri draw the blinds and let us become creatures of the night. I knew that the night had officially begun when Tina was safe in bed and the curling tongs and sprays made an appearance.

One year Terri took up tennis. She flounced around the courts in starched whites, working up a sweat, a most unladylike thing to achieve, but she said it was all worth it for the tone it brought to her biceps and triceps. This wasn't a particularly fashionable thing to do, in those days of the New Look, but she said she was thinking about the long-term benefits.

The next year, she joined the anti-bomb protest groups and found that this, with the tennis, filled her days. I did not go with her to either activity. I disliked strenuous movement, and the rights and wrongs of whether science should engage in any research at all any more were beyond me. Whatever the scientists did, however magnanimously they did it, it was only going to be exploited for evil. If someone somewhere could make a weapon out of it, they would.

Down there amongst the subatomic particles that were being discovered – it seemed like new ones every day – there were dangers lurking, so deep we couldn't see them yet, but I knew they were there. If exploration was going on, there would be exploitation to follow and worse to come.

Terri lit candles for Paul's memory, and for Josef and for Kätzchen, every Sunday in the neat white church down the street. Tina didn't change from one day to the next. There was nothing more that could bother us, if we didn't let it.

For old times' sake I still read an occasional copy of *Physics Today* or *Nature*. By now everyone knew, and somehow took it for granted that they had always known, that the universe was expanding. Despite this, the equations my father and I had written for our general theories of relativity still held. In his case, the equations could finally dispense with that cosmological constant, that little term that I had never liked, shoved in at the last minute for the purpose of holding the universe still. The equations held if you followed them back, almost all the way back to the beginning of time. Everything got closer and closer together, if you made time run backwards, until all the matter in the universe reached a point of infinite density. At that point, the equations broke down because everything broke down.

Still, the mathematical descriptions we had come up with took account of everything that had happened in the universe in the past 15 billion years, apart from that crucial first tenth of a second or so. I felt that this wasn't a bad achievement.

Apart from reaching agreement on the expansion of the universe, theoretical physics advanced to the point where it was in total chaos. If I followed the theories correctly – and there were a lot of them – then we might have a multiplicity of universes, each splitting off from another at the point where decisions were made. And a 'decision' could be an event as small and unremarkable as one particle interacting with another. And if you thought about how many particles there were in the universe . . . then anything was possible.

In some other universe, therefore, my father had never let me go. In another, my mother had brought me back. In these other universes, I had led a lifetime of happiness and the atomic bomb was not yet invented. In another universe, Paul was alive and Tina had never left me, and every night I could hold Josef tight in our bed in the sure and certain knowledge that he was mine for always.

I thought these theories belonged on one of those cartoons that Tina liked to watch, not in learned journals.

My father fought against these ideas, too, from his castle keep, sending aggressive slingshots of unified field theory over the battlements, still trying to tie classical theories together against the barbarian hordes of the quantum enemies. He spent years trying to come up with a theory that would allow the laws of quantum mechanics to derive from observable facts rather than statistical probabilities. But that was impossible. You couldn't observe the subatomic world very easily, and every time you did observe it, you changed it. The uncertainty principle was all we had, probabilities were all we could hope for, and we were going to have to put up with it.

So my father ended up as a character from history in a theoretical position that was a joke and in a place that was as much a joke as anything: New Jersey. He had ended up in New Jersey. If something strange happened in America, chances really were that it happened in New Jersey, to a man from New Jersey.

The Institute for Advanced Study in New Jersey paid my father to just sit around and think. And the whole time he was there, he never thought of a single right thing. Not in all those years. He tried. Of course he tried. He was hoping to put together a Theory of Everything, a grand idea that would explain the whole universe, from the edges of the galaxies to the smallest structure of the atoms we are made of. He failed. The fact that no-one else, even now, has managed to come up with a Theory of Everything, either, is no excuse.

I could understand why he was fighting. If you followed the

quantum theories through to their logical conclusion, my father would have to admit defeat over everything.

Imagine you take that partitioned box again, and split it down the partition into two halves. Take one half on a spaceship 10,000 light years in one direction, take the other half 10,000 light years in the opposite. In which half is the electron? You still don't know. The probability waves spread. You still have two ghosts in a state of uncertainty, but this time on opposite sides of the universe. Still, as always, when one observer opens his half of the box, the probability wave collapses. He either sees the electron, or he doesn't. It is either there, or it isn't.

And at the same moment, on the other side of the universe, because the ghost of one electron has been laid to rest, the ghost of the other is, too. The wave collapses. The electron is either there, or it suddenly isn't. The two things happen at the same time on opposite sides of a galaxy. One event influences the other.

Yet we all know that no influence can travel faster than light. My father had proved that – I had proved that – all those years ago. Yet in this case, *something* has travelled across the universe as fast as thought itself.

So, if the quantum physicists were right, relativity was wrong. And my father was dreadfully afraid they were right.

I was, too. The fabric of the universe seemed thinner than ever, as if any day it might simply tear itself apart under our feet and we would fall through into nothing. It sometimes seemed as if the whole universe was existing on nothing more than hope and goodwill and if we all stopped observing it for just one second, stopped looking, it would collapse completely.

I was tired most of those years. I was far too old to become a mother all over again, but Tina was going to need me to be a mother a lot longer yet and I was determined to give her everything she wanted. Nevertheless, my body betrayed me. I could not spring for her toys with the agility I'd had in Berlin. I found it hard to cope with her sudden and mysterious demands for honey or bread in the night, even when I brought them.

I looked after Tina and Terri looked after me.

Terri came into the kitchen one morning where I was giving Tina her breakfast as usual and said, 'I see your father has been proposed as President of the state of Israel.'

I stopped spooning sugar flakes long enough to say, 'He hasn't accepted, has he?'

'Not so far.'

Terri set up a mirror on the table and began dabbing at her face experimentally.

'What are you doing?'

She had a little brown pencil that I had never seen before which she was using to draw on her face.

'Chanel Faux Freckle,' she said.

I spooned another few mouthfuls. 'What's it for?'

'A little freckle speaks so much of youth,' she said. 'Don't you think?'

'How do you know whether what you've got is a freckle or a brown age spot?' I looked at my hands, which had plenty of the latter.

Terri, exhibiting that lack of humour for which I loved her so much, said, 'Age spots are light brown. My freckle will be dark.'

There wasn't much I could say to contradict her on that point: the facts were before me and the evidence was plain. With every day that I got older – as was only to be expected, and I didn't mind the wrinkles in the mirror as they made my face less haunted than it always used to be – Terri got another day younger. She moved as quickly as ever. No wrinkles, no lines. It was as if she were in constant free-fall, where all the effects of gravity are cancelled out.

Tina finished her dish of flakes and I put it in the sink.

19 November 1954

It looks like a picture, Dachau, where we took Tina, so that she could remember something of her father and brother, so that I could remember something of the people I had loved. So we were all back in Europe, but now like tourists, on a visit.

It was winter, and the snow covered everything and made the landscape softer somehow, less harsh than I remembered it, and I remembered Germany in some pretty bad snow.

But Tina, inside her head, was too young to remember, or perhaps old enough to want to forget. She responded only to the peace of the place, the calm lapping of the river against frosty banks and the winter birds calling warnings to one another in the trees. It was a blue, crisp day, leaves lingering on a few branches yet, but with the tang of winter in the sharpness of breath and the sprinkling of snow.

Whatever screaming had gone on there had died away, and whatever prayers had been thrown into the dark of the night as a plea for protection against the flames had been torn to shreds by time and the wind and covered over by the snow. And whatever words I said, they weren't enough, they weren't big enough or loud enough or strong enough to contain or describe the pain that shimmered over that shining snow. They could never be loud enough because some of the responsibility for that pain was mine.

I wondered all over again what my life would have been if I had not stood in the firelight in Desanka's kitchen and decided to haunt my father. There was even another avenue of my father's work in which I could have immersed myself: instead of exploring the white heat of fission, I could have explored the cold. In a temperature low enough – many, many degrees of sub-zero – all gases, solids and liquids will fuse their atoms together, in a form we can only guess at. My father, naturally, only ever wrote about this theoretically. But it might be possible. Instead of all of us apart in our separate states, split apart and cast asunder, we might be fused together, indissoluble and complete. I felt it might have been more satisfying, in the end, than chasing explosions.

Perhaps, if I had not danced in the firelight and chased the firelight, I would have Paul with me still, my little boy, and Josef, who had gone without saying goodbye.

For a moment I thought I felt them, that I could feel the reverberations in the air of the screams, that the last prayers were with us still, caught in the branches and whipping in the wind, but then I looked at Tina and her happy face, wide eyes and pink cheeks, and I knew that these fields were the past, they were history. I had spent all my life going back. I wanted to go forward, but not yet, not yet. It was necessary to have a last look and a remembrance before moving on.

The sky above us was perfectly clear and in the spring the grass would be green again and the meadowsweet would be growing over everything, blurring the edges, softening the outlines. And soon even those who remembered the truth would no longer be able to point to it; it would have crumbled and dissolved under that blue sky.

The fields where the soil had been wet with the blood of mothers' sons were turned into fields of cabbage, orderly rows of beets. It's been the same ever since the species walked upright, this paving over, this forgetting. Slowly and gracefully the forest was growing again. By autumn, mushrooms and ferns would slide in the dark over the bones.

As we watched, fresh snow began to fall and I shivered.

That night, as every night before bed, clean in her nightclothes, I combed Tina's long yellow hair free of knots then divided it into three strands and pulled each one in turn tightly over the other two. She wriggled her protest and I pulled harder. A neat and shining plait emerged, a perfectly interlocked, orderly procession, a credit to her grandmother. I tucked her into unfamiliar sheets and she was restless.

'We were born in the wrong time,' I said to Terri.

'Come off it,' she said. 'When do you think could be better than this?'

'Almost any time,' I said. 'Any time except this one. Any time except the one we lived through.'

'Every century before this one has horrors too hideous to mention,' she said. 'Think. Do you want to join a slave ship, huddle in a hovel without heating or fall prey to the latest wave of dysentery? Those are your choices. One of those, or something equally distasteful and similar, was the plight of most human beings who lived before now. You wouldn't last one day, Lisa. And what about Tina? They'd tear her apart like a pack of dogs.'

The woman who ran the boarding house was neat, efficient, and said that business was looking up this last year or so. Things were getting better in Germany now. You couldn't tell the difference any more between the guilty and the victims, the noble survivors and those who had got out by the skin of their teeth.

1 December 1954

'Are we done?' said Terri, folding clothes into a suitcase. She made it sound like a pilgrimage had been satisfactorily completed and a good point notched up in Heaven.

'No,' I said. 'Not yet.'

We had moved onward from Germany to Zurich to see the house where my mother had lived. We had stood outside the Burghölzli – the mental institution in Zurich where my younger brother Eduard had been locked away for years. I didn't want to meet him, I didn't know him, but I had seen his photograph in the newspapers after my mother died, when they were digging over the traces. I knew Eduard's sad bloated face, his tantrums, his childish delight that cherished ice cream as the best this universe could offer. I just wanted to stand outside and know that he was in there. He wouldn't know me. My other brother.

'Surely', said Terri, 'you've done enough trawling through old memories by now.'

'No,' I said. 'Not yet. Meiringen.'

I needed to go into the mountains to Meiringen because, in the asylum there, was an old lady – an old lady who, as a young girl, had been perhaps the only one to understand my father. Marie Winteler, the beautiful Marie, whose heart young Albert broke.

My father lived with Pauline Winteler and her family while he was at school in Switzerland. Pauline had a daughter, Marie. They fell in love but my father abandoned Marie for Mileva. A short while later, he wrote to Pauline, expressing his sorrow at having hurt the 'poor child'. It was perhaps the only time in his life he expressed sorrow, ignoring me, a poorer child, whose heart he also broke.

Pauline forgave him, would have gone on forgiving him if she had not been shot by her own son in the winter of 1906.

Terri was in the last throes of patience. She shuffled restlessly from one foot to another outside the iron gates where she was going to wait for me with Tina, anxious to be off. She didn't like this going back over old footsteps.

'Does madness spread through families like this?' I said to her. 'How much of what we do is inherited and how much of our own volition?'

We both looked at Tina, who smiled back and shivered. Where had her madness come from?

'Is this why you came here, because that is what you wanted to know?' Terri was sceptical. She always was.

'I think so.'

'You're looking in the wrong place for answers.'

'That's not the only reason I'm here. I want to talk to Marie because I think she is the last person alive who ever loved my father.'

'It's too cold to wait here,' said Terri, her breath white in the thin air, taking Tina by the hand. 'We'll be having hot chocolate in the town.'

If Marie had loved my father once, she did not any more. Yes,

Pauline Winteler forgave the young Albert but Marie never did, not for an instant. This is one of the few lucid comments she made in that asylum at Meiringen where I went to visit her in 1954, where the old lady was glad to talk with someone who was, as I told her I was, an old friend of the family.

In the turn of her head, there was something of the beauty she had shown in the early years of the century, when my father had fallen in love with her. But all she could remember was that he had abandoned her for Mileva, and there was nothing in Marie's head now except bitterness and madness. The depth of her hatred surpassed even mine. It was comforting to realize I was not alone.

'I think I know nearly everything now,' I said, packing the last item into the suitcase and sitting on it.

'I don't see the point,' said Terri. She had cleared the room ready for our departure early in the morning. You would never know we had been there.

'But I have to know,' I said. 'I have to know everything. It's all I have left.'

'No-one knows everything,' she said.

'Someone might.'

'That's only an hypothesis,' she said. 'You can't even know that.'

'But until we know what there is to know, what's the point in trying to know what we don't know?'

'Even knowing everything there is to know would not help you,' she said. 'Or me.'

'It will not help me understand the past,' I said. 'I know that much. But it might help me come to terms with it. Might help me see what might be.'

'Do you really think there's a "What might be" from here on?' said Terri.

'There might be,' I said. 'Who's to know?'

'Tina's crying,' Terri said, and she was. I went to her in her borrowed bed in the adjoining room as she dreamed about fields turned into beets and buttercups, fields that Tina could not remember seeing before, that Tina would not remember seeing again when she woke and was properly awake. Tina cried and I went to her. A crying in the night. A childhood that never ends. Tina – the child who taught me that there are only probabilities. No certainties.

I held Tina close and comforted her, brought her back from whatever memories had washed over her from that blue sky, that white snow, and eventually she calmed. I sat on the floor beside her and held her hands in mine all through the night. She was real. Tina was real and she was the most important thing I had.

You can criticize and rip a hypothesis to shreds – but that won't bring you a new hypothesis, a new theory. Where do they come from, these sudden theories? From what realm do they emanate, these glimmers of possibility? They are outside the raw data of the world, nothing to do with the analysis of facts. They seep into the brain in the dead of night, from the dark lake in which all my family sleep, in dreams, in warnings. I had dreamed the general theory of relativity one night to stave off starvation. I had hypothesized the atomic bomb out of thin air and vengeance, and now it was real. They were the theories I had bequeathed to the world and I did not think the world would thank me for either of them.

Perhaps Terri was wrong. There might be another hypothesis left for me yet. I might one morning wake and find myself saying, 'What if . . . ?' and feel that strange sense of something that might be becoming real.

But in my heart I felt Terri was right. I was going over old ground now, when I wrote notes that occurred to me when reading the physics journals. There was nothing original in my work. At times, errors crept into my calculations. I suspected that my days of theories were over. If there was something new to be discovered, someone else was going to have to do it.

*   *   *

'It's time,' said Terri. 'I've called the airport.'

I was stiff from sitting on the floor next to Tina all night and reluctant to move.

'We need to be there early to get three seats together on the plane home.' Terri was indomitable. 'Let's go.' She looked in the mirror and examined her face. She had done some serious research into dermatology lately with the result that earlier in the year she had had two chemical peels.

I decided that I had been right all those years ago: that time did pass differently in stationary and moving systems, and that somehow I had been stationary while Maja kept on moving.

'What's the verdict?' I said, watching her watch herself.

'I'm considering a collagen implant.'

'What for?'

'If they inject it from a syringe straight into the dermis,' she said, 'it should fill in these lines instantly.' She pointed at several under her eyes, with ruthless detachment.

'Where do they get the collagen from?' I said. 'Your legs?'

'The abattoir, I should think,' said Terri.

'Yeuch,' I said.

'It'll be worth it.'

'You don't need it. Look at you. You're already passing for someone in her early forties.'

'Lisa,' she said. 'Don't get me off the subject. It's time to go home.'

'Not yet,' I said. 'I'll come with you across the Atlantic, but then you take Tina back. She needs to be home. But I've got one last diversion. I've got one more thing to do.'

Terri went off to brush her teeth in a way that left me in no doubt of her feelings on this matter.

Not very far away, after all, my diversion, only to Berkeley, not so very far away from where we had been living all these years. But there I met someone whose accent and sensibility could only belong to someone brought up at the heart of that fractured, splintered collection of nation states that has been pleased from time to time to distinguish itself with the name of Europe.

It didn't take long to track him down. At lunch. In the cafeteria. If you really want to find someone, the clues are always there.

I knew who he was before he spoke. He had the same-shaped nose as I did, that same definite chin from Mileva, her dark eyes, as I did.

'*Szervusz*, Hans Albert,' I said.

He turned, and he knew immediately who I was. 'Lieserl.'

It didn't matter that the last time he had seen me I had been a little girl dressed in scorched cotton. I was his sister. Hans Albert is the only person who ever knew who I really was. That was why I had to find him.

He put down his tray and took my hand. 'I've known about you,' he said. 'I've always known about you. But no-one ever talked about you.'

'I remember you so clearly,' I said. 'You were so serious. This serious little boy in an ironed white suit.'

'I'm still serious,' he said.

'I'm glad. At least one of us should be.'

'I always wondered what happened to you. Mama wouldn't talk about it. Papa behaved as if you didn't exist. Then after a while . . . I prayed for you sometimes. I still do. We thought you were dead. We read what happened to Yugoslavia. We thought you were there.'

'You can have no idea where I've been,' I said.

People were walking around us. We were disturbing the orderly line.

'Come to my house,' he said. 'I'll cook you duck and cherries. Just like mother made.'

'You cook?' I said.

'Why not?'

So we went. Together, in his car. He was glad to talk. There was a lot of pent-up vitriol in my brother. After all, if, by the age of

twenty-six, your father has held space and time in the palm of his
hand, transformed science, altered the way mankind looks at the
universe, indeed, has explained the universe, then there's not much
left for you to do, is there?

'Certainly not much *I* wanted to do,' he said.

'Certainly not much I *could* do', I said, 'out there on that farm.'

'Except revenge,' he said.

'Exactly,' I said.

'It's been my life,' he said. 'One way and another. Perhaps no-one
except you can understand just how much I hate him.'

'Does he know that?'

'He knows that. But I never found the courage to tell him to his
face.'

When we got to his house, I left him to his dishes and pans for a
while and we talked of general things, of who he had been, and what
he had done, and who he had become. Sometimes whole lifetimes
can be dealt with in an afternoon in this way and you don't feel
you've left anything important out.

'You can cook,' I said. 'I haven't had this cherry sauce in . . . I
don't know how many years. Culinary arts.'

'To get cherries and duck like that?' he said. 'Culinary science. I
have the scientific training.'

'Either way,' I said. 'A culinary mystery to me.'

'No science at all?'

'I can't tune the radio to the right station,' I said. 'Or fix the car.'

'I don't believe you,' he said. 'You could if you wanted.'

'If I wanted,' I said. 'Yes. You know me too well. You left me your
magic stone.'

'Ah, the magnet.'

'The magnet. You knew I'd work it out.'

'You talked of revenge.'

'I got my revenge.'

'How?'

'I made the bomb.'

'That's revenge with a vengeance,' Hans Albert said, putting down his glass.

'Perhaps,' I said. 'It's guilt now.'

'Lieserl. Swords have killed more people through the centuries. Guns, road traffic accidents, bare hands. That is what war is. That is what life is. How many people do you know who have been damaged by the atomic blast?'

'None,' I said. 'But that's not the point. What I made out in the desert was primitive. The bombs that were dropped on Japan were babies in comparison to the giants we have now.'

'All that because our father was a pacifist?'

'It was the best revenge I could come up with,' I said. 'It was the biggest bang I could think of. It was the only thing I could do which he couldn't choose to ignore. But that's not the way it turned out. Afterwards, I just felt sick.'

'If you hadn't done it,' said Hans Albert, 'someone else would have.'

'That doesn't make me feel any better.'

'That's the trouble with revenge, I suppose.'

'That and guilt.'

'At least you tried,' said Hans Albert.

'I was misguided.'

Hans Albert looked at me suspiciously. 'Do you, er . . . ever do any good works?' he said.

I laughed. 'Like what?'

'Acts of charity?'

'No.'

'Voluntary work for the poor?'

'Never.'

'Rescuing starving animals from the gutter?'

I didn't even bother to reply.

'Good,' he said.

'Why', I said, 'are you so keen to bring out the lesser aspects of my character?'

'One saint', he said, 'in the family is enough.'

I laughed. 'Oh, Hans Albert, I agree.'

'Here. Let's drink a toast.'

'*Prost.*' I raised my glass.

'*Prost.*'

We drank. He was my brother. That night I was having the closest thing I was ever to going to get to an easy evening at home with a blood relative, and I was determined to enjoy it as much as I could.

My brother put down the glass. 'Lieserl, are you bitter?'

I slammed my fork down. There went my immediate chance of enjoyment. 'Of course I'm bitter.'

'I thought you would be.'

'No doubt they told themselves that it was for the best.'

'They were not married, they had no home, Lieserl, when you were born.'

'But this was my life they were throwing away. Even now, even as we sit here, Hans Albert, in this lovely room of yours, I think I have no home. You were born, what? Barely two years after me. Were you packed off to the edges of Europe? Of course not. You were relished and coddled in Berne. You had a mama and a papa. I didn't. Whatever warmth there was in our family, you, out of all of us, had the best of it.'

'Lieserl . . .'

'No, Hans Albert. The fact remains. You had a mother. I did not. If anyone should be after revenge, it's me, not you.'

'But you should know something. I envied you.'

'Why?'

'You were out of it. You could be your own person. You didn't have to live with those endless sly comparisons to your father all the time.'

'Was that such a problem?'

'They still look at me as if I'm a freak,' he said. 'Even now. As if any moment I'm going to start talking equations.'

'Well, you might. You know enough equations to build a bridge, after all,' I said. 'That's something more useful than I've ever managed.'

'There's one in Yugoslavia', he said, 'that I made. Did you know?'

'Yes,' I said. 'I knew.'

'I thought you might.'

'What would you like to do, Hans Albert? What do you normally do on a rainy Monday night?'

'I have a beer,' he said. 'I watch the football.'

'Then let's do that,' I said. 'A normal evening at home with my family, doing the things we always do. What more could I ask for?'

So we went through to watch TV, sitting comfortably on the sofa watching the game, the way it could have been, the way it should have been. We sat there watching TV and chatting, like a brother and sister who had not spent their lifetimes apart.

Out there, in deep space, in the hubs of stars, particles are created in pairs. They circle then collide, cancelling each other out. As if they had never existed. This is no scientific fairy story, though you can see why my father rejected it, can't you? It sounds ludicrous. Cancelling each other out. Matter and antimatter. Hans Albert and I watched TV and laughed till we cried.

'Mama taught physics in a high school for a while but, you know, it was difficult. Eduard needed someone around all the time.'

'And Papa had gone.'

'Long gone. Mama made him beg for a divorce, you know.'

I thought of Mileva and the set to her chin, that hard look in her eyes. Yes, I could see her fighting. She had given up everything for him, her own studies, her country, even her daughter so that the baby's screams wouldn't get in the way of the great man's science, and now he wanted to leave her.

'Yes, I can see her not giving in without a fight,' I said. 'What advantage to her was there in letting him get away? She had you boys to look after – she needed him there. It does not surprise me that she demanded a high price.'

'She got it.'

'The Nobel money.'

'Can you believe it?' said Hans Albert. 'She asked for that even before he'd won it. There was no guarantee he'd win it. But she bet on him. And she won.'

'Did she get it all?'

'All. Over a hundred thousand kronor.'

'They should never have given it to him, really,' I said.

'Why ever not?'

'The prize is supposed to be for work that is of the greatest benefit to mankind. But what use is there in a theory? What, exactly, are the practical applications of relativity in daily life? I don't need an explanation of gravity to give my daughter her breakfast, a description of spacetime to knit a baby's bonnet.'

'I'm glad you weren't there to argue,' he said. 'We needed the money. We had more than we needed for a while. Mama was even happy in those days.'

'I'm glad,' I said. 'I'm glad for you.'

He reached over and touched me on the arm.

'I'm glad you found me,' he said. 'I thought of you often.' His fingers were light against my skin.

And suddenly I had the explanation for those strange touches I had felt sometimes, out of the blue, unexpected, like someone was running a finger up and down my arm. It wasn't my father. It wasn't even my mother. It was Hans Albert thinking of me. I had been caught in the web of Hans Albert's thoughts, as if they could bring me home.

'You look like her,' he said. 'Very much.'

This surprised me. In photographs I had always been able to pick out features I had in common with my father, but now that Hans Albert mentioned it, I considered it was true. I had her dark hair and eyes. In later years I had her hardness of expression. It should not have been so surprising. I was like her in so many things. She had lost her daughter, I had lost my son. We had both had our lives transformed and distorted by the same man. We had both been abandoned by the same man.

'And the worst thing is,' I said, 'he was wrong.'

'For abandoning you?'

'No. Relativity. That's what he abandoned me for. His great theory. Some of the equations were wrong. All this we suffered and he was wrong.'

'Papa hated being wrong,' said my brother. 'What about all that "God does not play dice with the universe"? We had to live with stuff like that every day.'

'He was like most scientists,' I said. 'He was on rocky ground as soon as he started mentioning God.'

'That's because he was like most scientists and got himself confused with God.'

I thought perhaps Hans Albert beat even Marie Winteler in how deep his hatred went.

As it was the only evening we would ever have together and I wanted it to be as normal as possible, I decided we shouldn't talk about God any more, or science, or hatred, or revenge.

'What do you think is going to come along first?' I said. 'A touchdown or a field goal?'

'A touchdown,' he said. 'Bet you five.'

I won. Chance is built into the very fabric of the universe.

Hans Albert gave me the five, called me a cab in the early hours of the morning and hugged me close before I disappeared into the night.

CHAPTER TWELVE

The Institute

18 April 1955

I HAD COME ALONE. TERRI WAS RIGHT, THIS WAS PROBABLY MY last chance. She had watched me grow ever more restless with unfinished business ever since we had returned from Europe and had reminded me, more than once, that I should know as well as anyone that, to all intents and purposes, time only ran in one direction and, in my father's case, it was running out. He had been ill for a long time. Who knew how long I had got to put the final piece of the jigsaw puzzle in place?

And so I went. Marie Winteler had never told my father how much she hated him. Hans Albert had never had the courage to say it to his face. Mileva was dead, and Eduard couldn't speak for himself. So I would do it for all of them. I would put my father straight. I left Terri behind at home with Tina and got on the plane myself.

The hospital was a low grey block with long grey corridors and grey walls, and nurses in white shoes padding silently about. I passed the whole Sunday waiting and waiting. People were in and out all the time. I didn't know if they were relatives, friends or academic colleagues. I had no way of knowing what had been going on in my father's life the last years he was in New Jersey. He kept himself to himself and in the meantime people waited, to see if the old man would come up with his grand unified field theory, the theory of everything. But it had been beyond him: to marry everything together. Space and time, he could do; quantum physics defeated him completely.

I sat in the waiting room, unpeeling the tiredness of the plane journey from my neck and feet. As I got older, I liked flying less and less, that weightlessness, that removal from the forces of gravity. I took care to remain invisible, reading the sort of magazines that are found in hospital waiting rooms everywhere, magazines that told me about tribes in New Guinea and the best way of holding on to your man, and I drank cup after cup of bitter coffee from the hotplate, and paper beaker after paper beaker of cooled water from the flask in the corner. I kept up a stern but vigilant attitude, as if I might be expecting bad news at any minute and that warded off any stray enquiries. Relatives and nurses gave me sympathetic smiles and moved on with a nod of shared sorrow.

Perhaps the theory of everything eludes us all in the end, I thought. But it's not all of us who try to think of it.

During the evening, the stream of visitors got thinner, as if they had all gone home to their dinners and their warm lamplit rooms. I wanted to go home, too, to my warm room, and forget all this, the waiting, the edginess brought on by the caffeine and the tiredness from the trip. I was feeling nervous. I would only get one chance and I had to get it right. I rolled the words over and over on my tongue. Hate. We all hate. Despise. Detest. My shoulders ached. The harsh overhead lights came on in the waiting room and I looked and felt older than ever.

At eleven o'clock, just when I thought the coast was clear, someone new went in. I threw the magazines down in frustration and tapped my fingers, waiting for them to return and disappear. Did you know how much we hated you? Did you know how much we loathed you?

It was a brief visit. After the door banged shut, I waited an extra five minutes, just to be sure, but the whole floor was quiet.

Ten minutes before midnight, I crept into the ward where my father lay. It was at last deserted. I was safe.

He lay with his head on a white pillow, covered with a white sheet. He was unmistakable. The prominent nose, the shock of white hair. The skin over his scalp was as thin as paper. Underneath, I could see the blue veins, the hardened arteries in sharp ridges across that broad forehead, battling to maintain life. This was the man I had spent my life hating. Here he was, in front of me.

There was a bottle of mineral water and a spoon on the bedside cabinet and they glinted in the low light. Three or four plastic chairs had been brought to one side of the bed to accommodate the over-spill of visitors and hadn't been tidied away yet. Two extra pillows lay on the floor, half under the bed, as if they had fallen and no-one had bothered to pick them up. The room was very quiet. Not even the sound of breathing. But he was breathing. I could see his chest rise and fall in ragged jerks. I picked up one of the pillows from the floor. I could do it now, I thought, and no-one would ever know. I could put a stop to those ragged breaths.

We all hate. Despise. No-one would blame me. No-one would ever know.

I stood there holding the pillow, holding on to it tight, feeling for the first time in my life what it was like to hold real power, to hold power over someone's very life and death.

I thought of all the lives he had destroyed: my mother's, Marie Winteler's, Hans Albert's, Eduard's. My father had had power over people's lives, and he hadn't hesitated to use it. I thought of that little baby in Novi Sad, the baby he had never bothered to come and see, the baby he had abandoned for nothing more than a theory.

And then he opened his eyes.

'I've been waiting for you to come,' he said.

I stood there with the pillow. It would be easy. There was no strength left in those thin arms.

'You know who I am?'

'Of course,' he said. 'My little girl. The baby.'

They were long, deep, drawn-out, German words that he said. 'The baby.' Infinitely caring and infinitely sad. It was a gentle voice, if weak now, the sort of voice I would have liked to have grown up hearing every day.

I had not thought he would know me. I had envisaged having to remind him who I was, stamping my feet, spitting with hatred, a scrap of life thrown out half a century ago and forgotten, come back at last to haunt him. Instead I sat on the nearest of the chairs and put the pillow on my lap.

'You know why I am here, don't you?'

'Because I am dying.'

We spoke German without thinking, because it seemed easiest, because it was the language we were both most at home with, even after all this time dealing in English. And there wasn't time to waste on niceties. We both knew that.

'Yes, I'm here because you're dying. Because I have questions. Because you are the only one who can answer them. And because . . .'

He looked at the pillow on my lap. I didn't let go of it. He closed his eyes and said, 'I've spent my whole life asking myself questions. You must take after me.'

'I know I take after you. That's why I'm here.'

'So ask. Ask what you want to ask. You might as well get on with it.'

There was only one question, really.

'Papa, why did you send me away?'

Suddenly I was nothing more than a little girl in Desanka's kitchen, wondering if the day would ever come when I would be a princess.

He didn't answer immediately. He took time to think, under his closed eyelids, reaching back into his own past. 'My own father,' he said . . . He hesitated. I waited, knowing he would get to the point. 'Hermann. He was very gentle. Found it difficult to say no to anyone. And he achieved nothing at all because of it. Nothing. Nothing. And there were things I needed to do. Wanted to do. Had to do. So I said no.'

'No?'

'To your mother. When she asked. I did not want to be hampered by the "personal". I never did, all through my life. So when your mother wanted to bring you back with her . . .' He raised his hand from the sheet and brushed the air aside. 'I said no.'

'No.'

'That's right. I said no.'

'If she'd really wanted me,' I said, remembering her wide-boned hands, that hard look mixed in with the milk and the warm skin, 'she would have brought me back with her, no matter what you said. Isn't that right?'

'Oh no, she wanted you,' he said. 'It was me. I didn't.'

'But why?' Still it was incomprehensible.

'There were things I had to do. I wasn't going to sacrifice science for a screaming girl. You did scream, you know, all the time. That's what Mileva said.'

'I've been screaming', I said, 'ever since.'

He opened his eyes and looked at me closely, looking at my eyes which were brown like his, my hair which was turning white like his at the temples.

'I wondered, sometimes,' he said, 'what happened to you.'

'Not enough to ask.'

'No.' He sighed. 'You were out of my hands.'

'Did you ever think I'd find you?'

'I knew you would. Once you know everything about a situation, you can predict what's going to happen next. It was only a matter of time.'

'You're wrong there, Papa. You can't be sure of anything. Not at the quantum level.'

'Stuff', he said, 'and nonsense.'

'You're like Terri,' I said. 'She still insists that the cat in the box has to be either dead *or* alive as well. Still insists that God does not play dice with the universe.'

'If I'd had a little more time', he said, 'I'd have come up with a set of equations which proved it.'

'I don't understand why you have such strong objections to probabilities. To the uncertainty principle. To playing dice. After all, you played dice with me. You rolled me away and hoped I wouldn't come back.'

'I always knew you'd come back one day.'

'I could just as easily have stayed away.'

'No, you couldn't.' His eyes narrowed in pain. 'You couldn't have stayed away. You're my daughter.'

'But you have to admit it's possible. I might just not have bothered to get on that plane and come here. I nearly didn't. I hate flying.'

'No. Every action has its predictable consequences. I sent you away, but I knew you'd come back and I knew you'd spend your whole life hating me for what I'd done. You're not going to deny that, are you?'

'No,' I said. 'I did hate you.' I considered further. 'I still do hate you.'

He shrugged. 'I knew that, too.'

'What else did you expect? You abandoned me, Papa. You just let me go as if I were nothing. As if I were less than nothing. How could you do that to a child? How could you do that to me?'

'You mustn't think', he said, 'that I didn't feel guilty about what I'd done. That we both didn't feel guilty about it. Sometimes.'

'You never even asked about me,' I said. 'Not once.'

'I asked once or twice,' he said. 'And she told me you were fine. So how far can you take guilt?'

'Far enough,' I said. 'I know all about that. But did guilt make you regret what you had done to me?'

He looked at me carefully, at my face, at my hands, at the pillow. We were right at the edge here. What was the point of not telling the truth?

'No,' he said. 'Never.'

'That's why I hate you so much.'

'That's why I knew you'd come back.'

'You can't be so *sure* of everything.' I stood up, dropping the pillow. Never mind pillows, I wanted to hit him.

'Why not?'

'Because my laws are the laws of chance, too. You can't be sure of anything at the human level, never mind the quantum level. Tina taught me that.'

'Tina?' He raised himself slightly. 'Tina?'

'Your granddaughter.'

'Another girl.'

'She's named after you. Albertina.'

'Poor child.'

'She's lovely, Papa. She's beautiful. She has yellow hair and a sweet face. And about twenty-seven dolls. And she had a brother.'

'Had?

'Had. Paul is dead. The Third Reich killed him.' I hesitated a moment. 'No. I killed him. I was responsible. And my husband, Josef. I killed him, too.'

I watched my father's chest rise and fall, his thin hands and long fingers against the sheets.

'You would have liked Josef, Papa. You would have liked to have known Josef. I know you would. I loved him.'

The hands didn't move. My father was watching me.

'And do you know why they're dead, Papa? Because I am more like you than you can ever know. I sacrificed my children for science. I lost Paul because I was too busy planning my revenge on you. Josef died because I wouldn't let myself see the dangers. Wouldn't let myself think about anything but vengeance.'

'And are you going to tell me', he said, 'what this vengeance was?'

'That proves I've lost, doesn't it? If I have to tell you. If you don't already know.'

'If you don't tell me, I never will know.'

'Do you remember that young man on the ice, years ago? The one with all the papers? You turned him away. Told him his ideas were moonshine, poppycock.'

'Mass into energy. It should have stayed as moonshine.'

'You did the mathematics in the first place, Papa. You wrote the equation. You can't escape from the consequences of what you've done.'

'You can't hold me responsible for what happened.'

'Didn't you sign a letter to President Roosevelt telling him it was a good idea to go ahead and make the atomic bomb?'

He shifted uncomfortably against the pillow.

'You really don't have any principles at all, do you? What happened to your so-called pacifism? You were supposed to be totally against weapons. Arms of any kind. And here you were egging them on to make nuclear bombs.'

'There was some justification, girl. At that stage we still thought Germany would make them first.'

'At that stage', I said, 'so did I. It was when it was clear the Germans weren't going to get there at all that I went to Los Alamos.'

'Ah, so that was you was it?'

'Mostly me, yes. If it hadn't been for me, they wouldn't have done it. When they detonated at Trinity, I danced for joy. The fire brighter than anything the world had ever seen. That's what Trinity was. My revenge.'

He shrugged. 'So you have no principles, either.'

'It doesn't look like it,' I said. He wasn't telling me anything I didn't already know.

'And were you pleased with your revenge?'

'You know what happened after Trinity. It wasn't what I meant to happen.'

'That's no excuse. You said so yourself.'

'I know,' I said. 'I'm responsible. I took that one equation of yours
and I made it real.'

He sat up for the first time, as if I had at last made him think of
something he hadn't thought of before.

'Is that all you think people will remember from my life? That I
paved the path for the bomb?'

'No.' We were too close to the edge for me to lie, either. 'I think
you're as responsible as I am. That's one reason why I came today,
to hear you admit that. But I think what they'll remember you for
is relativity.' His shoulders relaxed and some of the tension went out
of his body. 'After all, once they took your stupid cosmological
constant out of the equations . . .'

He made a weak noise that I thought must be a laugh. 'Greatest
blunder I've ever made.'

'Once you took that out, the equations worked fine. Almost as
good as mine. I've got Mileva's gift for mathematics, you know.'

'You're lucky.'

'That's a matter of opinion. But they're good equations. And
there's no end to what they predict.' An idea from the *Physical
Review* came back into my mind. 'Have you thought what would
happen if there was a density of matter so large that spacetime
curved round it and nothing could escape?'

'Not even light itself?'

'Not even light itself.'

'Yes,' he said. 'I've thought about that. But someone else will
have to work out the calculations.'

'It won't be me,' I said. 'I'm done with physics.'

'So am I,' he said, 'I'm afraid.'

'As far as we know.'

'I'm going to know everything soon,' he said. 'I'll have no uncertainties left.'

'And what about regrets?'

I thought of Mileva dying alone, of Eduard in the insane
asylum.

'That my work did not make the world a better place,' he said. 'That is what I regret.'

He shifted against the sheets. The strain was beginning to take its toll.

'Sometimes', I said to him, 'I think that, if I had any sense of what was true and valuable, I would spend the rest of my days regretting, weeping for the dead and the innocent, for my mother, for Paul, for Josef, for all the children abandoned in the rain, for all those I should have helped, even for all those I could not have helped.'

'Oh, girl, what could you have done?'

'More than I did. More than I did. I want to say to them all, "I, I as a member of the human race, should not have turned my back on you." I was lonely all my life, Papa, because you turned your back on me. What must it be to have the whole human race turn its back on you?'

'I don't know,' he said. 'I don't know.'

'That's because we're survivors, Papa. That's why. For good or ill, whether we deserve it or not, we've survived. And that's a terrible burden to bear.'

'It is,' my father said. 'A responsibility.'

'And we both abandoned ours,' I said. 'We have that much in common.'

'Your first revenge failed,' he said. 'Have you possibly come here now for a second try?'

'I did,' I said.

'And now?'

I had a choice. I could go on hating, or I could stop.

I took hold of his hand. 'I've come to say goodbye.'

He smiled. 'Goodbye.'

Then, after a minute, he said, 'I'm sorry.'

'If the quantum physicists are right', I said, 'we could one day travel faster than light. And if we do that, we will travel back through time. And do you know what I would do then?'

'What?'

'I would not let you say no. I would make you keep me.'

'Do you know . . .' The words faltered. He was too weak by now to speak without difficulty. 'Do you know what I would do?'

'I don't want to know,' I said. 'I don't want you to tell me.'

I lay on the bed beside him, put my head on the pillow next to his. The hospital smell of scorched cotton was warm and comforting. I could not think why – I could not think why I relished its burned fragrance, until I remembered the last time I had smelled that smell: when Desanka had ironed my clothes into stiff sheets to await the arrival of my mother. I had sat on the bench in the kitchen for hours and it was the last time in my life that I was ever truly certain of where and what and who I was.

We think we are going forwards, we think we are creating things, moving on. But I began to see we only ever go backwards. And, if we are very unlucky, we destroy things as we go.

And then the tears that I had stored since the moment my mother had turned from me and gone away with Hans Albert in the carriage over the red dust, those tears spilled over and onto the bedsheets. It came kicking back, a mutant memory of rejection, painful and strong as the colours of the oleander and peppers that had run through my childhood. Years and years I had held back tears, waiting, waiting for I didn't know what – and now here they were.

My tears fell on his face, drop after drop, till we were wet with salt. Everything that had gone before collapsed to this point of singularity, and there was nothing else in the universe except me and my father.

He leaned toward me with some difficulty, up off the pillow. 'Lieserl,' he said. 'Lieserl.'

And then the pain took hold and the aneurysm in his veins ruptured and he fell back against the pillow. I watched as his eyes closed, as the last beats of blood through the veins in his transparent forehead faltered then stopped. The Theory of Everything was for ever beyond his grasp. The final set of equations would always remain unwritten.

I stayed a few moments longer, holding his cold hand in mine, and then I got up and wiped away the tears. I shivered. I had the same cold feeling as the one that comes over me every time I have too much to drink. The blankness of insensibility, down to the ends of my fingertips, that less-than-zero numbness, the freedom from pain.

By his bed were some papers. Not very interesting. Notes about the Middle East. Calls for the preservation of Israel.

As it was almost the last thing I could do, out of habit, I ripped them up and put them in the bin.

Lieserl. This, the one and only time my father ever called me by my real name, was reported in the papers next morning by the nurse who ran the shift as a 'mumbling in German'. She did not speak German.

She came in when she heard the mumbling but she did not see me. I had already gone back to being invisible. I had let go of his cold hand and melted into the shadows. She wasn't expecting to find someone there, so she did not look. There was some mild speculation as to what final secrets the old man might have been whispering to the universe, but I was not amongst the speculations.

Afterwards I stood outside the neat official residence at 112 Mercer Street where my father had lived, a comfortable place in a street of wooden houses and tidy gardens, where I did not belong, where I no longer had any reason to knock upon any of the doors.

I got the bus to New York to get the plane home and all the bright lights of the city were around me and they went on into the night without end. I reached out with my hands, to the ends of my fingertips, touching deep into the brightness of the hills and the darkness of the valleys and as far across the continent as Terri and Tina, and as long as they were there, I was safe.

Tina welcomed me home at more or less the same moment as they removed her grandfather's brain.

They studied the brain extensively but found nothing special. In formaldehyde they pickled the secrets. They cut thin slices, like Parma ham. They stained tissues.

My father's brain tested normal in every respect, although they knew it wasn't. That was the point. They don't dissect *everyone*'s brain after all. They were looking for something. Something they could use. But whatever it was, they didn't find it.

In the eulogies, I heard people talk of the man, his wives, his children, and I did not recognize him. They talked as if the modern universe was his child, a babe that he had nurtured.

In his will my father had made provision for both his sons. He made no mention of his daughter.

I was home. Terri took out a black lacquered compact and dabbed a vestige of shininess from the tip of her nose. The powder was golden, baby-soft. She poured me a very dry martini. The time was all the zeros. Midnight.

She patted the sofa next to her.

'Survivors,' said Terri, raising her glass.

'Survivors,' I said, sitting down and raising mine.

The End of Time

I DID FOR TINA ALL THAT I COULD. I BROUGHT HER TO THE END of her natural life. Tina died without warning in her sleep, in the autumn of 1963, of the heart defect that I had always known was there, because I had always known the irregular rhythm of her heartbeat. She simply did not wake when I went in to her in the morning. She died knowing her mother had tucked her up safely in bed that night, and I felt that there was no more I could ask. To have children, and to see them safely through, what more can any of us ask?

I never found out what happened to Tina in those years she had been away from me, but that didn't matter now. None of it mattered.

I buried her here, with all her dolls, in the place where we will end. The place where her childhood finally ended. So much of me died with her that I thought I would never be whole again. It was the last loss, and the worst.

We have always moved westwards, Maja and I. From the Austro-Hungarian Empire, across continents, across oceans. It is here, on the Pacific rim, with us looking westwards to the place where the west becomes the east, that we stopped.

We were free. After fifty years, Maja and I had reached a stage where we had enough money, enough time, and no responsibility to anyone except each other.

In fact, once I had accepted that Tina was gone, we were even happy.

As it was such a difficult choice, we took our time about making it. Maja brought home endless brochures and we compared the delights: conservatories, availability of twenty-four-hour nursing care if required, menus and temperature charts. Then there were reconnaissance visits.

'Look,' said Maja, pointing at the chair proffered in one establishment. 'Genuine veneer.'

In the end, and the decision was mutual, as you might expect, we chose the Sunset Home from Home in Mesa Verde, where we have fine and uninterrupted views of the Pacific coast and year-round warmth – important when coping, as I was, with the onset of arthritis and assorted other ills. Maja kept entropy at bay with manicures and a new hairdo every week and, once, an operation to have a varicose vein removed. I left her to it. I dislike surgery. I had seven stitches with the finest catgut when Paul was born, and when the first winds of winter blow, I can count every one of them still.

'Einstein?' The nursing home manageress laughed. Ruby, her name was. I liked the name and I liked her. She was the main reason we were at the Home from Home. 'Mrs Einstein? Any relation?'

We all laughed, as if such a thing was self-evidently ridiculous.

Yet I had insisted on being booked in to the nursing home under my given name, my true name. And it is a measure of the times that no-one suspects that this name is nothing but the truth.

I had to be Mrs on the registration form, not only to explain the fact that Maja was my daughter – for she couldn't pass for anything else now – but also because, from time to time, I did talk about my husband, Josef.

*   *   *

Josef. I have almost forgotten what his real surname was. I am on my own now, apart from Maja, but I still talk about Josef, and my other children, Tina and Paul. I don't know what past Maja has invented for herself. She is free to do as she chooses. But I am an Einstein and I will die that way.

In a neon lycra leotard, Maja does an hour of aerobics every morning, battling against the local effects of gravity before her bran and home-made yoghurt. In the same space of time, I might consider the superatom, and how one might best be created. I find physics too fascinating not to keep up with developments. Maja continues not to be impressed.

'The main dangers at the moment,' she said this morning, inspecting her reflection, 'are sagging buttocks and flabby pectorals. Not the superatom.'

Maja now goes every six months to a clinic in Switzerland where, in exchange for a couple of thousand dollars, they inject her with a suspension of dried cells from foetal sheep tissue. Maja is enthusiastic about the rejuvenation produced by this arcane process.

'Doctor Remagen keeps his own flock on the mountain behind the clinic,' she told me, as if that would make a difference.

She tried to persuade me to have some specific injections of my own: sheep pancreatic tissue to ward off my late-onset diabetes, cartilage cells to counter the effects of osteoporosis. I said no.

She has also recently had laser skin treatment, where the top layers of her skin were vaporized. Freed from encumbrances, the underlying dermis has started to produce collagen and elastogen once more, reforming the structure which naturally underpins young skin. She is jubilant and radiant.

'Your daughter's looking well today,' said Ruby, when Maja wheeled me past the office on the way to the garden.

'Thanks to the sheep,' I said.

'We are none of us getting any younger,' remarked Maja. 'Not really.'

'You are,' I said.

'It's the fashion,' she said.

The 'fashion' seems to be for everyone to look like babies. Pale skin, pale lips, dark eyes and romper suits. It is bizarre. Maja has been joining in.

'You go beyond fashion,' I said. 'People are beginning to notice.'

'People?'

'Me.'

'Lieserl,' she said. 'I can't hide the truth from you.'

She can't. Around midnight every night the one constant in my life comes back. I lie awake and listen for the familiar key in the door, the announcement that Maja is done and is back to me, that the world is restored to rights. I prepare to turn out the bedside light and put my arms about her in her accustomed place, to snuggle down warm in the borrowed glamour of her night in the city.

Does earth have anything to offer more fair? A room at the Sunset Home from Home, sinking back against the soft pillows and watching reruns of *The Lucy Show*.

Maja says that as far as she can tell, everyone in the city is talking about DNA and genes. No-one has ever talked about it much before, but now it is the happening thing.

I note it, duly, for reference.

Towards the end of 1965, my brother Eduard died, in the same institution he'd lived his days. Eduard's life was sadness and pain; in the end, I think he was glad to be dead.

Einstein's children – we did not seem fated for happiness.

'Lieserl,' said Maja sternly. 'Don't be self-pitying. You have to take happiness where you can. You have to grab it.'

Did Eduard's genes make him what he was? Did my genes make me dance in the firelight? I didn't think so. All I remembered was being alone, being abandoned, being left. My father made me who I was. After all these years, that was the only thing I was sure of, that loneliness the only thing I remembered. The farm, and the fire, and the stars.

I tell stories about the farm to Ruby and she looks at me as if it were another planet I were talking about.

'Not quite,' I say.

'It might as well have been.' Ruby, the pragmatist. I smile because I know she is right. Ruby deals, in the office downstairs, with a fax, a photocopier, a telephone, an answering machine and a computer. She disappears into the darkness and comes back covered in a rash of technology.

By now I think I recognize people I see in the afternoon movies on TV, even when – always when – they are perfect strangers. In this I am not alone. Ruby, who sits with me some afternoons when Maja is out, claims to be on intimate terms with a good proportion of them, too. For all I know, she might be. As she points out, I might be, too, only I've forgotten about it. Age does that. I tell Ruby that if my formative years had included hobnobbing with Joan Crawford and Greta Garbo, I would not be sitting here now eating scrambled eggs and milk toast and complaining that Maja has put too much butter in the eggs. She wants to know what I would be doing and there my imagination, unusually, fails. Ruby says it should involve money and lots of men and I say I have sun and scrambled eggs, what more do I want?

'Every time I eat a scrambled egg,' I tell her, 'I am increasing the amount of order in the universe.'

'What ever you say, darlin', what ever you say.'

She is happy. I am happy. What more could we want?

Every Wednesday Ruby travels across town to visit the place where her two sons are buried. Not to lay flowers down, not to think, to remember, even to pray, just to make sure no-one has sprayed the marker with paint, daubed slogans over their names or, worse, dug them up. Ruby has bad dreams.

I know what that feels like. Everything I did was recorded, documented, filed in cabinets of massive steel and kept under locks for the next hundred years. But, true to their scientific training, the Nazis kept records.

It is all there, if you know where to look. My equations. My calculations. My neatly typed reports. My foothold in history. It is all there, if you know how to look.

Occasionally Maja took me on a trip and we did things that only tourists do: buy postcards, support indigenous craftsmen, bring American cash dollars into the local economy.

Once she took me to Los Alamos, which is now a tourist centre.

Maja was very happy. She pushed me in my wheelchair and sang as she went along.

> And seldom if ever
> On the banks of the river
> Any poisonous herbiage grows.

Her clear voice rang out across the deserted buildings. She took my hand in hers and pointed out where our shared room with the temperamental wood-burning stove used to be, where they'd laid the duckboards to make a path to the Leisure Center.

I bought an effigy of my father. He had been turned into a fluffy badger or mole, something with a shock of endearing white hair and a scientific squint, something for little girls to take home and place on their pillows to keep them safe all through the night.

'What am I doing here?' I said to Maja, clutching the cuddly animal which was what my father had become. 'What am I doing here?' She pushed my wheelchair harshly, as if to stem the tears that she could see appearing.

'Tears are pointless,' said Maja. 'You told me that yourself.'

'They don't seem so pointless any more.'

Maja pushed me into the gift shop.

'Now and again, in this life,' she said, fingering a silver bangle, 'it is permissible to be a tourist.'

'As long as you don't gawp from a safe distance, as long as you don't refuse to take responsibility for what is going on before your very eyes.'

'I take responsibility,' said Maja. 'Desanka gave me the responsibility of you. And I still have it, don't I?'

'Yes. Oh, yes. No-one can accuse you', I said, 'of irresponsibility.'

Maja looked up surprised.

'I never thought I'd hear you say that,' she said.

When Apollo 8 went to the moon, the scientists thought it would be the pictures of the moon that we would be interested in. They broadcast hundreds, this way and that way, this view and that view, this crater, this shadow. They thought that the view of the dark side of the moon would be what we all wanted. It wasn't. Look back through the files. Rewind the videotapes. It wasn't the pictures of the moon people wanted to see – it was the pictures of the earth. For the first time we had proof that the earth was really round. Proof. Of course, we had been told this 500 years ago, when Columbus sailed to America, but now, for the first time, we could *see* it. The earth wasn't flat. At last, we sighed, we knew it. We looked at the blue curve of the earth falling through black space, and we knew it. We saw how alone we were.

There is no up or down in space, no north or south, no left or right, no right or wrong. I can see the attraction in that.

But here on earth, we see the edge to the picture. The frame to the photograph. In space, you do not. The universe goes on and on. If there is anything I would have liked in my life, it is that, the view with no edge to the picture. The universe going on and on.

* * *

'They're wrong about time,' I said to Maja. 'Clocks may run slow in a gravitational field, but not slow enough. Time is not a constant. It runs fast for all of us as we get older.'

'Unless', said Maja, 'you live in China.'

'What's China done to be immune to relativity?'

'In China, they value the old. In China, the golden vista of old age is a sunlit upland to yearn for, to aspire to. At nineteen, your opinion counts for nothing. At ninety, it is everything. Pigs are killed on your say-so. Whole villages bow to your whim. Rice in unlimited quantities is yours for the taking.'

'I see.' I was doubtful.

'As it gets nearer, therefore, for the younger ones, this time of unprecedented powers seems constantly to recede. Time slows. The golden day seems as if it will *never* come.'

'Unfortunately,' I said, 'I am not in China.'

'No,' said Maja. 'And I don't think you ever will be, either.'

So, of course, for me, time got quicker and quicker and then effectively stopped . . . when? Somewhere about the summer of 1973, I think, when what must have been a massive brain haemorrhage put paid to effective daily functioning and most of my logical thoughts. Twenty years ago? Twenty-five? I cannot count. I cannot keep track. There was warmth and movement one moment, cold and stasis the next. No-one knew then, least of all myself, that this temporary deficiency would last for the rest of my life. Everything began pouring together, coming closer, and has kept drawing closer since. Everything in my body gathers and gathers, shrinks down. I get smaller and smaller, shrunken. One day I will erase myself.

What I mainly see of the world these days is a grey mist. I walk, when I walk anywhere, when I have to walk anywhere, into walls. I move my hands over the table and knock over cups of coffee gone cold, my glass of water for medication. Maja shouts to tell me things, but I can hardly hear her so it doesn't matter.

I have no idea what she is saying. Did she have any idea, when she took me from Desanka, that her responsibility would last until I was nearly a hundred years old?

If I was asked to tell the story of this century, and many have been asked these days so I don't see why it shouldn't be my turn soon, I would say it was the century of Maja, who came round again and found herself and did not give up her responsibilities along the way.

It is her story, her century, in the end. Not mine, for I gave up when it was halfway over.

At some point they erected a statue of my father in Washington DC and he was set in stone for all to see and admire. My father's greatest theory predicted that all theories, including itself, would break down in the special conditions which reigned at the moment of the beginning of the universe. And they would break down again at the end. I feel them breaking down for me now. My memories break and splinter, the details are drowned in a fog. I no longer know what is true and what is not, what is real and what I dreamed.

Yesterday was my birthday. I think. Maja took me out to a place with Regency wallpaper in tasteful stripes; the fastidious roses – pink and beige but never red – against the mirror in the hallway. Maja ordered for me: vanilla and chocolate ice cream. It is something I can eat with only a spoon, that does not require cutting up, though it sets what few teeth I have remaining on edge.

Every so often Maja and her young friends gather round and there are candles on a cake, though I have long ceased taking an interest in trying to count them. I'll know when I've reached one hundred happy years, I guess, as there'll be more friends than usual and perhaps a photographer from the local freesheet, ready to publish my decrepit face over a hopeless amount of candles for the edification of the people of the valley.

When Slovenia became a war zone again, I took an interest in that part of Europe for the first time in years and got Ruby to read bits of the newspapers out loud.

I sucked on gums and considered what I heard. I heard Maja's voice over Ruby's: *If you do not know what happened, then for me to tell you would hurt your mind. If you do know what happened, then you will want to forget, as I do. There is only one thing worth saying now – that it should not happen again.*

But even as Maja spoke, as Ruby spoke, we knew that it would happen again, is happening now, and we are deaf to those who still scream.

The Croats turned on the Serbs and the Serbs turned on the Croats all through that plain and every surviving member of Desanka's family, of my family, was killed or scattered far away from their birthplace. Everything looks dark, in images of grainy black and white in the newspapers, even though this is happening now and the images could be in colour.

In the war, the record of my birth was burned. The crystal glass hidden in the rafters, in which Desanka had poured wine, the glass from which I had tasted my mother, after a hundred years of safety, was ground underfoot.

People came looking for me, of course they did, when the letters and the papers hidden in my father's house in New Jersey were finally opened to the public and they first got wind of me, sometime in the 1980s. But, if the people of Serbia don't want you to see a thing, you will not see a thing. We can make things appear and disappear: rabbits in hats, presents, sweets, borders and children.

I, Lieserl Marić Einstein, was invisible for most of this century. I wanted to hide, and everyone was only too happy to keep me hidden. Besides, don't forget, I was born in 1902, in a cold January, early in the morning, and it was only later, when they fought the wars that swallowed husbands and children, that the world began to see the benefits of paperwork. You need to keep track of people if you're going to conscript them. In that long-ago January, in 1902, I could be born and disappear like a pebble in a smooth pond. To a casual observer, it was as if I had died. As if I had never been born.

Of course I was born. Here I am, solid and reassuring and eating scrambled eggs with my friend Ruby, looking at the Pacific with my daughter Maja. But any last trace of me apart from this was rippled and scattered when the soldiers crossed and recrossed the Danube, their boots churning to mud the family fields, as refugees scurried across Europe, scattered like the random motion of tiny particles.

Some days Maja pushes me through the dunes and the scrub grass. I love to hear the first crash of waves, the boom of the surf. When Maja comes out of the sea, she lies on a towel and the water dries upon her and whitens her with its salt. She looks over the glassy waters. The sun is already high and there is scant shadow on the sand.

Sometimes we stay until night comes, though the sand holds the warmth of the day. In the dark, the waves roll towards us tumbling light. I used to think it was a trick of the eyes but Maja says no, it really is there, a phosphorescence from plankton in these southern latitudes, but it would be just as beautiful even if I was dreaming it. The light washes all through the night on the shore until we are as cold, despite the blankets, as we had been warm, so Maja says we should leave, and we do leave and go home.

When I think about it, I know that these are the happiest, happiest, happiest years of my life.

Maja shines for me, above and beyond the velocity of light.

A little way to the south of here is an airport, but I am too far away to hear the noise, or even see the planes in the daytime. In the nights, though, things look different, and I am often awake to see them. I need little sleep now, it eludes me, not because of nightmares, or even disturbing dreams, but simply because you need little sleep by the time you reach my age, the body being daily less inclined to expend the energy to repair itself. All the equations that I wrote show that the path of time forwards is an illusion. Illusion it may be on paper, but the illusion certainly won't go away if you blink your eyes. I am very old, and I know it.

In the nights, I can see the lights of the planes lined up, one after the other, over the rooftops and gradually getting lower to land. Sometimes, when you look up straight, you can see the steady curve of a space station, a tiny speck, moving inexorably on, silently, across the bowl of the sky like one of the clockwork planets in Frau Mehanovic's ether.

Where I grew up, I grew up without hearing a mechanized sound. No whirring of motors, not even the turning of wheels very often. In the kitchen we had oil lamps and the firelight; outside, nothing but the stars in the night, for we went to bed when it was dark and we rose when it was dawn. And now we have a multiplicity of universes. The glimmers of 'what might be' never stop. We never reach the end of what is possible.

By the 1990s, the technology had caught up with the theory enough for a group of single-minded scientists to demonstrate once and for all the fundamental strangeness I had always known was deep at the heart of the world. Light is a wave. If you shine light through two two holes in a board, the waves coalesce and overlap and produce a beautiful interference pattern on the screen behind. Remember this? But light is also little particles – photons. What happens when you send the photons, one at a time, towards the board with the two holes? This time you put a photographic plate behind the board, to catch where they fall. As each particle travels through one hole or the other, you'd expect there to be a build-up in just two bright spots, wouldn't you? That's certainly what you would get if you threw, say, 100 stones, one by one from your garden, through two windows of your house – a neat pile of stones in each room. You certainly wouldn't get an interference pattern along the carpet. Unfortunately, that's just what you get with photons. Even though you send them out individually, with long gaps in between, they still manage it. To all intents and purposes, each photon goes through both holes at once, interferes with itself and helps to form the pattern on the plate.

Never mind the fact that it's been in two places at once, the more interesting question as far as I'm concerned is, how does each individual photon know just where to place itself on the plate to contribute to the overall pattern? How does it know where all the rest will fall?

We like to think we are particles, acting individually, but we are all waves, together. We set out as particles, we end as particles, but somewhere in the middle we interfere with each other and create a pattern whose edges we can only guess at.

I am putting these papers in a locked box.

If you're reading these words, I am dead. Don't ever be sorry, Maja. I am not sorry. I lived longer than my time and suffered more than my share of hurt. If people knew the truth, knew what I had done, I would be reviled. I have not written this for people to know the truth. And I have not written this to hold you back. You can move on, faster and faster. Wherever you go, whatever you do next, you have fulfilled your responsibilities, Maja, and freedom is yours.

No, Maja. I have written this because I wanted to tell you that there are only two things I regret: one is not being able to save my children and my husband, the other is not finding a better way to vengeance than atomic fission. If I could blink my eyes and make time move backwards, those are the things I would change.

The Home from Home is high on a hill. The prevailing winds blow from the west – carrying the salt of the Pacific, pollen from Japan, spores from south-east Asia. They wheel me out into the sun on the hillside, with the soft and familiar blanket I brought from Novi Sad wrapped about my knees.

*   *   *

The sky above me is heavy and bright with stars. If you look carefully, you can see that some are of marginally different colours –
blue and red and orange. If I had been interested, I might have tried
to find out their names. I could walk along the beach saying, 'This
is Pegasus, that is Orion, there is Sirius.' But I was not interested
in their names, only whether they would fall on me, and I still do
not know why they do not fall on me, and now I never will.

They are things that do not matter.

What I am and what I have done will not matter. To me, maybe,
but no-one else. But these are my details and now you have them. I
am the detail of the twentieth century. I am what will be swept
under the carpet and forgotten. Now you know. And nothing and
no-one, although greater minds than my own have tried it, can reach
for that ultimate triumph of human reason and tell us what it was
all *for*; no-one can and no-one ever will know *why*.

All gone in the blink of an eye.

In a dark, dark wood, there was a dark, dark house, and in that dark,
dark house, there was a dark, dark room, and in that dark, dark
room, there was a dark, dark daughter.

Lieserl.

This house is high, high above the water and under the sun and the
stars. From here the waves crash against the beach and they make
no sound.

Mrs Einstein
The Background

In 1897, when he was studying at the Swiss Federal Polytechnic in Zurich, Albert Einstein met a Serbian student, Mileva Marić. She was from Novi Sad, a town in southern Hungary, then part of the Austro-Hungarian Empire, which later became part of Yugoslavia. Mileva had come to the polytechnic because it was one of the few universities in Europe to accept women. She was the only woman on the physics course.

Mileva and Einstein fell in love. The correspondence from that time in the Einstein archives consists of love letters between the two, and the letters are a mix of romance – he calls her 'Dearest Dolly' – and physics. Einstein felt Mileva was his intellectual equal; he talks of her doing his mathematics for him and she talks of 'our work' on the papers that he was to publish in the *Annalen der Physik*.

Einstein's family did not approve of Mileva; nor did many of his friends, who talked disparagingly of her limp (a legacy from a childhood dislocated hip) and her dark moods.

Yet in 1900, he writes, 'Dearest Dolly, I will overcome my parents' opposition to you', and they began making plans for marriage. But Einstein was out of work; he had been an awkward

student and had made few friends amongst the tutors at the polytechnic, and this told against him when he finished his degree and
tried to obtain a university post. He applied for many academic
positions and was refused them all.

In 1901, Mileva found herself pregnant. She had to break her
university studies, and went back home to her parents in Novi Sad.
Einstein did not accompany her, though they kept up a frequent
correspondence.

In between asking about her health and that of the child to be –
whom he calls Hanserl, insisting that it was going to be a boy –
Einstein talks in his letters about experiments with cathode ray
tubes that he wants to tell Mileva about.

Back in Serbia, Mileva had a baby girl, Lieserl, in January 1902.

On hearing the news, Einstein wrote, 'Is she healthy? Does she
cry? I love her so much and I don't even know her yet. All we have
to do is keep our Lieserl with us.'

But they did not keep the baby. Her birth was kept secret from
even their closest friends – the stigma of an illegitimate child in
conservative Switzerland would only have harmed Einstein's
chances of getting a job even further – and there is no evidence that
Einstein ever set eyes on his daughter. When Mileva rejoined
Einstein in Switzerland several months after the birth, she did not
bring Lieserl. Thereafter, there is no mention of her in their letters
for the next year and a half. It is not known who looked after the
child during this time, but the couple's economic precariousness,
together with Einstein's determination to continue work on the
theories he had begun to formulate, make it likely that they decided
to put her up for adoption.

There is only one more mention of Lieserl, in September 1903.
Mileva had returned to her family home and there discovered that
her daughter had contracted scarlet fever. When he was told,
Einstein wrote to Mileva, 'I am very sorry about what has befallen
Lieserl. It's so easy to have lasting effects from scarlet fever. If
only this will pass. As what is the child registered? We must take

precautions that problems don't arise for her later.'
Subsequently all record of her disappears.

In June 1902, Einstein obtained a post in the Patent Office at Bern, a lowly paid civil service post, but it was money enough. Mileva and Albert finally married in 1903 and went on to have two sons, Hans Albert in 1904 and Eduard in 1910.

Also in 1904, the work Einstein had been doing on gravity and light began to coalesce. He realized that if the speed of light was fixed and unchanging – an exception to all the laws of motion that hold good here on earth – then something else must vary in the equations which described the universe. His insight was that it was time itself which altered.

To say that time is not the same for all of us, that it moves at a different rate for someone who is moving and for someone who is standing still, is the insight at the heart of all Einstein's theories. It took Einstein several months to work this insight into the Special Theory of Relativity, published in 1905 in the *Annalen der Physik* as a paper called 'On the Electrodynamics of Moving Bodies'. Although he had written to Mileva about 'our work on relative motion', Mileva's name does not appear on the paper.

When you apply this theory to mass and motion, you get the equation $E = mc^2$. The energy (E) contained in any object is equal to its mass (m) times the speed of light squared (c^2): an enormous amount of energy. But the implications of this equation were not thought through for many years. Einstein himself seemed unwilling to explore the possibilities. At a meeting in Prague a young man battled through the snow and tried to get Einstein to acknowledge what his equation meant, but Einstein refused to have anything to do with him.

Einstein's genius was soon recognized from the papers published in the *Annalen der Physik* in 1905 and he obtained a series of university posts, finally settling in Berlin. Although Mileva and Einstein were now comfortably off, the marriage deteriorated.

Mileva and Einstein divorced in 1918 and shortly afterwards Einstein married his cousin Elsa. As part of her divorce settlement, Mileva asked for the money that Einstein would receive if he ever won the Nobel Prize. If this was a sign of her faith in his abilities as a physicist, she was justified; he won the prize in 1922 and the entire value of 110,000 Swedish kronor was paid to Mileva and the boys. In 1933, Einstein was denounced as an enemy of Nazi Germany while he was on a lecture tour of Europe. He decided it was too unsafe to return to Berlin and eventually settled in the US, where a post was created for him at the Institute for Advanced Study at the University of Princeton, New Jersey. He spent the last years of his life searching for a theory that would link quantum mechanics and relativity, but it eluded him.

Mileva settled in Zurich and became a teacher to support her family; she became increasingly melancholy and unhappy. Hans Albert pursued a career in engineering and followed his father to America, settling in Berkeley. Eduard was a diagnosed schizophrenic and was eventually institutionalized in the Burgölzli, the mental asylum in Zurich where he died in 1965. Mileva died in 1948, apparently penniless.

The existence of Lieserl was kept secret for many years. Helene Dukas, Einstein's secretary in the later years of his life, guarded Einstein's reputation as a scholar and a saint fiercely. She refused researchers access to Einstein's papers and kept secret anything that might detract from the reputation of her hero.

It was not until 1986, after Dukas had died, and after many legal wrangles between the trustees of the papers and the surviving members of Einstein's family, that the love letters between Mileva and Einstein were published and the existence of Lieserl became known.

Einstein never spoke of Lieserl publicly, and if those letters had not been found, we would not know she had ever existed. It is possible that she did not survive the scarlet fever, but it is possible that she did. That Einstein himself thought she had is clear from an incident that took place in 1935 when a woman, Grete Markstein, turned up, claiming to be his long-lost daughter. Einstein took her claim seriously enough to engage a private investigator to check on her story. Markstein was a fraud. Records showed she was too old to be Lieserl, having been born in Vienna in 1894. But Einstein's behaviour shows not only that he thought Lieserl might be alive, but also that he did not know what had become of her.

After the publication of the letters, researchers then tried to trace records of Lieserl's birth or adoption in the town where she was born, but Yugoslavia was at that point in the throes of civil war. Any records still surviving were destroyed.